A DEATH IN THE AFTERNOON

A DEATH IN THE AFTERNOON

BOOK 2

THE CLAPHAM TRILOGY

JULIE ANDERSON

This edition produced in Great Britain in 2025

by Hobeck Books Limited, 24 Brookside Business Park, Stone, Staffordshire ST15 0RZ

www.hobeck.net

Copyright © Julie Anderson 2025

This book is entirely a work of fiction. The names, characters and incidents portrayed in this novel are the work of the author's imagination. Any resemblance to actual persons (living or dead), events or localities is entirely coincidental.

Julie Anderson has asserted her right under the Copyright, Design and Patents Act 1988 to be identified as the author of this work.

All rights reserved. No parts of this book may be used or reproduced by any means, graphic, electronic, or mechanical, including photocopying, recording, taping or by any information storage retrieval system without the written permission of the copyright holder.

A CIP catalogue for this book is available from the British Library.

ISBN 978-1-915-817-76-1 (pbk)

ISBN 978-1-915-817-75-4 (ebook)

Cover design by Jayne Mapp Design

To

*Joseph Carlin and Ana Rodil
with thanks*

and to Angustias

PROLOGUE

'Wake up at the back there!'

A gust of laughter and applause was masked by the jaunty theme tune, which was overlaid, in turn, by the BBC announcer reading out the names of the programme's cast and crew. Chuckling, Winnie levered herself out of the armchair to switch off the wireless.

She took her empty teacup through to the tiny kitchen and began to think about supper. The growling rumble of traffic on the road outside signalled the start of rush hour. How people got the petrol, she couldn't fathom; Winnie shook her head — black market, probably.

Joe would be home soon.

There was Spam and a fresh egg in the pantry; he'd never taken to the powdered sort. She could dig up a potato for chips, to fill him up. And a bottle of pale ale too, for good cheer. Joe wouldn't be going to the pub, he had to be up early for work tomorrow and she reckoned he deserved the beer. She rummaged in the drawer for the potato peeler, gazing out of the window.

What?

Something... some*one* was falling from one of the higher floors in the flats, over the road. And there was a noise.

Oh my! Oh no! How dreadful! Awful!

Clutching her tea towel, Winnie hurried outside and down the garden path. There was a body... a person... a woman... lying on her back on the concrete of the parking area, hair splayed out. Or was that...?

The loud blast of a horn made her leap for the protection of the bollards on the central traffic island. She glared at the driver of the departing car and then turned back to look at the flats.

People were out on the balconies, shouting and pointing, but she didn't recognize the faces. Folk had come and gone since the war, moving in and out; they weren't from around here. Some had dark skin; those West Indians who had arrived a couple of months ago. For a moment a high-sided van obscured her view. When it passed, she saw people running from the building towards the prone woman. As she waited, anxious, for a gap in the traffic, the fallen body was encircled.

Winnie knew from her time in the WVS that it was surprising what people could survive, including falls from high places. That woman might be alive.

She considered.

If she was, the woman needed an ambulance and quickly. Ten to one those flats didn't have telephones, but there was a box on the corner of Culvert Road, which wasn't far. Winnie retraced her steps and scurried along the pavement, tea towel flapping, as she ran towards Culvert Road.

FRIDAY 20TH AUGUST 1948

1

FAYE SMITH

The fist came straight at her face.

Faye ducked. It missed by a whisker.

She swivelled, grabbed the wrist to which the fist belonged and yanked it forward over her shoulder, to flip her adversary to the ground. But her opponent was too tall and heavy and stood firm. Faye was almost caught in a bear hug and grappled to the ground. She managed to squirm free.

Shifting her weight from foot to foot, she waited for the next attack. That her foe was heavier and probably stronger didn't matter; given the correct application of force in the right place... Like a rugby player making a tackle, low around the legs; the bigger they are the harder they fall.

With a lightness of foot that belied her bulk, Faye's attacker came again, hands reaching, fingers ready to grab and grapple. But a sharp kick to the calf, followed up with a high kick towards the stomach, prompted a hiss and sent her stepping smartly backwards. Faye was breathing hard now, but so was her antagonist.

Subterfuge. A fake trip or slip, to make her come in close, leaving her vulnerable. Opponents sometimes underestimated Faye. It often worked, but not, she thought, with this one. She had to do something soon because she was tiring. Once she lost her speed the weight advantage would tell. They circled, each cautious, waiting for an opening to attack.

The afternoon sun cast long paths of light from the high windows across the ceiling to the top of the wall-bars on the opposite wall. Beneath them, a group of women sat on wooden forms or leant against the vaulting horse, intent upon the bout, shouting encouragement.

Who for? she wondered, in a part of her mind detached from the fight.

Many of them would like to see her beaten. Some of them were members of that little group of acolytes that had formed around her opponent, a woman named Mona Merchison.

She was circling closer now, moving forward with each pass to drive Faye back until she was against the wall and there was nowhere else to go.

Faye feinted left then propelled herself to the right, her pumps squeaking on the wooden floor. Mona was caught off-guard yet managed to catch her around the waist. Faye hooked her left leg around Mona's and, exploiting her instability, swept her foot out from under her. The woman hit the floor with a resounding and satisfactory thump.

Yes! She was away!

The yells reached a crescendo.

But Faye felt a hand grab her ankle and the breath was driven from her body as she crashed to the floor. Mona was on her, knee in her back, one hand around her throat, pressing her windpipe while the other scratched at her face. Gasping for air, Faye scrabbled at the hands. Then screamed as Mona's fingers pushed into her eye.

Stop! Stop!

She banged her palm on the wooden floor. She'd do anything to make it stop!

Then the fingers were gone and the weight was removed.

'What d'you think you're doing?' a male voice shouted, angry and loud.

Faye blinked as she sat up, her right eye seeing nothing but blackness, then stars, her head reeling. The shouting had subsided into a low muttering.

'That was a foul!' Faye croaked, massaging her throat.

'A foul?' Mona spat back at her. 'What d'you want? Queensbury rules? There's no such things as a "foul" on the street.'

'But we're not on the street,' the instructor retorted.

'She won't last five minutes out there,' Mona muttered. 'Without big brother to protect her.'

Still groggy, Faye felt John's hand reach for hers and she was pulled upright.

'Alright, sis?'

Faye nodded.

'So much for demonstrating that agility and brains can beat brawn,' he grumbled, close to her ear. 'Thanks for that.'

Faye said nothing, cursing her own stupidity. Mona had cheated, but she should have been ready for that. And the woman was right — there were few, if any rules on the street. It was a lesson.

Faye had always thought of herself as street savvy, not someone easily bamboozled or out-thought; it was a lesson she shouldn't need.

The gym doors swung open and a police sergeant strode through.

'Constable Smith!' The sergeant's voice echoed around the space.

'S'arnt,' John Smith responded.

'Constable *Faye* Smith,' the sergeant clarified. 'Come with me, please.'

'Ma'am.'

Faye rubbed dust from her cotton leggings and glowered at John. She trotted after the departing sergeant, breathing deeply. Behind her John called for the other women to form pairs on the rubber mats.

'Sarge,' she said as the doors swung closed behind them. 'What's up?'

'You're summoned,' the sergeant replied, but didn't lessen her pace. 'By Superintendent Bather herself, no less.'

Eh? Faye raised her eyebrows.

'Why, sarge?'

'Search me. I'm not party to the thoughts of the high and mighty.'

Not quite the all-powerful commissioner but very high up in the pantheon, Superintendent Elizabeth Bather (OBE) was commander of the women's section of the Metropolitan Police. Faye wiped her sweaty palms and tried, unsuccessfully, to tuck back the hanks of hair that were falling about her face behind her ears.

The sergeant rapped on a door at the end of the corridor and stepped into the room.

'Constable Faye Smith, ma'am.'

'Thank you, sergeant. Come in, Smith.'

On the far side of an office, in front of large windows overlooking the garden square, a uniformed figure sat behind a desk. Sunlight caught in her strawberry blonde hair and reflected from the bright white cotton of her shirt. Faye felt sweaty and dirty. She stood to attention.

'At ease. Do you know why I've asked to see you?'

'No, ma'am.'

'Hmmm. Chief Superintendent Morgan, of Scotland Yard, has contacted me. He's requested that you join a new unit he's setting up.' Bather paused. 'It is very unusual – *very* unusual – for a newly qualified WPC to move directly into the Criminal Investigation Department. It is even *more* unusual for her to join a specialist unit.'

The piercing blue eyes appraised Faye and the superintendent waited. Faye had no idea what she was meant to say, so she kept her mouth shut. Bather's chin rose and the suspicion of a smile crossed her face.

'The scope of the work of the women in the Metropolitan Police is widening every year,' she said. 'And I aim to widen it further. Your instructors tell me that you're conscientious and hardworking, you scored highly on the aptitude tests and have a good brain; your placement at Leman Street went well. You don't think in straight lines.' She glanced pointedly at Faye's clothing. 'I believe that the self-defence classes were your idea.'

'Yes, ma'am.'

'It was a good one. Like all good ideas, one wonders why it hadn't been thought of before.'

'Ma'am, it had — on several occasions.'

When Faye had told her brother that she was joining the Metropolitan Police, John had insisted that she improve her physical fitness. She began by running around the Common with him in the early mornings, rain or shine, and by doing regular physical jerks in the gym. It was a small step to learning how to defend herself and then to suggest including the others too.

'I found copies of requests in the files, for an instructor, for money to hire a venue and so on,' Faye explained. 'I looked in the archives, after I'd spoken with the women in the office.'

Faye knew how institutions worked; it looked to her as if the Met hadn't taken those requests seriously, but then, it was only relatively recently that they had begun to take the concept of women police seriously at all.

'The requests obviously fell on deaf ears, but now we've got a gymnasium it was easier to organise. My brother does similar training for the men, so...'

The superintendent gave a small snort of laughter.

'I think you'll do very well,' she said. 'But keep your nose clean, we need you to succeed. People will be watching your progress closely, Constable Smith, and some of them will be waiting for you to fail. I don't want to see you back here, with your tail between your legs — there's too much riding on this. I'm working hard to give women a real career in the Metropolitan Police, so you'd better not let me down.'

'I'll try not to, ma'am,' Faye replied.

Bather gave her a speculative look.

'You know Chief Superintendent Morgan?'

Phillip Morgan, godfather to Eleanor Peveril, her flat mate and close friend.

'Yes, ma'am. He took over a case I was involved with, as a civilian,' she explained.

'You obviously impressed him. Phillip is more forward-thinking than many in the Metropolitan Police and he's taking a risk with you. Remember that.'

'I will, ma'am.'

'Report to Detective Inspector Robert Kent at Union Grove station tomorrow morning at oh-nine hundred hours.'

'Ma'am.'

'DI Kent is based in District L. His team isn't bound by territorial jurisdiction, so Union Grove will probably be a base station only. Where is your local station?'

'Clapham, ma'am.'

The superintendent nodded.

'May I ask a question, ma'am?'

'Yes.'

'Will I still be in uniform?'

Bather considered. 'Tomorrow, yes. Allow DI Kent to tell you what he expects of you, you're on his team now. But I'd expect you to be in civvies when you start on Monday morning as a detective constable.'

'Yes, ma'am.'

'Good luck, Constable Smith. You're going to need it. Remember, there's a lot at stake with this appointment and not just for you. You're responsible for how women detectives will be seen in the Met in future. Make sure it's in a positive light.'

'Yes, ma'am.'

'Dismiss.'

Faye left the office in a happy daze. Wearing a broad grin on her face, she wandered back to the changing rooms. Yet the superintendent's cautionary advice made her pause. It *was* daunting. For a moment she doubted herself; could she make a success of it? There was so much riding on how she performed. But… she was going to get to do what she had joined the force for; she was going to be a detective!

'Detective Constable Smith' had a certain ring to it; was it *Detective* Constable or Detective *Constable*? She tried out the title under her breath.

As she pushed open the doors some women from the training class looked up and stood when she entered. They had been waiting for her.

Her grin disappeared.

2

FAYE

'Well, if it isn't Detective Constable Smith,' one said with an unpleasant smirk.

She couldn't have heard. Faye was certain that she hadn't spoken aloud.

'Off to join a special unit too. Nothing ordinary like a local station for Detective Constable Smith,' another added.

Faye shouldered her way past the women to the place beyond them where her clothes and duffel bag hung. News travelled fast.

'How much time did you spend on your knees to get that?' Mona called after her.

The woman had taken a dislike to Faye from the very first day. Like Faye, she was older than many of the recruits and quickly acquired a small cohort of hangers-on. Faye wasn't impressed; Mona was a lazy bully. So the woman goaded her followers into acts of spite and petty revenge against Faye.

'Jealous, Mona? Fancy being a detective yourself?' Faye responded. 'Better knuckle down to some work, then.'

She rummaged in the bag for her soap; she needed to wash before she dressed. Not shower, not this time — she didn't fancy being naked and exposed in front of these women.

'I don't suck up to the brass, that's for sure. Any more good ideas, Constable Smith?' Mona stressed the first syllable. 'I know how to take care of myself, I don't need teaching and I don't need big brother to save me, either.'

Faye bit back a retort as the sycophants grinned and nodded. That was the second time Mona had used that barb, she'd sensed that it had stung and she'd been right.

Don't let her get to you, she told herself. Mona would like nothing better than to restart the fight, but this time with help.

'I like being useful, Mona.'

'Like licking arse more like.' Mona's face contorted into an ugly mask. 'Or other parts of the male anatomy.'

'Last time I looked Superintendent Bather was female.'

'But Superintendent Morgan ain't and he's the one who's put in the request.'

'How would you know that?'

'Wouldn't you like to know?' Mona raised her chin and came closer until she was standing only inches away from Faye. She was just as tall and much bulkier. Her breath had a sour smell.

Faye didn't want another fight and she was hopelessly outnumbered. She couldn't take them all on and the last thing she wanted was to turn up bruised and battered at Union Grove the following day. Or worse, having to call in sick and not turn up at all.

Yet she couldn't back down. Let a bully win and they come back for more.

Mona smiled, nastily, her eyes calculating. Then she stepped back.

'Grab her,' she ordered.

'But…' one of the flunkies began to argue.

'But what? Go on!'

Faye's arms were pulled back.

Typical of Mona to get others to do her dirty work for her.

'Coward!' she yelled.

But one fist hurt as much as another when you were on the receiving end. There was nothing she could do as her arms were held fast. Faye clenched her abdominal muscles, bracing herself for the punch to the gut.

The doors to the changing rooms banged open, back against the wall.

'What's going on here?' It was one of the fitness instructors.

Her arms were dropped.

'Nothing, ma'am.' Mona looked straight ahead, her face blank. The others murmured the same.

The instructor looked at Faye.

'Nothing, ma'am,' she said.

The instructor narrowed her eyes.

'Then off you go,' she said to Mona. 'All of you. Out!'

As the women made their exit Faye reached for her clothes, but the instructor raised a hand to signal that she should remain.

'They resent you,' she said, turning to face Faye as the door closed behind the others. 'And they have reason to. A detective posting is something many constables have been working towards for years and you walk into one as soon as you're out of training. You've barely qualified for an ordinary posting and you get a special one. Advancement in the force is supposed to be on merit, not on who you know.'

But I am ordinary, I don't know anyone, Faye wanted to argue; it was how she thought of herself. Except, on this occasion, it wasn't true. She knew Chief Superintendent Phillip Morgan.

'You'd better be prepared for a similar reaction from plenty of others,' the instructor warned, her face stern, as she walked to the door. 'Don't expect everyone to be happy for you. And watch your back.'

Good advice, Faye decided, as she began, unwashed, to change into her uniform. The others might return.

Her good mood had dissipated.

First the superintendent's warning about failure, now this. Her new job came with plenty of expectations loaded on to her shoulders, as well as the resentment of some of her peers. And she hadn't even met her new colleagues yet. They might not take kindly to an inexperienced woman constable turning up to work alongside them, especially one who knew their super. Mona's snide comments probably wouldn't be that far from their thoughts and most, if not all, of them would be men.

She would have to be on her mettle if she wanted to be accepted.

With a sigh, she sat to put on her heavy police-issue brogues.

At least joining the detective ranks meant she could wear footwear more suited to the soaring August temperatures. The clodhoppers were useful in winter, but an encumbrance in summer. Now they could be consigned to the back of the wardrobe.

She stood, thrust her gym clothes into her duffel bag, drew tight its strings and headed for the door.

She would worry about it tomorrow – what was that bible quote of Ellie's? *Sufficient unto the day is the evil thereof?*

Faye smiled. Ellie would be delighted for her. So would Beryl. John would be proud.

They knew how much this meant, how very hard she'd worked for it – the physical slogging, day in, day out and the night times of study. The warm glow began to return.

A celebration was in order!

It was Friday night and, on Monday, she was going to be a detective. As the doors to the changing rooms swung closed behind her, a grin began to creep back across her face.

3

FAYE

The flat was hot and airless.

Faye tossed her keys into the shallow bowl on the bookcase by the front door. Ellie's keys weren't there; she must be working late again.

She sloughed off her heavy jacket and went from room to room, opening the wide, metal-framed windows. Returning to the living room, she flung ajar double doors that led onto their small terrace on top of the apron of the Underground station entrance below. The chatter of homeward bound commuters floated upwards, excited voices full of anticipation. It was Friday night. It would be the weekend soon.

Faye's heart lightened; a mixture of elation – her posting was, only now, sinking in — and some relief. It had been a gamble to join the police. She had given up a lot, including a secure and well-paid position at the South London Hospital, as well as the immediate promise of marriage and motherhood. All to pursue what, she believed, she had a talent for, what she was genuinely good at. Now it seemed to be paying off; things were going her way.

She hung her jacket and cap on the hook on her bedroom door. After tomorrow her uniform would go to the cleaners and then be put away. After tomorrow she could wear what she wanted. She sat to unlace and remove her heavy brogues.

Each shoe hit the back of the open wardrobe with a resounding clunk.

'Yes!'

Clad in lighter clothing and slippers, Faye wandered into the kitchen.

Beneath the window she saw the parched, brown grass of Clapham Common, dotted with trees and stretching into the middle distance. Nearest to her it was roped off into sections, marking out the site of the annual hospital summer fete. Ellie was organising it and she would have very little time to relax before next weekend. Faye knew how all-consuming a task that was, she'd done it herself several times in the past. She leant her forearms on the sill and inhaled deeply of the warm air.

That was the past.

What would her future be like? What sort of cases would she be working on? Would she have her own casework? And her new colleagues, what would they be like?

The front door slammed.

'Hello? Faye?' She heard Ellie call. 'Are you home?'

'In here!' Faye went through to greet her friend, unable to stop a triumphant smile stretching across her face. 'Ellie, I've had my posting. I start as a detective at Union Grove station on Monday.'

'That's super!' Ellie beamed and enveloped Faye in a hug. She took Faye's hands. 'Great news! I know how much you wanted this.'

'Tomorrow will be the last time I'll be wearing my uniform. Hurray! I'll be in civvies from now on.'

'Even better!'

'Your godfather...'

'Knew a good thing when he saw one,' Ellie said. 'You wouldn't have got the post if you weren't good enough. Phillip wouldn't have a weak link on his team.'

'Yes, but...' Faye began.

'No "buts"! It's true! Don't be ridiculous, you deserve this! Come on. You've worked hard for this.'

Yes, I have, Faye thought, and I do. So why am I so reluctant to believe it?

'And this calls for a celebration! Find the cocktail glasses. That manky old lemon in the cupboard might finally be useful and I think we've got some mint. We could make Southsides… if there's enough gin left.' She turned back to the door. 'I'll go and get Beryl.'

As Faye sorted through mismatched and dusty glasses in the sideboard, she thought about what her friend had said. Ellie came from the privileged middle classes, where preferment was assumed, she would think like that. Not like her own south London upbringing, without any 'connections' and in which you had to fight every step of the way to get on; doubly so if you were female. It made her doubt herself sometimes, to be too aware of her own shortcomings. She didn't have Ellie's in-built confidence.

She retrieved three coupes for washing and found the soda syphon.

'She's not there,' Ellie called, returning. 'I could have sworn she said she was on days this week.'

'Me too. Odd. Maybe she's decided to go out.'

'Maybe. I'll go and change.'

Faye chopped mint and squeezed the last drops of juice from the wizened lemon into the cocktail shaker, then reached into the cupboard for their precious bottle of gin. They'd used all their sugar ration, so they'd have to whistle for the sugar syrup. She shook the shaker and poured the drinks into two of the coupes, added a generous dash of soda water and topped each glass with a sprig of mint.

She carried them out onto the terrace and heard the lilting notes of a saxophone wind into the evening air. Someone higher up had their windows open and was playing the wireless.

It was the golden hour. The sun was low in the western sky and the shadow of their building stretched out before her. On the other side of the South Side the brick frontage of the hospital was dyed a deep red and its ranks of windows reflected the sun's glow onto the terrace and into their living room.

'Phew, it's not getting any cooler,' she said, fanning her face with her hand as Ellie joined her. 'There'll be plenty of folk on the Common tonight.'

'Yep. Look, there's the flight lieutenant.' Ellie pointed to a man emerging from the scrubby trees around a pillbox-shaped concrete building near the road, the entrance to the deep shelters. He wore the extravagant moustaches so beloved of the RAF. 'Are people still sleeping down there?'

'Don't think so. They've all left by now.'

The flight lieutenant was a Trinidadian who had come to Britain to fight Hitler and had settled in south London after the war. It was at his suggestion that Caribbean newcomers, arriving on the *HMS Empire Windrush*, were housed, temporarily, in the deep shelters at Clapham South.

'It must have been a shock to them,' Ellie said, with a sympathetic frown. 'To come from a country so warm and full of sunshine and to be billeted in the darkness deep beneath the earth.'

Faye cast an anxious glance at her friend. Neither of them had fond memories of the shelters.

'At least the summer heat would remind them of home,' she said, raising her glass. 'Cheers!'

'Chin chin!' Ellie did likewise. 'Congratulations to the newest detective in the Metropolitan Police Force! Detective Constable Faye Smith!'

'Thank you,' Faye said, taking a sip and wincing at the drink's tartness. 'I did it.'

'I never doubted that you would. Not for a minute,' her friend said. 'You always do what you set your mind to.' She grinned. 'It's one of your more admirable qualities.'

'Well, sometimes... eh?' She paused. 'So, what are my less admirable qualities then?'

Ellie made a zipping motion across her lips, eyes smiling.

'It's a shame Beryl's not here,' Faye said. 'She would enjoy these.' She raised her glass.

'Yes, but look!' Ellie said, pointing to the South Side. 'There she is, on her way.'

Faye lifted her hand to shade her eyes and peer into the reflected sunlight.

A short figure in a staff nurse's uniform was teetering on the far pavement, hesitant, waiting for a gap in the traffic.

It was Beryl, but not the usual Beryl, the Beryl who was afraid of nothing and nobody, who always strode out in life, decisive, demanding space and respect. As Faye watched, she drew the back of her hand across her eyes and Faye realised that her friend was weeping.

'She's crying, something's wrong.' Faye sat forward. Beryl was a tough cookie.

'Hey!' Ellie stood and waved. 'Beryl! What's going on?'

The nurse disappeared from their sight as she approached Westbury Court and Ellie went to open the door of the flat.

Minutes later Beryl was seated on the sofa in the living room, eyes red-rimmed and gulping in air between sniffs. Ellie sat by her side, holding her hand, as Faye knelt at her feet. The two women exchanged glances. It must be something serious to have upset Beryl so mightily.

'What's happened?' Faye asked.

At the second attempt Beryl managed to form words.

'Violet, Vi Taylor, one of my students, was bought into the SLH earlier this evening. She's dead.' Beryl inhaled heavily, trying to calm herself. 'She was only twenty, a bright, wee slip of a thing. She'd survived everything, had everything to live for.'

Beryl put her head into her hands.

'Take your time, it's alright,' Ellie said, stroking her friend's arm. 'Tell us what happened.'

'The police say it was an accident.' Beryl looked up, a fierce expression on her face. 'But I don't believe it.'

'Why?' Faye responded. 'What makes you say that?'

Beryl blinked and swallowed hard.

'Tell us,' Ellie urged. 'We might be able to help.'

The nurse sat up, squared her shoulders and thrust out her chin.

'There was a party, somewhere nearby – the Belvedere Estate, I think – those flats with the big balconies.'

Faye knew the blocks, barely ten years old, with their horizontal lines and creamy-white concrete balconies.

'It was in a flat on one of the upper floors. She… fell.' Beryl drew a breath. 'Onto the concrete below. Her head was all smashed in. I – I saw the body, in the mortuary.'

'Oh Beryl, I'm so sorry,' Ellie said.

'The police were called?' Faye asked.

'Yes, Doctor Horn reported the death. Someone came from Cavendish Road station to look into it.'

'D'you know who?'

'No, didn't see him.' Beryl sniffed. 'He can't have stayed long.' Ellie passed her a handkerchief and Beryl wiped her nose. 'Got the paperwork and went back to the station.'

'And…' Faye prompted.

'They're saying that she fell, that she was – drunk.' Beryl frowned. 'That she reeked of drink, of whisky.'

'And did she?'

'Aye, but…'

'Beryl?'

'Vi was temperance.'

'It was a party. Maybe she just had a drink or two,' Ellie suggested. 'That might've made her unsteady on her feet, especially if she wasn't used to it.'

'No, Vi never touched a drop.' Beryl's cheeks flushed; she was ferocious in her certainty. 'Never. It was her father, y'see. Always drinking away his wages down the pub and beating seven shades out of Vi and her mother when he came home. They ran, eventually. Got away from him. It's a common enough story, but that made Vi very strict about drink.'

Another young woman struggling out of poverty, trying to make an independent life for herself through nursing. Beryl probably saw herself in her student.

'So why'd she smell of whisky?'

'I don't know. Mebbe someone spilt a drink on her. Mebbe someone wanted it to seem as if she was drunk.'

'Why would they want to do that?' Faye asked. 'Really?'

'I don't know! I just know that she didn't drink. Ever!' Beryl thumped the cushion. 'And she was sensible – she wouldn't do anything silly, she'd make sure she didn't fall. There's something fishy about this, I can feel it.'

'If I'm thinking of the right buildings, those balconies have quite thick parapet walls, with guard rails,' Ellie said. 'It wouldn't be easy for someone to fall from one of them, but then… it was a party, maybe people were larking around.'

'How did Violet get to the SLH?' Faye asked.

'Someone telephoned for an ambulance. Robin and Stan picked her up, brought her in.' Beryl paused. 'Doctor Horn says she was dead on arrival.'

'What happens next?' Ellie looked at Faye. 'Will there be an inquest?'

'It's an unnatural death. It'll have to be reported to the coroner. Then the coroner will determine whether it was an accident. Doctor Horn can certify what Violet died of, but not how her death came about. The coroner does that. He could find it was accidental, death by misadventure, manslaughter or…'

'I told the doc about Vi being teetotal,' Beryl said. 'She wants to conduct a post mortem, to see what's in Vi's stomach. That would settle if Vi was inebriated, if that was the reason she fell. But the doc says she can't, isn't allowed to.'

'She's right,' Faye said. 'Doctors can't open up dead bodies without the permission of the deceased's family, or there are suspicious circumstances.'

'There are suspicious circumstances!'

'You believe there are, Beryl, but we need to have some evidence of that,' Faye said. 'I know it's sad that Violet has died and you don't want her good name defamed, but there must be some suspicion of wrongdoing if the police are to order a post mortem. And, right now, there isn't any.'

'Then find it! You're polis now. Find it!'

'Alright, calm down.' Ellie patted Beryl's hand. 'It isn't Faye's fault.'

'I know, I'm sorry, Faye. It's just…'

'It's alright Beryl,' Faye said. 'I understand.'

'I suppose Matron will be writing to the family.' Ellie broke the small silence.

'Her mother lives in Aylesbury,' Beryl said. 'I'll speak with Mrs Taylor by telephone to give her my condolences; I was Vi's nursing tutor after all. Matron's asked me to sort through Vi's things, to pack them up to be sent on.'

'I see,' Ellie said.

'But I'm certain something's wrong.' Beryl frowned.

Faye exchanged glances with Ellie.

'Beryl…' Faye began.

'Can't you find out more?' Beryl pleaded now; exasperation pushed aside. 'I feel that this is all wrong. I know it! Find out what really happened. If she fell, she fell, but it doesn't sit right with me that people will think it was her own fault. And she certainly wouldn't have been drunk. It's a stain on her reputation.'

Beryl looked first at Faye then at Ellie.

'No one else is going to stick up for her!'

'Alright,' Faye agreed. 'I'll look into it — informally, maybe. But I can't promise that I'll find anything.'

'As long as you look – look properly. That's good enough for me.'

SATURDAY

4

FAYE

Union Grove police station loomed over Faye. Four storeys of red-brick Victoriana on the corner of Union Grove and Smedley Street, it had a blue Police lamp above the door and a flagpole in the corner of its front garden. Inside was Detective Inspector Robert Kent and his new unit. Her new colleagues.

Faye was sweating; the sun was already warm despite the hour. She wore her full uniform, the belt around her waist cinched tight and the shiny buttons on her uniform jacket fastened. She had risen early to press and polish. First impressions were important and she had to get this first meeting right.

The constable at the front desk directed her to Kent's office on the third floor. Standing in the corridor, outside the half-glazed door bearing his name and title, she straightened her skirt and pulled her jacket taut. This was it. She mustn't make a hash of it.

Her stomach tightened. Faye took a deep breath and knocked.

'Come in.'

A man rose from his seat behind a large, wooden desk as she entered. Several inches taller than Faye, a shock of Brylcreem-defying black hair stood up from his high forehead, making him seem even taller. His white shirt was pristine, though his tie was askew.

'Constable Smith,' he said and offered his hand. 'Welcome. Please...' He indicated a chair opposite and retook his seat.

A swift glance around the office revealed very little about its owner, but, on the desk, a colour-tinted photograph in a mahogany frame showed an attractive brunette with two smartly dressed children, suggesting that DI Kent was a family man.

'You come highly recommended,' he said, but he didn't smile.

'I hope I can live up to my billing, sir,' Faye said.

'So do I, constable.' His tone was flat and dry. 'Take me through your background.'

'I joined Women's Branch fifteen months ago and did my training at Pembridge Hall, though I lived at home.'

'You're unmarried and Clapham born and bred?'

'Yessir.' Faye waited in case Kent wanted to comment further, then continued. 'I did my six months' probation at Leman Street in the East End, then passed as a WPC earlier this summer and have been awaiting assignment since. I live in Clapham. Cavendish Road is my local station.'

'Hm, your superiors at Leman Street seem to think highly of you,' he said. 'It says here that you were a hospital administrator before you joined the force.' Kent had opened a slim manila file and was reading its contents. 'Why the change?'

'I enjoyed my work at the South London Hospital, but it didn't stretch my mind.' Faye had her answer ready. 'I've always been interested in analysis and deductive reasoning and it seemed that I might have an aptitude for detective work, when I became involved in a police case. A nurse from the hospital was murdered.'

She didn't mention that she'd caused a great deal of embarrassment to her boss at the hospital, after discovering discrepancies in the record keeping systems that had led to drug thefts and two murders. The SLH had only been kept out of the newspapers thanks to the good offices of Chief Superintendent Morgan.

'My brother encouraged me to join the force, sir,' she concluded. 'He always said I'd be good at it.'

'Constable John Smith. He's at Battersea Bridge Road station.'

'That's correct, sir. And now at central training.'

'So far, it seems, he has been right, though we'll see how that translates into practical reality with the squad. You need to be able to think on your feet and handle yourself as a detective.'

Faye tried to read his expression, but all she saw was professional neutrality. Given who had recommended her, Kent would probably be as wary of her as she was of him. It would take time to establish a rapport.

'You're used to working within a hierarchy, I understand – within a chain of command. I hope you know how that works.'

'Yessir.'

'Hmmm.' He looked up from reading the file. 'Your previous job was at a woman only institution. You'll find almost the opposite is true in the police force. It will be very different.'

'I have four brothers, sir.'

This didn't seem to impress him.

'Ours is a special operations unit. Its commander, Chief Superintendent Phillip Morgan, is based at Scotland Yard and its remit runs across all local Metropolitan Police jurisdictions.'

Kent's gaze didn't flicker when he mentioned Phillip Morgan, though he must have been aware that Faye knew him. She made a mental note never to play poker with the DI.

'I and the team are based here in Union Grove and, broadly, we cover south London; our colleagues based in Highgate cover north London, but there are no strict demarcation lines. The gangs operate across the metropolis and so do we. I believe you were instrumental in shutting down an illegal drug manufactory two years ago, at the Clapham South deep shelters?'

'Yessir.'

She wasn't likely to forget. The scar on her side where the bullet had entered her body still ached when the weather was damp.

'So you've had some experience of how the gangs operate.'

'Not really, sir.'

It was clear that he knew all about her, far more than was in the thin file.

'This squad gathers intelligence about organised crime, with the aim of shutting it down. You will spend your first week here learning about the gangs, their structure and mode of operations and, where known, their personnel and hierarchy. We have an extensive library of information, collected from across the city. You can read the files here or have them taken to Cavendish Road station, but you may *not* take them home. The contents of those files, and any information about this unit, is confidential. Do you understand?'

'Yessir.'

'This is important.' He paused to let his message sink in. 'Criminals would pay a lot of money to find out what we know.'

'I understand, sir.'

'Good. I expect my people to work on their own initiative, so your daily attendance here isn't required. We don't keep office hours. You'll be out on the streets, sniffing out information. Our working practices can be... somewhat unorthodox. Standard procedure doesn't always apply — you'll have to get used to that as you go along.'

Faye wondered what that meant.

'I do, however, expect my officers to be careful of their own safety; the gangs are violent and can be deadly, so you must work with your colleagues, there'll be no going it alone. It's much too dangerous.'

The DI emphasised this with a stare.

'Everyone attends my weekly briefings at eight thirty on Monday mornings. Those will, in part, determine what your immediate focus will be. There will be specific case briefings as and when necessary. It is imperative that you keep me and the rest of the team informed of what you're working on, with regular updates, so you'll be here a few times a week.'

'Yessir.'

'Questions?'

'Are officers on your team assigned a specific case or area of investigation?'

'Yes, everyone has their own small specialism, though we all work together. We have to.'

'I – I see,' Faye said, although she didn't.

'I'd be very surprised if that was true, DC Smith, but you will.'

'Yessir.'

'I'm allocating the construction industry to you.' The inspector stood and collected a box file stuffed, untidily, with papers from the top of a filing cabinet. 'This is the most recent file. Building materials are in short supply and – thanks to the Luftwaffe — there's increased demand. We strongly suspect gang involvement, especially in regards to concrete.'

Faye gazed at the file as if it was a slap-up four-course meal. Responsibility for her own investigations, real sleuthing! She couldn't wait to get stuck in.

'Pre-fabs,' she said, forcing herself to concentrate on what the DI was saying. 'They use concrete. Councils are building plenty of those.'

The one hundred thousandth pre-fab in Britain had been built the previous year, in Clapham.

'There's big money in it, but councils use certificated providers only,' Kent pointed out. 'So how do the gangs get in on the business?'

'Using supposedly legitimate companies?' Faye suggested.

'You'd think so,' Kent said, dryly. 'The bosses want the contracts and, if they can't get them, will try to intimidate smaller contractors into giving them a slice. But they'll have competition from companies too large to intimidate, which exploit economies of scale and have experience in this business. How do our dodgy friends compete with them?' He handed her the file. 'Sort out this information and absorb it. See what you can discover, what connections you can make.'

He means find out exactly how they do it.

'Yessir.'

'You can drive?'

'Yessir. I learnt during the war.'

'Good. We have vehicles here, which you may use as necessary. Aside from absorbing information, you'll spend your first fortnight accompanying Detective Sergeant Daniel Walsh, an experienced officer, formerly stationed at Standish Lane. Danny will show you the ropes. And get rid of the uniform. The detective arm is plain clothes, detective constable.'

Faye fought to keep the smile from her face. This was the first time anyone had used her new title.

'I suggest that you talk with WPC Sweetham about the feminine practicalities. She can fill you in on the facilities and so on. She'll be in later this morning. But first you should meet Sergeant Walsh.'

DI Kent stood, as did Faye.

'He isn't in your direct line of command, but I expect you to treat him as if he is. He's senior to you and will be reporting back to me on your progress. Come with me.'

5

FAYE

Clutching the bulging construction file to her chest, Faye followed the DI.

'Union Grove is a local station,' Kent said. 'It belongs to L Division, but we have part of it as our base. Here's the squad room.'

A whisper of breeze blew through the open windows of a large, light and airy room. It held four or five desks, a number of chairs and a free-standing blackboard in the far right-hand corner. A solitary man sat at one of the desks, his head down, reading papers. He didn't look up when they entered.

'We use the cells and the interrogation rooms as and when we need them. Do you have a telephone at…?'

'Westbury Court. No.'

'Get one put in. Keep the receipts and charge it to the unit. Danny…'

Kent walked across to the man, who stood.

'This is our new arrival, Detective Constable Smith,' he said. The man nodded a greeting to Faye, who gave him a tentative smile. 'From Monday she'll be shadowing you. Show her the patch, educate her as to how we work. She'll also be doing some reading. Based at Cavendish Road station. I've given her the construction brief.'

'Yessir.'

'I'll leave you in the practised hands of Sergeant Walsh, constable. See you on Monday morning.'

'Yessir, thank you, sir.'

'Pull up a seat, constable.' Sergeant Walsh said as the detective inspector left. 'What shall I call you?'

'Faye, please.'

'Alright, Faye, I'm Danny, but I expect you to refer to me as Sergeant Walsh when we're out on the street.'

'Yessir.'

'"Sir" is good too.' He sat back in his chair, his right ankle over his left knee and folded his arms across his chest, contemplating her. 'Are you really straight from the training ground?'

So it begins...

'I became a WPC earlier this year, so I suppose you could put it that way,' she replied.

Faye knew she'd have to deal with scepticism about her appointment and she wanted to show that she was there on merit; also that she wasn't a fool to be taken advantage of. Yet she didn't want to seem arrogant or over-confident.

'Hmmm.' He twisted his mouth into a smile, but there was no corresponding smile in his eyes. 'And a friend of Chief Superintendent Morgan, I heard.'

'Chief Superintendent Morgan is the godfather of my flatmate. He took over a murder case in which I was involved, in 1946, in the deep shelters in Clapham. It was subsequently found to be gang related.'

'This was before you were on the force.'

'Correct.'

'I don't like amateurs.' Walsh scratched the stubble on his chin with his left hand and she noticed his wedding ring. His eyes were like chips of granite, impermeable and cold. 'Neither does the boss.'

'In the circumstances, and I'm happy to explain in detail if you're interested, I didn't have much of a choice,' Faye said. 'Afterwards, Chief Superintendent Morgan persuaded me to join the police.'

'Hmmm.' He contemplated her. 'At least you sound like south London?'

'Clapham.'

'I'm Lewisham…' The sergeant sat up, placing both feet on the floor. 'Right. What do you know about gangland London?'

He didn't sound like he came from Lewisham, but she had no time to consider that.

'Nothing.'

'Until the war London crime was largely run by the "Italians", the Spolletta gang – rackets, girls, drugs and gambling, especially gambling – they ran all the action at the racetracks, from Epsom to Ascot. What?' He paused.

'I need a notebook.'

'No, you don't. You'll find all this in the files, this is only my summary,' he said, then continued. 'Along comes the war and the Spolletas, none of whom was born closer to the continent than Billericay, are interned as potential enemy agents. This left a vacuum, which meant a number of would-be successors tried to fill it, with plenty of cottage-industry, black marketeering set-ups.'

'I see.'

'Post-war, things have started to settle down and we have two main rival gangs: the Caplan and Hunter gangs. It was a branch of Hunter's gang that operated out of Clapham South.'

So he'd known about that all along. Did he know that she'd been shot?

'Caplan,' she began.

'Sounds Jewish, doesn't it? Zack Caplan's a Yiddisher from the East End, though he lives in Mayfair now with a very good-looking goyim wife and two kids. Likes to act the Jewish godfather, giving to Jewish charities and the like, though most of the synagogues won't go near him. Hunter's closer to home, lives in a fancy mansion in our own Wimbledon.'

'Is he from south London?'

'No, another East Ender, though he married a south London girl, Abigail. She's the reason why they live where they do. One daughter and a son, away at a fancy boarding school during term time. What is it?'

'This isn't what I expected – gang bosses living in Mayfair and Wimbledon.'

'Would you live in the East End if you had plenty of money and could afford better?'

'No, I suppose not, it's just... that they're so... public. Do their neighbours know how they make their money?'

'In Wimbledon, I doubt it. In Mayfair, would they care? What's important is that these outwardly respectable citizens command small armies of violent thugs who operate their very dirty businesses for them.'

'Is there some sort of agreement between them?'

'Good question. We don't really know the answer. My money's on an uneasy truce. It's not in either of their interests to be constantly at war with each other. Bad for business. But they watch each other like hawks and steal a march when they can.'

'Do they communicate directly?'

The sergeant shrugged.

'Dunno, maybe, but it's unlikely. Communication is probably through their lieutenants.'

Faye nodded.

'The gangs expect and reward loyalty,' Walsh continued. 'We catch the small fry, but they keep schtum and do their time while their families are looked after on the outside. This doesn't help us link the crimes on the street to the big bosses in their fancy mansions.' He paused. 'Of course, we keep our ears to the ground to find out what's what.'

'Like what?'

'Raids, robberies, unusual or big events.'

'Isn't that for the Flying Squad?'

'Yes.'

'Don't we work with them?'

'Yes.'

There was an unfathomable expression on the sergeant's face.

'But...' she prompted.

'There's rivalry, 'course there is. What else would you expect? Kent would give his left arm to wipe the eye of some of the Sweeney brass and I hear there's no love lost between Morgan and Billy Chapman, his opposite number. Especially after the Heath Row caper.'

'The Battle of Heath Row, that's what the judge called it, wasn't it?' she said. 'I saw the newsreels.'

Footage had shown heavily bandaged members of the Flying Squad entering the Old Bailey, some on crutches. It had caught the imagination of the public.

'The Sweeney needed a result, after the Greville Street diamond job. I'll bet you haven't heard of that one.'

'No.'

The sergeant pursed his lips.

'Over a million's worth in jewellery half-inched and the Sweeney was nowhere to be seen. *That* didn't make the papers.'

Faye waited for him to say more, but nothing was forthcoming. Had the Flying Squad been outfoxed, she wondered? Or was it something more sinister? Even the trainees at Pembridge Hall had heard the stories about the Sweeney being too close to some of those who they should have been pursuing.

Either way Walsh wasn't yet ready to talk about it.

Now the sergeant was on his feet. 'Come with me.'

She followed him to a side room with floor-to-ceiling metal shelving around most of three of its sides, filled with box files.

'This is our library of crime,' he said. 'You can find every known gangster in London in here and a few from elsewhere.' He pointed to two diagrams taped to the wall opposite tall windows overlooking the street. 'Our "devil's diagrams" – the gangs.'

'Thanks,' she said, already studying them. Each was set out like a family tree. 'Is this right? Are there really that many people involved?' She paused, pointing to the Caplan gang. 'There must be a hundred of them, or more.'

'And those are the ones we know about.'

The sergeant looked pleased that she was impressed.

'There's a lot to take in,' Faye said, glancing around the room. 'I've got a lot of reading to do. May I take some of these files with me to Cavendish Road later?'

'Yes, so long as you take good care of them and bring them back. Keep them under lock and key.'

'Yessir.'

'Right, I'll leave you to it.'

Faye dumped the construction file on a desk and turned back to scrutinise the two diagrams. She began at the lowest level; the rank and file, the foot soldiers.

The street names scrawled beneath some of them she knew from her time in the East End. Its teeming tenements and docks had always bred crime and criminals, street gangs, wide boys, bruisers and strong-arms. These were now augmented by de-mobbed soldiers, men addicted to the danger they'd experienced in wartime or to its spoils, and unable or unwilling to return to steady employment.

Men who had seen the worst that other men could do, men who war had turned into killers. Faye shivered. This was what she was up against. She forced herself to concentrate on the diagrams.

A ranker could progress, if they were sharp and ruthless enough, to the next level; organising and leading jobs, working with the specialists – cracksmen and some women, forgers, drivers and confidence tricksters, who could command a bigger share of any loot. They, in turn, reported to the lieutenants. At the top of the pyramids were the bosses.

There was a cough.

'Excuse me.' A female voice. Its owner was a petite uniformed constable.

'Sorry, miles away.'

'I'm WPC Sweetham – Lydia.'

'Pleased to meet you.' Faye smiled and offered her hand. 'DI Kent told me about you.'

'And you're our newest recruit, a female detective.'

'I'm not the first.'

'No, but you're unusual around here, DC Smith.'

'Call me Faye, please. So what can you tell me about working here? First things first, where's the Ladies?'

Lydia inclined her head towards the door. 'Follow me.'

They went downstairs to the waiting room at the front of the building, where there were male and female lavatories.

'These are the only women's facilities, I'm afraid,' Lydia told her, as they entered the white-tiled room. 'We have our lockers in here too, well, more of a cupboard really. Here. I'll have another key cut for you.'

'But, how can we change if there are members of the public coming in to use the loos?'

'I bolt the door. I've complained, but… maybe you'll have better luck.'

'There are two of us now – it might make a difference, I suppose.' Faye was dubious.

'Someone said…'

'What?'

'That you're well in with one of the top brass.'

The second mention and it was only her pre-duty visit. What would it be like when she really started work here? Patience, she told herself. It was bound to happen and it would pass.

'I happen to know Chief Superintendent Morgan because of a case,' she said. 'And I know his goddaughter well, but I have no influence with him.'

Lydia cast her eyes down, saying nothing.

The two women began walking back up to the third floor.

'Now, what's your role here? You're not a detective, I assume?'

'I'm an SSO, a sex statement officer. I take statements if a woman has been raped, or assaulted and might not want to talk to a man about it. They talk to me.'

'I'll bet you hear some things!'

'Oh yes. Could quite turn you off men for life, believe me.' Lydia curled her lips in disgust. 'I take the statements of the working girls too, when they can be persuaded to make them, which isn't often.'

Faye raised a questioning eyebrow.

'Too scared. Though sometimes you get a youngster, or a foreign girl, who comes here thinking she's going to be a maid or a nanny and finds herself spending most of her time on her back. The ones like that, if they have some spirit, are sometimes prepared to stitch up their pimps if we offer to protect them.'

'And do we – protect them, I mean?'

'If we can. If they'll move.'

'Are there many foreign women?'

'French and German girls are brought over all the time. They're desperate – there's nothing over there, people are starving. Some are put to work in Soho, some in the northern cities. Fair-haired, pale-skinned women are shipped abroad, to Arabia or South America. Most of *them* don't go willingly.'

'White slave trade?'

'Yep. There's a lot of money to be made out of it — buying and selling people like merchandise.'

They returned to the squad room and the 'library'.

'There's so much to learn…' Faye indicated the files lying on the desk. 'I'd like to take some of these to Cavendish Road station, but I'll need a car. How do I go about getting one?'

'Pack up the ones you want to take – there are some boxes in the back – and we'll carry them down to the carpool. I'll sign for a car and drive you to Cavendish Road. I live near here, so I can bring the car back before going home.'

'Thanks, Lydia, that's kind of you.'

'Not at all,' the SSO smiled. 'It'll be good having another woman around here. Maybe I can make myself useful doing police work rather than spend my time between statements making the tea. If you ever need a hand.'

'Best offer I've had all day!'

6

FAYE

The desk sergeant beamed at Faye as soon as she and Lydia walked through the door of Cavendish Road Police Station.

'Hello, WPC Smith, or should I say detective constable?'

'Not until Monday.' Faye smiled in response, hoping she didn't look too foolishly pleased. 'And... how did you know?'

'Clapham's first woman police detective! Come on. News travels fast on this manor.'

Probably John, she concluded, telling his old muckers about his kid sister's success. Or maybe...

'Did DI Kent contact you about my being based here?'

'He did. Daisy's been clearing out the old filing room, you can use that as an office.'

'Thank you. And very appropriate, as I've brought some files with me. They're confidential, so I'll need a key to the room, or somewhere to lock them up.'

The sergeant gave her a level stare.

'We don't take backhanders here,' he said. 'You should know. Your John knows. And we're completely teetotal. Your information's safe here.'

'I *do* know, only I've been ordered by my boss that they have to stay under lock and key.'

'Lock and key it is then. I'll find the key to the room, there's only one. Will that do?'

'It will, thank you.'

Faye and Lydia carried boxes of files through to a narrow room with a sash window at its far end. It was sweltering, with a musty smell, and Faye crossed to open the window to let in some air. A table and chair stood opposite a row of empty wall shelves and cleaning equipment was piled in the corner. There were no radiators, she noticed, so it would be freezing in winter.

She didn't care. It was her office! Her very own. Besides, she wouldn't be spending much time there, once she was settled into the squad.

After Lydia had left to return the car to Union Grove, Faye sat down to read, starting with her own casework – the construction file.

A large-scale Ordnance Survey map tumbled out as she opened it, together with a booklet, 'How to Make Cement'. Construction might be located anywhere, but it occurred to Faye, as it had occurred to the creator of the file, that the source of materials was a good place to start looking. Limestone was a base material, so kilns tended to be built near limestone quarries and these were marked on the map. Clay, another ingredient, was found all over London. These two were fired and ground into cement powder, which was then mixed with sand and water to make concrete.

Faye focused on south London on the map. It was more sparsely developed than the north, with more waste ground and abandoned areas. Her eyes were drawn to Purley and the Rose and Crown Pit, a working quarry, with lime kilns. It wasn't far by road, or by rail, to Croydon, a transport centre with railway lines into central London.

Her head snapped up as the door opened. It was the sergeant, carrying a steaming mug and a door key.

'I don't care how hot it is, I always like my brew. I made one for myself so I thought you might like a cuppa,' he said. 'And here's the key.'

'Thanks.' Faye reached for the mug. 'I'm being spoilt today.' She sat back in the chair and took a sip. 'I remember this as a junk room.'

'Well... it was.' The sergeant grinned. 'I'm not disturbing you, am I?'

'Not at all. I'm glad of a break, I've got all this to get through.' Faye swept her hand over the pile of files.

'May I?'

The sergeant flicked open the top file. It was the file on Henry Hunter.

'You know it was his gang in the deep shelters at Clapham South?' he said. 'When, you know...'

'I got shot,' Faye replied. 'Oh yes.'

'He's a dangerous man, Hunter,' the sergeant continued. 'A killer before he was in long trousers. Owns swanky West End nightclubs now and has fingers in plenty of other businesses, though I'll bet none of them are square.'

'So I understand.'

Those businesses could be a link in the chain connecting criminal activities directly to Hunter. Were any of them incorporated, Faye wondered? Corporate accounts had to be filed with the Registrar at Companies House. Had DI Kent used an accountant to look at them? Even if he had, she would take another look. In her previous job she'd been responsible for drawing up the accounts for all the hospital catering. She knew what to put in and, if necessary, how and where to hide things.

'How'd he get started? Do you know?' she asked.

'Like so many others — thieving. Then war-time black-marketeering.'

'All the time building up his criminal contacts,' Faye added.

'He's got enough of *them* now.' The sergeant twisted his lips in a sardonic grin. 'Protection rackets at every racecourse and dog track and his bookies work the back streets. Drug factories, like the one you discovered, are all over the city and his people sell the produce in his clubs, as well as in pubs and on the street.'

'From Hornchurch to Harrow, Hounslow to Epping.' Faye returned his grim smile.

'That's what your lot's going after, isn't it?' The sergeant perched on the corner of the desk, one foot on the floor.

'Yep.'

'Well, a word to the wise. Have a mind to your own safety,' he said, looking at her from beneath drawn brows. 'Hunter thinks nothing of physically damaging those who cross him. Whoever they are. He won't care that you're a woman. And he'll do it himself, too – he's famous for it, proud of it. There are plenty that carry the scars, facial scars — his "calling card" – and they're the lucky ones.'

Faye swallowed hard. But, the bigger they are… she told herself.

Her mind slipped sideways.

'Actually, you might be able to help me with something else. I'm following up a case involving a nurse from the South London. Violet Taylor was her name – she was bought into the SLH yesterday evening, dead.'

'The nurse who fell? I wasn't on the desk yesterday, but I heard about it. Sad.'

'Who went to investigate it?'

'Harry Dawkins, I think.'

Faye knew Harry, he'd been at Cavendish Road a while.

'I understood that he thought the nurse was drunk? Something to do with a party?

'On the Belvedere Estate, Fairview House, flat number four hundred and ten.'

'Hmm… those balconies wouldn't be easy to fall from.'

The sergeant gave her a level stare and raised an eyebrow.

'A local woman called an ambulance and reported it,' he said.

'Who was that? Do you remember her name?'

'Mrs Winnie Pritchard, lives opposite the flats in one of those new pre-fabs. Number thirty, I think.'

'Thanks.' Faye scribbled down the name and address.

'Why the interest?'

'A friend of mine was the nurse's tutor at the hospital. She's adamant that Violet Taylor never touched a drop.'

'You think there's more to it?' the sergeant asked.

'I don't know, but I want to find out.'

'There were no witnesses to the fall,' he said.

'None at all?'

'None from the estate at any rate.'

'That's odd, isn't it?'

'Dunno.' The sergeant shook his head and made to leave. Then he turned back. 'Maybe it is. But that party was unusual. Lots of outsiders. Those newcomers, the West Indians. That flat is rented by one of them.'

'So? Weren't they questioned like everybody else?'

'Yes, but they weren't the most co-operative… And their neighbours don't like them. Some of our colleagues aren't impressed with them either, think they're troublemakers.'

'And are they?'

'Well, not *per se*, no,' he grumbled. 'But trouble follows them around.'

'Is that because they're new and look different and people don't know how to react to them?'

'They're not like us.' The sergeant shook his head. 'There have been complaints – playing loud music, that sort of thing. And there's been some trouble over Brixton way.'

Faye couldn't imagine trouble on Brixton's sleepy, middle-class streets.

'What kind of thing?'

'Fights, threatening behaviour, breach of the peace.'

'That's hardly anything new for south London.'

'It's not.' He sighed. 'But the locals get stirred up, claim the newcomers shouldn't have come here, should go back to their own country.'

'But we invited them!'

'That's as may be, but people are weary of the bad times, yet things aren't getting any better, so they look for someone to blame.'

Faye tapped her index finger against her lips, thinking. Bread had only come off the ration a month ago and there were plenty of other war-time restrictions still in place. At a time when there wasn't enough to go round among the existing population, new arrivals, even ones who'd been invited, might not be made very welcome. Especially ones who looked so different.

'I'll see if I can have a chat with Harry,' she said.

'Faye...' The sergeant paused, then continued. 'You might not want my advice, but you're going to get it anyway. Tread carefully with Harry. This is his case. The death of that nurse looks like an accident and we can't find anyone who was there who says any different. So that's where we are and that's what it is unless you can find any concrete evidence to suggest otherwise.'

'Harry—'

'Knows this manor, he's been here long enough. He might not be promotion material, but he knows his patch. He's been walking these streets for a long while. Treat him and those like him with respect; don't go marching in assuming they're wrong and you're going to get everything right.'

'I — alright, I'll be gentle with him,' Faye promised, smiling. 'I'll try and drop in on Monday.'

'And you can pay your tea kitty subs then too.'

'I will,' Faye said as the sergeant left her.

It was a warning, even if well meant. One that she would do well to heed, she thought, before knuckling down to read more of the files.

7

ELEANOR PEVERIL

'Where shall I dump these old invoices?' Jean, the office secretary, asked.

She and Ellie were surrounded by piles of paper. Since July, when the new National Health Service began, the hospital had been overwhelmed. It was the same across London, across the whole country; anyone with an existing infirmity or illness who'd been unable to pay for treatment before, now attended their GP surgery or hospital. The only way to cope was to create a paper queue, placing people's names on a waiting list. The list already stretched into next year and the office had to manage it, so Ellie had decided to reorganise, discarding old files and papers to make more space.

'We'll burn them,' Ellie replied. 'If they're from before the war. Put them on the trolley and get a porter to take them down to the furnace.'

'What about the personnel records?'

'I'll go through them,' Ellie replied. 'We might not want to throw out all of them.'

She tipped the contents of a filing cabinet drawer onto the desk and the files promptly spilled sideways onto the floor.

'Drat!'

She bent to retrieve them.

The topmost file belonged to Antoine Girard. Ellie quickly shuffled it back with the others, but a sharp intake of breath told her that Jean had noticed whose file it was. That was unfortunate; she really didn't want to have a conversation about *him*.

Ellie avoided the secretary's eye and concentrated on the other files. Jean bustled about, self-consciously, but she kept her thoughts to herself. Then she glanced at the clock and began gathering her things together.

'I'll be on my way soon, if that's alright?' she said.

Ellie looked at her watch.

'Blimey. It's almost lunchtime. I'd lost track of time. Yes, of course, you'll want to be on your way. Enjoy your afternoon.'

She reached out to prevent a pile of papers from fluttering away as a breeze blew in through the open door. Ellie went to close the window.

After the secretary had left, Ellie pulled out a chair, sat and opened the topmost file.

Doctor Antoine Girard had come to the SLH from the Free French forces billeted in Clapham in 1939, before returning to France in 1947. It was a temporary war-time arrangement – in peacetime the South London Hospital was staffed, exclusively, by women. He would have moved on anyway, post-war, but Ellie knew the real reason why he had left.

If, indeed, what he said could be trusted.

His photograph didn't do him justice. The dark curls seemed flat and lifeless, though the deep brown eyes captured the viewer, drawing them in. Ellie remembered his dash and *joie de vivre*. They had started seeing each other shortly after she arrived at the hospital. He was good-looking and charming and had a reputation among the nurses for being a lothario, so she hadn't taken it seriously, but over time their relationship deepened, or so she'd thought.

Then he'd told her that he was married.

She was fairly certain that he'd only confessed because Faye threatened to tell her if he didn't. Faye always got to know anything important in the SLH. Antoine swore that he was separated from his wife and they would have been divorced, but the war got in the way. He promised to go and finish the process. She didn't believe him, even though she wanted to, very much.

She threw him over, though her resolve had been severely tested when he looked so shocked and forlorn at the news. She suspected that this hadn't happened to him often, if at all, and he couldn't quite believe it.

Thereafter, she had lost all faith in her judgement when it came to men. Her former fiancé had proved to be a faithless, manipulative bully and Antoine had turned out to be an adulterous liar. Now he'd gone and she wasn't expecting his return. With a sigh she closed the file. She would have liked to add it to the pile of invoices, but it was too recent to burn.

A tap on the door heralded the entry of Matron.

'Hello, Ellie. Could I have the personal details for Nurse Violet Taylor, please?' Matron asked. 'I have the unpleasant task of informing her family about her sad demise.'

Ellie found Violet's slim record and handed it over.

It couldn't be easy, having to write letters like that, she thought. Senior officers would've had to do it all the time during the war, it was part of the burden of command. But it must be emotionally draining, knowing what the message would mean to its recipients. She hadn't forgotten the dread of the postman's knock on the door to deliver the black-bordered telegram.

In peacetime it must be doubly difficult and worse if there was any suspicion of foul play…

'Matron…' Ellie hesitated, unsure of how to approach the subject. The nurse looked up from reading the file.

'Has Violet's tutor, Beryl, Staff Nurse MacBride, spoken with you about the circumstances of Violet's death? She suggested that all might not be as it seemed.'

'Ah, I see.' Matron hesitated, then frowned. 'I'm not sure that you should place too much credence on what Beryl says in this matter, Ellie. She is very upset and might not be entirely rational about it. I wonder if perhaps she may have been too involved with the deceased to be thinking clearly.'

'Really? But... I'd understood that you had asked her to go through Violet's belongings and pack them up?'

'You're right, I did. And, on reflection, perhaps that wasn't a good idea – it could only upset her further, but Taylor was her student auxiliary. Can't be helped, what's done is done. Now for this unpleasant duty.'

She slapped her palm against the slim manila folder and, compressing her lips, left the office.

So, Matron thought Beryl was too close to her student to be objective when it came to her death. Maybe she was right and Beryl was overreacting? She was certainly more upset than Ellie had ever seen her before; perhaps she *was* too close to things? Of course, Matron also had the reputation of the hospital to consider, but Ellie knew from experience that the senior nurse wasn't someone to sweep bad news under the carpet.

Truth to tell, Beryl's distress yesterday had been so unusual, so unlike the wry, funny and hard-nosed Scot, that it had unsettled Ellie. She would go and find her friend, to see how she was. She didn't like to think of her suffering so. Ellie put the files away.

Violet Taylor had lodged with the other student nurses in the nurses' home. If Beryl was going through her belongings, that was where she'd be. Striding across the hospital gardens, Ellie kept in the shade of the trees as she headed towards the large red-brick building.

On the ground floor, at the far end of a long room lined with lockers and cupboards, Beryl stood at a table sorting through the dead nurse's personal effects. As Ellie's footsteps sounded on the wooden floor, she looked round, surreptitiously wiping her hand across her eyes. Her cheeks were puffy and her skin looked grey.

'Oh, Ellie, it's you.' She turned back to the table with a loud sniff.

'I thought you might be here,' Ellie said. She looked at her friend sidelong. 'Are you alright?'

'Yes, thank you.' Beryl's chin rose, but her bottom lip started to tremble. She took a deep breath and continued to sort.

'I'm so sorry, Beryl.'

The shorter woman looked up at her. There were tears in her eyes.

'Oh dear.' Ellie put her arm around her friend and Beryl turned into her embrace, her shoulders shaking with sobs.

Such harsh, raw grief. For a student and friend? Could there be more to their relationship than tutor and student, more than friends even?

When Ellie had first arrived in Clapham Beryl had described herself as 'different'. This, she had come to realise, meant that Beryl preferred romantic relationships with women not men. Could Beryl have been intimately involved with Violet?

'Beryl,' Ellie ventured, stroking her friend's wiry brown hair. 'Was Violet...? Were you and she... together?'

The Scot drew back, shaking her head.

'No, nothing like that,' she said, chin raised. 'Vi was my student. I was her tutor. I could never have taken advantage of that relationship.' She drew her fingers across her face, wiping away the tears. 'Besides, Vi had only recently got engaged. She was in love with a young local chap named Terry Carmody and, as far as I could see, he was in love with her. Vi wasn't... like me.'

Beryl looked wretched. Perhaps Terry Carmody wasn't the only person who was in love with Violet.

Poor Beryl, grieving for someone she loved, even if that love was unrequited. And she couldn't even share her grief with anyone. She must be feeling isolated as well as grief-stricken.

Coming across Antoine's personnel file earlier had reminded Ellie of the pain of lost love. She still missed him, his crooked smile, the way he would sweep her along in his plans for fun and pleasure. She missed being at the centre of someone else's life. Having someone to love.

If it was hard for her, it must be much harder for Beryl.

'It's hard.' Ellie had spoken before she realised it. 'Being alone.'

Beryl looked up at her taller friend.

'I mean, I miss Antoine, even though *I* finished with *him*. Loneliness is difficult to cope with.'

'Aye.' Beryl looked down at Violet's possessions. 'It is.'

'Are you going to parcel these up?'

'Yes. To send to her family. There are things that ought to go to Terry, like her engagement ring. It's still in the path lab safe, I suppose, but there's some other stuff for him too.'

'Wouldn't Violet want you to have something?'

'There's this.' Beryl held up a heavy text book on nursing practice.

'I thought that was yours…'

'It was, but I gave it to Vi, thought it might be more useful for her.' She put the book aside. 'Ellie?'

'Yes?'

'Would you come with me?' she asked, her eyes wide and glistening. 'When I go to Terry's. It'll be easier if there are two of us.'

'Of course I will,' Ellie answered. 'When do you want to go?'

'Now? Best get it over.'

8

ELEANOR

Terry Carmody's flat was on the third floor of a five-storey block in Clapham Park just off the south circular. The young man who opened the door was hollow eyed and looked like he hadn't slept.

'Oh, Beryl, it's you,' he said. 'Hello.' After a slight hesitation he opened the door. 'Come in.'

He pushed his tangled hair back out of his eyes and ushered them into a musty-smelling living room, where he began to clear away litter; empty bottles, a newspaper, an opened tin can.

'Please, excuse the mess,' he said, clutching items to his chest, one-handed. He tried to straighten an antimacassar over the back of an armchair with the other hand.

'Sit down, please. I'll go and...' He disappeared into another room.

Ellie opened a window to let in some air, then perched on the edge of the sofa. She smiled encouragement at her friend. Beryl was going to do the talking – she knew the young man – but Ellie would be ready to step in, if needed.

'This is my friend, Ellie.' Beryl introduced her when Terry returned. 'She works at the SLH too.'

Ellie gave Terry what she hoped was a sympathetic look. A brief, weak smile was his response, but then he seemed at a loss as to what to do next.

'Can I get you some tea?' he ventured.

'No thanks,' Beryl replied. 'I'm so sorry, Terry.'

'So am I.' The end of his sentence was bitten off in a gulp.

'I've brought some of Vi's things...' Beryl handed him a brown paper carrier bag.

'Thanks, thanks.'

Terry placed it on the coffee table and stared at it.

'I—'

His lips moved, but no words emerged. He blinked.

'Are you on your own here, Terry?' Beryl asked, glancing around the flat. 'Isn't Carl with you?'

'Nah.' Terry stared, vacantly. Then he shook himself and answered. 'He was out last night and I — I didn't have a very good night, so I slept in. He'd already left when I woke up... probably at work.'

'He's got a job then. That's good.'

'Yeah, well, sort of. He runs errands, picks up odd jobs here and there, mowing lawns, cleaning windows, that sort of thing.'

'Locally?'

'Yeah, some of the nicer places. There are one or two families that have taken to him – it brings some money in and it keeps him on the straight and narrow.'

Terry thrust his hands into his pockets, unwilling or unable to add more. There was a small silence.

'Do you work locally?' Ellie asked, anxious to keep him talking. 'What do you do?'

'Er, yes. I'm a mechanic, I work at a garage down on Northcote Road,' Terry said, adding, 'they told me to take some time off.'

He began to shake his head.

'Why couldn't she have waited for me?' he asked them, looking from Beryl to Ellie, as if they could answer. 'I had to work yesterday, but the party started early and Vi wanted to go with some of her

A DEATH IN THE AFTERNOON

new friends from your hospital. Someone they knew was having the shindig.'

Ellie didn't know what to say, so she said nothing. Beside her, Beryl bit her lip.

'If she'd have waited we could have gone together. I should have been there. It would never have happened if I'd been with her.'

Terry's face closed upon itself. His gaze lingered on the bag of belongings.

'It's mainly bits and pieces,' Beryl said. 'The clothes are being sent to Aylesbury. I haven't been able to bring her jewellery yet – it's still in the safe in the path lab, where they took her when she was brought in. I know you gave her an engagement ring... I thought you might like it returned.'

Terry sat down abruptly; his legs seemed incapable of supporting him. He put his head into his hands.

'I can ask for it, if you want?' Beryl volunteered.

'Yes. Yes, please.' Terry looked up. His cheeks were wet.

'Is it worth much?'

'Just paste.' He shook his head. 'But Vi liked it. She was so happy when I gave it to her... proposed to her... you know. Did it properly, went down on one knee and everything. It would be good to have it.'

'I'll get it and bring it round.' Beryl's voice was tremulous, the phrase cut off. Her smile was tight and too bright.

'We should be going now,' Ellie said, standing.

Best to get Beryl out of the flat. She mustn't break down here.

'Come along, Beryl.'

'Thanks,' Terry said. 'Let me show you out. Thanks Beryl.'

The front door closed behind them and they began to walk down the stairs. Ellie sneaked a look at her friend. Beryl was silent, introspective, but she seemed to have regained her self-composure.

'Is it just Terry and his brother?' Ellie asked, hoping to distract her. 'No other family?'

Beryl took a deep breath and answered. 'Both parents are dead. Killed in a V2 raid. Young Carl was taken in by neighbours until his brother was demobbed. Terry does well in the circumstances. Carl can be a handful, always getting into hot water when he was a bairn. He's only fifteen now.'

Another family fractured by war, Ellie thought.

'At least he's earning some money,' she said.

'I think Terry could use it,' Beryl went on. 'Carl's medication used to cost plenty. He's got brain problems, can't concentrate, has a tendency to lose his temper. He takes drugs daily. One of the physicians at the SLH sees him.'

'Hard for Terry.'

'Even harder now. Vi was like a big sister to Carl.'

'Will her death affect Carl's mental state?'

'I don't know. Something else for Terry to have to worry about.' Beryl compressed her lips and shook her head. 'I feel for the lad.'

The heat hit them as they left the building and began to walk across the grassy area towards the south circular.

Ellie winced at the noise blaring from a Tannoy on the roof of a passing van. The flags attached to its roof were fluttering, advertising a public meeting in Brixton. She didn't recognise the flags' device.

'What's that?' she asked, pointing.

Beryl wrinkled her nose in distaste.

'The Union Movement. Oswald Mosley's new party; that's their flag. The fascists are on the streets again.'

'Really? Already? I know there were riots in Liverpool and Leeds last year, after those soldiers were killed in Palestine,' Ellie said. 'I wondered if there might be more to it.'

'It's closer to home than that. Go down Ridley Road on a Sunday afternoon and you'll see them, marching and pontificating against the Jews, even after everything that's happened. Home-grown Nazis.'

'Frightening people and then taking advantage of their fear.' Ellie shook her head. 'I thought we'd left that behind.'

Both women returned the waves of a couple of nurses on the other side of the road.

'It never ends,' Beryl said.

Ellie caught the note of sadness in her friend's voice. She sounded tired.

'Come and have a cup of tea at number twenty-two,' she urged. 'Maybe Faye'll have more to tell us about the case.'

'I can't right now, I've got some tutorials to do,' Beryl replied. 'It's all very well getting promotion, but now I've got to do the job. I'll come over later, when I've finished work, if that's alright with you?'

'Of course. See you later.'

9

ELEANOR

'So, what have you learned about Vi's death?' Beryl asked.

The three women sat on the terrace at number twenty-two as streetlamps flickered into life, their light as yet indistinct. Despite the dusk the air was hot and the concrete radiated heat. The mercury hadn't been below the mid-eighties all day.

'The constable who went to investigate wasn't at the station this morning,' Faye replied. 'I'll speak with him when he is. The party Violet attended was on the fourth floor of Fairview House, flat four hundred and ten.'

'Terry seemed to think that the party was organised by one of the newcomers,' Ellie said, looking at the deep shelter building on the Common. 'Violet had befriended some of the new Caribbean nurses at the SLH.'

'Terry?' Faye asked.

'Terry Carmody, Violet's fiancé,' Ellie explained. 'We went to see him this morning, to take him some of her personal effects. He was very upset. Understandably.'

'I'll find out who Terry meant,' Beryl said. 'Vi made the new people welcome; she was a generous soul. Plenty of SLH people went to that party, there's talk of little else over the road.'

'What's the consensus?' Faye asked.

A DEATH IN THE AFTERNOON

'People are shocked, saddened by Vi's death. She was well liked.'

Beryl paused, looking inwards.

'What do people think happened?' Faye pressed her after a short pause. 'And what did people see?'

'Nobody really knows. Apparently, the party was to celebrate the birthday of a chap called Lionel – he and two other men rented the flat. They came over a couple of months ago, on that ship, the *Empire Windrush*. Others from the ship were there, as well as local people and folk from the SLH, like Vi.' Beryl took a sip of iced water. 'I was talking with a couple of nurses who went along. They said it was a good do, music playing. The doors on to the balcony were open and the sun was shining, everyone was enjoying themselves.'

'What happened to spoil it?' Ellie sensed something had.

'Hmmm, there was a disturbance. Young louts came out onto the next balcony along and started shouting abuse. Everyone went inside.'

'Did that make them stop?'

'No. I was told there were chants and... noises, but Lionel turned up the wireless to drown it out and they got bored and went inside too.'

'It must have been distressing, upsetting...' Ellie suggested.

'Some, those who'd been outside on the balcony when it started, were upset, some were angry,' Beryl replied, scowling. 'I would have been.'

'Was Violet one of them?' Faye asked.

'I don't know, but I know she would have hated it.' Beryl cast her eyes down. 'But — listen to this — she left the party shortly afterwards.'

'She left!' Ellie exclaimed. This changed things.

'Yes. She left the party.'

'Where did she go?' Faye asked.

'Nobody knows,' Beryl said. 'But, about five minutes later, there was a commotion, and someone shouted that a woman had fallen from the flats. Then people rushed out onto the balcony and saw her body on the concrete below.'

'Were the nurses you spoke to certain,' Faye asked, 'that Violet had left the flat *before* she... fell?'

'They seemed to be.'

'Did they tell this to the constable who went round to investigate?' Faye continued.

'I suppose so, if they were asked.'

Faye raised an eyebrow. 'Did anyone actually see Violet fall?'

'I don't know. I don't think so.'

'Hmm...' Faye paused, then continued. 'One other thing. Did anyone see Violet drink any alcohol while at the party?'

'None. They all confirmed that, just like I said.' Beryl raised her chin, looking defiant.

This too shone a different light on Violet's death. Perhaps Beryl was right, Ellie thought; there were questions to ask about the death. How did she fall, where did she fall from and why?

Faye would ask the questions. Once she got her teeth into a mystery she would never let go until it was solved.

'I see. The nurses who you talked to, they did make statements, didn't they?' Faye asked Beryl, expectantly. 'Somebody did make a formal statement of what happened?'

'I don't know,' Beryl answered, her face screwed up in frustration. 'I didn't ask. Sorry.'

'I'll take a look at the case notes,' Faye replied.

'Have you reported the death as suspicious?' Beryl went on. 'Is there going to be a post mortem?'

'Not yet...'

'Why not?'

'Because I don't have any more proof of that now than I did yesterday. Evidence is what's needed.' Faye answered.

'But if Violet left the party...' Ellie began.

'*If* she did,' Faye answered, 'and someone is prepared to give a statement saying so.'

A DEATH IN THE AFTERNOON

'What's the point of the police if they can't investigate?' Beryl's frustration was beginning to get the better of her.

'Beryl, you've only just told me about this,' Faye protested, then sighed. 'Look, I'll speak with those nurses who talked to you, unofficially, if you tell me who they are. Get them to make statements... though time has passed since the incident now so that won't be as persuasive as if it was given immediately after the incident. People forget things.'

'You don't need to do that, I'll talk to them,' Beryl said. 'I want to help. I feel so useless.' She blew air from lips that curved into a wry smile. 'That's why I'm such a mardy so-and-so. What do they have to do? Go to Cavendish Road?'

'Yes. They should ask the desk sergeant if they can make a statement about a recent unnatural death. Tell him that they were at the party.'

'Right.'

'I have learnt who called the ambulance. It was a local woman. I'm going to speak with her when I get the chance, to find out exactly what she saw – it might help. I've got her address.'

'That's something, I suppose.'

Beryl sighed. Then she slapped her palms on her knees and rose.

'Right, I'd better be going. There's a Party social this evening, raising funds for the Decolonisation Committee. I said I'd help behind the bar. Got to keep cheerful.' She raised one eyebrow. 'It's being so cheerful that keeps me going.'

Ellie accompanied her friend to the door. Returning to the terrace, she found Faye staring into the distance.

'She's disappointed,' Ellie said.

'I know, but I can't conjure up evidence out of nothing,' Faye replied. 'And without it I can't get authorisation for a post mortem. The problem is, Beryl's never really come to terms with my joining the Met.'

'She knows investigating is what you're good at, that you want justice. But you know her background.'

'Yes, I do.' Faye sighed. 'But I'm not sure Beryl appreciates the difficulty – there's a limit to what I can do. The young nurse was her student, I know, but…'

'Rather more than that, perhaps,' Ellie said. 'I think Beryl had quite a crush on Violet, I suspect she was in love with her. I found her in tears earlier today when she was clearing through Violet's things.'

'Ah. That might explain things. Poor Beryl.'

There was a pause. Disembodied voices floated up to them, from the entrance of the Tube station below. People going up west on a sultry Saturday night.

'I want to help, but I'm barely through the door,' Faye murmured.

Ellie realised that she'd forgotten to ask about Faye's new posting.

'How was your visit to Union Grove this morning?'

'Alright, although it'll be very strange having to get used to working with men, after…' Faye gestured towards the large building opposite.

'Are there no women office workers, clerks or typists?'

'I didn't see any, but it's Saturday, so they might not be working today. I did meet a WPC, Lydia Sweetham, she's stationed there. She was very welcoming, likes the idea of having another woman around and was keen to help. I got the impression that the male detectives didn't include her very much.'

'Well, you can.'

'I intend to.'

'Ha! You've got an ally already,' Ellie said. 'What's your new boss like?'

'Hard to tell. Detective Inspector Kent is very different from Miss Barnett. Much harder to read. He seems alright. Professional.'

Relations between Faye and Miss Barnett hadn't been the same after the deep shelters case, even though Faye had worked for the hospital administrator for many years before that. Faye had subsequently resigned. Ellie hoped that DI Kent was a better boss, someone who would appreciate her talents and give her licence to use them.

'I'm to follow a detective sergeant around for a fortnight,' Faye was continuing. 'Sergeant Danny Walsh. I'm going to have to work hard with him, I can already tell he's not an admirer. Can't blame him, I suppose. A woman constable, fresh out of training, being placed directly into a specialised CID unit.'

Ellie didn't know what to say.

'Oh, I almost forgot to mention... we're going to have a telephone installed,' Faye said. 'DI Kent told me to organise it and charge it to the unit. Is that alright with you?'

'Of course! It'll be very useful!'

The Deanery, Ellie's parents' house, had a telephone, but that belonged to the church, so Ellie was rather impressed with the idea of them having their very own.

'I'll speak with the telephone people on Monday,' Faye added.

Good news, yet her friend seemed so weighed down with care. She would find it difficult after working at the SLH. There would be plenty of barriers placed in her way in her new, chosen career.

It had been a brave decision to leave the hospital and an even more courageous one to join the police force, but that was Faye. She thought hard about something, then did what she'd decided to do, however daunting. Ellie had reason to be thankful for her friend's determined and resourceful approach. It had saved her life.

'You'll manage,' she said, encouragingly. 'You'll win him round.'

'I hope so.' Faye sighed.

Faye had her detective posting, things were going her way. She ought to be happy.

But Ellie was feeling maudlin too. Perhaps Beryl's grief was affecting them all.

She had a job she loved, good friends and excellent prospects, even if she was almost thirty. She should snap out of it! Stop being so self-indulgent. She should buck up and count her blessings.

A joyful heart is good medicine, Proverbs 17:22, she could almost hear her father's voice saying.

Don't let the bastards grind you down. She could hear Beryl's voice in her head too.

It made her smile and her spirits lifted. She missed her friend's dry, laconic humour. It would return when the mystery of what really happened to Violet Taylor was solved.

Now. No more moping, lounging around waiting for the world to change. It was Saturday night, even if she was working tomorrow morning.

'How about we go to the Odeon?' she proposed. 'Cheer ourselves up a bit. The early performance is a try-out – a film called *The Red Shoes*.'

'What's it about?' Faye asked.

'Love versus art. Anton Walbrook and Moira Shearer. The heroine must decide between her lover and her dancing.'

'Huh. Why is it always women who must choose?' Faye said. 'When we get even a sniff of doing something meaningful.'

'Blame biology,' she replied.

'Blame the system! Blame men. We could have both if we were allowed to. Poor women have always had to work as well as bring up children, it's nothing new.'

'I'm determined to have both,' Ellie said, tilting her chin up and laughing. 'But not a husband. I shall have a string of adoring lovers, who fall at my feet and encourage me to do whatever I want.'

'*You* might actually do it! Throw one or two my way when you've finished with them! Make sure they're the rich ones.'

'I shall carry on being a hospital administrator, only with three bonny children.'

'Unmarried? Even the SLH might not countenance that!' Faye said, but she was laughing too. She looked at her watch. 'Evening showings start in just over half an hour. If we're going, we'd better get a move on.'

'Right! I bag the bathroom first!'

SUNDAY

10

ELEANOR

At the lectern in the canteen Ellie checked off another name on her list, then stamped the ration book of the nurse who was next in the queue for the food counter. Many of the tables in the canteen were already taken and the tall room rang with high-pitched talk and chatter, the clink of cutlery on crockery. Sunday lunch was always popular, even if the temperature was up in the eighties outside.

A raucous crowd of porters clattered, laughing, through the double doors and she noticed her boss, a look of stern disapproval on her face, enter behind them. Miss Barnett carried a rolled-up newspaper and looked as if she was going to use it to swat the porters, like flies.

The administrator now spent most of her time at Regional Health Board meetings or in discussions with the local SLH trustees. The daily running of the administrative side of the hospital and its catering fell, mostly, to Ellie, helped by Jean in the office and by Cook and the team in the canteen, but Miss Barnett was still the person in charge.

'Are you looking for me?' A counter server took over at the lectern as Ellie approached her boss.

'I am.' The older woman indicated that they should sit. 'Did you see the front page of yesterday's *South London Gazette?*'

'No.'

Miss Barnett slapped the newspaper down flat on the table. The front page carried a lurid report of Violet Taylor's death beneath a photograph of the Belvedere Estate. It concluded that the police were treating the death as an accident, the student nurse having fallen from a fourth-floor balcony while drunk.

'This doesn't reflect well on the SLH,' Miss Barnett said, lips compressed. 'Three people "commiserated" with me about this at yesterday morning's meeting. One also recalled the death of the unlucky Nurse Cooper. I can only imagine what Rosalind might be feeling right now – another nurse dies and a student to boot.'

More pressure on Matron. Ellie winced in sympathy.

'I don't need to tell you what conclusions some people will draw.'

Ellie needed no reminding. Ever since it had been set up, the South London, a hospital run by and for women, had attracted an unfair amount of criticism from those who disapproved of its very existence. She sighed. There would, doubtless, be letters from 'Outraged' of Streatham, former officers and, possibly, medical men.

The police investigation into Violet's death could hardly help matters. Should she tell Miss Barnett about it, about the likelihood of foul play and Faye's involvement?

The hospital administrator's face wore a pinched, tired and sour look.

No. The reference to Jane Cooper's untimely death was unfortunate; it would raise the spectre of Miss Barnett's own failings during that case and the current investigation would remind her further, especially given Faye's involvement. She looked as if she had enough on her mind at present.

'At least we should get some good publicity next weekend,' Ellie said, offering this by way of solace and reassurance. 'Arrangements for the fete are in place and all the local press are invited.'

'Good. We need the press on our side. The SLH needs to be well

A DEATH IN THE AFTERNOON

regarded, especially now we don't have as much control over our own destiny. I can't overstate how important it is that the Fete goes well. It's our public face. Have we got our usual local supporters involved – the Women's Institute, the Rotarians, the Workers' Education Association?'

'Yes, they've all taken stalls. So have several local businesses,' Ellie replied.

She didn't mention that she had turned some away. Several building firms competing for the new Preston House contract had offered donations to the fete committee. It was regrettable, but she couldn't allow there to be any hint of corruption, so she had refused to take their money. The SLH had to be seen to be totally above reproach.

'The funfair arrives on Friday night and will set up then—'

'But they're not to open until Saturday and the fete,' Miss Barnett interjected. 'You need to watch them – they always try to open on the Friday night, but I've always said no. If they're part of the fete they need to open when the fete does and it's the fete that delivers their customers. Is it the Deptford Fair people again?'

'Yes.'

'Good. We know them. And the stage and stalls?'

'Will mostly be erected on Friday evening and Saturday morning,' Ellie continued.

'The speeches?'

'Begin at twelve thirty.'

'Who's doing them? The Mayor, the Chair of the Board of Trustees…'

'Yes. One of the consultants will act as the host.'

'Good, that's very good. Thank you for the report, Ellie, it's cheered me up somewhat.' Miss Barnett retrieved the newspaper.

'I thought it might,' Ellie said, giving her a reassuring smile.

Perhaps, she thought, now Miss B was in a better mood, it might be an opportune moment to mention Faye.

'I have other news too,' she continued. 'Faye Smith has been made a detective.'

'Good. I'm pleased she's got what she wanted,' Miss Barnett said.

'She's worked very hard for it.'

'I'm sure she has,' Miss Barnett answered, as she stood. 'She was never afraid of hard work. *That* wasn't a problem.' She turned on her heel and marched off.

So, Miss B still hadn't forgiven Faye.

Ellie watched as the hospital administrator departed. The woman's usual rigid, upright stance was bowed. All the extra responsibilities must be weighing her down. Miss Barnett was totally dedicated and worked ridiculously hard. The hospital was her whole life. It would be easy to get sucked into that existence, she supposed; to let the job take over. It was certainly important, but one needed to have a life outside work too; it was healthier that way.

She thought about joking with Faye the evening before, about lovers and children.

One of the servers at the counter was looking, expectantly, in her direction. The queue had grown. Once lunch service was over, she would go and join Faye and her family on the Common, but for now she needed to get back to her place. Ellie rose and walked over to the lectern.

11

FAYE

'Head towards Mount Pond,' Faye called to her brother John. 'Avoid the area along the lane it's all cordoned off for the fete.'

Five members of the Smith family, and Nick Yorke, trekked across the grass of Clapham Common, laden with folded deck chairs, a large picnic hamper (carried between Nick and John) and various bags and blankets.

'We're having a picnic, Ma,' John had said. 'Not trying to climb Everest.' But Esme had insisted that it was all necessary.

'Find a good spot,' she instructed. 'Nice and flat for the deckchairs.'

Nick Yorke's arrival surprised Faye. She and Nick had only recently decided to go their separate ways. He was a thoroughly decent man with modern ideas, a University College sociologist and teacher and she'd hoped very much that their romance would thrive. It hadn't.

'Under a good tree,' Phoebe shouted after the two men, who were forging onwards across the Common. 'For some shade.'

Phoebe walked beside her mother, her pale face flushed in the heat, Faye noticed. It was remarkable that she was there at all. Tuberculosis had almost killed her, but a drug trial had led to a complete cure. Now she worked in the planning department of the council and, although she would never have a strong constitution, she could, it seemed, live a long and normal life. Her mother chatted to Phoebe as they walked. Her younger daughter's death would have destroyed her completely. It was a wonderful reprieve.

Faye's gaze switched to her father.

Reg strode along on his own, sweating and uncomfortable in his Sunday best jacket in the midday August temperature. He'd insisted on wearing it and was probably now wishing he hadn't. Not that he'd ever admit it.

She caught her older brother's eye as she caught up with him and Nick beneath the large chestnut tree that they'd chosen. He, too, was watching their father labouring in the heat; probably wondering how long he would stick it out before removing the jacket. They should've had a bet on it. Faye's mouth twitched into a smile.

A large tartan blanket was spread on the grass and the picnic hamper unpacked. Reg put up the deckchairs, one for himself and one for Esme, promptly took off the jacket and sat down.

'Bet that's sooner than you thought,' he announced, to no one in particular.

Faye and John met each other's gaze, both trying not to laugh.

Cups and plates were handed around and food distributed. It was a Sunday feast, with assorted sandwiches, early apples and plums from the garden and Esme's jam made from the summer berries on brambles and bushes growing around the train yards where Reg worked.

'Is that potted shrimp, Ma?' John asked, pointing to a jar of spread. 'Where'd you get that?'

'Phyllis went to Whitstable for the day, talked one of the fishermen at the quayside into selling her a bag full of shellfish, whelks, shrimp, the lot. He didn't even ask to see her ration book.'

'It's probably contraband,' John said with a sigh. 'You've got two police in the family now, but you still buy this stuff!'

'I didn't buy it. It was a present and never you mind,' was Esme's response. 'Here. These won't stay cold for long.' She handed out bottles of homemade ginger beer.

'Ahhh, that's good.' After taking a long swig, John lay back on the dry grass, putting his hands behind his head.

Faye curled her long legs beneath her, acutely aware of Nick's closeness. He sat beside her, sleeves rolled up, balancing strong, tanned forearms on his knees.

'How are things at the depot, Reg?' he asked. 'Many changes?'

'Some,' Reg replied. 'I'm employed by British Railways now, not Southern – they were going broke.'

'Same as the others,' Nick said. 'It'll take some time, I suppose, for any real changes to happen.'

'Yes, though they ought to get some security at the yard pdq. I've never seen so many things go missing so quickly!'

'Pilfering?' Faye asked.

'Bare-faced robbery, more like,' her father said. 'Three large bales of copper wire walked out by themselves last week. You can't put one of those in a wheelbarrow. There must have been a truck to take those away. And there was a consignment of sand went missing too. How'd they transport that?'

'Somebody wants their own private beach,' Phoebe giggled.

'Those are restricted materials,' John said. 'That means chokey. Did anyone report it?'

'I don't know. Pearson, the site manager, is rarely there these days.' Reg shrugged. 'He's always in meetings. British Railways, or whoever is running things, had better get their act together or they'll find half their stores missing. I swear those thieving 'aporths would take the rolling stock if they could.'

John sat up.

'I'll speak with someone at the station,' he said. 'Though it might be something for you.' He looked at Faye. 'It could be gang related – isn't that your lot…?'

'It certainly sounds like it's organised,' Faye responded.

Reg said nothing although she noticed that he was watching her through narrowed eyes. He had made his opinions about her joining the police very clear. She waited for the sarcastic put-down, but it didn't come.

'Look, there's the ice-cream man!' Phoebe gestured towards Mount Pond. The arrival of Nardulli's van distracted them both. Other picnickers on the Common had noticed it too and there was a general movement.

'I'll go and get us some.' John got to his feet.

'I'll come too.' Faye did likewise, brushing dust from her skirt.

'You think gangs might be involved?' she asked as she and her brother joined the rapidly growing queue on the tarmac path to the pond.

'If it's on any scale, yes,' John replied. 'See what your new boss thinks.'

'Maybe. I'll have to get more out of Dad first,' Faye said, looking back towards the Smith family picnic. 'He seems to be taking this morning's announcement well, about my new posting. That wouldn't have anything to do with you, would it?'

'We had a little talk.'

'I knew it!'

'He was worried. Thought you, as an unmarried woman, might be taken advantage of.'

'I can look after myself.' Faye gave him a sour smile. 'And it's not likely, given Phillip Morgan's patronage and with a brother on the force.'

'He just needed some reassurance; you know what he's like.'

'But I'm constantly having to reassure him. And Mum, to an extent. Constantly explaining.'

'Well, you're breaking the mould, what d'you expect?' John replied. 'You will go your own way.'

'I fully intend to,' Faye said, emphatic, then softened. 'Thanks for speaking with him, though I can stand on my own two feet, you know.'

'I thought you had enough on your plate. And you *have* gone from one extreme to the other.' John cast a look in the direction of the SLH. 'How's it going so far?'

'Give me a chance, I haven't started properly yet. I went to see DI Kent yesterday.'

'And...?'

'He seems alright, though he didn't really explain how things work there, not in detail. The SSO was helpful, Lydia Sweetham. I'm to accompany a sergeant for a couple of weeks to see what's what and find my feet.'

'Makes sense – your DI wouldn't expect to have to teach you, you've qualified.'

'Hm, I got the impression that things might be done rather differently there.'

'The sergeant will put you right.' John jingled change in his pocket as they reached the front of the queue. 'Six cornets please. Got any money, sis?'

'Here.' She handed him a threepenny bit.

'I notice Nick's here.'

'I'd be surprised if you hadn't, he's six foot three and hard to miss.'

'You know what I mean,' her brother said. 'Are you two...?'

'Mum and Dad invited him.'

'Ah.'

'They're still hoping.'

'And they're wrong...?'

'Nick and I want different things.' She took three cones from the vendor as John paid. 'Why?'

'Just wondered. I liked Nick. Still do.'

'So did I! More than like! It's just that he wants to settle, start a family and I'm not ready for the whole marriage, children, housewife life,' she said, as they began to stroll back to the picnic. 'I've got other things to do. I've only just become a detective and I want to be a successful one.'

'Hmm, you're not getting any younger...'

Faye gave her brother a withering look.

'Listen, you're my sister and I love you, but you're an independent, stubborn cuss,' John said. 'Nick's a good bloke and I think he's still very attached to you. You could do a lot worse and he won't hang around forever waiting for you to change your mind. Do you want to end up an old maid?'

Faye pressed her lips together. It wasn't that simple! How could she explain? Where should she start?

'I haven't seen you walking out with anyone recently, *elder* brother of mine.'

'It's different for a man.'

Always, always, it's different for a man. Bloody men!

'Hey... stop it!'

Faye was flicking blobs of ice cream at her brother.

'Come on, it'll melt if we don't hurry.'

Beneath the horse chestnut the cornets were handed out and all conversation ceased.

Faye's gaze swept around the group, resting, finally, on Nick. He was laughing at something Reg had said and his eyes twinkled. He'd shaved off his Navy beard, which made him look younger, with a strong jaw and expressive mouth. The breeze ruffled his hair and she fought down the desire to touch him. The physical attraction was still strong. She admired him too; he'd been a good friend and companion, as well as a lover. Ideal, some would say.

It would be so easy to fall in with what he wanted.

She dismissed the memories. It would never work.

At least he'd been honest with her. After all the death and destruction he'd witnessed, it was natural to want to build, to create, to nest. But she had her own goals. Right now, her work won out over love and family, especially if, as it seemed for Nick, one couldn't have the love without the family. So, she would have neither. She would have her work.

'Hey, is anyone at home?' Nick was waving his hand in front of her face. 'Ellie's here.'

Faye looked round to see her friend striding across the grass towards them, dark hair flowing back from her face. Heads turned at her passing – Ellie never failed to attract attention.

Some things never changed. Life must be so much easier when

you were beautiful. To be envied by women and desired by men. But that would, doubtless, bring its own complications. Besides, Ellie couldn't help her looks and she certainly had problems enough of her own.

'Hello, Ellie. Come and sit down.' Esme patted the grass beside her. 'I've kept some potted shrimp for you, I know you like it.'

'Thanks, Esme, that's kind of you.'

'Busy?' Faye asked.

'Of course, it's Sunday lunch,' Ellie replied. 'Though the sunshine's kept people outside, so not as busy as we could be.'

'Everyone will be outside next weekend,' John said. 'Let's hope the good weather doesn't break.'

It felt as if it had been hot and dry forever; it would be such bad luck if it changed on the very weekend of the hospital fete. Faye's memories of wet weather summer fetes were not fond ones.

'Some of the nurses came over with me,' Ellie said. 'They've got stakes and string and are marking out the plots for the stalls.'

John swung to his feet.

'I'll go and see if they want any help.' He dropped a wink at his sister before he began to leave. 'See you in a bit.'

'Is everything organised, Ellie?' Esme asked.

'Everything that I can do has been done,' Ellie answered. 'The parade's arranged and we have plenty of games and stalls. Can I rope you in, Esme, to help on the "Lost and Found"?'

'Yes, of course.'

'Just as one of my sons departs, another arrives.' Reg indicated the curly-haired figure of Matthew, sauntering across the grass towards them. 'Pass me another of those bottles, Esme, while there are still some left.'

'Hello there. This is a very bucolic scene, I must say,' Matthew said.

'Hello, Mattie.' Phoebe waved up at him, shading her eyes.

'Greetings, brother,' Faye said. 'You've just missed the ice creams.'

'Have some jam and bread instead.' Esme pressed a plate of food on her son as he sat, crossed legged, at her side.

'Lots of people coming out late this lunchtime,' Matthew said, raising his chin to indicate a group of picnickers who were sitting down about twenty feet away.

Faye watched the young Caribbeans settle, taking bottles and food wrapped in brown paper from shopping baskets. They were an exotic-looking group, the women wearing brightly coloured dresses, lemons, pinks and blues, while their men wore loose suits and ties, one with a hat pushed onto the back of his head. She noticed other people looking at them too, but they seemed oblivious to the stares. Maybe, she thought, they'd already become accustomed to being looked at. Like Ellie.

'At least it's warm, not the usual British summer – it'll be more like home for them,' Esme said. 'They might get a surprise when the weather turns.'

'I think they might've found out what the climate was like before they travelled,' Nick said. 'Wouldn't you? Most of them are well educated, you know.'

'How'd *you* know?' Matthew asked. 'Are you studying them?'

'Not specifically,' Nick explained. 'But their arrival will change Britain. It's already beginning to.'

'Arriving at the same time as the ex-pats,' Reg said. 'The population's rising again.'

'Just as well,' his wife added.

'When are we going to bring all our troops home?' Reg grumbled. 'From Malaya. How many will have to die there for the rubber and oil?'

'Sometimes, Reg, I think you and Beryl MacBride have more in common than you'd think,' Nick said, smiling as he caught Faye's eye.

Faye grinned as her father harumphed.

'Anyway, we need the money,' Faye said. 'To repay the Americans with.'

A DEATH IN THE AFTERNOON

'Oh, we're bankrupt, alright,' Reg agreed. 'Stoney broke, like the rest of Europe. We can't afford to keep an empire anymore.'

'We're better off than most,' Esme said, trenchantly. 'I've seen the newspaper photos of those German cities. And there's what the Jerries did to the French towns on their way out of France.'

Esme's general benevolence was something Faye loved about her mother, whose sympathies took no account of national borders. And she was right. They *were* lucky. They'd survived when many hadn't; they had places to live, food on the table and lives to lead.

The war had been over for three years, but nothing seemed to be getting better. People were impatient and, even though Faye knew changes were happening, she couldn't help but be affected by the general mood of disatisfaction. She ran through the changes already underway in her head – the nationalisation of transport, of electricity, coal, the new National Health Service and so on. Things would improve, she told herself; they would. She had to keep believing that.

Anyway, who said making a new society was going to be easy?

She missed discussing it with Nick.

'So, how many colonials are likely to come here?' Phoebe asked.

'A lot, I should think,' Nick said. 'Britain needs people, that's why we invited them. There are thousands of vacancies, especially in transport, the Royal Mail and the new health service. About eight hundred Caribbeans arrived on the *Windrush* and almost all of them have found jobs by now.'

'In two months, that's good going,' Esme said.

'There are some at our garage,' Matthew said. 'London Transport employees, good drivers, men who served. Clippies too.'

'How are they fitting in?' Reg asked.

'Alright, though they keep themselves to themselves.' Matthew took a swig of now warm beer. 'It was better at the start when there was only one or two of them, they mixed more. Gil was a real laugh. Now they tend to stick together. It all gets a bit... cliquey.'

'It's natural to congregate with your own kind,' Esme said. 'Do you think they'd like some of my jam?'

She reached for the unopened jar.

'Hang on, you put half my sugar ration in that,' Reg said, taking it from her.

'And mine,' Phoebe added.

'Actually, they don't come from the same places,' Nick said. 'The majority are from Jamaica, but others are from Trinidad and Tobago, British Guiana... There are distinct differences between the islands and great rivalry between them too. We shouldn't think of the Caribbeans as all the same.'

'There are meetings and marches in the East End, I'm told,' Ellie said. 'Mosley and his ilk. Anti-semitic mostly, rabble-rousing.'

'It won't be too long before that sort turn their attention to our new arrivals,' Reg said. 'Mark my words. A black man is easier to identify than a Jew. It'll be something else to whip up trouble about, to frighten folk. It won't matter that we asked them to come, that we need them; people will forget about that when they've been scared.'

Faye and Nick exchanged glances. There had already been questions in Parliament.

'The SLH has new Caribbean nurses,' Ellie said. 'They're very competent.'

Some of them had been at the party in Fairview House. Faye wondered if Beryl had persuaded any nurses to make statements yet.

'Any one for an ice cream?' Matthew asked.

12

ELEANOR

Ellie stepped into the cool, tiled foyer of Westbury Court.
She was alone. Faye was helping to return the picnic gear to the Smith home and Ellie didn't want to presume on Esme's hospitality. Faye's mother would insist on feeding her and the family's rations were meagre enough to begin with; though quite how potted shrimps were available on the ration was a mystery she didn't want to go into.

'Ellie!'

It was Ron, the concierge, coming towards her. His expression betokened news.

'You've got a visitor.'

Beyond him, coming out of the little cubby hole that Ron called his 'office', was the unmistakable figure of Antoine Girard.

'Thanks.'

She gazed, wide-eyed, over Ron's shoulder at the Frenchman. His cream linen suit was crumpled and his cheeks slightly flushed. The liquid, dark eyes were the same.

'Thanks, Ron.'

'S'alright...'

Ron wittered on, but she hardly heard him. Her heart fluttered. Joy. No, definitely not joy, she told herself. Shock.

Antoine came to stand behind him and their eyes met. She found it difficult to look away.

'Thanks, Ron,' she mumbled again.

She managed to focus her gaze on the concierge, though Antoine's appearance had knocked her sideways.

'I'll... umm...' Ron jerked his thumb towards his room and retreated, leaving her with Antoine.

Say something!

'You're back. When did you arrive?'

As if there wasn't something less banal to say. She wasn't thinking straight.

'Yesterday.'

'Are you staying in Clapham?'

'No.'

'Well, I'm glad to see you well.' She made as if to walk to the lift.

'Ellie, I promised I'd come back. Don't walk away from me, Ellie, please. I want to talk with you. To tell you what I've been doing.'

Ellie opened her mouth to speak, but no words came out.

'We could go up...' he said.

'No.' She didn't want him in the flat. It would be too much like old times. And too tempting. 'Let's go for a walk on the Common.'

He frowned, but then nodded acceptance. 'Very well.'

They walked, in silence, out onto the lane, where Ellie turned left, to avoid the SLH staff who were still pegging out pitches for the fete. She saw John stand up as he noticed them, but she put her chin down and carried on without acknowledging him.

'Slow down,' Antoine said. 'You're marching like a guardsman.'

'Sorry.' She slowed.

'Let's go over to the pond.'

They walked across the dry grass. Nardulli's van was still there.

'Would you like an ice cream?' he asked.

'No, thank you.'

They walked side by side, but Ellie felt an enormous distance between them. Children were still playing rounders on the grass.

'I know you lost trust in me, Ellie,' Antoine began again. 'And I was a coward not to tell you about Delphine. I acknowledge that I should have done, but I was afraid that I would lose you. And the longer it went on, the more afraid I became. Please, can we sit and talk?'

There was a wrought iron bench seat just ahead, overlooking the pond. Ellie sat at one end of it.

'It was true, what I told you, though I accept that I should have told you earlier.' Antoine sat halfway along but didn't attempt to get any closer.

Ellie said nothing. It seemed to disconcert him. She concentrated on watching the ducks.

What did he expect? That she'd been storing up questions and arguments to test him with? That she'd been living his return in her head? She'd stopped doing that many months ago.

'Delphine and I lived separate lives before the war. In the ordinary course of things she and I would have divorced years ago. But when I went off to fight and Ligugé was occupied... it became impossible. Anyway, I have begun divorce proceedings now. Given no objection from Delphine – and there won't be any – I should receive my decree within six months. Then I will be completely free.'

He waited.

Still Ellie said nothing.

She wasn't sure what to say. She wasn't sure what to think. Or to feel. Just the sight of him had upset her equilibrium.

'I'd, I'd like us to start again,' he went on. 'If you will permit?'

'I don't know, Antoine.' The words came out in a rush. 'I wasn't expecting to see you again.'

'But I told you I would return.'

'I didn't believe you.'

She stared at the pond without seeing it. His voice cut across the fuzz in her brain.

'I – I have a temporary visa and a position at St Thomas's if I want it,' he said. 'But the only reason for me to stay in London is you. If you'll have me?'

'Antoine, you deceived me, by omission if not by outright lying. You knew I wouldn't have anything to do with a married man.'

Ellie forced herself to keep the emotion out of her voice.

'Then you leave, go back to France. I had no idea if you were really coming back, or when. Now after a year and a half, you turn up and want everything to go back to the way it was. But things don't work like that. I'm not sure I *want* us to get back together.'

His face and lips were pale and he looked like someone had kicked him in the stomach.

'You've met someone else?'

'No, but—'

'Ellie... please,' he persisted. 'Everything I've done, I've done for this.'

'I'm not sure I could ever trust you, Antoine. I – I don't see that there's a future for us.'

'Didn't you miss me, at all? Shouldn't "absence make the heart grow fonder"?'

'Of course, I missed you. I missed you terribly, even if you did deceive me. But that's not the point.'

'Look, my reappearance seems to have shocked you – at least wait before dismissing me, wait until you've given my proposal some thought. Will you think about it?'

She sighed.

'I don't know, Antoine—'

'And it *is* a proposal – we could marry, if you want. Once my divorce comes through. I love you, Ellie. And I thought that you loved me.'

'I did,' she wanted to shout. 'Until you spoilt everything.' But she said nothing. She needed to think. He was right about that.

'My visa is for one month. If, by the end of that time I haven't applied for full leave to stay I will have to return to France. Even if I have a job, I need permission to remain. Think about our future and, if you'll have me, I'll apply for leave to stay. If not...' he raised his hands and shrugged, 'I'll go back to France. You need never see me again.'

But I don't want to decide! Why are you putting this responsibility on me?

'When may I expect your answer?'

'When I've had time to think.'

'Can we meet? I'll come to Westbury Court. Or to the canteen if you'd rather.'

For a split second she wondered if she could contrive to avoid him. No. He would find her. Besides, that was the coward's way out.

Antoine stood and she looked up at him. Swiftly he bent over and kissed her, so quickly she couldn't react, on the lips.

'*Au revoir*,' he said.

She exhaled in a great gust as she watched him walk back along the path around the pond. That had been so completely... unexpected. She'd spent the last eighteen months convincing herself that she'd done the right thing to end their relationship. That he wouldn't be coming back. That he wasn't worth pining over. Now here he was and hoping that they would get back together.

And how dare he put it all on her!

She didn't want to decide.

As she rose, she scrunched her hands into fists and thrust them into her pockets, then started out for Westbury Court.

13

ELEANOR

Ellie turned the key in the door of number twenty-two. As she entered, Faye and John got to their feet, anxious looks on their faces.

'Ellie.' Faye hurried over, hands outstretched in front of her. 'Is everything alright?'

Of course, John had seen her with Antoine and he'd told his sister.

'Yes. No.' She raised her palms as if to fend off any questions. 'Yes. I don't know.'

Beryl entered from the terrace.

'Ellie… is he back? Has Antoine returned?'

'He's back, but I don't know how long for. That depends…' She couldn't explain. Not here and now, in front of everyone; she needed to think about it first. 'I don't want to talk about it now…'

She wanted to escape to her room, but that would only worry them further. There was an embarrassed silence.

Beryl coughed.

'About Violet Taylor's death,' she said. 'I've found out more.'

Thank heaven, a change of subject.

Ellie exhaled.

A DEATH IN THE AFTERNOON

'The nurses I spoke to will make statements, so the police will know that Vi wasn't drunk.'

'Good,' Faye said.

'Also, an auxiliary nurse named Prudence Green came to find me this morning,' Beryl continued. 'She'd heard I'd been asking questions. She and her fiancé, an ex-RAF man, arrived from Jamaica last month. They were both at the party in Fairview House. She says there's a witness who saw Violet outside the flat *after* she left the party, knocking on the door of another flat on the same floor.'

Ellie saw and heard, but she didn't really take in what Beryl was saying. Very gradually her composure began to return.

'Eh?' John looked puzzled. 'What?'

'Violet Taylor, a young nurse, one of Beryl's students, died on Friday,' Faye began to explain. 'She fell from a fourth-floor balcony and we — the police — have been treating the case as an accident; drunken nurse falls from party flat. There were no witnesses, other than the lady who reported it.'

She began to concentrate on the conversation in front of her.

'Fairview House? On the Belvedere Estate?' John asked. 'And no one saw anything?'

'Nothing.'

John raised his eyebrows.

'Beryl's convinced that there was foul play; Violet never touched alcohol and there is some suggestion, though nothing concrete, that she'd left the party before she fell to her death. Now, it seems, we have a witness.'

'You'll have to do something now, Faye,' Beryl insisted.

'I'll need to speak with this new witness and ask him to make a statement—'

'Ah well…' Beryl looked uncomfortable. 'I'm not sure he'd do that.'

'Why?'

'He's already had a run in with the police. Sorry, but…' she cast a glance in John's direction, 'a lot of the West Indians don't trust you.'

Ellie saw the look exchanged between brother and sister.

So did Beryl.

'And with good reason, I say.' She glowered from under lowered brows.

That was a glimpse of the Beryl of old, the one who never took a step backwards. Heartening, but not, perhaps, at the most opportune moment.

'Take the copper who spoke with Prudence and the others. Pru tried to tell him it wasn't an accident, but he ignored her, asked her lots of questions about the others at the party, where they lived, what they did for a living, was very unpleasant. He'd got it in for them from the start.'

'You can't be sure of that,' Faye said.

'Maybe not, but I've got a good idea. It's prejudice; something they're familiar with.' Beryl wouldn't be deterred. 'Soul destroying, being treated like that. I know, it's happened to me; though nothing, I suspect, compared to what they've experienced, even in the few weeks they've been here. Have you seen those posters?'

Ellie knew of the notices in the windows of some of the lodging houses. *No dogs, no blacks, no Irish* they said. It was vile and unacceptable, but it wasn't against the law. Guesthouse owners and landlords chose who they rented to.

'That copper seems to have put the wind up them completely.'

'You can't hold me responsible for the actions of every policeman, Beryl,' Faye responded.

'Why did *you* have to be polis anyway?' Beryl retorted. '"The enemies of the working class", that's what Orwell calls them!'

Oh no. This was getting much too heated.

'What's important is finding out what happened to Violet.' Ellie interrupted.

'The police are saying Vi's death was a self-inflicted accident and that's wrong, we know it is,' Beryl said, vehemently. 'And even if this new witness won't make a statement, we could nail the story about her being drunk by commissioning a post mortem. Doctor Horn wants to do one. Why can't you get permission for that, Faye?'

'I can't do that without evidence…' Faye began.

'I'm giving you evidence.'

'No, you're not! You're telling me that someone has said that there's someone else who saw Violet after she left the party, but that whoever that is won't make a statement to back that up!'

'Well, what about you, then?' Beryl turned to John. 'Can't you do something?'

'Not my patch,' John replied. 'I'd only have to pass it to Cavendish Road, anyway.'

'You two would stick together,' Beryl said. 'Class traitors, the pair of you,' she muttered.

'Steady on, Beryl!' John responded.

Faye blinked; she looked shocked.

'Beryl, if you want to solve the case we must work together,' Ellie said, keeping her voice calm, but not prepared to take any nonsense. 'Faye can't just order a post mortem, she has to find new evidence of wrongdoing. It's got nothing to do with class.'

Beryl looked like she was going to argue, but Faye answered.

'Claims and accusations must be substantiated by evidence, by facts,' she said, firmly. 'Those are the rules. Otherwise, anybody could accuse whoever they liked, whether they'd committed a crime or not. A court of law must be a place where facts hold sway, not opinion, falsity or make believe.'

'Evidence and facts! The truth is that the law works for those who run it,' Beryl declared. 'It works for the wealthy and powerful, or people like them. For those who can afford it and those whose faces fit.'

'That's not true—' Faye argued.

'Hang on I don't think we should—' Ellie attempted to intervene.

But Beryl carried on, she had her dander up.

'Yes, it is!' she countered, her face flushed pink. 'The law doesn't work for outsiders, or anyone who's different. It didn't work for me and plenty like me in the Gorbals.' She pointed to her chest. 'I can't help where I was born, but the coppers didn't see me as a person, an individual, just as an address.'

Ellie knew about Beryl's impoverished and difficult childhood and how it explained her politics, but none of this could be laid at Faye's door. Yet the Scot was working herself up into a passion.

'It doesn't work for people like Pru, perfectly respectable people. All the coppers see is her black skin and they make judgements,' she continued. 'They think people like Vi, who can see beyond the superficial and shallow, are "letting the side down". I'll bet that copper thought Vi got what she deserved, that it was her own fault for being at the party!'

Tears began to run down Beryl's face.

'I don't think that's true...' Faye began, aghast. 'You don't know what that constable was thinking. It's the police's job to investigate all unnatural deaths, regardless of who has died, or who they were with when it happened.'

'Well, they're not doing their job then!'

'That's hardly Faye's fault, Beryl.' Ellie interjected to pour oil on troubled waters, before one of them said something they would regret later. 'She's trying to help.'

Faye took a deep breath, about to speak and Ellie shot her a warning glance.

'I'm going to talk with the woman who called the ambulance tomorrow,' Faye said, her voice measured. 'To see if I can find out more. And I'll speak with the constable who went to investigate the death. But a witness who's not prepared to go on record isn't a lot of help.'

Beryl seemed to have shrunk; her arms were wrapped about herself. She sniffed and opened her mouth to speak.

'Did they say that they'd speak with us? The Caribbeans?' Ellie jumped in ahead of her. 'Can we talk to them about this face to face?'

'Yes,' Beryl answered grudgingly. 'They said they'd meet us tomorrow evening, if you're free.'

'Alright. I'll make sure I am,' Faye said. 'Where are we meeting?'

'A café over Brixton way.'

'Alright. I'll come and hear this for myself.'

MONDAY

14

FAYE

Faye loped past Long Pond, feet beating a steady rhythm on the path. The water reflected the blue of a sky unsullied by clouds, but its surface was still in shadow; the sun hadn't yet risen above the tall houses on Clapham South Side.

The daily morning run around the Common had been John's idea, but Faye took pleasure in it. She exhilarated in the physical motion, stretching her legs, feeling her body working and it almost always lifted her mood. She enjoyed seeing the changing seasons day by day.

This morning it was the crisp coolness in the air that she liked; it would disappear as the sun rose higher. She swung northwards into the sunshine and passed the eastern embankments of the war-time gun emplacements, now almost hidden by grass and dotted with the flowers of knapweed and bird's-foot-trefoil. The barracks had been dismantled long ago.

The morning run usually allowed her some unencumbered time to think. Today, however, she expected John to join her. He would want to see her before her first day as a detective. And she wanted to speak with him, somewhere private, away from other ears.

Sure enough, as she approached the halfway point a tall, male figure wearing shorts and a singlet emerged. He slotted in beside Faye, pacing stride for stride.

'Alright, sis?'

'Yep.'

'All ready and correct?'

'As ready as I'll ever be. And as for correct...'

His cheeky grin made her smile; she had seen that grin for her entire life. But now she wanted John's advice.

'Can I ask you something?'

'Sounds serious. Fire away.'

'On Saturday Sergeant Walsh made a remark about the Flying Squad being nowhere to be seen at the site of a major robbery. It sounded... a bit off.'

'Off?'

'It might have been him taking a pot-shot at another police department, inter-divisional rivalry, maybe, but I got the impression he meant something else.'

'Like what?'

'Corruption, bribes. Everyone's heard rumours...'

John frowned.

'It happens,' he said.

She waited, guessing that there was more to come. John was considering how to answer. They swerved, synchronised, into an avenue of mature trees.

'Some of us are less fastidious than others about how we get our money,' he said, eventually. 'You'll be able to spot them – the individuals who are on the take; not right away, perhaps, but you'll soon learn. You develop a sense about it.'

He paused as they ran past the bandstand, where some dog walkers were chatting.

'It starts with small things and it's easy to fall into; turning a blind eye when an old mate on the street makes a book or flogs contraband out of a case. Then it gets a bit more serious, like helping yourself to the contents of a shop that's already been robbed, that sort of thing. I've seen people fall into it, despite themselves, especially when all their colleagues are doing it. There's pressure to conform.'

'But you've never—?'

'No. Never. How can you apply the law to everyone else if you don't follow it yourself?'

Faye looked down at her pounding feet.

She expected no less from her brother, but she felt a twinge of guilt. At the hospital she'd been scrupulous in enforcing the rigid wartime rationing rules, ensuring the hospital wasn't cheated of anything. But that hadn't stopped her bending the same rules when it came to taking foodstuffs home for Phoebe. She understood very well how easy it was to justify something like that to oneself, when, really, it was an abuse of one's position. Like getting preferential treatment perhaps…

But she had more questions.

'You said it begins with small things, so sometimes it gets more serious then?'

'Yeah, sometimes it's protection money.'

'Like any other gang!' Faye flushed, slowing her pace. 'Just one with a uniform or a warrant card.'

John came to a halt.

'It goes on,' he said. 'Again, it starts small; maybe a pub landlord gives you free drinks, because your being there keeps his place trouble free, so you get something for nothing, just because you wear a police uniform. But that leads on to having expectations that you'll get something for nothing and then that leads on to asking. That becomes demanding money with menaces.'

Faye screwed up her face in disgust. 'You get away with that and you start to feel invincible, I suppose.'

'It's then that a policeman becomes worse than the average criminal. Those are the really dangerous ones; they've got everything to lose. But all of it's corrosive, it breaks down the trust there should be between colleagues.'

'The desk sarge at Cavendish Road said something I didn't understand,' Faye continued, remembering his comment. 'It seemed weird at the time, but I didn't get a chance to ask him about it. He claimed that the station was teetotal, but I've seen coppers from there drink alcohol, including you. So what did he mean?'

John looked at her sidelong.

'It's a way of making everybody culpable,' he answered. 'Even those who won't take part. You'll find an envelope thrust into your hands as you're walking down a corridor, from a colleague, someone more senior to you perhaps. "Take a drink," they'll say as they pass you. The envelope will have money inside.'

Faye's jaw dropped. She snapped it closed.

'What if you don't take it?'

'You'd have to make an effort to return it,' John replied. 'Then you're a marked man, or woman. Ostracised. You'd have to watch your back when you're out on the beat, you couldn't depend on your fellow coppers.'

'But…' she hesitated, thinking. 'That's clever.'

'Isn't it. And, before you ask, I've managed to avoid it so far. I was lucky. Cavendish Road was kosher and I spend most of my time at central training now. But I'm implicated too, I haven't reported those that I know do it.'

'Never grass to the brass.'

'The ranker's mantra.'

'Except the brass are often in on it. You'd better get clued up about it, you're right about that. Especially where you're working.'

'What's that supposed to mean?' Faye bridled. They started to stroll towards Mount Pond.

'Not what you've just thought. Don't be so touchy,' he admonished. 'Listen, one way of getting money is by selling information. A tip off as regards a raid that's about to take place, a nudge towards an area a specialist unit, like yours, might be particularly interested in. That sort of thing.'

Faye recalled DI Kent's warning about confidentiality and what information criminals would pay for.

'I see.'

'The thing is, it could be anybody.'

Faye thought about the gang bosses, who wined and dined the rich, powerful and famous in their clubs, procuring influence in return for favours and services. It was rumoured that senior policemen, judges and politicians were on their payrolls. The whole of public life was corrupted.

'Keep your head down, sis and play dumb until you know who to trust. Yours is a new unit, you said?'

'Yes.'

'So it probably isn't embedded there then. Yet. You'll probably be lucky. There are some places, some stations, where it's rife.'

'Like the Flying Squad?'

'I'm saying nothing…'

He sprang forward and Faye set off in pursuit.

15

FAYE

Faye took a seat next to Sergeant Walsh, who was deep in conversation with the man to his left.

This was it. Her first day with the squad. It was so important that she didn't make a pig's ear of it. She glanced around the room, but no one was paying her any attention. There was a rumble of conversation. It was the Monday morning briefing at Union Grove police station.

She took out her notebook and pencil. As her fingers brushed against the warrant card wallet in her handbag, she felt a brief spurt of happiness.

Don't mess it up.

In a semi-circle around the blackboard sat the entire team. Faye was surprised by its size; five detectives, aside from herself and three uniformed officers. All of whom were men. Lydia sat by the wall with two women, who looked like clerical staff. Was this a self-imposed segregation, she wondered? The policewoman nodded a greeting and Faye raised her hand in a wave, but she didn't have time to say hello before Detective Inspector Kent strode in, holding a sheaf of files.

'Good morning, everyone,' he said, perfunctory. 'First this week, an introduction. We are pleased to welcome Detective Constable Faye Smith to the unit. Stand up, Faye, so everyone can see you.

Faye half stood, smiling, self-consciously around the room, then quickly retook her seat.

'One of Superintendent Bather's finest. Please afford DC Smith every courtesy, as a new squad member.'

Was there a hint of disdain in his voice? No, she was imagining it.

'DC Smith will be shadowing Danny for a couple of weeks, until she gets the lie of the land. Now, let's go round the room. First, Steve.'

The DI sat on the edge of a desk at the side of the room as a fleshy man in an ill-fitting suit came to the front.

'Detective Sergeant Stephen Turner,' Walsh hissed into her ear. 'Gambling, tracks and clubs.'

'If you count Spooky Johnson last Friday, thirty-seven street bookies have been arrested and charged for illegal gambling during the Games,' DS Turner said. 'Racetracks are quiet, after the recent Kempton Park fracas and attendances are up at horses and dogs. It's business as usual in Soho now all our Olympic visitors have gone home, though there's word of a new Caplan spieler operating in the Charing Cross area.'

Looks were exchanged; this appeared to be news.

'Any information you might pick up about it gratefully received,' the sergeant continued. 'Tables, we think, though I sense there's something unusual about it. I don't know what, but it could have some specific purpose.'

'Boxing?' a detective asked.

'Mebbe. Brian's doing the rounds of the gyms and ABA clubs to find out what people might have heard.' Turner gestured towards a short, red-haired man, who was sitting amidst the group.

'Sending the short arse again,' a voice from behind her said and there was laughter.

Brian looked unperturbed. Faye wondered how he'd been

recruited. There was a minimum height requirement and he couldn't have met it.

'Bri, DC Brian Ford...' Walsh whispered, 'was amateur national flyweight champion a few years back. He knows a lot of people in the game. And don't be fooled by the "short arse" claptrap, he could flatten any one of us without breaking sweat.'

So, Faye thought, the squad recruited by reference to skills, not rules. Maybe that was how she'd got in. But what special skills did she have?

'Keep ears to the ground and tap up any snouts.' Turner went on to list the meetings for the coming week at racecourses and dog tracks, mentioning specific individuals, track bookmakers or their henchmen. Faye couldn't keep up with all the names, though everyone else seemed to know them.

'Thank you, Steve,' the DI said, after the DS had finished. 'Bob, wagons?'

'Detective Constable Bob Lowe,' Walsh whispered, as a big, flat-headed man took centre-stage. His eyes were bloodshot and his chin stubbly, even though it was Monday morning.

'Probably out on the lash,' Walsh said, in response to Faye's questioning look. 'Trying to get the information.'

Where? If a pub or club was open on a Sunday night, it was somewhere illegal. But not off limits to squad members, Faye noted, if there was information to be had.

'He's transport and haulage.'

The gangs were deeply involved in that world, intimidating competitors and frightening drivers into transporting contraband.

'It all seems relatively quiet at the moment, although...' He went on to list and update the team about ongoing cases, all unknown to Faye. 'Any questions?'

Faye tentatively raised her hand. In for a penny, she thought.

'DC Smith.'

'I have a question,' she said, pausing briefly. 'I've heard reports of large quantities of railway yard stores going missing. The security at some of the yards seems to be lighter now that the railways have been nationalised. Maybe a case of no one really taking responsibility for looking after the assets. I wonder—'

'What kind of stores? Petty pilfering?' Kent interjected. 'That's not what we're about, DC Smith.'

'Three bales of copper cable, two steam chests and an unknown number of stores, within the last fortnight from Nine Elms, sir. I can't find any reports made about this property being stolen either.'

People sat up and the DI looked more interested.

'Not petty at all. How did you hear about that, DC Smith?'

'Not the sort of thing you take away in a wheelbarrow,' Faye said, reluctant to answer. 'They would have needed transport. Hence my question.' She nodded to DC Lowe. 'My intelligence is good. The yards keep an inventory of stores and equipment, I understand.'

'Definitely worth a look. Bob, can you take that please? Talk to DC Smith about it.'

The DI gave her a speculative glance, one eyebrow raised.

Faye kept her expression neutral. She wanted him to think she was intelligent and hardworking, but not that she was pushy. 'Too clever by half' was a phrase she was familiar with.

'Right, anyone else?' DI Kent asked.

No one volunteered anything.

'Court reports?'

A young constable stood and reported on a protection racket in Wandsworth market, a case that was up in court later that week. An older man spoke about the progress of cases involving enforced prostitution and living off immoral earnings. DI Kent handed a sheet of paper to one of the women seated at the side, who tacked it to a noticeboard.

'The schedule for this week in the courts,' he said. 'We're providing witness testimony in four cases, all Lambeth.'

As he rattled off a list Walsh spoke, *sotto voce*. 'The local stations take the cases to court and sometimes make the arrests, but we appear as witnesses.'

Something else that was different from usual police procedure. She would have to see exactly how that worked in practice.

'Any other questions?' The inspector scanned the room.

There were none.

'One last thing – now we finally have extra personnel I want to open a line of investigation into construction,' he said. 'We all know that the gangs are involved, but we don't know how they manage to operate in such a highly regulated business. So Faye, DC Smith, will have the construction brief. Talk with her if you've any pertinent information, or any questions. Now, if there's nothing else...?'

Conversations had already started around the room and the meeting ended.

'That was a good piece of intelligence,' Walsh said to her. 'Saving it up to impress the boss on your first day, eh.'

'I happened to come across it at the weekend. Chit chat. You know how it is, you're from south London,' Faye answered. 'What do I do now? More reading?'

'No. We'll take a little trip out east to see an informant of mine, a snout, see if he knows anything about Zack Caplan's new joint.'

Faye gathered up her things and had begun to follow the sergeant when the DI beckoned her over.

'Come in,' he said and she entered his office as indicated. 'Close the door. Sit down. That was a good piece of information. Where'd you get it? And please don't prevaricate any further.'

'My father works at the yard,' she answered.

'I see. Make sure Bob knows about that, he'll come up with an excuse for asking questions. We don't want your old dad getting into hot water, now, do we?'

'Yessir.'

'Right, good start on your first day. Now, off you go with Danny.'

16

FAYE

Danny Walsh drove like he was late for a fire.

Faye bit back exclamations and sat rigid, her palms pushed down on the passenger seat, as they barrelled around corners far too quickly, narrowly avoiding oncoming vehicles.

'Where are we going?' she asked when they'd stopped at a set of traffic lights.

The sergeant was eyeing the highly polished saloon car idling next to them. Its driver was slightly elevated and studiously ignoring the battered Wolseley alongside.

'Brockley Cemetery,' Walsh replied, putting the car into gear and flooring the accelerator as soon as the lights turned green. He looked back over his shoulder at the shiny new Vauxhall, only now pulling away. 'That stuffed you, you arrogant bugger,' he muttered under his breath.

'Danny, *why* are we going to Brockley Cemetery?'

'To meet Soapy, Soapy Davis, a snitch of mine.'

'Why's he called Soapy?'

'You'll know when you get down wind of him.' Swerving wildly, they overtook a slow-moving Morris and only just avoided the bollards in the centre of the road. 'Sunday driver!' Walsh yelled out of his window.

'Do you always drive like this, or is it for my benefit?' Faye asked, tetchily.

'Drive like what?'

'Never mind. Watch out— Oh well.'

Faye turned to see the milkman shake his fist at their departing car, as a mangled metal milk-bottle carrier bounced away across the road, milk splashed white across the asphalt.

Walsh chuckled.

'Soapy's a low life who sniffs around on the edge of the Hunter gang. If they think a task is beneath them, they give it to Soapy or someone like him. Which makes him useful, especially if I can set him on to find specific information.'

'Is he southeast London?'

Walsh nodded.

'Did you find him when you were at Standish Lane?'

'I don't have much to do with the people at Standish Lane now I work for Kent,' Walsh replied. Not, Faye noted, answering her question. 'I'm careful who I talk to outside the team and you should be too.'

That was the third time she'd been told to keep her mouth shut in as many days.

Yet Standish Lane was Walsh's old station; surely he must have friends there? Or was there some sort of south London police rivalry? Local stations often resented central units descending on their patch and Walsh might not want to tread on former colleagues' toes. Yet she couldn't imagine the man in the driving seat next to her being particularly careful of colleagues' sensitivities.

It was tranquil in the cemetery, an oasis of birdsong and wildflowers amid the brick and tarmac of south London's terraced streets. Danny Walsh looked completely out of place in the sun-dappled shade. Faye watched him. Just because she was the pupil now didn't mean she couldn't observe and do some detecting, about the case and about the sergeant.

They forged a path between moss-covered grave markers, passing an obelisk, a memorial to the dead of the First World War, as the vegetation became wilder. Many of the gravestones were crooked or askew, undermined by tree roots or the shifting ground. Walsh stopped in front of a large plinth holding statues of an angel and a girl child.

'The Cain family, including their little girl,' he said, his voice sombre. 'And their son, Barry. He was RAF, killed in action over Norway, 1942.'

'You knew him?'

'Know the family — fairground people, ran the Showground at Deptford.'

Faye knew them too, she realised; they brought their funfair to Clapham Common every year for the SLH fete.

'Look.' Walsh strode off to the right. 'Hannah Cain, the matriarch; my uncle worked for her. I spent many a happy hour as a nipper on their gallopers. Barry and me used to pretend we were working in the central gearing room, so, when the mirrored walls were turned outwards, we could see up the girls' skirts as the horses were on the rise.'

Faye didn't respond. She couldn't work out how much of this was Walsh trying to provoke her and how much was his usual attitude. Or maybe provocation *was* his usual attitude.

'There's Soapy.' Walsh indicated a thin man with sloping shoulders skulking behind a large stone mausoleum. 'I'll take the lead.'

Faye followed Walsh over to him.

'Soapy.'

'Sergeant Walsh.' The man flicked his cigarette end into the bushes. 'Who's this then?'

'Detective Constable Smith; just joined us. I'm showing her the ropes.'

'I'll bet you are.' The man leered at Faye as she nodded a straight-faced greeting.

'What've you got for me then?'

'Depends what you're going to give me in return, Sergeant Walsh.' The snitch's voice had a wheedling quality that set Faye's teeth on edge. 'I want a retainer.'

'You'll get nothing until you give me some information. Anything else on Kempton Park?'

'Nah, s'all gone quiet. Tanker's taken his medicine and is paying his dues again.'

'What about this new spieler near Charing Cross, then? Zack Caplan's expanding and I'll bet your mob ain't delighted. What's the word on that?'

Soapy shrugged. 'Dunno, too high up for me to hear much. Word is the boss sent Brodie to parley with Caplan's mob, some sort of re-cip-ro-cal arrangement.'

'Hmm...' Walsh looked thoughtful. 'What else? I've heard nothing worth paying for so far.'

'We've bin recruiting,' Soapy said. 'Dealers. Some of our dusky brethren.'

Faye wondered how a man who had sounded out all the syllables in 'reciprocal' so carefully could use a phrase like 'dusky brethren'. A phrase he'd heard others use, perhaps.

'Names?'

'Nah.' Soapy shook his head. 'Not yet anyway.'

She supposed it made sense for the gangs to recruit inside any newly arrived group. Was there a chance that this had anything to do with events at Fairview House?

'What do you know about the death on the Belvedere Estate?' she asked, watching Soapy closely.

His eyes narrowed a little as he glanced at Walsh, then back at her.

'Accident. Woman fell,' he barked out. 'Party.'

Faye's skin prickled. She let the silence lengthen. He knew something, she was certain.

'Are you sure?' She raised an eyebrow. 'Nothing to do with drugs then?'

'Not that I know about.' Soapy relaxed. 'Might be some of the new dealers, I don't know.'

'New dealers?'

'The blacks. I told you—'

'How did you know there were Caribbeans at the party?'

'I – I didn't. Just assuming.' Soapy began to scratch frantically at his chest. A nervous tic when he was lying, perhaps? 'They get everywhere. They'll be taking over soon.'

Faye half expected the litany of complaints and prejudices that followed, but she sensed that it was mere camouflage. Soapy knew something about what had happened on Friday evening, or had suspicions, but he wasn't about to share them.

'Alright, alright, we can do without your views on colonial citizens.' Walsh shut the conversation down. 'Seems to me you haven't got anything for us, right now.'

'Come on,' Soapy argued. 'I'm taking a risk talking to you.'

Walsh handed over a note. Faye couldn't see its value, but she surmised, from the disgusted look on Soapy's face, that it was probably only ten bob.

'Brassic, are you, sergeant? Spending your money on other things.' Soapy shot a venomous look in Faye's direction.

'Piss off, Soapy and be grateful for what you've got.'

Muttering, the informant started to shamble away.

'And make sure you've got more for me next time!' Walsh called after him. Then he turned on his heel and marched back to the car at double time. Faye hurried in his wake.

At first she'd been unsure about Beryl's allegations and her certainty that there had been foul play, though she would have trusted Beryl with her life. Yet if what Beryl had been told by those at the party was correct, there was something very dubious about Violet Taylor's death and the snitch's reaction to her questions confirmed it. The convenient story about an accident didn't add up. Violet Taylor hadn't fallen to her death while drunk and, maybe, it was drugs and gang related.

She had to follow this up.

'I'm sure Soapy knows more than he's saying about the Belvedere Estate episode,' Faye said as the car pulled away. 'Did you see the tension in him when I mentioned it?'

Walsh said nothing as they circled a roundabout.

'There's something suspicious about the whole incident, I'm certain, even if I don't know what. It seemed worth asking about.'

Walsh glared at Faye, but remained silent, a silence that continued as they drove back to Clapham.

'Don't you think?'

There was still no response.

Faye's chest felt hollow. She'd made a mistake. She had somehow offended Danny Walsh. What was it Walsh had taken against? Was it asking Soapy about the Belvedere Estate?

His driving, she noticed, while much too fast, was now performed with a clinical efficiency as he stared at the road ahead.

Would explaining help?

She doubted it.

As the Wolseley roared through the streets, she sat, wondering, no doubt as Walsh intended, when he would let her know, in no uncertain terms, just what she had done wrong.

17

FAYE

Walsh slammed the driver's door and stalked off across the car pound towards the station building. Faye hurried to keep up, as the sergeant took the steps up to the back door two at a time.

'Danny...' she said, when they reached the top.

'What?'

He swung round, stepping forward so far that she was forced to step back against the metal rail at the top of the steps. It cut into her skin. She felt the warmth of his breath on her face.

'It's time for you to learn some of the rules around here and I don't care who your fucking friends are.'

He raised his right hand and for a split-second Faye thought he was going to hit her, but he pointed his index finger, jabbing the air, at her face. She recoiled further, gripping the rail on either side of her to prevent herself from falling. The metal was hot against her palms.

'Soapy might be small time, but he's *my* snout.'

Jab.

'Understand.'

Jab.

'If you want to ask questions, you ask *me*.'

Jab.

'Otherwise, get your own grass.'

'I didn't think—'

'Too fucking right you didn't.'

He teetered on the balls of his feet as if he would launch a punch at her, but, instead, whirled around and barged his way through the door.

Faye was left, breathless, to straighten up. She looked around the yard. Had anyone seen?

It was empty.

As she pushed at the entrance door, Faye noticed her hands were shaking. She took a deep breath and concentrated until they stilled. In the Ladies she strode back and forth in the small space, trying to calm herself. Stooping over a sink she splashed cold water onto her face, patting her cheeks dry with paper towels the texture of sandpaper.

She'd made a mistake.

How was she to know that she shouldn't have asked questions? Maybe Walsh's instruction 'Let me take the lead' meant 'Keep your mouth shut'?

Probably.

Of course it did. She'd misinterpreted. It was her fault.

Yet his reaction was out of all proportion. Faye's sense of justice kicked in. She might be in the wrong, but so was he.

Yet she got the distinct impression that Walsh's belligerence was, quite simply, his normal MO. How he did things. That jabbing finger, she realised, would normally be prodding a colleague's chest... Her lips began to twitch into a smile.

Regardless, she was convinced that Soapy Davis knew something about last Friday's events on the Belvedere Estate. His whole attitude told her so. But, after Walsh's outburst, Soapy was off limits. How else could she get the evidence needed for a post mortem? Because she was, now, certain that a post mortem was needed.

A DEATH IN THE AFTERNOON

The door to the Ladies opened and Faye nipped inside a cubicle, snibbing the door after her and sitting down. She put her head in her hands and closed her eyes as she heard the other occupant use the facilities. There was nothing to be done, she realised, other than ask Walsh's pardon and she doubted *that* would be swiftly forthcoming. There would be no point in complaining about his behaviour and it would only make her more disliked. Right now, she was the new woman copper who'd been given a dressing down by Danny Walsh; that, she could live with.

She flushed the lavatory and left the cubicle. She needed to get back to work, to be seen at her desk. She couldn't 'go missing' on her first day.

Keeping a look out for Walsh, she returned to the squad room, made herself a restorative cup of tea and took it into what she already thought of as 'the library', where she consulted the very large-scale Ordnance Survey map pinned up beside the gang hierarchies.

She knew that a consignment of sand had been stolen from Nine Elms Depot. To make concrete with it, the thieves would need to add cement and aggregates. On Saturday she had identified the Rose and Crown pit, near Croydon, as being one possible source of limestone for cement and the railway line from Croydon came directly into central London via the Battersea Locomotive Depot at Nine Elms. Would cement powder be the next consignment to go missing?

Bob Lowe would be following up the depot thefts and she could see him sitting at his desk.

'Hello, Bob,' she said as she approached him. 'Have you got five minutes?'

'Pull up a chair,' he said. 'Nine Elms?'

'Yes. My informant is my father, he works there. Can you take care not to...?'

'Don't worry, I'll find another reason to take a sniff around.'

'Thanks,' she said, gratefully. No one liked an informer and it could make her father's life difficult, or even dangerous, if the gangs were involved.

'Now, when did all these stores go missing?'

'Almost immediately after nationalisation. He doesn't know if the officials are in on it; the site manager is away from the site a lot.'

'I see. I'll drop by later, take someone from the Battersea nick with me.'

'Not my brother, please. He's stationed there.'

'So you're from a police family! I'll make sure it's someone else. Now…?'

'Can I pick your brains about something else? It's probably linked.'

'Pick away.'

'I've been thinking about how the gangs get in on such a highly regulated business. I suspect they scare off smaller competitors – classic intimidation tactics — but, if they want the big contracts, they'll be competing with companies too big to frighten. So, I reckon they'll be looking to undercut them on price.' Faye paused. 'If they could cut their costs, by stealing raw materials, say, that would help. Limestone quarries are all monitored and clay's everywhere – two out of the three ingredients necessary to make concrete; the third is sand and plenty of it.'

'And not from a beach,' Bob said. 'Taking large amounts of coastal sand would soon be spotted and it could still be dangerous… I know they're supposed to have cleared the mines, but more are always being discovered, as well as unexploded bombs.'

'Exactly. But they could steal it…'

'From places like railway yards, like Nine Elms. I'll do some digging.' He raised an eyebrow, waggishly. 'Other rail depots might've had consignments of sand stolen too.'

'And cement powder,' Faye said. 'Check for thefts of that too. That'll be transported by rail.'

'Leave it with me, I'll let you know what I find.'

'Can you concentrate on south London first?' she asked. 'I've got a feeling this is happening under our noses.'

A DEATH IN THE AFTERNOON

'Okey-doke.'

'Thanks, Bob.'

Lydia looked up as Faye walked over to her.

'Any chance you could help me some more?' Faye asked.

'Yep, what d'you need?'

'Come with me.'

They walked to the library and Faye closed the door behind them.

'I need to find someone on the edges of one of the gangs who I can tap for information,' she said, indicating the two hierarchy diagrams. 'I'd guess that that won't be easy.'

'Impossible, more like,' Lydia answered, ankles crossed as she sat on the table in the centre of the room. 'They've all got their snouts. Danny Walsh uses Soapy Davis, Bob Lowe has Chick Thompson and Steve Turner uses Rosey Rose. Those are the ones I know about, but they'll have others, perhaps higher up in the organisation, or not on the diagrams at all. They're very protective of "their" men – they don't like anyone else trying to speak with them.'

As she'd discovered.

This squad was all about gathering information; perhaps it was understandable. Anyway, it was the way of things – that much was clear.

Both women contemplated the diagrams. It was then that Faye realised what was *not* shown.

'What about the women?' she asked.

There were no female names, aside from Abigail Hunter's.

'There must be female criminals? Nightclub manageresses, bordello madams, bookie's runners, con artists. There must be.'

'Yes, but… we've never put them on the charts.'

'Why?'

'We just don't.' Lydia shrugged again.

'I think we ought to.' Faye reached for a thick red pencil. 'Tell me, why is Abigail Hunter on here, yet not Zack Caplan's wife?'

'Abigail Hunter is a business partner as well as a wife,' Lydia said. 'It's said that Hunter treats her as one of his lieutenants.'

'But one who shares his bed.'

'Yes, keeping it in the family, though word is that Hunter often plays away. You wouldn't think so to look at him... Anyway, Susan Caplan restricts herself to family and home.'

'Hmmm.' Faye frowned. 'Does she have a bank account?'

'I don't know. Only if her father or her husband set one up for her,' Lydia said. She twisted her lips. 'And I don't think it would be her dad. Susan was brought up by her mother.'

'If she has an account then Caplan must have sponsored it, she couldn't open one herself. So, what's to stop him using it? Let's find out if she has one. Can you do that?'

'How?'

'Talk to the tax people, see if you can get some information out of them. Now, is there anything else missing from these diagrams?'

Faye and Lydia added names in red to the Caplan and Hunter gang diagrams, identifying the females involved in the illegal activities.

'Maybe we should list family members too,' Lydia suggested. 'At least for those higher up in the ranks.'

'Good idea. Collate what we know already and then check with Births, Marriages and Deaths at Somerset House.'

'Looks like I'll have plenty to do between taking statements.'

The women smiled at each other. Lydia flushed.

'Faye,' she began, hesitant. 'You know you said that you were acquainted with CS Morgan?'

'Ye-es.'

'Well.' She seemed to make a decision. 'I think you should know that half the men in this place think you're Morgan's floozy.'

'Why doesn't that surprise me?' Faye grimaced. 'Does DI Kent think that?'

'I don't know. He knows the Chief Super, so I wouldn't think so...' Lydia gave her a wary look. 'I hope... I hope you didn't mind me mentioning it, only... you've been so kind... and I thought that you ought to know. If you hadn't worked it out already.'

'No, Lydia, of course I don't mind. I'd much rather know than be left to speculate.'

'Oh, there's more than enough speculating goes on round...'

The door opened and DI Kent walked in.

'Here you are,' he said to Faye. 'I've been looking for you. My office in five minutes please.'

Heart sinking, Faye answered 'Yessir.'

18

FAYE

'What did you do to piss off Danny Walsh?' DI Kent asked her, exasperation written in the lines of his face. 'You were supposed to shadow him, not antagonise him.'

'I—'

'Danny is a good, effective policeman, who has his ear to the ground. He knows how things work. You, on the other hand, have yet to establish that you deserve to be here.'

Faye kept her mouth shut. The DI was right.

'It's not difficult – all you have to do is watch and learn.' His tone was sarcastic. 'You're to continue doing so tomorrow.'

'Yessir.'

She reckoned it was ten to one that Danny Walsh had demanded rid of her and Kent had told him 'No'. The sergeant had scowled at her from across the room as she followed Kent to his office.

'So mind your p's and q's. And, in future, you do as you're told and follow Danny's orders. Do you understand?'

'Yessir.'

'As regards the diagrams... you and Lydia have made some additions?'

Surely he couldn't object to those.

'Yes, sir. We've added the names of the women.'

'It's a good idea to set out what we know about them – the higher-ranking ones at any rate, you couldn't include all of the working girls, there are too many of them.'

She relaxed.

'We thought we'd include family ties too, to make links between gang members. People here might already know, but new team members like me won't be aware of those links, so, shouldn't we show them? Lydia's going to the Public Record Office to track down any who aren't already in the system. She'll update the central diagrams. As you said, it's all about information.'

'Good.'

While she had his attention, there was the question of the gang's businesses…

'Sir, there are the "legit" businesses. Like nightclubs?'

'Yes, the bosses own clubs, even if their placemen are the nominal owners. What about them?'

'Are any of them incorporated? And have we looked at the company accounts?'

'No, though other businesses are,' Kent snapped. 'We engaged an accountant to go through *those* accounts when the unit was set up. He found nothing useful.'

Faye swallowed.

'Perhaps it's a fool's errand then, but I used to draw up accounts, it was part of my previous job,' she explained. 'I'd like to take a look at them, just in case I spot anything. And I can review the accountant's findings too, if you don't mind?'

'Not at all. Be my guest.'

Faye ignored the caustic tone.

'Lydia can get the latest details from the Registrar at Companies House. They should tell us who the company officers are, who else is involved and which accountants audit the accounts.'

'Lydia is going to be a busy girl.'

'She wants to help, sir. And she can do more than make mugs of tea and help the secretaries.'

The DI gave her a level stare.

'This is your first day here, DC Smith and you seem determined to turn things upside down,' he said.

'I — I don't intend to, sir. I'm sure most of what occurs to me has been thought of and discounted, maybe for good reasons, but it seemed like a good idea.'

'It is. Have you begun work on construction?'

'I've had a look, Bob's helping me. Sir?'

'Yes.'

'May I ask, are there any specialisms in the hierarchies? I don't mean criminal skills, like safe breaking, I mean special focus. So, does one lieutenant have responsibility for certain areas of operations? Like brothels? Or—'

'Construction.'

'Exactly.'

'Not really, not as far as we know, although arrangements tend to be because of physical location. So, one person might oversee business at Kempton Park and Sandown racecourses, which are close together, while another deals with Ascot and Windsor for the same reason.'

'I see. Thank you, sir.'

'Good. Is there anything else?'

'Yessir.' Faye took a deep breath. 'I've reason to believe that a recent death, being treated as an accident by local police, is suspicious. It was a young nurse from the hospital where I used to work. I asked Soapy Davis about it.'

'Ah. I was aware that you spoke with him...'

Walsh had told him.

'...but I didn't know what about.'

'He knows something, sir, but he wasn't saying.'

'Why is the death suspicious?'

'She's supposed to have fallen from a balcony during a party. She smelt of whisky when she was brought into the hospital. But she was a strict teetotaller and there's a witness who saw her, after she left the party, but before the fall. So, the "accident at a party" theory doesn't add up. I'd like to request a post mortem, to see if she was drunk, as was claimed. It needs to be done quickly; the incident occurred late on Friday afternoon.'

Kent pursed his lips, but, before he could speak, Faye pressed on.

'The pathologist at the hospital agrees, I know her. She was a police pathologist during the war, but she can't go ahead without the family's permission or a request from the police.'

Kent considered for a moment. 'Very well, if you sort out the paperwork you can tell your pathologist to go ahead. An extra pathologist to call on might be useful to us in future. Sometimes our designated pathologists are difficult to get hold of. Did you know the nurse personally?'

'No, sir.'

'Very well. And remember, if there isn't a link to gangland, the case isn't for us. Let the locals sort it out.'

'Yessir. Thank you, sir.'

Excellent!

Faye hurried through to the squad room and rang the number of the SLH office.

'Hello, Jean. It's Faye. How are you? Is Ellie there?'

'Hello, Faye. I'm well, thank you. Detective now, eh? Well done you. No, Ellie's probably in the canteen.'

Faye looked at her watch. It said two thirty. Blast, she should have realised; Ellie would be overseeing the cleaning and preparation for reopening the canteen at four.

'Alright, Jean. Can you take a message? It's for Miss Horn, the pathologist.'

'Fire away.'

'Could you tell her that the police are requesting her to carry out a post mortem on the body of Violet Taylor? By the authority of Detective Inspector Kent of Special Operations Unit D7. Did you get that? I'll fill in the paperwork and be round with it later this afternoon. She'll be anxious to begin, given the amount of time since the death, so I thought I'd let her know and she can make a start straight away if she's free.'

'Wilco. Pop in and see me if you're here before five.'

'I should be,' Faye said. 'See you later.'

She replaced the telephone handset on its cradle, pleased that her boss had seen fit to trust her, even after the episode with Walsh. Or was Kent simply giving her enough rope to hang herself with? Let the DCS's floozy screw things up and be sent back to uniform.

No, that wasn't going to happen.

She would listen more carefully in future and do exactly as Walsh told her.

Now for Harry Dawkins and Mrs Winnie Pritchard.

19

FAYE

'Hello, sarge. Told you I'd be back soon.'

Faye mock saluted the desk sergeant as she walked through to the large office.

'Don't forget your subs!' he shouted after her.

She spotted the solid form of Harry Dawkins hunkered in front of a typewriter at a desk beside one of the windows, tapping at the keys with one finger. The blind was drawn against the sun.

'Constable Dawkins,' Faye said as she approached. 'Harry.'

'If it isn't Johnny's little sister,' he responded, in a jolly tone.

Faye gave him a tight-lipped smile. Dawkins was all of three years older than she was.

He assumed a serious expression as he stood and offered his hand. 'Congratulations, detective constable.'

'Thank you.' She shook hands. 'Actually, I wanted to ask you about a case. Violet Taylor.'

'Misadventure,' Dawkins said. 'Nurse was drunk, fell from a fourth-floor flat during a party.'

'Thing is, Harry, she was SLH and I've been asked to look into it.'

'You don't work there anymore, Faye, and this isn't your patch either.'

It was tempting to point out that the whole of London was her 'patch', but she didn't want to antagonise Harry. She might need his help and she remembered the sergeant's warning.

'I know, but I still have contacts there and I've said I'll look into it. Besides, my DI's requested a post mortem.'

Harry sighed and rolled his eyes.

'Why? It's open and shut. A witness — the only witness — saw her fall; lady who lives opposite. Those nurses who made statements this morning didn't see anything new, you know. I assume you had something to do with their coming in?'

'They wanted to. Violet Taylor was a well-regarded and popular nurse.'

'She was dead on arrival at the hospital. Stank of spirits. Had been at a party with a rum crowd.' He chuckled at his own black humour. 'Lots of those newcomers there, Caribbeans.'

'You spoke to some of them, I understand.'

'Yes. They weren't so keen to make statements. One of them, another nurse, was prepared to, though her so-called "fiancé" wasn't.'

'So-called? What are you saying?'

'It's just an excuse, isn't it? Anything goes these days. 'Specially with the blacks.'

Faye told herself to be patient.

'Did you look at where Nurse Taylor fell from?'

'Course I did.' He bridled. 'I do my job properly. I've been doing it for long enough.'

By implication, longer than I have, Faye thought.

Yet, whatever Harry's personal views, it was local police like him who were the front ranks against crime and criminals. They were the indispensable ones, not detectives, she told herself.

'And what did you conclude?'

'It would have been difficult for her to just "fall",' he said, to Faye's surprise. 'The balcony had a guard rail.'

'So?'

'Must have been some larking around going on. Horseplay.'

'Sufficient to topple her over the edge?'

'Well, yes. She fell, didn't she?'

Faye stifled a retort. This wasn't getting her very far, so she changed tack.

'Did you take the names of those at the party?'

'Certainly did. Just typing up my report now. Daisy's off sick. You just can't get the help these days, what with babies and women doing men's jobs.'

Undeflected, Faye pressed on.

'Could I have a copy of your report, please? I'd like to see who else was there.'

'When I've finished it.'

'Did anyone you spoke to mention some shouting from the balcony of the next door flat?'

'Don't think so. They weren't exactly forthcoming about anything. Seemed very suspicious to me.'

'Harry, could it have been that they felt threatened?'

'Threatened? Who by?'

'You! The police.'

'They've got no reason to feel threatened. Unless they've done something wrong. Unless they're hiding something. All they've got to do is co-operate.'

'Yes, but I'm just saying—'

'How long have you been doing this job?'

Faye sighed.

'I've just finished my training.'

'So you're still wet behind the ears. Just because you've got yourself a detective post, doesn't mean that you can come in here and tell me how to do *my* job.'

'I—'

'You've got your step; they're wanting women these days, so that's good for you, even if it means good chaps are overlooked. Specialist teams...' He tutted. 'What's needed is more police on the beat. Just because you're a detective now doesn't mean you know better than people who've been walking these streets for years.'

'I grew up here! I know these streets.'

'Not like a copper does.'

'That's as may be, Harry, but times are changing and the streets are changing with them.'

'I know. You don't have to tell me. Not everyone likes the way they're changing neither.' Harry's voice was growing louder. 'And you don't have to look down your nose like that – there are plenty of folks who think like me. Ordinary people. The majority. We don't have enough to go round in this country as it is.'

This again. Faye groaned inwardly. And besides, she *was* ordinary.

'And remember, you might find yourself out on the street when you could do with back-up from the likes of me.' He pointed at her. 'I wouldn't antagonise us if you know what's good for you.'

'What d'you mean by that?'

That was a direct threat. She wasn't going to stand for that.

'Just saying,' Harry backed down when he saw her anger. 'But you might need us, some old-fashioned blokes, at your back, doing the real business.'

The real business. Old fashioned blokes.

Faye snapped her mouth shut. Arguing was pointless. There was nothing she could do, nothing she could say, that would change Harry's attitude. It was hopeless. To be seen, not as a person, but a woman, or a black man, or a Jew, someone marked out as not of the tribe. Such was the nature of prejudice.

Right now, she needed Harry's help with the Violet Taylor case, so she would bite her tongue. She would do what so many women always did, mollify and stroke, but it went against the grain.

Ye gods, this was so different to the SLH! Maybe she hadn't really appreciated how fortunate she'd been to work in a place where women were treated as professional people, without this casual misogyny.

'This is going to be my base station, Harry, so I don't want to get off on the wrong foot. Let's agree to differ about the newcomers, shall we?'

The constable harumphed.

'Will you let me have those names?'

'I'll get Daisy to make a list for you.'

'Thanks.'

20

FAYE

The single storey pre-fab stood the one end of a small row of similar dwellings along one side of the busy south circular. To Faye it resembled a child's drawing of a house, with a shiny brass knocker and letter box on the central front door and asters and roses growing beneath the square windows to either side of it. A neat garden lay behind a wooden fence and ran around the whole of the property, separating it from the next pre-fab along. Tidy ranks of vegetables lined the narrow side strips and tall bamboo cane pyramids carried dangling green beans.

Faye opened the gate and walked up the path to the front door.

Concrete. The house was made of cream-painted concrete panels inside a steel frame.

She rapped the knocker, warrant card at the ready.

The door opened to reveal a tiny woman, with huge eyes and tight, unfeasibly black curls. A suitable occupant for the little doll's house.

'Good afternoon, my name is Detective Constable Faye Smith,' Faye said, enjoying a moment of pure pleasure as she held out her warrant card in its new leather case. 'Are you Mrs Winnie Pritchard? May I speak with you?'

'Yes, that's me,' the woman answered, peering at the card. 'Women police now, I don't know. Come in, please.'

Faye was led into a small kitchen that overlooked the front garden. She sat at the kitchen table.

'What's this all about, then?' Winnie Pritchard asked, as she filled the kettle.

Faye explained her involvement in the case of Violet Taylor, saying that the police were awaiting the results of the post mortem, but that she was looking into the death.

'Poor girl. I was in here, making the tea, when I heard the noise from across the road.'

Mrs Pritchard pointed to the housing blocks opposite.

'At what time was this?' Faye asked.

'It was a few minutes after five o'clock, *Take It From Here* had just finished. My Joe comes home at six, so I came through to get tea ready.' She put cups and saucers, a jug of milk and an almost empty sugar bowl on the table. 'I told the other policeman all of this. What's his name? Constable Dawkins, from the station along the way.'

'I'm sure you did,' Faye reassured her. 'And I'm sorry to be asking you again, but sometimes it's better to speak with someone directly, rather than merely reading a statement.'

'She was at that party, that's what the *Gazette* said.'

'Did you know at the time that there was a party going on?'

'No. I could hear music, but that often happens, so I didn't think anything of it.'

'And you heard something? A cry? A scream?'

'I'm not really sure. I think there was a noise, that's what attracted my attention, but I saw her fall.' A teapot in a crocheted cover joined the other items. 'I didn't clock that it was a person at first, it was a blur. Then I realised. She was a nurse, the newspaper said.'

'Yes, she worked at the South London. If I could ask—?'

'My sister's girl had her first baby there. Milk?'

'Please. Did you see where she fell from?'

'Not really, but it was from one of the upper floors – fourth or fifth.'

'Can you tell me what happened next?'

'I ran outside. To see if there was anything I could do.' Mrs Pritchard poured the tea. 'She was on the ground, just over there. Past the pavement and the lamp post, near to the grass.'

Faye glanced over at the flats as she sipped her tea.

'I couldn't cross immediately, there was too much traffic. It's getting busy again in rush hour, you know.' She replaced her cup in its saucer. 'By the time I was halfway there I could see others were ahead of me. So I thought it'd be of more use if I went round to the call box on the corner and called for an ambulance.'

'That was quick thinking,' Faye said and Mrs Pritchard beamed.

'It wouldn't have far to come,' she said.

'You said that people were there, at the – by where the nurse fell?'

'Yes, four or five people. Men. Then a woman came, one of those West Indians.'

'I believe she was a nurse, a friend of the woman who fell.'

Mrs Pritchard winced. 'Oh dear. That must have been horrible, to see her friend like that. I didn't notice anything else, I went to the telephone.'

'Did you recognise any of the men?'

'No, although I thought one or two of them were locals.'

'Can you remember names?'

Mrs Pritchard shook her head. 'I can't remember anything these days.'

'If you do, please let me know,' Faye said. 'I'm afraid I don't have any cards yet, but I can write down my station's telephone number, or you can leave a message at Cavendish Road police station. I'm often there and, even if I'm not, a message will reach me.'

'Alright. Would you like a top up?'

Faye accepted another cup and gazed around the kitchen.

'I haven't been inside one of these pre-fabs before,' she said. 'They're small, but they're very neat.'

A DEATH IN THE AFTERNOON

'Oh yes, this suits me and Joe down to the ground. Look.' The woman sprang up and opened a door. 'Indoor bathroom, with hot running water. What d'you think of that?' She beamed with pride. 'All the pre-fabs have them, as well as a kitchen water heater too. Better than the outside lav and heating a copper on the range. And look at this.'

She pulled back a washing up towel that happened to be lying over the edge of a work counter, as if it was a stage curtain.

'Ta–da! A Frigidaire! Built in!'

'My!' Faye was genuinely impressed. The kitchen might be small but it was very well fitted out.

'We got bombed out and had to sleep on a mattress on the daughter's floor for months, but it's almost worth it for this. Built of concrete and steel, not bricks and mortar, but it's warm and dry – no creeping damp from a cellar – a decent patch of garden to call our own and all the mod cons.'

'I'm glad you like it so much,' Faye said, meaning it. It was impossible not to be charmed by Mrs Pritchard's enthusiasm for her new house.

'We came to see it being built, Joe and me,' Mrs Pritchard continued. 'It didn't take 'em long, everything came on the back of a lorry. The foundation slab had been laid before and they built the whole row of houses in a day, had the houses up by lunchtime and did the fitting out in the afternoon.'

'Impressive,' Faye replied. 'Who built them, d'you know?'

'Oh yes…'

Faye's eyebrows rose. Could it be…?

'…Lambeth Council.'

Ah.

'You didn't see which builders they used, I suppose?'

Her hostess shook her head.

'Well, thank you, Mrs Pritchard, but I'd best be going.' She stood. 'Thank you for the tea.'

'My pleasure, dear. Let me show you out.' They walked into the tiny hallway. 'Oh, I don't suppose I should call a copper "dear".'

'Not a good idea, in general, perhaps, though this one doesn't mind.'

'I'll go into the station if I can remember anything else.' Mrs Pritchard stood in the doorway. 'Such a shame, that young nurse. I hoped so much that she would survive. It was quite a shock when I saw in the *Gazette* that she'd died.'

'She probably died immediately,' Faye said.

'Hmm, not necessarily. I know from my volunteering at St George's that quite a lot of people survive a fall from that sort of height,' Winnie said. 'You'd be surprised. That's why I went to telephone for an ambulance.'

'In case she could be saved?' Faye said.

'Exactly.'

21

ELEANOR

Ellie and Jean scrutinised a large plan showing the detailed layout of the tents, stalls and amusements of the SLH fete.

'The plots have been staked out with pegs and string.' Ellie indicated the squares and rectangles. 'Here's the list of what goes where.' She indicated a key at the side of the diagram.

'What's this?' Jean pointed to a large, empty square near to Nightingale Lane.

'That's the stage. For the dignitaries and speeches. Here, in front of it, is where we put up rows of chairs.'

'And the funfair?'

'Over here,' she stabbed a finger at the map. 'Further away from the South Side, it's safer for the children. The fair will be there throughout the weekend.'

'And very popular too, I've no doubt.' Jean made a moue of displeasure.

The secretary expressed disapproval of anything that Miss Barnett might consider unseemly, but, Ellie suspected, Jean would enjoy the funfair as much as anyone when the day arrived.

'The shooting range will be here.' Ellie pointed to an area adjacent to the entrance of the deep shelter. 'We need to make sure it's set up so that the rifles point at the concrete, not at the rest of the fete.'

She lifted the plan.

'Can you divide this up and run it through the duplicator to hand out, so our helpers know what should go where on Friday. Have the programmes gone to the printers?'

Jean nodded.

'First thing this morning.'

'Good. No one else can ask me to change the running order.' Ellie pressed her lips together and reached for her bag. 'Now, I must go down to the canteen. I should have been there over half an hour ago!'

There was a knock at the door. Both women turned.

'Antoine!' Jean almost clapped her hands in delight. 'You're back! Lovely to see you! How are you?' The last was delivered in a low, confidential tone.

Ellie blinked and snapped her gaping mouth closed. What was he doing here?

'I've come about my records,' the Frenchman blurted out. 'I thought... I'm sorry to intrude.'

'What about them?' Ellie demanded, then moderated her tone. 'That is to say, they're your records – of course, if you want them, you must have them.'

Jean was already at the filing cabinet where personnel files were kept under lock and key.

'I wonder if you could send them over to St Thomas's?'

'If you wish,' Ellie replied, trying to speak normally.

'Are you working there, now, Antoine?' Jean asked. 'I do hope you'll come and see your old friends at the SLH now you're back.'

There was an awkward silence.

'I'll leave you two to chat...' Ellie said.

'No, please don't go on my account...'

Ellie escaped into Miss Barnett's empty room, closing the door behind her.

Get a grip, she told herself. This couldn't keep happening; she couldn't be completely thrown off balance every time she came across him. He had friends in Clapham – he'd be around for a month at least. She would likely run into him again.

And she needed to consider what he had asked. Once the summer fete was out of the way…

The voices next door ceased. It was probably safe to go back in.

Jean looked up from the typewriter.

'I'm sorry,' she said, with a tentative, sympathetic smile. 'That was awkward. I did always like Antoine.'

'There's no reason why you shouldn't,' Ellie said, crossing the office to her desk.

'Did you know… that he was back, I mean?'

'Yes, as it happens, I did.' Ellie sat, focusing on a file on her desk, but not seeing any of the writing on it.

'He looked very anxious not to upset you…'

Ellie was saved Jean's special pleading on Antoine's behalf by another knock on the door. A porter's blonde head poked around it.

'Ellie, there's a kerfuffle in reception, can you come?'

'What kind of a kerfuffle?' Ellie said, following the porter into the corridor.

'It's a young man,' she explained. 'Not visiting a patient, I'd say. Looks distressed and… a bit dodgy.'

They walked along the corridor towards the hospital entrance.

'He came in asking for Beryl MacBride. I told him she wasn't here. Then he started shouting and swearing, waving his arms about; I was glad I'd not told him where Beryl was. I was going to go and get a couple of the girls, just to help him on his way, but then he asked for you.'

'Me?'

'Demanded to see you, in fact. Wouldn't take "No" for an answer. I told him I would get you if he settled down.'

They pushed open the double doors into the marble-floored formal entrance hall of the hospital.

There was a short queue at the reception desk. Sitting on a bench seat against the far wall, with a space around him, was Terry

Carmody. His face was grey and drawn and his eyes bloodshot; he looked even worse than when she and Beryl had gone to see him on Saturday.

He caught sight of her and rose.

'Terry, what is it? What's happened?'

'I'll be over here if you need me,' the porter murmured, before she went to stand by the entrance doors.

'Ellie.' Carmody blurted out as he stumbled forwards. 'I... it's... I...'

'Calm down, calm down. Tell me.'

'I—'

His face crumpled and he began to weep, silently, wiping his nose on the back of his hand. Some of the other people waiting looked at him with sympathy; most chose not to notice.

'I can't cope with this. I've tried to find Beryl, but... Please say you'll help me.'

'Of course, I'll help you—'

'Terry, Tel...' A short man wearing a mechanic's overalls bustled into reception. 'There you are. I've been looking all over.'

'Sid, this is Ellie. She works here.'

Ellie acknowledged the other man. 'Now, let's get out of here and go and sit somewhere quiet and you can tell me what's going on.'

Within ten minutes, Ellie was sitting with Terry Carmody and his friend on a shady bench in the rose arbour in the SLH gardens. A blackbird's liquid song floated above the 'click click' of secateurs as a gardener dead-headed roses in the beds nearer the hospital. A muted drone of traffic rumbled from the South Side beyond.

Terry teetered on the edge of the bench, rocking back and forth, his elbows on his knees. He rested his head in his hands, then sat up again, shuffling back on the seat. Tears leaked from the corners of his eyes. Sid placed a hand, awkwardly, around his friend's shoulders, patting him on the back.

What could have happened? Whatever it was had wounded an

already desperate man still further. Ellie sat back, keeping very still and calm.

'Now, tell me what's happened,' she urged in her most gentle voice and handed Terry her handkerchief. 'Start at the beginning.'

'Thanks.' He sniffed. 'It's Carl.'

Of course.

'He didn't come home after work on Saturday. He often goes to the football,' Terry said, in a defensive staccato. 'Sometimes he stays with one of his friends. Overnight. I can't make him come Home. I do try.'

'I'm sorry,' Ellie said, soothing. 'It must be hard for you.'

'Being on my lonesome will be even harder.'

Terry's face was pained, his mouth turning down and scoring deep lines into his face.

'And—?'

'By yesterday lunchtime, I was starting to wonder where he was. None of his old mates had seen him. Not even at the Palace on Saturday afternoon and he never misses a home game. That's when I got really worried.' Terry gave her a despairing look. 'I don't know where his new friends spent their time. There was nothing else I could do, so I went home. Then this morning...'

The tears returned and the other man took up the tale.

'The police came round to the garage this morning. I work there, with Terry. They told him that they'd found a body, with Carl's medication card in the jacket pocket. Brought him here to identify it. I came too.'

Terry put his head into his hands again and his shoulders shook with silent weeping.

'I'm so sorry, Terry.' Ellie leaned forward. 'Did they say how he died?' She directed her question to Sid.

'Drugs. An overdose. He was found in the basement of a derelict house – been bombed in forty-two and never rebuilt. It was where addicts go, they said, somewhere the police visit regularly.'

Addicts? Beryl hadn't said anything about Carl being a drug addict. Was he?

'Terry, did Carl ever—?'

'No. Never.' Terry sat bolt upright, shaking his head, his lips pressed together until they were white.

'Can you be sure? Sometimes even close family members don't—'

'He couldn't be, not with him taking his medicine, he'd be vomiting all the time. The doctor checked when she prescribed it, that Carl didn't ever take narcotics.'

'I see.'

'They showed me the needle marks on his arms, the arms of his body.' Terry began to weep again. 'I'd never noticed those. I don't think those marks were there before.'

'So how did he get them?'

'I don't know!'

'Alright Tel, calm down – it's not her fault.'

A young man who didn't, who couldn't, take narcotics found dead from a drug overdose; a young nurse who never drank alcohol is dead after falling, while inebriated, from a high balcony. The hairs on the back of Ellie's neck began to rise.

'Terry, do you think there could be a connection with—?'

'Vi's death? There must be.' Terry gazed at her as if she might be able to explain it. 'Though, at the moment, the only connection that I can see is me!'

It had crossed Ellie's mind, but she hadn't liked to mention it.

'Do you think Carl could have been at Fairview House, last Friday, Terry?'

'Eh? I dunno. I'm sure he wouldn't have had anything to do with what happened to Vi, he loved her. She looked after him like a big sister. He would never hurt her.' Terry's grief was very close to anger; he was growing belligerent again.

'I'm sure.' Ellie calmed him. 'Maybe someone he knew was there, a friend? They might know something.'

'Yes, I suppose so,' Terry conceded. 'I'll ask his mates, though I'll have to find them first. How else can I find out what happened to him?'

'You could request a post mortem, for a start,' Ellie suggested. 'Then our pathologist could determine whether Carl was a habitual drug user. Yes – I know what you said, but it's always useful to have science on your side to back you up.'

'That's a good idea, Tel,' Sid urged.

'How do I do that?'

'Come with me to the office and I'll find the forms. You can fill them in then and there. Sidney and I can help you, if you want.'

'Yes. Let's do that now.'

Ellie nodded a silent greeting to a group of nurses as she, Terry and Sid followed the winding path back to the hospital building.

'I should have looked after him better,' Terry said. 'I thought he was settling down, working for some nice families, but he'd got in with the wrong crowd. Older than him, mostly and rough.'

'You couldn't follow him around, Terry, he had a life of his own.' Sid tried to console his friend.

'I know, but…'

'Do you know the names of Carl's new friends?' Ellie asked. 'Could you write them down for me? If they're of dubious character, I know a police detective and I could ask her to check if they have criminal records.'

Terry gave her a guarded look.

'If Carl got mixed up in what they were up to, that might help explain why he died.'

His expression relaxed. 'Alright. But you must tell me what you find out.'

'Very well, I promise I will.'

She led them through the building, ignoring questioning looks as she did so.

'This is Mr Terry Carmody,' she said to Jean when they arrived at the office. The secretary looked down her nose, her mouth turning down at the corners. 'His brother's body is currently in the mortuary and Mr Carmody wants to request a post mortem. Could you find the necessary form, please?'

As Jean went to do so, Ellie pulled out a chair. 'Please, take a seat,

Terry. Here, Sidney, have this one. I'll get a pad and pen for Terry to use.' She rummaged in a desk drawer.

'Here's the post mortem request.' Jean put the form on the desk in front of Terry, who looked at it, then at Ellie.

'Thanks, Jean,' Ellie said, ignoring the secretary's distaste. 'Let me start to fill it in, Terry, while you write down those names.'

It didn't take her long and Ellie handed the partly completed form to Terry for his signature. He handed it back to her, with the list.

'Thank you. I'll see the authorisation gets to the pathologist,' she said. 'She can conduct the post mortem as soon as she gets it. I suggest you call at the hospital tomorrow and ask for the mortuary.'

'And the names…'

'Don't worry, I'll pass them on. Oh, one other thing that might help. Do you have a current photograph of Carl that I might borrow?'

'Yes, we had some taken at Margate last month.'

'Good.'

'I'll find them when I get home, pick the best. I'll bring one with me tomorrow.'

'Thank you. Will you take him home, Sid?'

'Yeah. Come on now, Tel.'

22

ELEANOR

Ellie sat down at her desk, thinking. Carl's death couldn't be a coincidence, could it? She must tell Faye about it.

As if summoned by magic, her flatmate's head poked around the office door.

'Hello. Where's Jean?'

'I've sent her to find Beryl to tell her to come to the path lab,' Ellie replied, rising and slipping Terry's completed form into her pocket. 'Do you have the post mortem authorisation for Violet?'

Faye waved an envelope. 'Here. But I suspect Dr Horn has already carried it out,' she said.

'Let's go and see.'

Their footsteps echoed on worn stone flagstone floors as they approached the pathology laboratory and mortuary, which were in the oldest part of the hospital. Pushing the doors open, they entered a chilly, windowless room fitted out with steel tables and sluices. A diminutive figure wearing a mask and a surgeon's gown was at work at one of the tables at its centre.

'Dr Horn.' Ellie called out in greeting and Faye waved the envelope so that the pathologist could see it. They went to wait in the tiny cubicle that served the pathologist as an office, while she finished the post mortem she was working on.

'Terry Carmody, Violet Taylor's fiancé, came in this morning,' Ellie said, taking the opportunity to bring Faye up to date with developments. 'His brother, Carl, was found dead earlier today, in an abandoned house, apparently having taken a drug overdose.'

Faye whistled. 'That can't be a coincidence,' she said.

'My thought exactly. His brother says Carl never took drugs; they would have played havoc with his medication. Our local police, on the other hand, are happy with the drug overdose explanation.'

Faye frowned and muttered something under her breath.

'Hello, Ellie, Faye...' Dr Horn greeted them as she removed her mask and stripped off her gloves. 'Can't keep away from the old place?'

'It keeps drawing me back,' Faye said with a smile. 'Though today the reason is a sad one. Violet Taylor?'

'I carried out the post mortem as soon as I received your go-ahead,' the pathologist said. 'Follow me.'

She led them over to the far wall and its mortuary storage cabinets and pulled open the nearest one. On it lay the naked corpse of Violet Taylor, freckles livid against the skin of her bloodless face. Her skull, what was left of it, was supported by a paper pillow.

Ellie grimaced in distaste.

'Was her head so badly smashed?'

'I'm afraid so,' Dr Horn replied. 'The parietal and occipital bones were shattered when her head hit the concrete.'

'So there would be no way of knowing if someone had struck her on the head first?' Faye asked.

'None,' Dr Horn replied. 'So you think there was foul play?' she asked, after a second's hesitation.

'That's what I hope the post mortem will help us to determine,' Faye replied.

The pathologist looked down at the body.

'After what Beryl MacBride told me, the first thing I looked for was alcohol. Usually, humans metabolise alcohol quite rapidly, though not so quickly after death, so there was a strong chance that there would be evident traces of alcohol if she had drunk a significant amount. But I could find hardly any. If Violet Taylor had drunk a large quantity of alcohol, I'd expect to see far more. She certainly wouldn't have been inebriated sufficiently to lose control of herself.'

'So she wasn't drunk?' Faye clarified.

'Exactly.'

Ellie exhaled.

Vindication for Beryl; and it would allow Faye to get her teeth into the case.

'That's not one hundred percent foolproof, however and could be challenged in court, especially given the time elapsed before I examined the body.'

'Your opinion's good enough for me,' Faye said. 'What else did you find?'

'Miss Taylor died of injuries incurred when she fell from a high place, most obviously when the back of the head came into contact with the ground.'

The pathologist had paused but clearly had more to add.

'And?' Faye asked. 'There's something else?'

'There are some suggestive details,' Dr Horn replied. She raised one of the body's arms by the wrist. 'There's bruising to the wrists and forearms.' The yellow bruising was clear to see. 'This is distinct from post-mortem *livor mortis*. It was caused before death occurred.'

'When the ambulance men picked her up to place her on a stretcher, perhaps?' Ellie suggested.

'Highly unlikely. Ambulance men are trained in how to lift; they don't haul on the wrists.'

'Stan and Robin brought her in,' Faye said. 'They're experienced ambulance men. Could this mean that she was manhandled before she fell, or was pushed, from the balcony?'

'I think it's possible,' Dr Horn said. 'Although, bear in mind, that could be because someone was trying to stop her from falling or jumping. Trying to save her. There is, however, something else.'

She produced a small plastic spatula and a torch from the pouch in her gown. Opening Violet's mouth with the former, she shone the torch onto the teeth.

'Look at the front upper incisors.'

'What is that?' Ellie peered into Violet's mouth. 'Are they broken?'

'Not broken, but the enamel's cracked and chipped,' Dr Horn replied. 'And recently.'

'Done when she fell?' Faye asked.

'It's possible. Her upper and lower jaws could have clamped together when she hit the ground, cracking or breaking the teeth. If that was the case, however, I'd expect upper *and* lower teeth to be affected.'

'How else could this have happened?' Faye asked.

'Could someone have tried to force something into her mouth?' Ellie suggested. 'Like a bottle? Pouring alcohol down her throat.'

'Maybe,' the pathologist answered. 'Though there may be other explanations.'

'Is there any indication of death from anything other than the fall?' Faye asked.

'None. And a head injury like this is almost impossible to survive.'

'Thank you,' Faye said. 'So, if I read this right, the marks on the body and its contents are suggestive that Violet Taylor *did not* fall to her death from a balcony while inebriated and that she *may* have been manhandled beforehand. Does that mean she could have been thrown or pushed? Is that a reasonable conclusion to draw from the forensic evidence?'

'My post mortem report will say that is possible. The evidence isn't definitive, but I would say that there's enough to warrant further investigation.'

'A murder investigation.'

'Murder is certainly a possibility given the forensic evidence.'

So Beryl was right all along.

'Thank you.' Faye's face was grim.

'I understand that you have another body, of a young man, brought in this morning,' Ellie said to the pathologist.

'Yes. One Carl Carmody, a local youth.'

'Carl is the younger brother of Terry Carmody. Terry was Violet Taylor's fiancé.'

The pathologist's eyebrows rose. 'Do I have authorisation to conduct a post mortem?' she asked.

'Here.' Ellie handed the completed form to Dr Horn. 'Terry Carmody filled a request form earlier this morning.'

'Good. I should be able to get to him this afternoon.'

'I spoke with the woman who reported Violet's death before I came here,' Faye said. 'A housewife, who lives opposite the flats where it happened. She said she saw the body drop and a small crowd gather round it shortly afterwards. She recognised a number of the people who surrounded the body as locals but couldn't remember their names.'

'Could one of them have been Carl, I wonder?' Ellie asked. 'His brother said he'd begun to hang about with a bad crowd. He had mental problems, couldn't pay attention and was on medicine. I think there was a doc from here who was seeing him.'

'Who?' Dr Horn asked. 'She'll know more about his medication. That might help me.'

'I don't know, but Beryl does.'

'Violet Taylor, fiancée to Terry Carmody dies and, less than three days later, his brother's body is brought here,' Faye said. 'Much too much of a coincidence for my liking.'

'What's too much of a coincidence?' Beryl came through the double doors into the path lab.

'That Carl Carmody was found dead so soon after Violet died,' Ellie summarised.

'What!' Beryl exclaimed, mouth agape. 'Carl's dead! How?'

'Drug overdose, we're told, but we have our doubts,' Faye answered.

'My God, poor Terry.' Beryl shook her head and frowned. 'First Vi and now his brother. I must go round and see him.'

'Terry came here this morning,' Ellie said. 'He was looking for you but found me. He was in a desperate way, looked like he'd just been driven over by a tank, poor chap. He signed post mortem request forms and promised a photograph of Carl tomorrow.'

'That'll be useful,' Faye said. 'But we need it now, to show to our interviewees this evening and find out if they saw him at the party or afterwards.'

'I'll ask for the photo when I call on Terry later,' Beryl said. 'His flat's on the way to Brixton.'

'Ladies, this is all very interesting, but may I have my laboratory back, please? I have more work to do.' Dr Horn began to usher all three of them out of the lab. 'By the way, Beryl, who was the SLH physician overseeing Carl's medication?'

'Miss Souter,' Beryl answered.

'I'll speak with her.'

'Oh, one other thing before we go,' Beryl said. 'Vi's jewellery. I promised Terry I'd collect it and take it to him.'

'It'll be in the safe.' Dr Horn marched into her office and spun the dial of a small wall safe. 'Here.' She took out a transparent, sealed plastic bag. 'Here it is.'

She handed it to Beryl.

'But...' Beryl held up the bag.

'Hmm?'

'There should be a ring, an engagement ring that Terry gave to Vi. That's what he's interested in being returned,' Beryl said.

'This is what was on the body when it was bought in,' Dr Horn said. 'My assistant is very conscientious when it comes to recording the personal effects of the arrivals. Here's the entry in the ledger.'

She handed a thick file to Beryl, pointing out the entry. It recorded a set of gold stud earrings and a small pocket purse containing sixteen shillings and eightpence.

'If you could sign for it, please?' The pathologist handed Beryl a pen and Beryl did so.

'Right, now...'

They were ushered out into the corridor and the laboratory doors closed behind them.

'Vi was so proud of that ring,' Beryl said. 'She always wore it. I had to instruct her to remove it when she was on the wards. It didn't look like a cheap ring, either, despite what Terry said. He must have saved up to buy it. Do you think it could have been stolen when she was lying on the concrete, her head smashed in?'

'Would anyone do such a thing?' Ellie exclaimed.

'Remember the black-out and the Blitz,' Faye said. 'When we were all supposed to be pulling together. Plenty of looting and theft then, including stealing from the injured or dying. Cash, jewellery, the lot.'

'A very poor show,' Ellie said.

'There'll always be some looking to turn a situation to their own advantage,' Beryl added, lip curling. 'One way or another.'

The trio walked back to the modern part of the hospital, stopping in the entrance hall.

'So, d'you believe me now?' Beryl challenged Faye.

'I believed you before, Beryl,' Faye responded. 'But I needed independent evidence.'

'And now you've got it! There'll be more tonight. I'll go and visit Terry, take this with me and pick up the photograph,' Beryl said, still grasping the small plastic bag. She headed towards the hospital's front doors. 'See you in Brixton at seven.'

23

ELEANOR

The bell on the door jingled as the three women entered the café on Coldharbour Lane. There was a split-second lull in the babble of voices, before the lilting buzz of chatter resumed. The café's clientele was exclusively Caribbean.

There were some speculative glances coming their way and a perceptible change in atmosphere. Not hostility, but a general wariness. Accustomed to being noticed, it meant little to Ellie, but, from Beryl's fidgeting, Ellie suspected that the nurse found it uncomfortable. Faye was, as always, hard to read; watchful, giving nothing away.

They sat at a Formica-topped table with a clear line of sight to the café door and ordered three cups of tea.

From beneath lowered lashes, Ellie observed a group of men at a table opposite playing dominoes with an exuberance she'd never associated with the game before. They slapped tiles down on the table as they joked and ribbed each other. Her lips twitched into a smile; their *joie de vivre* was infectious. They were exotic and new and she wanted to speak with them but knew she couldn't. Why should they want to talk with her? Here *she* was the interloper.

What had Esme said? That it was natural for people to congregate with their own kind; this was the perfect example. Here people could unwind because they felt more at home among their own, not aliens in a strange and often hostile land.

Ellie loved her country, never more than when it was under threat from the Nazis, but she knew that there was no turning the clock back; time moved, inexorably, on. Yet many of her compatriots wanted to return to how life had been before the war. The arrival of the Caribbeans made that impossible. Society was changing, just when people wanted to return to a normality that already belonged to the past. Life would be difficult for the newcomers, even without the day-to-day prejudice they would face because of the colour of their skin; it must be very hard.

Faye stirred her tea for the tenth time.

'Where are they?' she demanded. 'They're late.'

'They'll be here,' Beryl answered. 'Pru said they would be, so they will be.'

'I think they're here now.' Ellie tipped her head towards the door, its bell ringing as it opened.

A neatly clad woman led two men in their direction. Given the look of recognition on Beryl's face, this must be Prudence Green. The woman had an air of quiet assurance, her posture upright and composed; someone who took pride in her appearance, but without any vanity or pretension. Ellie warmed to her on sight.

The taller of the two men with her, who had an open, pleasant face, touched Prudence's elbow to steer her around a jutting table. He must be her fiancé; what had Beryl said his name was? Another West Indian followed, wearing a sour expression and radiating hostility, but he broke into a grin when greeted by others in the café. His name was Gilbert. It was clear that they were all well known to their fellow Caribbeans.

They stood and Beryl presented Ellie and Faye to Prudence, who introduced her companions.

'Maurice Grover, my intended.' Prudence gestured towards him and he smiled as Ellie shook hands with him.

'Pleased to meet you,' she said, then looked at the other man, then at Pru, but no introduction was forthcoming. She raised an eyebrow and smiled.

'You can call me Gil,' he said, his expression guarded. 'But I don't want my name to be bandied around.'

'I – I see,' Ellie said.

'I've come here for Pru and Mo,' he said, glaring. 'That's all. Not to help no polis.'

Ellie saw Beryl glance at the other nurse and Prudence's slight shrug.

'Tell me, Gil,' Faye addressed him. 'D'you know my brother, Matthew Smith? He works on the buses.'

'Matt, Matt Smith, yes, I know him, we work out of the same garage.' Gil's eyes narrowed in suspicion. 'You his sister? Humph, a woman copper. I knew he had a brother who was polis, but not a sister too.'

'It's turning into a family business,' Faye responded.

'Detective,' he said, giving Faye the once over.

Faye didn't react but held his gaze.

'Haven't I seen you at the SLH?' Prudence asked her.

'Yes, I pop in now and again, usually to the canteen,' Faye replied. 'I used to work there not so long ago.' She placed her notebook on the table. 'Thank you all for coming. Shall we sit? I'm going to make notes, so that I don't forget anything, I hope that's alright with you.'

The Caribbeans acquiesced wordlessly.

'Right. Can you confirm that you were at the party at Fairview House last Friday and tell me why you were there?'

'Yes. We were all invited,' Prudence replied. 'Though Mo and I arrived first.'

'With Violet?'

'Yes, she came with us. Terry was going to join us all later.'

'How did she seem?' Beryl asked.

'Happy, I'd say,' Prudence replied. 'She was showing off her engagement ring. Though that all changed...'

'I understand there was some unpleasantness, shouting and abuse from the next balcony along?' Faye prompted.

'That's correct,' Pru said. 'Racialist slogans and shouts. We all went inside and, soon after, Violet said she was leaving.'

'Why? Why change her plans?' Faye continued.

'She didn't say, but she had a determined look on her face.'

'She didn't give any indication of what she was planning to do next?'

'No.'

'And then she left? You saw her go?'

'Well... actually, no,' Prudence said. 'I didn't, did you...?'

Maurice shook his head in the negative.

'So we can't be certain that she left,' Faye said.

There was a small silence.

'Yes, we can,' Gil volunteered. 'Because I saw her outside, in the corridor.'

Tea was brought to the table, although Ellie hadn't seen the West Indians give an order of any kind.

'In the corridor,' Faye repeated. 'Can you tell us what happened?'

'I arrived later,' he continued. 'After work. When I came out of the lift on the fourth floor, I turned the wrong way and ended up walking the whole way around the central well before finding flat four ten. There was a woman knocking at the door of a flat on the same side as the one I was going to. A slight woman with reddish-brown hair and a freckly face. I walked past her.'

'That was Vi,' Beryl said.

'Did you notice the number of the flat?' Ellie asked.

'No. It wasn't the one I wanted, so I walked on by. It was the next one along, I think.'

So, Violet was knocking on the door of the adjacent flat.

'What happened then?' Faye continued the questioning.

'I heard the door open after I'd gone past. There were raised voices. Male and female.'

'Was it the door to the flat with the louts on the balcony?'

Gil shrugged.

'Gil didn't arrive until after the unpleasantness,' Maurice said. 'He wouldn't know about that.'

'It must have been the same flat, the one next door,' Prudence said. 'Violet was upset by those half-wits, we all were, but I think she saw someone she knew on that balcony. That's what dismayed her so much. Not the racial slurs, which were distressing, but not surprising, but that someone she knew was making them. I think she went round to tackle them. That was very brave of her.'

'Did *you* recognise anyone on the balcony?'

'No,' Prudence said and Maurice concurred. 'No one.'

'They were all young men?'

'That's right.'

'This *proves* that Vi didn't die in a drunken fall,' Beryl said. 'We have witnesses who say she left the party before she fell and one who saw her going into another flat on the same floor.'

'I didn't say that,' Gil interrupted. 'I saw her outside the flat. And I don't know if they let her in, either.'

'Of course, but this is important,' Ellie said. 'Isn't it, Faye? It places Violet somewhere else when she died.'

Faye didn't respond.

'There was some noise outside in the corridor as well,' Prudence volunteered, frowning with concentration. 'After the shouting. Do you remember?'

'Yes. It was the thugs again,' Maurice said. 'Making a racket as they were leaving.'

'And this was before Violet's accident?' Faye asked. 'They left *before* that happened?'

'Before,' Prudence answered.

'Definitely before,' Maurice agreed.

'Did all of them leave?'

'I can't say,' Prudence answered. 'We heard them. We didn't see them.'

'But someone opened the door to Vi,' Beryl said. 'So someone was still there.'

'And the doors to the balcony were still open,' Gil said. 'I noticed that when I went out onto the balcony later, to see what was going on down below.'

'Was this young man on the balcony of flat four eleven?' Faye showed them the photograph of Carl.

'Yes, he was there,' Maurice said, 'making a lot of noise.'

'Who is he?' Gil asked.

'He's a local youth,' Faye said, then corrected herself. 'Was, past tense. His body was brought into the South London earlier today. He was killed, possibly murdered.'

All three Caribbeans looked shocked and surprised.

Faye wasn't usually so tactless and insensitive, but... Then she realised, her friend had sprung this on the West Indians deliberately. They realised it too.

'You didn't need to tell us like that,' Gil said, accusing. 'You wanted to see how we'd respond.'

'What's going on?' Maurice asked, sharply. 'We had nothing to do with any murder.'

Ellie became aware that the noise around them had diminished, the domino players grown quieter. She cast a glance around the café; people were looking over to their table. The jolly atmosphere had disappeared.

'We don't know anything about that.' Prudence pushed her chair back and stood. The café was silent, everyone focused on their drama. 'Beryl, I thought you said—'

'I apologise.' Faye tried to forestall their departure, half-rising and reaching out her hand towards the nurse. 'I'm sorry. Please don't leave. I needed to know if you knew about his death.'

Prudence seemed to be in two minds, vacillating. Gil moved to push past her to the door.

'Please don't be offended,' Ellie interjected. If they left now, working out what really happened to Violet would be so much harder. 'Please. She's only trying to get to the bottom of who killed Violet.'

Gil snorted in derision and Prudence shot him a fierce look.

'May I ask some more questions?' Faye asked. 'Please.'

The trio exchanged looks. Prudence retook her seat. The chatter in the café resumed.

'Alright,' Maurice said.

'Another witness to the incident told me that, after Violet fell, a group of people formed around her.' Faye pressed on, before they changed their minds. 'Is that so?'

'Yes,' Prudence responded.

'What did you do?'

'Violet was our friend. When we realised what had happened, Pru and I immediately went downstairs,' Maurice said.

'Were other people standing around Violet when you got there?'

'Yes,' Prudence answered again.

'Did that include some of the men who had been on the next-door balcony?'

'Not as far as I know, I thought they'd already left.'

'I went out onto the balcony,' Gil added. 'I could see everyone down below.'

'Was the dead boy there?'

'The kid in the photo? No. At least, I don't think so.'

'What was going on?'

'Nothing much, people were just staring down at the body.'

'I called out that I was a nurse and people let me through,' Prudence said.

'And what did you see?'

'Violet was lying on her back, one leg bent beneath her, her arms spread out. There was a pool of blood.'

'What else?'

'Nothing else. She looked the same.'

'Wearing the same clothes, the same jewellery. She didn't look different in any way?'

'Unless you count having had her head stove in,' Gil added.

'She hadn't been... interfered with, had she?' Prudence asked. 'Is that why you're asking about her clothes?'

'The post mortem showed no sign of it,' Faye answered.

'Good,' Prudence said with relief. 'I didn't notice anything different. She was a bit dishevelled, but then, she had just fallen from four floors up, so...'

'Was she unconscious?' Ellie asked.

'Yes. People can survive a high fall, you'd be surprised, but her head had been too damaged for her to be conscious.' Prudence paused, then continued with her tale. 'Anyway, I took her pulse, it was irregular and faint. Then the ambulance men arrived and she was taken away.'

'And what did the onlookers do?'

'Once there was nothing to see but a large bloodstain, everyone drifted away,' Maurice said. 'The party was over. Then the police came.'

'Constable Dawkins.'

'That was his name,' Prudence said, exchanging a look with her fiancé. Gil looked away, a sneer on his face.

'Did you tell him about seeing Violet outside the flat?' Faye asked Gil.

'I wasn't saying anything to that po-lis man,' he replied, scornfully. 'I've learnt it's better to keep my head down and say nothin'.'

'I see.' Faye looked down at her notepad, her lips whitened as she pressed them closed.

'When you were watching from the balcony all of that time, did you see anyone bend or kneel down by the body?' she asked Gil.

'No.' He shook his head. 'They were all just standing round. Pru was the only one who was close to the… to Violet.'

'Right.' Faye asked a more general question. 'Do you know who owns the party flat and the next one round, may I ask? Who does that belong to? Is it rented?'

'Lionel told us all the flats along that side are rented,' Prudence added. 'The same man collects the rents once a month, but he's from an agency, Golden Properties.'

'That's useful, thank you. That'll help me track them down,' Faye said. 'Thank you.' She went to put her notepad away then stopped. 'Is there anything else that you've remembered that might be unusual, or out of the ordinary?'

'No.'

'No, except…' Maurice hesitated.

'Yes?'

'I'd forgotten until now, and I don't know if it means anything, but... one of the lads who had been so noisy earlier, the one in the photograph who died. I saw him after Vi fell. He was on his own, up by the traffic lights near the junction with Cavendish Road. He was running away.'

'He'd run away?' Beryl asked, a look of astonishment upon her face. 'Carl ran away! Vi was like a sister to him.'

Maurice shrugged apologetically and raised his hands.

'Thank you,' Faye said, making a note. 'That's all very helpful. It may be that I'll ask you for a formal statement later, if we charge someone and need to go to court. Would you be willing to give one?'

'We've already spoken with the police,' Prudence said. 'We told Constable Dawkins everything we knew.'

'And we were treated like we were the criminals,' Maurice added. 'Asking questions about our lives, our jobs, where we lived. No respect.'

'And he didn't even listen to what we said.'

'I'm not going anywhere near a polis station,' Gil said, emphatically.

'We want to stay out of any controversy,' Prudence said. 'Our experience with the police hasn't been positive. And we haven't broken any law, or even come close to it.'

'Except being here,' Gil said, with a sour look.

Faye sighed.

'I understand. I won't ask you unless there's no other way,' she said. 'And I'm sorry that you've been treated disrespectfully. That shouldn't have happened.' She put her notepad away. 'Thank you very much for all that you've told us. It's been very helpful.'

They all stood to leave and Ellie sighed with relief; she hadn't realised how tense she had become. The interview was over.

24

ELEANOR

'You think Carl Carmody is mixed up in whatever happened to Violet Taylor?' Ellie asked.

The trio were walking back towards Clapham, keeping an eye out for a bus.

'Don't you?' Faye replied.

'He was on that balcony.'

'And Maurice saw him running away – I can't understand that at all,' Beryl said. 'He was so fond of Violet.'

'Carl was seen on his own and he was seen later, after Violet had fallen,' Faye said.

'Which means…?' Ellie asked. 'What?'

'I don't know, but it might be significant. That he didn't leave with the others. Also, what was he running from and why?'

'Anyway, now we know that Vi left the party before she died and *didn't drink* anything!' Beryl said.

'Dr Horn told us that too,' Faye said.

'Yet she smelt of liquor,' Ellie said.

'Someone had made sure of that,' Beryl added. 'I told you so!'

'It *could* have been an accident, the liquor I mean,' Faye said, but didn't sound convinced. She was looking pensive. 'What's puzzling me is, who was next door when Violet went round there? And what was going on in that flat? Violet may have seen something she shouldn't have done, something that got her killed. But I don't know what.'

'Could it be drugs?' Ellie asked. 'Carl died of an overdose, even if he didn't administer it himself. And we know that the gang would have needed somewhere new for their bagging and boxing operation after the deep shelters were denied them.'

'Maybe, but, if that's what the flat was used for, it'll have been cleaned up by now,' Faye went on. 'Still, there might be some trace if I could get in there to find it. And I would have thought that someone – a neighbour, a tradesman – would have suspected something illegal was going on there.'

'Could you ask around the estate?' Ellie asked.

'The estate that saw nothing?' Faye gave her a sceptical glance. 'But you're right, yes, we could. I don't think we've asked the right questions in this case. We need to do it again now.'

'What else could have been going on in the flat?'

'Whatever it was, it must have been obvious to Violet, if she got a look inside. I'll track down the owners of flat four eleven and speak with them, try and persuade them to let me have a look around the flat, but I can't insist upon it without a warrant.'

'Couldn't you get one?'

'I doubt it. I might be able to if this is gang-related and it's my instinct that it is, though that won't convince my boss. Otherwise, it's for the local station to deal with, or for them to bring in the Yard.'

'And we know they're not doing that!' This from Beryl.

Faye said nothing.

'Do we know *why* they're not doing it?' Ellie asked.

'Aside from Winnie Pritchard, who reported it, no one saw the fall, either at the party or elsewhere in the flats,' Faye answered. 'Everyone's claimed they noticed nothing, so there are no witnesses.'

'I've given you witnesses, what else do you want?' Beryl threw up her hands in frustration.

'But they won't take the witness stand,' Faye replied. 'And they won't make statements. No. It wouldn't ever get past my boss and I'd look bloody stupid.'

'You can't blame them for wanting to keep their heads down,' Beryl said, chin raised, challenging Faye to contradict her.

'No, I can't,' Faye said, after a pause. 'There's too much bad feeling. We invited these people, we should have been prepared. Now it's too late and they don't trust the police.'

'There are plenty of folk in London who don't trust the polis,' Beryl said. 'I hate to say I told you so, but I told you so!'

Faye said nothing, but her jaw tightened.

Beryl continued. 'The police are prejudiced and bigoted and—'

'Not all the police, Beryl,' Ellie interrupted, anxious to forestall another argument. 'Don't generalise.'

'And on the take, the lot of them!'

Ellie glanced at Faye, expecting a rejoinder, but none came,

'You know that's not true, Beryl. Faye isn't corrupt and neither is her brother, or my godfather. They work hard, doing a difficult job. Just because some of their colleagues are... you can't criticise them all.'

'A few "bad apples"?' was Beryl's rejoinder. 'That old argument. Rot spreads.'

'You want us to be perfect,' Faye said. 'Held to a higher standard and above suspicion, is that it?'

'Yes!'

Ellie knew that this was what Faye believed. And Beryl knew it too, if only she would stop and think.

'So do I.' Faye held up a hand, palm outwards, to forestall Beryl's objections. 'And maybe we're not, but that shouldn't stop us from doing our job.'

'So what are you going to do next? Did you speak with the constable who went to Fairview House when the death was reported?' Beryl asked.

'Yes, I did. I know Harry,' Faye said. 'So does Ellie.'

'Really?' Ellie's eyebrows rose.

'He was the constable who got your things back from Mrs Packham a couple of years ago.'

'Ah. He was kind, though he had very definite, very traditional views about women and their place in the world.'

'Surprise, surprise,' Beryl said out of the side of her mouth.

'I suspect he may not have filled Prudence Green and the others with confidence in the British police,' Faye said.

Beryl harumphed.

'He *has* promised me a copy of his report.'

'What will that tell us?' Beryl asked.

'Who else was at the party, but little else, I fear. You never know…'

'I have the names of Carl's friends that Terry gave me,' Ellie said. 'Would that be helpful?'

'Yes. I'll see if anyone at the station knows those names and Lydia can check with central records. If any of them has a record, we'll have photos we can show to the other partygoers. We need to find out who was on the balcony next to the party flat. Then I can put some pressure on them to find out what they know. I think whoever killed Violet was in flat four eleven.'

A delivery truck rattled past them.

'I'll also ask Terry for the names of the families Carl worked for,' Ellie said.

'Good. The results of the post mortem of Carl's body should be available tomorrow,' Faye added. 'That might tell us more. Given that Carl's death is almost certainly linked with Violet's.'

'What can I do?' Beryl asked. 'I know I've been complaining like a stuck gramophone record, but I want to be useful.'

'Can you speak with Prudence again, see if you can persuade her or Gil to co-operate, formally?'

'Alright,' Beryl said, with some reluctance. 'I'll speak with Miss Souter, too, find out about Carl's state of mind if he wasn't taking his medicine.'

'Yes, good idea,' Faye said. 'Once we can identify some suspects, I could visit Mrs Pritchard and show her their photographs. She might be able to identify those who surrounded the fallen Violet, though it's unlikely; they were probably fifty yards away.'

'Look, here comes a thirty-seven.' Ellie raised a hand to flag it down. 'Anyone got any change?'

TUESDAY

25

FAYE

'It's an empire,' Lydia said.

'It is when you see all the info gathered in one place,' Bob Lowe added. 'It gives a real sense of the scale of things.'

Faye, Lydia and Bob stood in the library at Union Grove contemplating a new diagram on the wall.

'Six limited companies and that's not counting the clubs and other businesses,' Faye said. 'And we're sure they're all Hunter's.'

'His name isn't on any of them,' Lydia replied. 'They're all run by proxies and there's often a complicated trail of ownership. But there is evidence that he's either the hidden owner, or backer.'

'A way of using his dirty money,' Faye said.

'We know he's linked with the limited companies because of Abigail Hunter, she's on the board of all of them. Four own land and property; their income is rents, that's all,' Lydia explained. 'A lot of the property is in the poorer parts of town, though some isn't. Some of the land is in very good positions, so probably bought after the bombing, when it would have been cheap.'

'There are plenty who've done similar,' Faye commented. 'And they are slum landlords too.'

'The working companies are London & Surrey Limited, a building company and London & Kent Limited, which is in haulage.'

Lydia pointed to the new diagram and glanced at Bob. 'Arthur Comstock is the company secretary of them all, but he holds no shares.'

'Old Arty Comstock, I didn't know he was still around.' Walsh sauntered in carrying a very large mug of brown liquid.

Faye stiffened, remembering their set-to of yesterday. Yet today, if not all smiles, the sergeant seemed to want to build bridges.

'Who is he?' she asked.

'Dodgy brief. Time was you'd find his card pinned to the noticeboards in every nick in south London and some of the prisons too.' He took a sip. 'I thought he'd retired though.'

'It seems not,' Faye said.

'The accountants are Field & Wainwright, a respectable Battersea firm.'

'This is good work, Lydia,' Faye said.

'Yes, well done, Lydia,' Bob said, taking his leave.

'Thank you.' The SSO blushed.

'Yeah, saves us from doing the paperwork.' Walsh's smile was smug.

'You've done well,' Faye reiterated, ignoring Walsh. 'Having this information helps make connections, that's what it is all about. There are more types of detective work than pounding the streets.'

Walsh opened his mouth to retort but Lydia got in first.

'One other thing, while I remember. The man at the records office mentioned that there was a recent rights issue in London & Surrey, a large injection of cash; he said he wouldn't be surprised if the Inland Revenue was interested. They'd want to know where the money came from.'

'So would we,' Faye interjected.

'Well, well,' Walsh said. 'Large injection of cash, eh?'

'I've got copies of the accounts, but I don't suppose they'll tell us that sort of detail.' Lydia indicated a small pile of manila folders lying on the table.

'Maybe, maybe not, but they're worth having. I'll look at them when I get the chance,' Faye said.

'Accountant, are you?' Walsh asked.

'No, but I used to prepare accounts for audit in my previous job. I might be able to find something useful. If the auditors are respectable they might include information that seems innocent to them, but could be more meaningful to us.'

Walsh raised his eyebrows and made a face as if he was impressed.

'I don't suppose you came across a firm called Golden Properties, Lydia?' Faye asked.

'No.'

'Danny?'

'No. Why?'

'Could you track it down, Lydia?'

'I can try.'

'Thanks. Oh, and one more thing… Would you find out for me if two men, brothers named Terence and Carl Carmody, have criminal records? The second of them, the younger one, came to our attention as a child, I think.'

'Rightio.' The policewoman made a note.

Walsh followed Faye into the larger room.

'Where'd you get those names?' he demanded. 'They don't mean anything to me. And what's Golden Properties?'

'A firm I came across in another case. Rent collectors,' she said and went back to her desk. She wasn't going to make the same mistake as yesterday. He wanted to keep things to himself. So would she.

To her surprise, Walsh followed her.

'Faye, look, I – I'm supposed to be helping you.' The DS looked down into his mug. 'So that's what I should do. I was angry yesterday when you started questioning Soapy — he's my snout. You don't do that, d'you understand?' He paused. 'Though, I accept… that you mightn't have known. I'm prepared to take it as an honest mistake.'

What did he think it was? Deliberate? A flouting of his authority?

'Anyway, I thought you were going to complain about me, but Kent... when he and I spoke... he didn't know about our... little *contretemps*. You hadn't told him about it. That counts with me. You were out of order, so you got a bollocking, but you didn't complain, so...'

She suspected that this was the closest she was going to get to an apology from Walsh. On one hand it wasn't acceptable; on the other, she needed his knowledge and contacts, so she had little choice but to accept it.

Strike while the iron's hot. She pulled her notebook from her handbag.

'Actually, I wanted to ask you about some more names. Look. D'you know any of them?'

'Oh yes. A couple. Low level hoodlums, on the periphery of the gangs. Soapy Davis level, but in the muscle line. How'd you come across them?'

Faye hesitated. Walsh was being helpful now, but she didn't entirely trust him.

'I want to talk with them about the death of a nurse on the Belvedere Estate,' she said, eventually.

Walsh's chin jutted out and he looked down his nose.

'That's what you asked Soapy about.'

'Yes. And I still say he knows more than he's saying.'

Walsh frowned.

'What's that got to do with us?' he said, his sweeping arm indicating the squad room.

'I don't think the nurse fell. What's more, I think perhaps she saw something she wasn't supposed to, in one of the flats nearby. There might be a gangland connection.'

'Hmmm.' Walsh sipped his tea. 'D'you know which flat?'

'Yes, four eleven, Fairview House. It's probably been cleaned up now, but still...'

'Warrant?'

'Doubt it: not without more evidence.'

Walsh looked at her over the rim of his cup for a moment, then inclined his head towards the door. She followed him out into the corridor.

'I might be able to get us in there,' he said, keeping his voice down.

'What? How?'

Walsh gave Faye a level stare. Then he seemed to make a decision.

'Keep this to yourself. I unburdened a set of keys from a burglar before he went to the cells recently,' he said. 'Skeletons. If that flat has a standard warded lock we'll be able to get in.'

'But isn't that—?'

'Illegal. Yes. Look, we'll knock at the door and see if there's anyone in the flat. If no one answers we'll go in. We can always say we smelt gas.'

Instinctively, Faye rejected the idea. She began to shake her head.

'Do you want to take a look inside that flat or not?' Walsh demanded. 'I'm offering you a way in. No one need know.'

She began to back away.

Just because you can, doesn't mean you should.

'Oh well, if you're going to be high and mighty about it…' Walsh shrugged.

Would it really be so wrong? To go into an empty flat. It wasn't corruption, just bending the rules a little and she wouldn't profit, personally, by doing it. And there was Walsh to consider. He had trusted her with his secret, offered to help her… she would lose all credibility with him if she didn't go along with his proposal.

The clue to finding the killer or killers of Violet Taylor and Carl Carmody might be inside that flat. No one else was going to follow up their deaths. She had to follow this to the very end, regardless of where it led her.

'Alright. You're on,' she called, to Walsh's retreating form.

He stopped.

'Come on then,' he said.

26

FAYE

Walsh parked the car in Belvedere Road, a few minutes away from Fairview House. They walked through the estate of identical five-storey buildings, their balconies forming continuous cream horizontal stripes against the blue-grey brick walls. Faye scanned the area, looking from side to side as the sun beat down.

'Faye, will you stop looking so furtive? You're drawing attention to us,' Walsh said.

'We shouldn't be here,' she said. 'I don't want anyone noticing us.'

'What d'you mean, "We shouldn't be here"?' Walsh retorted. 'Don't be ridiculous. We're old bill and there's been a death. We've every right to be here.'

'I know that, it's...'

What we're about to do, she wanted to say. Break the law.

'So, what's the story with the dead nurse?' Walsh asked.

'I'm not sure yet, but I think her death is linked to a subsequent one. A local youth. One of those names I gave Lydia to check on.'

'Was he at this party?'

'No, but he was on the balcony of the flat next door. His body was found in the basement of a derelict house in Billingdon Road nearly three days later, after an overdose. He's a local lad, so the body was brought to the SLH. His brother claims Carl never took drugs, the medication he was on would have meant he would have been very sick if he'd tried. His brother was the nurse's fiancé.'

'Hmmm.'

'It's too much of a coincidence. A teetotal nurse dies in a "drunken" fall and a young man who can't take narcotics dies of an overdose.'

'I'll grant it seems suspicious,' Walsh said. 'If they were all connected it's probably a domestic. Remember, if it's not our case, you shouldn't be spending time on it.'

'I used to work at the hospital,' Faye said, by way of explanation. 'My friends knew the nurse.'

'Alright, you're doing them a favour, but that's neither here nor there. We've plenty of work of our own.'

They rounded the corner of one large block into an open space. Communal metal waste bins were lined up at one side and an area of grass ended at the main road; on the other side of it was the neat row of pre-fabs where Winnie Pritchard lived. This was where Violet had fallen.

Faye opened her notebook and read Mrs Pritchard's comments aloud.

'"Past the pavement and the lamp post, near to the grass." That's what a witness from across the road said.'

'I don't think we need to be told,' Walsh said, pointing to a dark patch on the ground. 'Someone's tried to wash it away, but this won't go until we have some rain.'

Faye stood beside the stain and looked at the L-shaped building. She was standing in its elbow. The party flat could have been on either arm of the 'L', but, from Winnie's description, Faye thought it was on the arm nearer to the road. Sure enough, a sad, half-deflated red balloon still floated defiantly from a balcony on the fourth floor.

'Up there, I think,' she pointed out to Walsh.

'Hmmm, and no one saw anything.' He glanced around, sounding incredulous.

Faye knew what Walsh meant. Anyone standing on any of the balconies along the other arm of the 'L' would have been able to see what was happening when Violet fell. The building was five storeys high. That was a lot of balconies. Where were the witnesses?

'People could still have been at work...' She cast around for explanations. 'Or getting ready to go out on a Friday night.'

'Or are keeping their mouths shut.' Walsh headed over to the entrance. 'Come on then.'

They took the lift to the fourth floor.

'Turn right,' Faye said. 'The party flat was number four ten. The flat I want to investigate is next door, four eleven.'

As she'd been told, the corridor ran around an internal light-well with opaque windows opening onto it at regular intervals. The doors to the flats were opposite the well and they soon passed the party flat. The door to flat four eleven was next.

Walsh rapped on it.

No reply.

He tried again, but still no one answered.

'Well?' He pulled a set of long keys out of his pocket and raised his eyebrows in a question.

She couldn't back out now. Beryl would never forgive her.

'Alright.'

The third key turned in the lock and the door opened. They were inside.

'Don't touch anything,' Walsh said, as he pulled on a pair of rubber gloves.

Damn! Faye cursed herself for not bringing gloves herself. Yet... she felt a chill in the pit of her stomach. He'd come prepared. It seemed this wasn't the first time.

Inside, the flat looked tidy, if sparsely furnished, but closer inspection revealed its shabbiness. Sunshine poured through the wide glass doors to the balcony, filling the living room with light.Walsh began to take a look around.

'No clothes in the wardrobe,' he called from the only bedroom. 'And the bed isn't made up.'

Faye nudged open the bathroom door. Bleach and cleaning

materials sat on a shelf, but there was none of the usual clutter of a bathroom. Where were the toothbrushes, toothpaste and soap?

'There's not a lot in the bathroom either,' she shouted. 'What about the kitchen?'

'Some tea and tins in the cupboards. Plates and dishes, a kettle and some mugs.' He came back into the living room. 'I'd say that this place is used, maybe used regularly, but not lived in. There's no one here permanently.'

'But what's it used for? That's the question.'

'No johnnies – not a knocking shop.'

'Not a drug den either – no scales, bags, other paraphernalia.' Faye frowned. 'Can you open the doors to the balcony?'

A couple of minutes with the skeleton keys and the doors were ajar. Faye stepped outside.

The balcony was empty; no detritus, no rubbish, nothing. To her left, on the other side of a narrow gap, she saw the party flat with its single balloon. Anyone over there would have got a good look at people standing where she stood. Prudence's story was verified – not that she had ever doubted the nurse.

On the other arm of the L-shaped building the balconies were empty. No one was outside. Maybe everyone was at work, or it was the time of day. She looked down at the dark stain on the concrete below. It stood out clearly, seeming nearer to where Faye stood than to the party balcony, but Violet could have fallen from either. Faye imagined the trajectory.

'Was it someone from Cavendish Road who came round here?' Walsh asked, as he joined her on the balcony. 'Didn't they bother to check how your nurse "fell"?'

'They assumed it was an accident and spent a lot of time trying to intimidate the partygoers, many of whom were West Indians.' Faye kept her voice neutral; she didn't know what Walsh thought about the new arrivals. For all she knew, he might share Dawkins' views. 'Without witnesses, what evidence was there that it was anything else? Though they didn't look too closely either.'

She felt Walsh's gaze upon her as she looked down at the stain.

He seemed to be about to say something more when there was a noise behind them. A key turning in the lock.

'Leave the talking to me,' Walsh said, *sotto voce*, as he stepped back inside.

The door to the flat was opening. Someone was coming inside.

They would be discovered! She'd known this was a mistake!

Faye held her breath.

The arrival, a skinny young man, took one look at them and took to his heels.

'Hey!' Walsh rushed after him, the door slamming back against the wall on its hinges before it closed slowly.

Faye stood, unsure of what to do next. Should she wait? Yes, Walsh had the keys. She couldn't leave an unlocked flat.

Her eye fell upon the balcony rail. All the other balconies carried tell-tale daubs and splashes on their rails. Even those that were well kept with flowerpots and washing lines bore evidence of frequent visits from pigeons. The party balcony, too, was slightly encrusted. But not this one.

It must have been cleaned and very recently.

Faye re-entered the living room and nudged aside a wooden-framed easy chair. The threadbare carpet beneath it was the same colour as the rest of the carpet. There was no fading, nor was there any dust to suggest that someone had cleaned around the chair. The carpet wasn't newly laid so that suggested that whoever had cleaned the flat had been very meticulous and moved the furniture to clean beneath it.

The whole place had been cleaned very thoroughly indeed.

Yet that didn't explain the lack of fading on the carpet. Some difference was to be expected, especially given the long and sunny summer. Unless the curtains were kept closed for much of the time.

Whatever went on in this flat, those doing it didn't want to run the slightest risk of being seen. Could Violet have seen it? Was that the reason why she died?

The door opened and Walsh returned, breathing heavily.

'Lost him.' He answered her quizzical look. 'I swear I'm getting too old for this.'

'Did you recognise him?'

'Certainly did. One of the louts on your list,' he said. 'Thomas O'Shaughnessy, a low-grade fence. We should be able to pick him up, I'll put out an alert on the way back to the station. Something's going on here, you were right.'

'Good. And look,' Faye said. She tapped the chair with her foot. 'No fading of the carpet in the sunshine. Whatever goes on here happens when the curtains are drawn.'

Walsh pursed his lips and nodded.

'The place has been cleaned up, carefully and methodically, I'd say,' she added. 'Furniture moved, the lot.'

'We'll get a team round anyway, there might be some prints somewhere. I'll speak with Kent, get a warrant, do things legally.'

'Will he allow that? After we broke in?'

'I think I can persuade him.'

Faye wondered at Walsh's certainty. Was DI Kent as elastic about the letter of the law as Walsh was? She hadn't imagined that the DI would be the type, but what did she know? Could this be what Kent had meant when he described the way the team worked as 'unorthodox'?

John had told her it wasn't just the junior ranks who made their own rules.

'Come on, we've got to get out of here.' He closed and locked the balcony doors. 'O'Shaughnessy might come back with some mates.'

He shepherded Faye into the corridor and locked the door behind them.

'So you agree with me,' Faye asked, as they descended to the ground floor. 'Violet Taylor's death is suspicious?'

'Yes. I don't think that nurse died in an accident,' Walsh replied. 'And maybe something dodgy was going on in the flat – not that this means it's gang related, mind. I need to speak with Soapy again.'

27

ELEANOR

In a hospital full of women, a man tended to stand out.

Ellie noticed Terry as soon as he entered the canteen. He wore a jacket and a tightly knotted tie, but his attempts at smartness were marred by his thick denim work trousers. Yet she liked him for making the effort, especially given his own sad circumstances. She signalled to one of the servers to take over from her as he approached her lectern.

'Terry, would you like some tea?'

'No, no thanks.'

'Do come and sit down.' She led him to a table.

'I wanted to thank you,' he said. 'For helping me and Carl. I've just been speaking with your Dr Horn; I went to the pathology laboratory.'

'Has she done the post mortem?'

'Yes.' He looked down at his hands, which were shaking. After a moment's concentration they stilled.

Ellie waited. It seemed to be important to Terry that he tell her about the post mortem findings. She could go and speak with Dr Horn later to get the full story.

Terry licked his lips and continued.

'Carl died of an overdose of heroin. His arms have injection marks, but the doc thinks that these were recent. His body doesn't show the signs she would expect of a regular, long-term user.'

'So...?'

'But there are lots of injection marks, so it's a contradiction. Apparently. But Doc says he might not have injected himself. Somebody else could have done it, maybe when he was drunk.'

'Oh, Terry, I'm so sorry.'

'No, no, it's good. Don't you see?' he said. 'It exonerates Carl. He wasn't some sort of druggie. Someone did this to him, he didn't do it to himself.' Terry's voice grew strident. 'The police have got it all wrong.'

Heads were beginning to turn. Ellie caught the questioning glance of one of the servers behind the counter and she shook her head. She would deal with this.

'They have so far,' Ellie said, her voice soothing. 'But there is a detective on the case now, who knows about Violet and about Carl. I've given the names you gave me to... them. Rest assured there's someone working on this right now.'

'Good. 'Bout time.'

Terry gulped in a great mouthful of air. Anger chased sorrow across his face.

This was the second death of someone close to him in days. In the circumstances, Ellie thought, he was doing well.

'I thought things were getting better,' he gasped, swallowing hard. 'I knew there were the rough types, but he still saw his old school friends and had plenty of work, with some respectable families. It's not been easy since our parents died. And Vi was such a help.'

'I suppose you'll have to tell them, the families he worked for, to explain that he won't be coming to their homes anymore.'

'Yeah.' Terry sniffed. ''Spose.'

'Do you want me to do that for you?' she offered. 'I could telephone them from here.'

And they might know something. Faye could do it, officially and maybe ask some questions too.

'Would you? They're in the book. The Redmonds in Dulwich and the Hunters in Wimbledon. The Redmonds are on Mayflower Road and the Hunters on Ridgeway Drive. Thank you. That's very kind of you.'

Ellie made a mental note of the names.

'I'll do that. Now... I'd best get back to work.' She began to rise.

'Just... one more thing, please?'

'Yes?'

'Vi's jewellery. Beryl brought some of it back, in a bag, but the ring, the ring I got for her, wasn't there.'

'I know. It isn't here, I'm afraid. I don't know why.'

'But she must have had it on, she never took it off, except to wash. It must be here.'

'Dr Horn gave us all the jewellery Violet was wearing,' Ellie explained. 'It had been logged in the path lab on arrival and the ring wasn't listed.'

'Then somebody took it!' He stared at her, eyes wild. 'Somebody in this hospital took it!'

'All the jewellery was locked away in a safe, Terry,' Ellie said, quietly. 'I saw Dr Horn, the lady you've just met in the pathology laboratory, remove the bag it was kept in from the safe. There wasn't a ring in it. We asked about it and looked in the Effects Register, but a ring wasn't mentioned. If Violet was wearing it when she arrived at the SLH, it would have been in the book.'

'Who brought her in? I want to speak to them!'

'Terry, the ambulance brought her in. The men who drive it and help the injured are professionals. They did that sort of thing in the war, they...'

'There was a lot of things people did in the war! Some of them not good at all.' Terry eyes were filling with tears.

'It's much more likely that the ring was taken, if it was taken, before the ambulance men got to Violet,' Ellie persisted. 'We know that there were people standing around her.'

Terry was fighting the sobs welling up inside him. He looked very close to breaking down entirely.

'Well, that'll be it then,' he said. 'Some thieving bastard robbed my Vi's ring. The only thing I have left to remind me...'

He put his head in his hands.

Ellie felt helpless.

'Can I get you something?' she asked.

'No. Nothing that I want. What I want is impossible.' Terry sat up and wiped his face with the back of his hand. 'Thanks. You've been very kind. I'm sorry I shouted at you.'

'Apology accepted. I know you're upset.'

'I'll be on my way. You're working and I've taken up enough of your time.'

Ellie stood and watched him leave, his shoulders hunched and arms pulled close to his body. He seemed turned in upon himself, emotionally as well as physically.

She sighed. Such a lot of tragedy in so short a time. He would need time to grieve. It was so sad. She seemed to be surrounded by sadness.

Pull yourself together! she admonished herself. Do something useful.

She needed to be active, to be doing something. But something other than the bloody summer fete!

Service was almost over; she could check in at the office and then go and speak with Stan and Robin, the ambulance men who had brought Violet Taylor to the SLH. She'd have to be tactful, but she would check if Violet was wearing her engagement ring when they saw her.

'You've had a couple of telephone calls,' Jean told her as she entered the office and handed Ellie a note of the number. 'I said you'd ring back.'

'This looks like St Thomas's number.'

'Erm, it is.' Jean gave a stretched, pressed smile. 'It's Antoine Girard.'

'Tsch.' Ellie began to walk to her desk.

'I think you ought to ring him,' Jean said. 'Otherwise he'll keep telephoning.'

Ellie stopped herself from saying that she didn't care what Jean thought. Besides, the secretary was right. She knew Antoine, he would persist.

'I'll telephone in here,' she said, going into Miss Barnett's empty room and closed the door behind her.

The operator put her through immediately and she heard Antoine's baritone.

'You telephoned me,' she said, looking out onto the South Side. Groups of nurses and other SLH staff were walking back to the hospital after spending their lunch break on the Common.

'Yes. To ask you if you would meet me sooner than we agreed.' His voice was measured, but she sensed an underlying urgency.

'Why the rush? You've got your job at St Thomas's now, I assume.'

'Temporarily. Look, I don't want to have a conversation like this over the telephone.'

A conversation like what, she was tempted to ask, but realised that she was avoiding the issue.

'I'm very busy at the moment, the SLH summer fete—'

'Yes, I know, but I'm being pressed to decide about my future here – the offer of the job won't be available for much longer, so I have to make up my mind.'

'You don't need me to do that. You can decide for yourself.'

'Oh yes, I do need you. You know I do. I'm only here, in London, because of you, because of my feelings for you. If you won't have me, my path is much clearer.'

Ellie sighed. He was placing all the responsibility on her shoulders. She couldn't decide for him. She didn't want to and besides, she needed time to think.

'Please, Ellie, if I ever meant anything to you.'

'Alright.' She gave in. 'I can be free tomorrow night after work.'

'Tomorrow.' He sounded relieved. 'Thank you. Shall I come to the hospital?'

'No.' She didn't want tongues to start wagging. 'Come to the flat. At seven.'

'Seven. Very well, I'll see you then. And Ellie, thank you.'

'See you tomorrow.'

She put the phone down and slumped down into Miss Barnett's office chair.

She already regretted giving way. She didn't want to think about it, about him; she'd done too much of that after he'd left. Blaming herself for ending the relationship, when it was he who had been the deceitful one.

She dismissed her thoughts about Antoine. It would only upset her further. Concentrate on the case. Give Faye those names and addresses.

Ellie picked up the telephone again and dialled the number Faye had given her for Union Grove police station. After the third ring someone answered, and Ellie asked for her friend.

'Sorry, she's not here right now. Can I take a message?'

'Yes, could you tell her that Ellie telephoned, I'm her flatmate? I've got some more information for her from Terry Carmody. Could you ask her to contact me, please? She's got the number. Thanks.'

She replaced the handset. What could she do now?

A noise brought her back to her surroundings. Jean had knocked on the connecting door.

'Ellie, it's Marjie Pargeter's "do". You're expected.'

Damn. She'd forgotten.

'Yes,' she said, getting to her feet. 'Coming.'

Marjorie Pargeter was the only Lady Almoner left at the South London, no longer needed now the NHS existed. Marjie was a pleasant old girl, though those who petitioned her wouldn't have thought so; she treated SLH funds like her own money and was miserly in ensuring that only those who really couldn't pay got treatment for nothing. She'd been at the SLH for almost twenty years. Probably too old to go to another hospital.

Her farewell gathering was taking place in the board room.

Ellie could hear the buzz of chatter and the clink of teacups from along the corridor as she walked towards it. What would

Marjie do now? The SLH had been a huge part of her life. A spinster with a small private income, supplemented by her stipend as an Almoner. Ellie wondered if Marjie had any savings put by. Would she have enough to live on and, if she didn't, would she apply for National Assistance funds from the state? Many people were too proud to do so, or believed others, far worse off than themselves, needed the help more.

Was Marjie Pargeter's fate what the future held for her, she wondered? A penurious and lonely old age.

She shook off the gloomy thoughts as she fixed a smile to her face and opened the door to the board room.

'Ellie! Come in, please,' Miss Underwood said. 'Would you like some cake?'

28

FAYE

It was, Faye reflected, a measure of the growing trust between them that Walsh no longer drove like a complete maniac when she was in the car, just someone who didn't understand the concept of a speed limit. They were on their way to an address in Merton that Lydia had tracked down; it belonged to Golden Properties, the rent collection agency.

'There it is,' Faye said as they passed a parade of shops. 'Number seventy-eight.'

Walsh parked in a nearby side road and they walked back. Number seventy-eight was a tobacconist and confectioners, but a door to the left of it carried a small column of names belonging to the businesses that occupied the offices above. Golden Properties was one of them.

Narrow, uncarpeted stairs led them to a first-floor landing with a series of half-glazed doors, one of which belonged to the rental agency. Walsh knocked and went in, Faye following behind.

Filing cabinets ran around three sides of the office, partly obscuring the single sash window. A sandy-haired man in his thirties sat behind several piles of manila files at a desk at the centre of the room.

'Hello.' He stood and came around the desk. 'How may I help you?'

'Detective Sergeant Walsh and Detective Constable Smith.' Walsh showed the man his warrant card. 'We'd like to ask you a few questions, Mr...?'

'Peters, Mark Peters.'

Faye made a note of the name in her notebook.

'This is your business, Mr Peters?'

'Yes, I own it.'

While Mr Peters answered Walsh's opening questions, Faye took a covert glance at the files lying open on the desk. All seemed to contain the same, or similar, papers; a schedule showing an address, or addresses, rental due, collection dates, sums collected and sums paid over to the owners. A column on the far right showed commission earned. Standard administration. It looked above board.

'Fairview House?' Peters was saying. 'Yes, I make collections there for a client who owns several flats.'

'On the fourth floor?' Faye asked.

'Er, yes, flats four hundred and eight to four fourteen.'

It was Walsh's turn to scribble.

'And the owner is?'

'I'm afraid I don't know an individual name. The rents are sent to a company, less my commission, of course.'

'The company being?' Walsh asked.

'London & City (Estates),' Peters replied.

Surely this must be another of the Hunter companies; its name was so similar to 'London & Surrey' or 'London & Kent'. Too much of a coincidence not to be. They were getting somewhere at last.

'Are all the company's flats in Fairview House occupied at present?' Faye asked. 'Do they all have tenants?'

Peters picked up one of the manila files from the desk and riffled through it.

'No, as it happens,' he said. 'Flat four hundred and eleven is empty.'

Faye shot Walsh a conspiratorial glance, which held more than a glint of triumph.

'Thank you, Mr Peters,' she said.

Walsh added his thanks and they made their way down to the car.

'That company...' he began.

'Sounds like it's one of the companies on Lydia's diagram,' Faye said. 'We need to get back to the station and check. If it's associated with Hunter, it's a link between the Hunter gang and the death of Violet Taylor.'

'Hold your horses...'

'And of Carl Carmody,' Faye added, slamming the passenger door.

'We know the companies own a lot of properties,' Walsh said as he slid into the driver's seat. 'It'll be very difficult to tie one flat to Hunter; a half-decent brief would tear that apart.' He adopted an excessively refined accent and a pompous manner. 'How can you expect my client to know what takes place in one of the many properties owned by a company in which he has no material interest? The only connection being that his wife sits on the board? My client has no knowledge of any of the individual properties.'

'There are too many coincidences,' Faye responded.

'But it's all still circumstantial,' Walsh countered. 'I grant you, the nurse's death is suspicious, but that doesn't mean it's a gangland case. It might be for the Yard. Let's check it out some more, then see if the boss needs to know about it.'

He put the car in gear and they pulled away.

Traffic was nose to tail and Faye drummed a frustrated rhythm on the dashboard. An accident had closed off a major road. Where was Walsh's usual speed when you wanted it? They were forced to travel at a crawl towards Wimbledon.

As they approached a railway bridge, she glanced out of her window. At first, she wasn't sure what she was seeing, then she realised what it was — a cement works, with a high cylindrical tower and the mounds of sand at its base. Right next to the railway tracks.

At the apex of the bridge, she craned her neck and looked to either side. Around twenty train lines raced away into the distance. This must be the Wimbledon Park Depot. Not as large at Nine Elms, or with as many passenger lines as Clapham Junction, but with plenty of railway tracks, nonetheless. Faye was convinced that the railway would play a key part in whatever the gang were up to with concrete. But they would also need a base where the concrete panels were made.

Once back at Union Grove they went straight through to the 'library' and Lydia's latest diagram.

'Yes!'

Faye slapped the wall in triumph. The diagram showed that London & City (Estates Holdings) was one of the companies controlled by the Hunters.

'This paperwork detecting is paying off,' she said, looking pointedly at Walsh.

'Alright,' he conceded. 'It is. Good work. And to you too.' This to Lydia, who had joined them. 'Didn't I say that before?'

'No, you didn't,' the WPC snapped, adding, grudgingly, 'but better late than never.'

'But it doesn't link the death of the nurse with Hunter,' he reminded Faye. 'We need real, solid evidence to build any case against him. Proof positive. Unless we can get that evidence, there isn't a case and this isn't for us.'

Faye recalled her recent argument with Beryl. Now she was the one who was frustrated. She had to get more evidence.

'I checked those brothers out, Faye.' Lydia interrupted her thoughts. 'The older one doesn't have a record, but the younger, Carl, got into hot water as a minor. Nothing serious, but it earned him more than one clip round the ear. He was diagnosed with a mental disorder, otherwise it would have been court, possibly Borstal, but his medicine must have helped, because there's been nothing recent. And there was a message for you, Faye. Someone trying to get hold of you earlier.'

The chit that Lydia handed over had the telephone number of the SLH office on it. Ellie must have telephoned.

'Excuse me,' she said and crossed to use the phone on her desk in the squad room.

'Hello, Ellie. It's me. You rang?'

'Yes, Terry Carmody has given me the names of the families that Carl used to work for. I said that I'd telephone them and explain why Carl wouldn't be turning up to do their odd jobs anymore, but I think it might be better if you did it, officially. You might be able to find out more.'

'Good idea.'

As Ellie read them out Faye's jaw dropped in amazement. One of them was a Wimbledon family, the Hunters of Ridgeway Drive.

'Thanks, Ellie, that's great. See you later.'

A second link between the Hunters and two violent deaths. The first might be tenuous, but this... Surely Walsh would acknowledge that the deaths were gang related now.

The sergeant was speaking with a group of colleagues and, as Faye went to tell him about this latest development, they looked in her direction. And laughed. Her feet slowed as Walsh turned towards her. The group dispersed.

They'd been talking about her, laughing at her. Damn them.

'Danny!' she called, sharply. 'I've got something!'

'What?' He came over.

'Carl Carmody, the dead boy, worked for the Hunter family,' she said, indignant. 'Did gardening and odd jobs at their house in Wimbledon.'

Walsh's eyebrows rose.

'So,' she continued, 'the Hunter odd-job lad dies, hours after the death, in suspicious circumstances, of a nurse who was engaged to his brother. Who fell, or was pushed, from a flat owned by a company associated with Hunter.'

'That is certainly suggestive,' he conceded, frowning. 'But it's still circumstantial. Everything you have is circumstantial and we need hard evidence. Who killed them? Was it the same person? Can you prove it was on Henry Hunter's orders? What has a nurse to do with Hunter anyway? I still say we need more.'

Shaking his head, he walked away.

Walsh wouldn't ever admit she was onto something. Not without cold, hard proof. If they had to have evidence to build a case she would have to get it.

Faye returned to her desk and reached for a copy of the A to Z. They had passed relatively close to Ridgeway Drive earlier that afternoon. Where the enemy lived. Where *her* enemy lived.

A plan was forming in her mind. She would carry the news of the sad demise of the young odd-job lad to the families who employed him. She had legitimate questions; how had he behaved when they'd seen him last, had they noticed any signs that he was taking narcotics? The sort of questions she would ask the Dulwich family too, where she would go first.

Then Wimbledon.

She would watch and wait until she knew Hunter was out, then pay Abigail Hunter and the rest of the household a visit.

Who knows what she might find out? Faye felt the surge of adrenaline, the energy of excitement, flowing through her veins. The DI had told her to act upon her own initiative and that's what she would do. She would, however, follow his orders as regards never going it alone.

'Fancy a jaunt, Lydia?' she said.

29

FAYE

Ridgeway Drive, Wimbledon was the sort of leafy, suburban London street where only the wealthy could afford to live. The large houses were set back from the road within spacious grounds, often behind high walls and gates. The Hunter house was a mock-Tudor edifice at the far end of a looping gravel drive, with a mature cedar of much older vintage standing in the oval of grass in front of it.

'That's it. You've seen where Hunter lives. We can go now,' Lydia said. She had grown more and more nervous the longer they sat there and now sounded disapproving. 'It was all very well going to see the Redmonds, but we shouldn't be here, Faye. Even sitting outside. They'll notice. We've been here at least an hour and a half.'

'We're police officers and Hunter is a criminal, we've every right to be here. And this is my case.'

'Hunter isn't just your case, he's everyone's case and the boss needs to know about any approach. He'll do his nut! You can't do this without checking with him.'

'Danny said we needed more evidence before we went to Kent with the Violet Taylor case,' Faye said. She would get some. Then no one could avoid investigating Violet's death.

'We're following protocol, Lydia. There are two of us. Though I think it might be better if you stay in the car. A uniform might cause alarm.'

Avoiding any more objections, Faye shoved the car door open and climbed out.

'Faye, you're not going in there. Faye…'

Lydia's pleas grew fainter as Faye strode towards the gravel drive.

She scrunched her way to the porch. The massive wooden front door was studded with metal bosses, like that of a mediaeval church, with a large brass push-button bell to one side of it. Faye held her finger on it.

Waiting in the sunshine, Faye glanced back at the car. Lydia caught her eye and began gesturing for her to return, but Faye pretended not to see. She stood back to take a closer view of the house frontage. Very grand.

As she stepped forward to press the bell again, the door opened, to reveal a good-looking woman, probably in her forties, though she could have been older. Her tailored trouser suit showed off a neat, slim, if full figure and her auburn hair was brushed back from her forehead. Elegance and understatement, marred slightly by the amount of jewellery she wore. Her necklace reflected the sunlight.

'Mrs Abigail Hunter?' Faye asked, politely.

'Who wants to know?' The question was delivered in a nonchalant drawl; it seemed a habitual reaction – the woman didn't sound suspicious of her in particular. Perhaps mistrust went with the territory.

'My name's Detective Constable Smith.' Faye produced her warrant card. 'I understand that a young man named Carl Carmody does odd jobs for you.'

'Yes. What of it?'

'I have some bad news, I'm afraid. If I might come inside?'

Abigail Hunter thrust wide the door and Faye followed her into a spacious, wood-panelled entrance hall, a highly polished staircase rising to the upper floors.

Her feet sank into a thick piled carpet in a living room which seemed as big as the entire flat at Westbury Court. A family portrait hung in a gilt frame above a large fireplace and there was what looked like a fully stocked bar at the far end with at least six months' worth of spirit rations on its shelves.

Heavy footsteps creaked overhead. Henry Hunter's? Was he at home? She hadn't seen him from outside.

Faye felt a tingle of excitement.

'Now, what is it you want?' Abigail Hunter was barely polite.

'I'm afraid—'

The front door banged. A young girl, aged about thirteen and bearing a strong resemblance to Mrs Hunter, hurtled into the room.

'Belinda!' Mrs Hunter looked equally surprised. 'You're home early. I thought you had sports club.'

'Cancelled... oh.'

'Hello.' Faye said to the girl.

'This is a policewoman, Belinda. My daughter. Now...' Mrs Hunter raised an eyebrow.

'Yes. Perhaps you would prefer if...' Faye inclined her head towards the girl, but her mother put an arm around her daughter's shoulders.

'What is it that you have to say?'

'I'm sorry to have to tell you that Carl Carmody, the young man who used to do odd jobs for you, won't be continuing in your employ. I'm afraid to say that he's dead.'

She watched them both closely. The girl was obviously shocked at the news and, Faye could have sworn, Abigail Hunter was also astonished.

Didn't she know? If Hunter had ordered Carmody's death, surely she must have done. Yet Faye was convinced that it came as a surprise to her.

'Mum!' The girl reached for her mother's embrace and Abigail Hunter put her arms around the child.

'Yes, love.'

'What happened?' the girl asked, squirming round to look at Faye, tears in her eyes.

'Carl was brought into a local hospital having taken an overdose of narcotic drugs,' she answered, quietly. 'He didn't survive.'

'That's a shame,' Abigail Hunter said, handing her daughter a large handkerchief. 'He was a good worker.'

'He used to play cricket with Bertie in the garden, when he was home from school,' Belinda said. 'He was always laughing and joking. He wasn't a flaky.'

'Where did you learn a word like that?' her mother demanded.

Somewhere else in the house a telephone rang.

'Will there be some sort of service, a funeral?' Abigail Hunter asked, ignoring it. But it continued to ring.

'I don't know. His brother might be organising something. The parents are dead, I believe.'

The woman's patience snapped.

'Excuse me, I'll have to answer this.'

'Did you know Carl?' the girl asked Faye, as her mother left the room.

'No. What was he like?'

'He was fun, was always busy, but he would stop and talk to us. Joke with us. My brother and me. He wasn't much older than us. Although…'

'Although…?'

'Nothing.' The girl frowned.

Faye smiled, tilting her head and raising her brows, wordlessly encouraging the girl to speak.

'Last time he was here he didn't speak to us at all, just concentrated on his work and kept to himself. He was different; distant and jumpy. Not how he usually was at all.'

'Do you know why?'

'No. I wondered if I'd done something to upset him…'

'When did he start acting like that?'

'Only a week ago.'

'Still here, Belinda?' Her mother had returned. 'Go on, off to your bedroom now.'

'Wonderful things, telephones.' Faye made conversation to prolong the visit. 'I'm about to get one.'

'They're very useful.' Abigail Hunter's eyes were cold. 'Belinda, to your room, please.'

The girl opened the door to the hall and almost collided with a tall, broad-shouldered man. His shirt was open at the collar and he had a rakish air. The girl stepped aside, with a scowl on her face.

Was this Henry Hunter? She didn't think so.

The man watched the girl leave, then his gaze fell upon Faye. His eyes flicked over to Abigail Hunter with a question in them.

Abigail shook her head, almost imperceptibly. An understanding passed between them.

'This is Detective Smith,' she said, emphasising Faye's title. 'She has some unwelcome and surprising news. Young Carl Carmody's dead.'

Faye sensed that Abilgail's words carried a hidden meaning, but she couldn't discern what it was.

'She's just leaving now.'

'Detective...?' the man began. His mouth turned down at the corners and he seemed to grow larger, his chest expanding.

'Yes, well, thank you for your help,' Faye said to Abigail Hunter, unwilling to cede her authority. 'I'm sorry to be the bearer of bad news.'

But discretion was the better part of valour.

The man moved to stand between her and Abigail. He was light on his feet for such a big man.

'This is the way out,' he said, indicating the door to the hall.

Once there he caught her arm and pulled her towards him until his face was close to hers, lowering down at her.

'Tell your boss that he'll regret this, this is a private home.'

Faye blinked.

'Oh, don't tell me, this is all your idea! Proper girl guide, aren't you? Now, fuck off back to your station.'

He propelled her across the entrance hall and pushed her through the open front door.

It slammed behind her as she staggered out onto the gravel, her heart beating rapidly. She hadn't anticipated that. It was – unsettling.

Who was the man? Where had he come from? Not through the front door; she would have seen him. Had he already been in the house when she arrived? Was it his footsteps she had heard upstairs?

Not Hunter, she was certain; Abigail's reaction hadn't been that of a wife. But she sensed that there was something – an intimacy – between them. Their conversation had carried a weight of meaning. Of what kind she wasn't sure, but it was worth noting.

It was interesting, too, that Carl Carmody's attitude towards his work and the children had changed very recently. It was such a shame that she hadn't had more time alone with the girl.

She reached the pavement and Lydia started up the car.

'Get in!' the policewoman hissed through the open window.

As Faye opened the passenger door she looked back towards the house. A large figure stood in the window, watching. He was speaking on the telephone.

30

FAYE

As Faye tossed her keys into the bowl, she was relieved to see that Ellie's were already there.

The visit to the Hunter home had left her disturbed and anxious; she needed to talk about it, to get it out of her system. She was beginning to think she'd made a mistake in going there. She had had to get some evidence, otherwise Danny and the DI would never accept that Violet's death, and that of Carl Carmody, were related to the gangs. But... had it really been the right thing to do?

Faye could see her friend sitting by the small table out on the terrace, her hand around a beaker, staring into space.

'Hello there,' she called.

'Oh! You're back.' Ellie jumped, looking abashed. 'You startled me!'

She looked as if she had been rudely awoken from a very pleasant dream and didn't like the reality she found.

'There's some iced water in the kitchen if you'd like it.'

'In a minute,' Faye replied. 'I'll change and join you.'

What was the matter with Ellie? She hadn't been herself at all recently. Faye couldn't remember when she had last seen her friend carefree and laughing. Was it working so hard on the fete?

She frowned and pushed aside her own worries.

Was it Antoine's reappearance? No, Ellie's worries began before that, but it couldn't have helped. They hadn't talked about it on Sunday; others had been there, and Ellie was reticent, so Faye hadn't pursued the matter. They hadn't talked about it since, either.

Her friend had been very badly hurt when she learnt Antoine was married. She had, only recently, begun to get over the whole episode. And now he was back. She should have talked with Ellie as soon as Antoine returned.

Faye sighed as she changed.

She'd known about the wife – seen his personnel file – and she had insisted that he confess. He'd prevaricated until she threatened to tell Ellie herself. When he eventually told her, Ellie had ended the relationship. This, Antoine had said, was what he'd been afraid of. He'd left for France soon after, to seek a divorce, he claimed. Something, in Faye's view, he should have done as soon as he began to court Ellie with any seriousness.

It had been difficult to see Ellie's pain after he left. Her friend had lost all confidence in her own judgement, believing that she was a fool when it came to men. That love itself was a fool's game.

Faye thought she'd seen the last of Antoine; she'd never believed he would return. Someone else would come along for Ellie, she was convinced; her friend could take her pick from a legion of suitors – men fell at her feet. But Ellie wanted none of them. She had thrown herself into her work and remained alone. Yet she seemed increasingly dissatisfied.

Faye filled a glass with the iced water, now rather less icy, and went to join her friend.

'Penny for them?'

'Just thinking,' Ellie said. 'It's been a busy day.'

Faye sipped her drink.

'How are you, Ellie? Now that Antoine's back?'

Ellie raised her hands, then let them fall.

'I don't know,' she said. 'It's thrown me out of joint. I wasn't expecting him to return. I'd reconciled myself to my decision, for good or ill.'

She frowned, her expression suggesting the latter.

'And why is he here?'

'He's getting a divorce and wants us to take up where we left off.'

'Do you want to? Do you think it's even possible?'

'I don't think so. I'm not sure I could ever trust him, again.' Ellie's face was drawn and sad. 'But there is a large part of me that wants to believe it could work, that we'd get over it.'

It must be pleasant to inspire such devotion, Faye thought. For a man to offer to give up his country, reorganise his whole life, to be with the woman he loved.

Romantic poppycock, she corrected herself.

'So, what happens now?' she asked.

'He's here on a temporary visa and must decide if he's going to apply to stay. So, he's pressing me for an answer as regards seeing him again. He's proposing marriage if I want it.'

'And do you?'

'I – I used to want marriage and motherhood and, if it's going to happen, time's running out for me, but that's not a reason to rush into it. And I'm not sure Antoine is the right man. The thing is, he's putting all the responsibility for making decisions onto my shoulders.'

'So don't let him. Be honest but make him decide.'

'That's what I'm trying to do. But… I don't know if I can.'

Faye said nothing but reached out and stroked her friend's arm.

'He's coming here tomorrow evening to talk things through. Can you…?'

'Make myself scarce. Of course. When shall I…?' Faye said.

'He's due at seven.' Ellie gave a sad smile and lifted her chin.

'I'll work late.'

'Anyway, how are things at Union Grove?'

'Fine, though most of my colleagues think I'm your godfather's "lady friend", to put it politely.' Faye made light of it. Her friend needed cheering up.

'Hah! About time Phillip got himself a new woman, even if only in people's lurid imaginations.' Ellie started to grin. 'He's divorced,' she clarified, in answer to Faye's questioning look. 'It's a long story. Of course, it could make your position even more difficult.'

'I'll survive.'

'Oh, by the way,' Ellie continued. 'Dr Horn did the post mortem on Carl Carmody. I haven't spoken with her, but Terry said she'd concluded that Carl wasn't a regular user of narcotics. That, in effect, she thought that someone may have killed him by injecting him with the heroin overdose. And I spoke with Stan and Robin, the ambulance men. They confirmed that Violet never regained consciousness.'

'You *have* been busy.'

'They also confirmed that Violet wasn't wearing her engagement ring when they picked her up, or, at least, they didn't notice it. The ring seems to have gone missing. Terry's rather upset about it. A minor mystery compared to the two deaths, of course.'

'Nothing's minor in this case,' Faye said. The missing ring niggled away at her. 'Did you ever see this ring?'

'Only once. Violet was showing it off to a group of nurses in the canteen, passing it around. It was a fine ring, I was surprised when Terry said it was paste. It had a hallmark, a "V" above a crown, which is unusual on a piece of costume jewellery. I pointed it out.'

'And what did Violet say to that?'

'Only that it made the ring extra special.' Ellie's brow puckered. 'Beryl was there. It must have been hard for her to see; Violet was so happy at her engagement.'

'Yes.'

There was a moment of silence.

'You look as though you've made discoveries too,' Ellie said, her mood seeming lighter now.

Faye smiled; her friend could always sense when she wanted to talk. She began to describe her visit to the Hunter home.

'The man that Carl worked for is a gangster!' Ellie's eyes

widened, as Faye inclined her head. 'But Terry thought the family was respectable.'

'So he said.'

'He had no reason to lie,' Ellie replied. 'Could he have known?' When Faye didn't respond she continued. 'Though I'm sure I know the name in another context. I wonder…'

'What?'

'Nothing. But – I don't understand.' Ellie seemed perplexed. 'Why shouldn't you go to their home?'

'I had a legitimate reason to be there, but… I hadn't realised how… territorial it was, how they might react. I thought I might be able to find some evidence linking Violet's death with the Hunters. And I… I thought I could handle things.'

'And didn't you?'

'I — I made a mistake. They saw through me immediately. And I hadn't told my bosses at the station what I was going to do.'

Faye paused, remembering the thrill of excitement because she was going to do what no one else had. She'd been such an idiot.

'The truth is, I wanted to get in there, see what I could learn.' Faye shook her head in incredulity at her foolishness. 'And I certainly shouldn't have gone inside alone.'

Ellie pressed her lips together and exhaled through her nose.

'I can't see what's wrong with it. You're investigating a case.'

'That's it, you see. Violet Taylor's death isn't my case, it's not even a case the squad would usually consider. Without direct evidence to link it to the gang or Hunter, it'll stay that way.'

'The Hunters… gangsters… and in Wimbledon of all places!'

'We also found out who owns flat four eleven in Fairview House,' Faye continued. 'A company called London & City (Estates Holdings) Ltd. It's one of a collection of companies owned by the Hunter family.'

'Well, there's a link for a start.'

'Yes, but it's circumstantial. The company owns lots of properties.'

'Quite a web they weave.'

'Oh, you wouldn't believe... and I think that the flat is being used for something illegal. It isn't tenanted, but people go there.'

'The hooligans...' Ellie prompted.

'Yes, and more, I suspect.'

Faye found herself telling Ellie about what they had found in flat four eleven.

'So you got a warrant after all,' Ellie said.

'I – um, we – not really.' She glossed quickly over Walsh's set of burglar's skeleton keys. 'While we were there one of the young men whose name was on the list of Carl's new friends barged in. Danny says he and another of them are low level thugs, on the periphery of gangland.'

'Like this Dopey, or Soapy?'

'That makes him sound like one of the seven dwarfs!' Faye laughed. 'He really isn't that pleasant. But yes, a low-level hoodlum. We've got an alert out for him; he could have been on the balcony on Friday evening. If we can bring him in for questioning, we'll be able to find out more.'

Ellie was looking at her with concern.

'Faye, you know how to do your job, but... isn't going into someone's flat like that illegal?'

Faye opened her mouth to justify it; to explain that moral purity wasn't something that effective police detectives could afford; that they could always give an excuse, like smelling gas. To explain that the normal rules didn't seem to apply in her new squad. She stopped.

'Yes,' she said. 'It is. But it seems to be how things are done at Union Road, or how Danny Walsh does things, at any rate. It isn't what I'd expected, though the DI did tell me that their methods were sometimes unorthodox. It's all very... on the edge. I know that at least one of my new colleagues haunts illegal drinking dens in pursuit of information. Truth is, I'm not really sure what is and what isn't permitted.'

'Perhaps you could talk with Phillip—'

'No,' Faye countered, quickly.

'I thought you'd say that.'

'And you shouldn't either, Ellie, please.' It would destroy any credibility she had with her colleagues. 'What I've told you was in confidence. It would be damaging for me if it went any further. I really shouldn't have told you any of this.'

'I won't tell anyone, Faye. You know that. But... this is your career.'

'Yes.' Faye paused. 'But it's difficult when you're new and don't know how things are done. I've only been there a few days. I'm supposed to be learning from the sergeant, but...'

His actions had certainly been 'unorthodox', not to say illegal, whatever excuse he might have given. Going to Ridgeway Drive without the DI's approval had been a mistake, but it wasn't illegal and she had reason. Going into the flat was different, even if there had been a reason for that too. It was confusing: she needed to properly think it through.

'Maybe you should talk to John about it,' her friend said, leaning across to her. 'I really think you should. You need to talk to someone about this, someone who knows more about it than me.'

'Yeah,' Faye said, but she wondered.

Would John understand? She loved her brother and he had always looked out for her. But he was so... incorruptible. And he wasn't a detective and didn't work in a special squad. Anyway, she needed to be able to look out for herself; she should be able to work things out without him. She remembered Mona Merchison's jibe.

Sink or swim.

'By the way.' Ellie changed the subject. 'I'm told there's a man coming round tomorrow afternoon to install our new telephone.'

'That was quick. I didn't expect it to happen so soon.'

'The building already has a telephone line, the one in the foyer, so it's easier to install another, I'm told.'

'Well, good.'

Ellie's smile looked sad.

'What a pair we make,' she said. 'Sometimes I feel old.'

'I know what you mean,' Faye answered. 'Come on, let's go for a walk on the Common, blow this miserable mood away. It's warm and balmy, there are still lots of people out – let's go and speculate about their lives rather than be gloomy about our own.'

'I'll show you how the fete is laid out,' Ellie said, rising. 'You can tell me where I'm going wrong!'

'Oh no. This is your fete. I've done enough of them!'

She followed her friend indoors, her spirits lightening.

WEDNESDAY

31

FAYE

The silence was stony; arid and harsh.

Detective Inspector Kent stared out of the window into the sunshine, his back to Faye. His jacket stretched taut across his shoulders because his arms were folded across his chest. Faye sat, stunned, her head sinking into her shoulders as she tried to make herself disappear.

'What the fuck did you think you were doing?' had been his opening comment, the door to his office barely closed.

In vain she had tried to explain; that she had a good reason to visit the Hunter home; that it might provide good intelligence; that the Hunter family, not only the gang, could be linked, personally, to two murders. None of her arguments made a jot of difference to the black scowl on the DI's face.

'You're bright, you're keen and you've had some good ideas, but *this could never* be one of them. You have been a member of this team for three days. Three fucking days! And you're running round like Tigger in a china shop. That isn't how my squad works! There is a chain of command. Familiar with that concept, are you?'

'Yessir,' Faye whispered, as he paced up and down the room.

'There are rules! And one of *them* is that you don't go waltzing into the family home of one of the most feared and dangerous men in London unless you go with the full knowledge of your superiors and officers in support. Or you have incontrovertible evidence and you're about to arrest him! Have you? *Have you?*'

'No, sir.'

'Hunter's lawyers are already claiming intimidation and persecution. All you have achieved is to stir things up and, believe me, Hunter will take his revenge, though it might not be you who pays the price for your little jaunt. And, whatever happens, this unit will be blamed. You've increased the level of risk, jeopardised the safety of your fellow police officers *and* got nothing to show for it.'

'We know that Carl Carmody's behaviour changed very recently.'

'What?' He glowered at her, frowning.

'I, it's my case. Sir...'

'Don't you understand?' Kent's jaw was clenched tight as he explained, slowly and quietly. 'Two deaths, however regrettable and deserving of investigation, are drops in the ocean compared with the criminal business of the Hunter gang. It kills, hurts, damages, enslaves and steals, every day across this city. We exist, as a unit, to destroy them, to bring as many of them as we can to justice. We exist to take a strategic approach.' His voice rose. 'That's what we're for! Do you understand that?'

'Yessir.'

'And we don't move until we're ready, however much we'd like to! Our objective is to amass sufficient evidence to put Hunter, and Caplan, away for a long time. Until we can do that, we do what we can, while keeping our eyes on the ultimate aim. We *do not* go charging in at half cock on a fishing expedition. And my officers most certainly do not go charging in alone, without proper authorisation.'

'I—'

'I really hope you're not about to say that you weren't alone because SSO Sweetham was in the car with you. I really hope not. Because then I'd have to assume that you were taking the almighty fucking piss out of me with an excuse even a schoolgirl would blush at.'

Faye dropped her head even further.

'Where do you think this is? Malory fucking Towers?'

She wished the floor would open up and swallow her.

'And don't blame Sweetham for telling tales. She tried to cover for you, however misguided that may have been. I'm taking away her access to vehicles and she's going to stay behind a desk for the foreseeable. She can restrict herself to taking statements and making the tea.'

Faye stared at him.

Poor Lydia.

And it was all her fault.

'I knew it was a mistake, a novice on the team and a woman at that! Get back to your desk and stay there while I think exactly how I'm going to handle sending you back to Superintendent Bather. And make no mistake.' He pointed at her. 'That is where you are going. This experiment is over.'

Faye's jaw dropped. No. Not that!

'And don't imagine Phillip Morgan is going to come riding to your rescue either.' He pointed his finger at her again. 'He'll have my resignation if he doesn't back me on this. There is a chain of command and it cannot be ignored by the likes of you.'

Faye blinked. He turned his back on her and stared out of the window.

'Out! Now.'

She scrambled to her feet, trying to get out of that room as quickly as humanly possible.

In the larger room it was unusually quiet. The people who were there had their heads down, working, at their desks. They were studiously avoiding looking in her direction, looking anywhere but at her. They'd probably heard every word. They knew she was in disgrace and would soon be packed off, back whence she came.

Lydia sat with her back to her, looking pointedly in the opposite direction. There was no look of sympathy or commiseration. Faye didn't blame her.

Faye sniffed, raised her chin and walked over to her desk, lips pressed tightly together. She picked up the files containing the accounts of the Hunter companies, then crossed to the 'library', her vision blurring as hot tears of shame began to well. She closed the door behind her and hoped that her colleagues would be kind enough to leave her to mourn the crumbling of her hopes in private.

She sat and opened the files and began to look at the accounts, but the words and numbers danced before her eyes.

She was going to be shipped out; DI Kent had left her in no doubt of that. A detective no longer.

It was all sinking in. The DI's dressing down, her feeble excuses, her being bundled back to uniform, and she'd only just arrived. What an utter, utter disgrace.

She remembered Superintendent Bather's exhortation that she mustn't make a pig's ear of her posting, that more than her own fate rested upon her being successful. Other female PCs wouldn't get the opportunity to be detectives – because of her. And Phillip Morgan, who had taken a chance on her, would be made to look foolish. Because she had been stupid. Because she'd tried to go it alone, despite all the warnings. She'd been so arrogant, so sure she was doing right.

She wouldn't get another chance. She'd let everyone down, including herself.

John would have to take some stick too. He'd been so proud of his kid sister, the woman detective. She would have to own up to making a complete mess of her golden opportunity, to him and to the rest of her family.

There were those who would rejoice in her failure, plenty of them; the Harry Dawkinses, the Mona Merchisons, the naysayers of this world. All the people who thought women shouldn't have jobs in the first place and certainly not serious ones.

Faye laid down her pencil, put her arms on the desk and wept.

32

FAYE

She heard the squeak of the door opening and jolted upright, back straight, swiftly wiping her fingers across her cheeks.

'It's me.'

Walsh. Her shoulders relaxed a little.

'Did you hear all that?'

'Half the station heard all that.'

'Oh, God.'

Faye hid her face in her hands, shrivelling with shame.

'If it's any consolation, it could have been worse. He has been known to physically throw people off the premises.'

She looked up at him, amazed, but he had a crooked grin on his face.

'No, that shellacking was up there – force ten on the Richter scale,' he continued. 'But he'll probably calm down.'

'Not soon enough to save my bacon,' Faye said. 'I'm being packed off back to uniform.'

'Yeah, I'm sorry about that,' Walsh said, frowning. 'Just when we were getting somewhere.'

Eh?

'Look, Kent'll have to talk to the Chief Super, which gives us some time. Not a lot, but some. I've got a meeting set with Soapy and I'll press him about the nurse's death and what happened on the Belvedere Estate. He clearly knows something, you're right about that. He might know something about the second death too, the Carmody lad.'

Faye grunted an acknowledgement.

'And, for what it's worth, I think this is worth investigating,' he said. 'I'll pick it up after you've gone.'

So Violet's death was a case worth pursuing when it was his case, but too circumstantial when it was hers.

'But, barging into the Hunter home,' Walsh continued, grinning. 'That was stupid. Like Tigger, wasn't it?'

'Tigger…' Faye rolled her eyes. Over enthusiastic, dim and chaotic.

'Actually, I think your instinct is sound,' he said. 'It's possible that this could give us the link we've been looking for between the day-to-day activity of the gang and Hunter, or at least his family. And I'll tell the boss so, too. You've been right so far.'

Faye blinked in surprise. The fulsome support was totally unexpected.

'Thank you.'

But then, she was on her way out. That was why he was being nice to her. Faye stared at him.

'My point is, do you want to come along? This death is your case until you go and, given the boss's attitude, you might not have a lot of time left to solve it. I take it that you *do want* to find out who killed your nurse and why?'

'Of course! But the DI's made it plain that I'm shackled to my desk.'

'Hmmm, maybe I can persuade him otherwise, now that he's vented the full force of his fury. I want to talk with the pathologist who examined the nurse's body and you could introduce us, that might loosen your chains. I've read the post mortem report she submitted on the nurse.'

That's more than I have, Faye thought.

'Dr Horn used to be a police pathologist,' she said. 'But Danny, all you need to do is to show your warrant card.'

'I know, but I might get more co-operation if I'm with someone she knows and trusts. Not everyone is a whole-souled admirer of His Majesty's boys in blue.'

'Yes, I've noticed. What could we have done to deserve that?' Faye gave him an accusatory stare.

'Anyway, a personal introduction might come in handy, she could be useful in future. If I can get you released from your desk, will you take me to talk with the pathologist?'

'Yes.'

'That gives me something to work with. But you stay by my side, understand? You never leave my sight. No rushing off following leads of your own.'

Walsh's powers of persuasion with the DI were obviously superior to her own, as within twenty minutes they were driving towards the SLH. Faye directed him to the staff car park and led him through the hospital. In the path lab she made the introductions.

'Sergeant Walsh would like to ask you about your findings as regards the deaths of Violet Taylor and Carl Carmody,' she concluded.

'What do you want to know?' asked Dr Horn, rinsing her gloved hands in one of the sluices.

'In your considered opinion, did Violet Taylor fall from Fairview House in a state of advanced inebriation?'

'No,' Dr Horn replied. 'Violet Taylor died because she fell from a high building, but the physical evidence is that she hadn't drunk alcohol to excess. Besides, there are other injuries to her body that suggest that she may have been man-handled before the fall and, possibly, a bottle or funnel was forced into her mouth.'

'Thank you, and—' He stopped, interrupted by the doors to the path lab swinging open.

Beryl bustled in.

'Faye, I was told you were here. What's happening?'

'Beryl, this is Sergeant Walsh,' Faye said. 'Danny, this is Staff Nurse MacBride, tutor to Nurse Taylor and the person who refused to accept the initial police response. She's the reason I investigated this case in the first place.'

'Staff Nurse MacBride.' Walsh nodded.

Faye glanced at Beryl for an acknowledgement, but the Scot was staring, speechless, at the sergeant.

'Hsst, Beryl,' Faye prompted.

'What? Oh yes. Hello, sergeant,' Beryl said.

'Doctor, I've seen your report on the death of Violet Taylor; may I have a copy of your post mortem report on Carmody?' Walsh addressed the pathologist. 'And, if you will, could you give me the salient points now?'

'Of course.'

She beckoned them over to the mortuary storage drawers and pulled one open. The cold, chemical smell of the laboratory was overlaid with the scent of decomposition. Faye covered her nose and mouth. It emanated from the corpse of Carl Carmody. The boy had been big for his age, with a muscular and sinewy body. It was covered with livid black and purple bruises.

'He's been badly beaten,' Walsh said.

'Yes, though the beating wasn't the cause of death,' Dr Horn said. 'Carl Carmody died from organ collapse due to respiratory failure and oxygen deprivation. The blood toxicology shows us this was brought on by an opiate, probably heroine, combined with alcohol.'

'Time of death?' Walsh asked.

'Difficult to determine with any accuracy. High temperatures accelerate decomposition. I would say several days ago. My best guess would be the early hours of Saturday morning.'

'Soon after Vi was killed, then,' Beryl said.

'Yes.'

'How did he die?' Faye asked.

'Look.' Dr Horn lifted up one of Carl's arms. The livid red blotches of needle entry into the veins were clear to see. 'Studded with puncture marks. Yet his body doesn't show the usual signs of

A DEATH IN THE AFTERNOON

regular narcotics use. Indeed, his prescribed medication would have meant that any continued use would have massive side effects and complications, none of which were evident in his body.'

'So...?'

'My considered opinion in *this* case is that it's extremely unlikely that the young man took the heroin voluntarily. The needle marks were made by other people injecting him, probably when he was drunk.'

'So Carl was murdered too?' Beryl said, aghast. 'Are you sure?'

'No, I can't be certain. I can only draw conclusions from evidence found on and in the body.'

'Have you found anything else?' Faye asked.

'Yes, as it happens. Here and here.' Dr Horn pointed to faint weals of red around the boy's wrists. 'There are similar marks around his ankles. I'd say he'd been restrained.'

'Caught, trussed, force fed alcohol and then killed,' Faye said.

'I talked with Miss Souter, who was treating him,' Beryl said. 'She told me it was likely that Carl would've been mentally unstable without his medicine. Easier to catch, maybe, if he wasn't thinking straight.'

'That's about the size of it,' the pathologist replied.

'Thank you, Dr Horn, you've been very helpful,' Walsh said. 'If I could leave you my card...'

As the pathologist took the card offered Faye turned to speak with Beryl, but the staff nurse had gone, the swinging path lab doors testament to her passing.

Why on earth had she rushed away like that?

'So, we'll be on our way,' Walsh concluded. 'Faye. Faye?'

'What, oh yes. Thank you, Dr Horn.'

'Happy to help,' the pathologist replied. 'You know your way out.'

33

FAYE

'Carl Carmody didn't commit suicide,' Faye said. 'Though somebody tried to make it look like he did.'

'It was a very half-hearted attempt,' Walsh replied. 'Perhaps his killer thought no one would bother about the death of a petty offender, a bit of a wild boy.'

Or knew that the police wouldn't look too hard, Faye thought.

Carl's body had been brought to the SLH because he was known to be a local; ordinarily a body found in Billingdon Road would fall within the jurisdiction of Standish Road station, it would be taken to the mortuary that station used. Faye considered asking Walsh about his old station but decided against it; he'd been reticent about it before and she didn't want to sour the recent fragile improvement in their relationship.

Once again, they were walking through Brockley Cemetery, past the WW1 memorial and the Cain tomb.

'So, why *did* you go to Hunter's gaff?' Walsh asked.

'It seemed like a good idea at the time,' said Faye.

'It took some guts, I'll hand it to you.' His expression was deadpan. 'Only a beginner would even consider it! How, *how* did you think that would be a good idea?'

'You said we needed evidence. I thought I might find some or learn something useful relating to the case.'

'And did you? Was it worth it?'

'Yes. And no. Carl Carmody did odd jobs for the Hunter family. It was Abigail he had dealings with and, as it turned out, the Hunter children, not Hunter himself. I thought I'd be on safe ground talking to them and yet I still might get some information. And I might've got away with it, too, if that heavy hadn't shown up as if from nowhere. I didn't imagine that he, that they, would be so territorial. And I had reason to be there, the news of Carl Carmody's death...'

'Which Hunter may have ordered.'

'Alright, alright.' Faye rolled her eyes. 'Anyway, I learned that Carl Carmody used to chat and play with the Hunter kids, until last week. Then his behaviour changed. Young Belinda had no idea why. She said he seemed nervous and jumpy.'

'Hmmm, and? Anything else?'

Faye considered.

'I'd swear that Abigail Hunter didn't know about Carl's death. She looked genuinely surprised. Yet, she's her husband's lieutenant and partner as well as his wife. If Hunter had ordered Carl's killing, why didn't she know about it?'

Walsh shrugged and shook his head. 'Maybe he didn't want her to know. Or maybe she's a good actress?'

'I think the man I saw there was Derek Brodie – large, broad shoulders, black hair and a square jaw. Handsome in a crudely drawn way.'

'Sounds like Brodie.'

'Well, this is going to sound speculative, but I got the feeling that there was some understanding between him and Abigail Hunter.'

'What kind of understanding?'

'I'm not entirely sure, but...' The more she thought about it, the more convinced Faye became that there was something going on between them, something she had interrupted. 'They were very familiar with each other's thought processes. That suggests a closeness, maybe an intimacy, that I found... unusual. Also, he was there, in the house; no one came and went for at least an hour before I went in. Hunter wasn't at home, so I'm not sure what Brodie was doing there all that time. I heard what sounded like a man's footsteps upstairs when I arrived. And the girl, Belinda, didn't like him, though she wasn't surprised to find him in her home. I realise this was only my impression and it may or may not be significant.'

'Hmmm, it'd be a brave man who'd mess around with Hunter's missus,' Walsh said. 'And a foolish one. I don't think Derek Brodie's that brainless; he'd be risking everything he's got. He's worked for Hunter for years, he's one of his right-hand men. Maybe that's why he knows Abigail so well?'

'As I say, it was only an impression, but there definitely seemed to be something between them.'

'There's Soapy.'

Up ahead Soapy was loitering near the same mausoleum as before.

'Now this time, if you want to question him, let me know.'

The snout nodded a greeting as they approached, but kept looking around, as if he expected to be ambushed.

'Soapy,' Walsh said. 'What've you got for me?'

'Dunno, Sergeant Walsh. What've you got for me?'

Faye recognised the familiar ritual, which, she suspected, opened every exchange between Walsh and his snitch.

'Depends,' Walsh said. 'The Hunter flat on the Belvedere Estate. What goes on there?'

'Don't know anything 'bout that.'

'Where the nurse "fell" from.'

'I heard it was from a party,' Soapy said.

'Next door to one. Been cleaned up, but the forensics might find something. What's it used for?'

Soapy shrugged his thin shoulders.

Faye exchanged a glance with Walsh, who blinked agreement.

'Carl Carmody,' she said, adopting Walsh's staccato delivery.

'Boy's body was found in a basement in Billingdon Road. What do you know about that?'

'Nothing.'

'He was the young lad who did odd jobs for Abigail, Mrs Hunter.'

A sly look crossed Soapy's face.

'What's it worth?'

'It's worth you not getting hauled down to the station, that's what it's worth,' Walsh said. 'And I'm not talking about Standish Lane.'

'And the moolah.'

'Two quid and you keep your arse out of gaol.' Walsh squared up to the snitch.

'Alright, alright.' He licked his lips. 'Word is the Carmody kid had it coming.'

'What?' Faye was astonished.

'Did something to cross Derek Brodie. Nobody disrespects *him* and gets away with it.'

'What? What did he do?' Faye demanded.

'Dunno.' Soapy backed away from a threatening Walsh. 'I don't, I don't!'

'If I find out you're lying…'

'I'm not. I swear.'

Walsh glowered at him and peeled two notes from a roll in his pocket.

'Here,' he said. 'Now piss off.'

Soapy grabbed the notes and stuffed them into the inside pocket of his scruffy jacket as he shambled away.

Faye's mind was buzzing with questions as they made their way back to the car.

Had Carl really crossed Brodie? If it was a matter of disrespect, how come Carl was still working at Ridgeway Drive?

Could that fit with Carl's change of behaviour? If he'd transgressed in some way, maybe he'd had reason to be nervous – he was afraid of being found out and dismissed, or worse?

She needed to speak with someone who had known Carl; she

needed to speak with his brother. Ellie or Beryl could persuade him to talk with her, if Beryl was around, after her disappearing act that afternoon.

Now, she sensed, they were getting closer to who killed Violet and why. Just as well; the clock was ticking. Time was running out.

34

ELEANOR

Ellie opened the door of number twenty-two to a thick-set man wearing brown overalls and carrying a toolbox.

'Telephone installation,' he said, with a slight lisp. 'Flat twenty-two.'

'Yes, come in please.'

Once inside, the engineer put down his box and rummaged in it.

'I need to find the telephone point, miss,' he said. 'All these flats have' em, even if the builders didn't install the telephones themselves. Usually next to an electricity socket. I might have to look around, if that's alright with you?'

'I see. Alright. There's a bedroom through here and another just along that corridor, but surely the telephone line would be here, near the front door.'

He shrugged. 'It probably is. Not for me to say.'

'Can I make you a cup of tea?'

'Yes, please, love. That would be nice. Thank you.'

Ellie wandered into the kitchen and filled the kettle. She was pleased that the engineer had arrived and installation was underway; she wanted it completed before Antoine's arrival.

Everything had to be just so. She had planned what she wanted to say and ran through it again in her head. They had had some good times; their relationship had seemed to be developing into something deeper and more long-lasting. Yet, throughout that time, he had known that it could not lead to anything. He had allowed her to believe otherwise, had led her on, had deceived her.

She had finished the relationship when she found out that he was married and – this was the main point she wanted to make – she didn't see how his reappearance could change her opinion of him. It couldn't change what he'd done.

He said he'd begun divorce proceedings, but she had no reason to trust what he said. She also wanted to point out that it wasn't fair that he should put all the responsibility for any potential future they could have on her shoulders. She understood his situation, but that wasn't for her to resolve.

Truth to tell, she was very nervous about the whole meeting. Him being here, in the flat, was bound to bring back memories and she wasn't at all convinced that she wouldn't weaken and capitulate. Antoine could be very persuasive.

'S'cuse me.'

The engineer knocked on the open kitchen door.

'Where do you want the telephone put, miss?'

'I thought – in the living room, please.'

'Not a bedroom? Some people like it there, in case of burglaries or break-ins, during the night, like. It's to hand if they need to contact the police.'

'No. The flat is shared, so both occupants need to have access to it. It should be in the living room,' Ellie replied.

'Righty-ho. Living room it is.'

'Milk?'

'Yes, please.' The man reached out for the cup handed to him. He was wearing surgical gloves. 'For my eczema,' he explained, when he saw her notice.

He sipped the tea.

'Having a telephone's really useful,' he confided. 'There've been a lot of break-ins recently, as well as fraudsters talking their way into people's homes. Having a telephone makes people feel much safer.'

'Yes.'

What was he wittering on about? Why didn't he get on with the job?

'They're nice, these flats.'

Ellie wished she hadn't offered him the tea; he seemed to be taking his time drinking it and the afternoon was passing. She wanted to get ready for Antoine's visit; it wouldn't be long now.

'Yes.'

The engineer returned to his previous topic.

'You can't be too careful,' he said, seemingly relishing the possibility of a crime. 'And a woman on her own…'

'I'm not on my own. As I said, I have a flatmate.'

'You're Miss Smith, aren't you?'

'No. My name is Peveril.'

'Oh, only I had Smith down on my chitty.' He frowned.

'That's my flatmate,' Ellie said, becoming impatient. It was obvious that he was in the correct flat, so why all the questions? 'I'm actually expecting a visitor very soon, so I'd be grateful if you could get a bit of a move on.'

It would be uncomfortable if the engineer was still here when Antoine arrived.

'Alright, I'm just drinking my tea.'

The man didn't move.

'Well, I need to get ready,' she said, walking past him into the living room. 'He'll be here very shortly.'

'Oh, gentleman caller, is it?'

'A doctor, actually,' she said, sharply.

It was no business of his and she didn't like his tone.

The engineer put down the mug and crossed to his toolbox.

Finally! She thought.

But he clipped the box closed and stood.

'I'll be on my way then,' he said.

'What?'

First he dawdles, then he can't wait to be on his way!

'You don't know where the telephone point is and it'll take time to detect it. I don't like to be rushed and interruptions make the job more difficult. I'll come back at another day, when I have time to do a good job. Here's our card.'

He handed a card to Ellie with a smirk.

Bloody effrontery!

'The office'll be in touch to make arrangements. Goodbye. Thanks for the tea.'

She closed the front door firmly behind him and tossed the card into the key dish. What a waste of time.

In her bedroom she opened the wardrobe and took out a cotton summer dress, holding it against her body as she posed in the mirror. This would do nicely, with just a touch of lipstick and a pair of sandals. She kicked off her house slippers and began to change.

Halfway through she stopped.

What was she doing?

This wasn't a romantic assignation, a 'date', as the Americans would say. She didn't have to look her best. Merely neat and tidy. The blouse and cut-off trousers she'd been wearing would be perfectly acceptable, though the slippers would have to go. She put the dress back into the wardrobe. And the lipstick? She only had a nub left.

She would make the flat neat; that was acceptable preparation for a visitor. Tidy the living room.

But before she left the bedroom, she drew the red lipstick over her lips and pressed them together. It made her feel better.

That would be tickety-boo.

35

ELEANOR

The doorbell rang at six thirty precisely.

Antoine stood in the doorway, a posy of fresh flowers in his hand. His face was pale against his dark hair.

'For you,' he said, proffering the flowers as he entered.

She wondered if he'd bought them at the florist's downstairs.

'Thank you, but you shouldn't have, really. I'll put them in water.'

He followed her through to the kitchen.

'The place hasn't changed much,' he said, looking around.

'No, although we are having a telephone installed, the engineer was here this afternoon. All the mod cons.'

'Oh.'

For some reason this seemed to dampen his spirits.

'Would you like some tea?'

'No, thank you.'

He followed her back through to the living room, where she placed the vase of flowers on the sideboard.

'Ellie, I—'

'Please sit—'

Antoine sat in an easy chair; Ellie perched on the sofa. She shifted her position, acutely conscious of the physical distance between them. She had never used to feel awkward in his company, but she did now.

He licked his lips and began again. 'My employers at St Thomas's are pressing me to decide about a new contract,' he said. 'I would like—'

'I'm not going to allow you to turn this into being my decision, Antoine,' Ellie interrupted him. 'What you decide to do is up to you. I'm not going to make the decision for you.'

'I have every intention of making that decision myself,' he replied, quickly. 'But I need to know where I stand with you, *cherie*, in order to make it.'

'My position with you is as it was when you left,' she said. 'You deliberately deceived me—'

'Only because I didn't want to lose you.'

'For whatever reason, that is what you did. So I cannot trust you, Antoine, and, without trust, there can be no intimacy between us.'

'So, you reject me. Again.'

His face had grown even paler and his dark eyes were moist. Something lurched inside her chest.

'I don't see what has changed. The facts haven't.'

'I'm getting a divorce. I will be free. That's changed. I no longer have any reason to keep anything from you.' Antoine's jaw was set, his lips compressed.

'How do I know that's true?' Ellie said. 'What you did destroyed my trust in you. I don't see how that can be restored.'

Antoine stood, face drawn taut, tension in every limb. He strode to the open terrace doors and looked out, keeping his back to her.

'So that's it?' he said, quietly. 'That's your answer?'

'I – yes, that's it.'

'You won't even let me try? I thought that our relationship was worth something, enough at least to try to rebuild it?'

'I thought it was worth something too,' Ellie said, standing. Antoine swung around and strode to catch her hands in his own.

'Then—'

'Unfortunately, the relationship I thought we had wasn't real.

You were married, all along. Playing me for a fool.' She disengaged her hands.

'I wasn't, I wasn't. Ellie, I was terrified that, once you found out, you'd drop me.'

'And you were right!'

'I — I tried to obtain a divorce almost immediately after I met you,' Antoine said. 'But it was impossible. There were no records. People were displaced, many had fled the occupation. Delphine was hard to trace. At first, I believed she might have died. Many had.'

She knew that Ligugé, Antoine's town, had been occupied by the Nazis. What he said was plausible. But then, hadn't he always been plausible?

'So why couldn't you have told me this then? Why keep me in the dark? And how do I know that's even true?'

'I swear it, Eleanor. Please, please let me make it up to you,' he beseeched her.

Ellie shook her head, determined to stick to her guns. At the same time, she wanted him to persist, to beg her to take him back. Could there really be a future for them?

'Antoine, what's done is done. Go back to France, or stay in London, that's up to you, but I'm not going to promise you anything.'

'There is some hope for me, then?'

Did he sense her weakening?

'I didn't say that!'

'But you don't dismiss me. You will see me again?' There was a desperate yearning on his face.

'Antoine—'

'*S'il vous plait*, Eleanor. Promise me nothing, but don't dismiss me, *belle dame sans merci*.'

She felt her resolve dwindling, but also knew that it wouldn't be fair to allow him to hope when she really thought there was none.

'I cannot offer you any hope, Antoine. It wouldn't be fair to you.'

His mouth twitched; he seemed to be working hard to keep his emotions under control.

'Don't dismiss me, *cherie*, but know that, if you do, I will never return.'

'Antoine, you're doing it again. I—'

'You can destroy me, Eleanor, but I beg you to give me another chance.'

The absurdity of the situation struck Ellie. It seemed that Antoine thought so too. One corner of his mouth was curled into a wry smile, though there was deep sadness and fear in his eyes.

'Eleanor, I'll go now. May I call again?'

Ellie felt backed into a corner. Yet all she had to do was say 'No' and he would be gone for ever.

'Yes,' she said, almost in a whisper.

'*Merci.*' Relief and gratitude chasing across his face. 'Thank you.'

Ellie stepped back, away from Antoine, who, it seemed, was going to embrace her.

'I'm going,' he said. 'I won't… I'm going.'

36

ELEANOR

Ellie sank down onto the sofa, exhausted.

All her resolve, all her determination had melted away. She did, it seemed, want him back after all, even if she might regret it later.

The door opened. It was Faye.

Ellie shook herself. She must have been sitting there for longer than she thought.

'How did it go? Are you alright?' Faye asked.

'Yes, I think so.'

'Ron says Antoine has gone.'

'Yes.'

'And that he looked, not exactly pleased, but not entirely dejected either?'

'Yes.'

'So…?'

'I told him that I couldn't trust him, that I didn't think we had a future… but he wants a chance to prove that I can. He thinks the relationship is worth saving.'

'And what do you think? What do you want?'

'I want it to be how it was, but I'm not sure it can be. At least, not for a long time.'

In the silence, she heard shouts and calls from the Common.

'I gave way,' she said, eventually. 'I couldn't dismiss him for ever.'

'Oh, Ellie.' Her friend hugged her.

'So we might be seeing more of him. Is that alright with you?'

'Whatever you decide is alright with me,' Faye assured her. 'I haven't enjoyed seeing you unhappy these past months. If Antoine is the man to make you happy, maybe giving him another chance is what's best. He seems to have done the decent thing, even if belatedly.'

'He's bound to call again.' Ellie gave her friend a sad, rueful look.

'Speaking about calling, did the telephone engineer turn up?'

'Yes, but he couldn't do what he needed to, had to have some different equipment, he said. We'll be contacted to arrange another appointment, apparently. His card's on the key plate. He was a bit of a rum character.'

'How d'you mean?' Faye rose and walked over towards the key dish.

'Asking lots of questions, talking about burglars and the police.'

'Ellie, was this the card?' Faye's voice was urgent.

'Yes…'

Something was wrong.

'What is it?'

'London & Surrey (Household).' Faye read the card. 'Ellie, I think this is to do with my work. I think the man you saw wasn't a telephone engineer at all.'

'What?' Ellie frowned.

How could that be? Oddly, it didn't seem surprising.

'Did Ron let him up?'

Ron, the caretaker, was usually the first port of call for any workmen arriving at Westbury Court. He would let residents know of their arrival using the internal intercom system.

'I don't know, although, now you mention it, he didn't buzz me to say someone was coming and he usually does.'

'Let's find out.'

The cubby-hole that Ron called his 'office' was just off the tiled foyer. A rap on its window brought a startled Ron out, away from his wireless.

'What can I do for my two favourite ladies?' he asked, affecting a proprietorial tone.

'Ron, did a telephone engineer check in with you before coming up to number twenty-two, this afternoon?' Faye asked.

'Short fellow, wearing brown overalls, carrying an over-sized toolbox,' Ellie added.

'No. If I'd seen someone I'd've buzzed you.' Ron shook his head. 'He can't have checked in with me and I've been here all afternoon. Saw your Antoine arrive, Ellie, he said "hello". He's back now, is he?'

'Er, yes.'

People would ask; she had better get used to it.

'Thanks, Ron,' Faye said.

'S'alright. He wasn't a problem, was he?'

'No. At least, I don't think so,' Ellie answered.

The two women returned to the flat.

'Ellie, listen. The card that man gave to you is for a company owned by Henry Hunter, whose house I so misguidedly visited yesterday. I suspect that man wasn't a telephone engineer at all,' Faye said.

'The gangster in Wimbledon? Hang on, you're saying that one of this man's henchmen has been inside our flat?' Ellie said.

She had been alone in the flat with him. There was a creeping shiver down her spine.

'It's possible.' Faye answered.

'Why would he be here?' Ellie asked, quietly.

She could have been in real peril that afternoon. The 'engineer' had been strange and... suggestive. Yet all she'd been thinking about was Antoine's visit.

'We must report this. So that something can be done, the man can be warned off... though I don't know who will deal with it...' Faye sighed. 'Was he alone during the time he was inside?'

'Yes, I went into the kitchen to make him a cup of tea.'

'So he could have taken an impression of its key – was your key in the bowl by the door? We usually throw our keys in there.'

Faye was pacing up and down, face drawn and anxious.

'Yes, I suppose he could have done,' Ellie murmured. 'I'd better speak with Ron about getting the lock changed.'

'And have you checked the flat, after he left?' She stopped pacing.

'No, I've been into my bedroom and that was undisturbed. So was the bathroom,' Ellie answered.

'Good. I'll check mine.' Faye went to do so.

Ellie began to scan the living room. Had anything been moved or was missing? Everything seemed to be in place.

What?

It was a shout, a scream. It was Faye!

Ellie ran.

She barged through the door to Faye's bedroom.

Inside, flimsy scraps of tissue paper fluttered around the bedroom like snowflakes, blown by the breeze once the door had opened. Faye stood, both her hands at her mouth, staring, wide-eyed, at her bed. She looked up at Ellie, shock and fear on her face.

On the bed, devoid now of its wrapping, lay the newly cleaned police uniform that Ellie had picked up for her friend earlier that day. It had been hanging on the wardrobe door, but now it was laid out as if someone was wearing it, with the waist of the skirt inside the jacket and the cap placed on the pillow.

From the jacket, just above the waistband, protruded the dull metal of a heavy bayonet, plunged deep into the bed beneath.

37

ELEANOR

'I know this is distressing, Miss Peveril, this sort of intimidation is supposed to be,' Detective Inspector Kent said to her in measured tones.

Kent sat in an armchair in the living room at number twenty-two. Besuited, neat and professional, he was frowning, which made him seem bad tempered and harassed. Ellie thought that his black hair gave him a slightly satanic look.

Attempting to intimidate the police. This sort of thing must have happened before.

Earlier Ellie and Faye had both made formal statements to Sergeant Danny Walsh, Ellie's first sighting of the man who thought nothing of entering a private home without a warrant. Yet he seemed professional too, if somewhat bothered by the heat.

'My godfather...?' Ellie began.

'Is on his way,' the inspector replied. 'He'll be here as soon as he can.'

A constable joined them.

'The prints team is almost done,' he said to the sergeant. 'Is there somewhere they can wash?'

'Yes, the bathroom,' Ellie said. 'I'll show you.'

Ellie rose and indicated where to go, then stepped into the

kitchen; she wanted to be by herself. Why were they looking for fingerprints? She'd already told them that the man was wearing gloves.

She shook her head to clear it – she hadn't yet come to terms with a criminal being in their home; it was difficult to accept. Standing at the sink, she pressed her hands down on the metal rim, tensing her arms.

Behind her, someone came to stand in the doorway. She turned to see the sergeant.

'The man, the intruder, stood where you are standing, drinking a cup of tea,' she said to him. 'Unfortunately, I've washed up the mug he used.'

'I don't think we'll get any prints, you said he was wearing gloves, but we have to try,' he replied. Could he read her mind? 'The knife wasn't one of yours, I take it. He didn't help himself to it from the kitchen?'

'No, he didn't really come in here at all. He must have brought the knife with him, in his toolbox.' She swallowed hard. He could have attacked her at any time and she would have been defenceless. 'I do hope you catch him.'

'There's more than a chance that he's already known to us,' Sergeant Walsh said as they went back to the living room. 'Our best bet as regards identifying him is you.'

'Sergeant Walsh is correct,' the inspector said. 'If you could come to Union Grove station with Faye tomorrow morning, he'll take you through our rogue's gallery of photographs.'

'My description doesn't help, I suppose,' Ellie said. 'He was very average looking. Apart from the slightly sibilant "esses".'

She was certain that a glance passed between inspector and sergeant. Faye sat forward on the edge of the sofa; she had noticed it too.

'You already have an idea who it might be,' Ellie said.

'It's possible,' DI Kent said, reluctantly. 'But we don't want to prejudice a formal identification.'

There was a prolonged buzzing from the intercom. Ellie answered it.

'Ellie, I'm coming up.' Chief Superintendent Phillip Morgan had dispensed with Ron's services as intermediary. She opened the door. Behind her everyone stood.

'Are you alright? How are you feeling?' he asked, looking down into her face as he put an arm around her shoulders.

'I— it's quite frightening to think about what could have happened,' she replied, leaning into him. 'But I'm alright, really. It was Faye he was interested in, not me.'

'Faye.' Phillip walked over and took Faye's hands. 'How are you?'

'I'm alright thank you, er, sir.'

The senior policeman waved away the honorific and acknowledged DI Kent and Sergeant Walsh.

'It's classic intimidation, sir,' the inspector said. 'Faye — Detective Constable Smith — has been working on the case against Hunter. This... incident... may be a message to back off. Though there may be other elements in play here, that we know nothing about.'

'Arrogance.' Phillip's face was grim. 'Sheer arrogance.'

'Sir?' the sergeant spoke.

With a sharp nod of his head, Phillip indicated that Sergeant Walsh should speak.

'This afternoon, DC Smith and I found what we believe are links between two recent suspicious deaths and the Hunter gang, or Hunter and his family. I think this incident might have happened because Faye, DC Smith, was getting close to the truth. Her instinct's sound, sir.'

Phillip harrumphed and looked, questioningly, at Kent. The inspector glared back at him, saying nothing.

So, they've spoken about this before, Ellie thought. She knew her godfather was a supporter and the sponsor of her friend's career; but, it seemed, DI Kent was not. There were undercurrents here that she didn't understand.

'There is a chain of command, sir,' the inspector muttered

'The detective inspector and I will discuss our next move on the way back to Union Grove, but DC Smith will remain *at her desk* for the immediate future,' Phillip said. 'And *I mean* at her desk. You understand, Faye?'

'Yessir.'

'In the meanwhile, a plain clothes police officer will be stationed downstairs. He can keep your concierge company for a while. You should alert your boss, Ellie. Tell the hospital.'

Ellie nodded. She would.

'Sergeant Walsh will arrange for a car to pick you both up tomorrow morning at nine o'clock.'

Her godfather was angry; his lips were compressed and white, always a telltale sign.

All this reflected unfavourably on the police, it reflected badly on him. He was personally as well as professionally affronted.

'Are your people finished here, Robert?' he said.

'Yes, sir.'

'Right. We'll be going then.'

DI Kent and Sergeant Walsh made their way to the door, but Ellie's godfather lingered.

'What's happened is frightening,' he said to them both. 'But it's over now. Your home is safe and will be even safer when the locks are changed and you have a telephone installed – we'll arrange for a genuine telephone engineer to do that straight away. There's a locksmith on his way. I know it sounds impossible, but try and relax now. Goodnight, Faye.' He inclined his head towards Ellie. 'If you'd walk with me for a moment, Ellie?'

When they were in the corridor outside, he stopped.

'We need to consider what, if anything, to tell your parents.'

'This won't make the newspapers, will it? I didn't plan to tell them anything,' she spluttered. 'There's no need to worry them unduly.'

Phillip looked unconvinced but agreed.

'Very well.'

He kissed her forehead and began to leave, then turned back.

'I know you'll put this behind you, Ellie. And Faye too. Your friend's having a tough time at the moment – she's made some mistakes and this is something of a baptism of fire for her, but I'm sure she'll work through it. She's too intelligent and tenacious a character to give in. I have every confidence in her and in you.'

'Thank you, Phillip.'

'Chin up. 'Bye now.'

Ellie closed the door and leant back against it.

She just wanted it to stop. For the villains to get caught. For normality, and safety, to return. But she knew it wouldn't and she had her part to play in stopping it. She'd played her part during the war and she'd do so again now.

She pushed herself away from the door and went to confer with Faye in the kitchen.

THURSDAY

38

FAYE

Faye flicked through the pages of the file, not seeing the words written there. She was at her desk in the squad room at Union Grove, having delivered Ellie to Danny Walsh to look at the photographs. The large room was empty. Everyone seemed to be somewhere else.

It seemed that her colleagues knew about the events of last evening. She had found a fresh mug of tea and a biscuit on her desk, perhaps a peace offering from Lydia, although the SSO was nowhere to be seen. The desk had been tidied too.

When she'd asked Walsh what was going to happen, he'd muttered about cracking heads together, but like all of them, he didn't really know. He hadn't been included in the discussions between Kent and Morgan. Walsh's knee-jerk reaction might be a common one, but she doubted DI Kent would share it and Phillip Morgan would only use those methods as part of a calculated strategy, if at all.

How would they decide to respond to the 'message' from Hunter? Everyone was waiting to see what would happen next.

There was, however, one silver lining.

Yesterday DI Kent had been ready to ship her back to uniform, but it seemed that that would be delayed. To do so now could be seen as an acknowledgement that she, and, by definition, the police, had been at fault. It would also look like a craven act, as if they were running scared of the Hunter gang.

She had a reprieve.

But it might not last for long and, if she was to solve Violet Taylor's murder and find out who had killed Carl Carmody, she had to make best use of the time.

Think. Think about things differently.

Think about the people.

She knew quite a lot about Violet, thanks to Beryl, but little about Carl. Fifteen years old, just out of school, with mental problems and taking medicine to minimise their effects. In trouble with the police when younger but trying to go straight now. Belinda Hunter had described a jolly sort of character, but one whose behaviour had changed radically only a week ago. Faye believed the girl. She had no reason to lie.

Soapy had claimed that Carl had crossed Brodie in some way and that seemed believable too. Why had Carl's behaviour changed and how had he transgressed? Had he defied or thwarted Brodie, or was it his bosses, the Hunters? He had worked at the Hunter home. What could he have done?

There was one other, associated, mystery niggling at Faye.

What had happened to Violet Taylor's missing ring?

Violet had been wearing it when she was at the party, but it wasn't on her finger when the ambulance came for her. It had gone missing at some time between her being at the party and her body being collected.

Had it been filched, as they supposed?

According to Terry it was paste, of sentimental value only. Yet Ellie knew good jewellery when she saw it and it was hallmarked. What if it wasn't a cheap ring at all? Then it might be worth nicking. Yet Terry couldn't have afforded an expensive piece of jewellery.

Unless... An image of Abigail Hunter flashed into Faye's mind. She was standing in her doorway, sunlight reflecting on her jewellery, heavy gold and diamond encrusted. Rings. Had Terry got the ring from Carl, who had helped himself to it from the Hunter home? Was it possible that Violet's engagement ring had belonged to Abigail Hunter? Was that how Carl had transgressed?

If so, he'd been very foolish. Abigail Hunter, it seemed to Faye, was the sort of person who would notice immediately if anything of hers went missing and would want it back, plus punishment for whoever had taken it. Would that explain Carl's change in demeanour; if he had taken Abigail Hunter's ring, he was right to be jumpy.

This was speculation. And she could have sworn that Abigail had been surprised to learn of Carl's death. So it didn't fit. Damn. Maybe she was over-thinking things?

On the subject of rings and jewellery...

Walsh had told her about the Greville Street jewellery robbery. She would have a look at that file.

The robbery had taken place in daylight at a diamond merchant and jeweller's in Hatton Garden. Masked, armed robbers had stolen the pieces in the display cases and the unset gems in the workroom behind the shop. They knew what they were looking for. The haul was carried out in their pockets and in one of the jeweller's own bags, to a car waiting outside. There were no witnesses. The raid took less than five minutes.

The loot had been worth a small fortune, but none of the stolen pieces had surfaced since. Some would have been broken up, the metal melted down and the stones recast. Some stones would have been spirited away, out of the country. Faye wondered what had happened to the remainder.

The file contained a list of what had been stolen, with photographs and sketches. Most of the pieces carried the jeweller's stamp, an inverted V-shape above a crown.

That was it!

A 'V' above a crown – that was what Ellie had described only yesterday. Could the ring that Terry had given to Violet be one of the rings stolen from the Hatton Garden jeweller's?

If Henry Hunter's gang was behind the raid, had Hunter given his wife a ring, or allowed her to take her pick of the spoils? She was a woman who liked jewellery.

And could Carl Carmody have helped himself to that ring, one among so many that she owned, so that his brother was able to court Violet Taylor? Could it all be connected? Was that why Violet died?

If that ring linked the Hunters with the jewel raid... it was evidence that could put them away for a long time.

It was a tenuous hypothesis, but it did hang together.

Faye had always assumed that Violet had been killed because she saw something in flat four eleven that she shouldn't have done. But perhaps it wasn't that at all. Perhaps it was the occupants of the flat who had seen something. Maybe they'd been told about a missing ring, which they then saw on Violet Taylor's finger?

She had to speak with Walsh.

Faye was on her feet, when a flood of colleagues suddenly entered the room, glancing, not unkindly, in her direction, but saying nothing. It appeared that there had been a meeting held elsewhere to which she hadn't been invited.

Lydia Sweetham came over to Faye's desk.

'I wanted to say how sorry I am to hear about what happened yesterday,' she said. 'Everyone is. It was way over the top.'

Walsh joined them.

'Exactly,' he said. 'Out of order. Completely out of order.'

'Danny, I've been thinking...'

'Oh-oh.'

'Could Hunter have been behind the Greville Street robbery? You said that no one knew who the mastermind was.'

'It might have been Hunter, or Caplan. Neither of them would have actually done the job, though. It was more likely to be organised by one of their lieutenants. Why? What are you thinking?'

'It's just a theory.'

She explained her thinking to Walsh and Lydia.

Walsh whistled.

'It makes sense,' he said. 'But pond life like O'Shaughnessy wouldn't have seen Abigail Hunter's ring before.'

'Hmm, perhaps Abigail had the word put out, with a reward. Or she could have set someone to find Carl, someone who knew what the ring looked like.'

Walsh acknowledged this possibility with a tilt of his head.

'But why kill Violet?' he asked. 'Why not simply take the ring and frighten her into keeping quiet?'

'From what I know about Violet, I don't think she was the easily frightened type.' Faye remembered Beryl describing the young nurse's background. 'And I don't think she would have willingly given up her engagement ring.'

'If there was a struggle…?'

'Violet may have been killed accidentally, although if she was going to be a problem she would have to die,' Faye continued. 'Either way there was a body to dispose of – they couldn't leave her corpse in that flat without attracting suspicion.'

'So her killer dowsed her body in alcohol, tried to pour some down her throat and threw her off the balcony,' Walsh concluded.

'Once her killer saw that ring on Violet's finger, it wouldn't take long to put two and two together and realise how she'd come by it,' Faye continued.

'So it's curtains for Carl Carmody.'

'Though he was able to make his escape,' Faye said. 'He was last seen running away. Anyway, the ring on Violet's finger had to disappear, because it was one of the pieces stolen in the Greville Street robbery. Ellie and I were told that she wasn't wearing it when her body was brought into the SLH.'

'It all fits,' Lydia said.

'It's still speculative.' Faye was anxious to play it down until they got some hard evidence. 'But Ellie and others saw the ring, they can describe it. If we can place that ring in the stolen stash and trace it to the Hunters, we've got them! Unless Terry Carmody can come up with another explanation for how he came to have such a ring, from a Hatton Garden jeweller.'

'Which he won't be able to do,' Walsh said.

'I want to get to the bottom of Violet Taylor's murder – because that is what it was – and put away whoever was responsible,' Faye continued. 'But, if my theory is correct, it will also give us a case against Hunter and his gang.'

'You should tell Kent,' Walsh said.

'I know. We might need his help.'

But Faye didn't relish the thought. She knew she was only in the DI's team on sufferance; he didn't want her there. On the other hand, was this a chance to prove her worth, to persuade him to keep her?

'I'll speak with him later, or maybe tomorrow, *if* we can certainly identify Violet Taylor's ring as being from the Greville Street jeweller's,' she said. 'Solid evidence only.'

'By the way,' Walsh said. 'Your telephone has been installed. Your caretaker left a message with the switchboard. I suspect, after yesterday, the boss insisted it was done immediately.'

'Good. That'll make us feel safer.'

The doors to the room opened to admit Ellie.

'Did you identify our bogus telephone engineer?' Faye asked her.

'I think so,' Ellie replied. 'Someone named Vincent West.'

'Has an alert been put out for him?' Walsh asked and Ellie nodded an affirmative. 'Not that I think we'll find him. He'll have left London by now or be lying low.'

Faye stood and beckoned Ellie through to the filing room and the diagrams. Sure enough Vincent West featured fairly low down on the Hunter gang hierarchy.

Ellie pointed to London & Surrey.

'That was on the card left by West,' she said. 'And…'

'What?'

'The company, London & Surrey, has bid for work from the SLH. I'm sure of it. They want the Preston House contract.'

'The new midwives' home, that's a big contract.'

'We haven't ruled them out yet,' Ellie said. 'I think we should.'

'No,' Faye answered, quickly. 'It'll be interesting — and possibly helpful — to see what sort of a bid they submit. It might be an opportunity to see where they get their materials, their concrete in particular. Any bid would contain the names of their suppliers.'

'Why's it so important?'

'That's something else I'm working on,' Faye explained. 'Construction. I'll fill you in later.'

'I won't allow anything that might rebound upon the reputation of the SLH,' Ellie said.

Just as I wouldn't have done, Faye thought. Maybe she'd have to persuade her friend.

'Last night, the sergeant said that you and he had made a link between Violet's death and the Hunter gang. Do you think her killer is somewhere on this chart?' Ellie asked, scanning the diagrams.

'Maybe, yes.'

'And Carl Carmody's?'

'Almost certainly.'

'Do you have any more leads?'

'Now you mention it, yes. It's about Violet Taylor's ring. You saw it. What did it look like?'

Faye flicked through the Greville Street file as Ellie replied.

'I only saw it once. It was made of gold metal with a row of white gemstones across the outer half. Why?'

'Look at these. Do any of them resemble Violet's ring?'

One by one, Faye handed the photographs and sketches of the missing jewellery to her friend.

'This... this looks very like it.' Ellie pointed out a ring in a photograph. 'I think, though I only saw the ring for a moment. Beryl saw it more often, you should ask her.'

'Hmm, she might remember it better, I suppose.'

Especially given that it meant her beloved was going to be marrying someone else.

'Ellie, would you take the photograph and ask her? I can't do it, I'm grounded and anyway, Beryl and I haven't been great pals recently.'

Faye felt bad about that; it didn't feel right to be at odds with

Beryl, who she'd known and been fond of for years. Especially when Beryl was at her lowest ebb.

'She's grieving and in pain, she'll get over it,' Ellie said. 'Of course I'll ask her. Phillip might not appreciate my confronting any gangsters, but I can do this at least. Not at all dangerous.'

'Thanks. How are you getting home?'

'Your sergeant's arranged a car to take me back to the SLH. I'll see you later back at the flat.'

39

ELEANOR

'Ellie!'

Ellie whirled round to see Beryl waving at her.

'You were looking for me earlier?' the nurse called out, making her voice heard over the canteen's chatter.

'Yes.' Ellie led her to a quieter table over by the windows. 'I wanted to ask you something.'

'I've got some questions for you, too. You and Faye wouldn't happen to know anything about those three police cars parked outside Westbury Court last evening, would you?'

'As it happens...'

Quickly, Ellie sketched out the previous evening's events.

'By Jesus!' Beryl looked shocked. 'That must have been frightening. For you and for Faye. And you're both alright?'

'Yes, no damage done, just a scare,' Ellie replied. 'I went along to Union Grove station this morning and identified the so-called engineer from their album of photographs and they're trying to pick him up. But Faye thinks he's probably left London or is in hiding. Sergeant Walsh agrees.'

Beryl's expression changed; her face clouded with distaste.

'That's the chap who was here with Faye yesterday?'

'I don't know, was he?'

'I think Walsh was his name.' She hesitated. 'Look, Ellie, I'm pretty sure I've seen him before and somewhere you wouldn't expect.'

Ellie raised an eyebrow. Beryl was being mysterious.

'I told you about the marches down the Ridley Road on a Sunday afternoon in the East End.'

'Mosley's mob?'

'And the others. Well, on Sunday, me and some others from the Party went down there to see what was happening. We went in mufti, so to speak and it was just as well. If they'd clocked that we were communists we'd have ended up the worse for it.'

'There was violence?'

'It was in the air from the start. There were one or two speakers on a cart, under a Union Movement banner, raging on about Jews and immigrants, trying to get the crowd worked up. Thugs and bully boys stood around the cart, dressed in black shirts, pseudo-fascists if not the real thing.'

Ellie recoiled. 'I thought we'd seen the last of them. Wasn't this what we fought the war to stamp out?'

'Like I said before, they never went away.' Beryl's tone was jaundiced. 'But here's the thing – after about an hour there's a stirring in the crowd and it's Mosley himself come to speak. He's escorted by a phalanx of tough-looking gadgies carrying staves. That's where I saw Sergeant Danny Walsh, he was one of Mosley's bodyguards.'

'What? Are you certain it was him?'

'Completely. When I saw him yesterday I recognised him immediately.'

'Were there any police there?'

'Yes, in uniform, but they didn't interfere. They would've been out-numbered anyway, I suppose.'

'What happened?'

'Mosley spoke, talking about a new Europe, linking up with like-minded foreigners, but that didn't get the crowd's attention. Then another man stood up. He was more of a firebrand, started inciting the crowd to "destroy the enemy within".'

A DEATH IN THE AFTERNOON

'And who did he mean by that?'

'Jews, I think. That's when it all kicked off. There were men in the crowd who started shouting and fighting the thugs around the cart. Some of them were wearing yellow stars. Jewish ex-servicemen, I think. There's a group of them who disrupt the fascist rallies. The crowd started to run and that's when the police stepped in. It was complete chaos.'

'And the sergeant?'

'Last seen shepherding Mosley away.'

Ellie stared at Beryl. This was news indeed. One of Faye's close colleagues was a fascist sympathiser.

'I'll have to tell Faye,' she said. 'She needs to know, even if she can't do much about it.'

'Of course, Faye should know! She can't trust him. I wouldn't if I was her.'

Policemen were entitled, Ellie supposed, to have political opinions, just like anyone else, but parading alongside a noted fascist, someone who had been interned during the war for fear that he would aid the enemy, might attract comment from his superiors. Especially if Walsh was taking part in rallies that were likely to end in violence and would involve his colleagues in the police.

'Anyway, why were you looking for me?' Beryl asked.

'Oh, it's about Violet's missing ring.'

Ellie had almost forgotten, the news about Sergeant Walsh having driven it from her mind.

'Hasn't that turned up yet?'

'No, but... Faye gave me a photograph of a ring. She wanted me to ask you if it was Violet's.'

'You saw it too,' Beryl said, taking the offered photograph. 'Yes, this looks like it. I particularly remembered that row of small, glinting stones.'

'Good. I thought it was the same. I'll tell Faye, she'll be pleased.'

'Why does she have a photograph of Vi's ring?'

'I don't know. I should have asked her,' Ellie replied. 'I don't suppose Violet told you where Terry bought it from? Did they choose it together, at a jewellers'?'

'I don't know, she didn't mention it. Why'd you ask?'

'I was just wondering how Terry came across it, that's all.'

'Can't help you there.' Beryl stood. 'Are you going to tell Faye then, about the sergeant?'

'Yes, I will. Tonight.'

'I'm turning into a right grass,' Beryl said. 'I should start charging; I'd make a profit. Anyway, I'd better get some lunch. I'm due back on the ward in half an hour and I've got a long shift. Probably won't finish until late.'

'Alright, see you tomorrow, perhaps. Come round tomorrow night.'

It would be exactly one week since Violet Taylor had fallen to her death. Ellie didn't want Beryl spending that evening alone.

'That'd be good. See you then.'

40

ELEANOR

Clapham Park was only fifteen minutes' walk from the SLH. The five-storey blocks, set back from the road, were surrounded by lawns, with thin, white birch trees giving inadequate shade. Terry's block was in the middle, if she remembered right.

There were few people about, though she noticed a couple of men hanging around by the entrance to the next block, smoking cigarettes and chatting. They watched her walk past and she half expected a wolf whistle, but none came.

On the third floor she knocked on the door to the flat Terry had formerly shared with his brother. She was determined to ask him where he had bought the ring he had given to Violet, the same questions she had asked Beryl.

She knocked again. He might not have heard the first time.

After another thirty seconds she knocked again.

Was he at work? No, she could hear someone coming towards the other side of the door. It opened a crack and she saw half of Terry's face. The chain was across.

'Terry?' she said.

His face was very pale.

'Oh, it's you. You shouldn't be here, Ellie.'

'Can I speak with you?' she asked. 'It's about Violet, about her ring.'

He shook his head, violently.

'I don't want to talk about it anymore.'

He began to push the door closed but Ellie shoved her foot into the gap, wincing as it was caught between door and doorjamb.

'Please. You asked for my help and I gave it. I—'

'Take your foot away, please. It'll only get hurt and I don't want to hurt you. You've been kind, but you've done enough, now you can leave things with me. There's nothing for you to do anymore.'

'But Terry—'

'Leave it alone, I said.' His voice was rising, in pitch and volume and he peered out of the gap as if he could see into the corridor. 'Don't do anything more. And go now. Just go.'

He looked and sounded frightened.

He opened the door a further crack, clearly intending to slam it, even if her foot was in the way.

'Alright, alright,' she said. 'I'm going.'

The door slammed, almost cracking against her toes. Ellie skipped backwards.

Terry was terrified. His fear clouded around him, a tangible thing. He was like a completely different person; he'd been grieving before and angry, but not fearful – why had he changed? Had Vincent West paid him a visit too? She began to feel uneasy as she slowly descended the stairs.

As she left the building, she checked for the two men who had watched her, more alert now to any threat, but there was no sign of them. They'd gone. Good.

She strode out across one of the lawns, head held high, towards the South Circular. At least she could be sure of being back at the SLH before it was time to reopen the canteen for tea.

She stopped at a crossing point and looked right and left to cross the road.

Further along the pavement were two figures. With a shock she realised that they were the two men she'd seen earlier. They must

A DEATH IN THE AFTERNOON

have been waiting for her to leave and then followed her. Could they be the reason why Terry had been so frightened?

With assumed nonchalance she looked right and left again, pretending not to notice them, but she crossed quickly, despite the oncoming car. Once on the opposite pavement she lengthened her stride.

Don't look back, she told herself; it would signal that she'd noticed them. Maintain the illusion of normality for as long as possible. But it was hard to keep facing forwards, stretching her legs, striding out.

From behind her came the loud blast of a car horn and she took a quick look over her shoulder. The two men had hurried across the road. It was they who had caused the driver's ire. She quickened her pace again but as she stole a glance behind her, she saw that the distance between them had narrowed. They were hurrying too. There was no doubt in her mind that they were pursuing her.

What should she do?

Abandon any pretence and run like crazy to try to get help?

Run into the road and flag down a car? Given the sort of people she was dealing with, this would simply mean putting someone else in danger too.

The traffic lights were immediately ahead and the police station wasn't far away. She could go there – if she could stay out of the men's clutches for long enough to reach it. Or she could cross straight over at the lights and try to get to the back entrance to the SLH.

Either way she had to get to the lights before they did. She quickened her stride, beginning to trot. A brief glance over her shoulder showed her pursuers much closer than before. Panic flooded over her.

Ellie took to her heels.

Above the sound of her own pounding heart she could hear footfalls behind her. The men were running too and they were making ground on her. Gasping for breath, she redoubled her efforts.

Get to the SLH!

The lights turned red, but she ran on, into the road. A car screamed to a halt inches away from her, horn blaring, but she dodged around it and carried on running. As she reached the pavement she could glimpse the rear entrance to the hospital about fifty yards away. So near...

She felt a sharp pain in her side. Stitch.

Ignore it. Keep running.

Her pursuers were so close behind her that she could hear one of them panting for breath. She wasn't fast enough. They would catch her. Then what would happen?

At all costs she had to evade them.

Heavy breather was almost alongside. She saw a stubby-fingered hand reaching out to grab her arm and veered to the left, out of its grasp. But she could hear the second on her other side. It was no good. Tears of desperation stung her eyes.

'Ellie!'

'Ellie, what's going on?'

What?

Up ahead, a group of nurses was hurrying towards her, concern on their faces, half a dozen of them at least, with one or two still by the gate into the hospital. Within seconds she was surrounded by friendly faces and voices. She was safe!

Ellie halted, bending double and gasping. She felt her heart rate slowing and the pain in her side abated. She straightened up.

'Two men.' Breathe... 'They were following me...' Gasp.

'Who? Where?'

She looked back to the traffic lights. The men seemed to have vanished. Where were they?

'What did they want?'

'I don't know, but they were chasing me.'

Ellie took a few steps back and her gaze was snagged by the glint of metal on the ground. What was that? A knife.

'Did this belong to them?' A nurse picked the knife up by its curving blade, held between the tips of her thumb and forefinger. 'Looks like an army knife.'

'Blimey!'

'A Bowie,' another said. 'It's evidence. Check for fingerprints.'

'Give it to Faye Smith,' her companion interjected.

Ellie nodded. She would.

'Ellie, are you alright? Ellie? You're very pale, do you want to lie down?'

'I'm alright. Really. I must get home.'

But she didn't feel alright. Alright was a long way from how she was feeling.

'We'll go with you, see you inside.'

Surrounded by a phalanx of nurses, Ellie walked into the grounds of the SLH.

41

ELEANOR

'Did you get a good look at them?' Faye asked.

'Not really, I was too busy trying to stay ahead of them.'

Reclining on the sofa in the living room at number twenty-two, Ellie could see the early evening sun reflecting from the windows of the SLH opposite. The chase had left her shaken and feeling assailed. The knife lay on the coffee table. Her head ached and, right now, she wanted Faye to stop marching up and down.

'And they were waiting for you outside Terry Carmody's block?'

She sighed.

'I don't think they were after me, specifically. I think they were watching for anyone visiting Terry. When I emerged after seeing him, I thought they'd gone, but in fact they were lying in wait near the road. If I hadn't decided to cross the lawns where I did, I would have walked straight into them.'

'Yesterday's incident here, then today this attack on you, although, I wonder...'

'If they thought I was you.' Ellie finished Faye's thought for her. 'That's occurred to me too.'

'We'd be difficult to mistake for each other.' Faye half-smiled. 'The police detective who looks like a film star.'

'Would they even know what you looked like?' Ellie argued.

'We're the same age. I arrived from the right direction... They might have assumed I was you.' The more she thought about it, the more likely it seemed. The gang was after Faye, just like the day before.

'Hmmm... as soon as you ran, they'd have suspected you were involved with the case; you'd just been to Terry's block. Yet Terry wouldn't let you in, you say?'

'No. Too scared. He was positively sweating fear. He'd been properly frightened.'

'By the same men who followed you, perhaps.' Faye sounded pensive. 'The question is why. Why have they put the frighteners on him? I only hope Terry doesn't become the next body found in an abandoned house. It's probably too late to offer him police protection.'

She stopped walking.

'This is escalating and it worries me, Ellie. You shouldn't be involved in this, it's too dangerous.'

'I think I am involved, like it or not. These criminals have been to my home, threatened my best friend and probably killed one of the SLH's nurses. I don't think I have a choice *but* to be involved. Do you?'

'I'm sorry.' Faye's voice was full of self-reproach. 'I didn't think my new job would place you in such danger. I'm police, I've got the whole of the Metropolitan Police Force at my back, but you...'

Beryl's warning.

Everything else that had happened had driven it from her mind. Faye needed to know that not all her police colleagues might be as loyal, or as trustworthy, as she thought them.

'There's something I must tell you, something Beryl told me,' Ellie said as she pulled herself up into a sitting position. 'It's about the sergeant, Danny Walsh.'

'What about him?'

'Beryl's seen him down Ridley Road, during the Mosley meetings...'

'So, someone's got to be on duty—'

'No. Not as a policeman, as a bodyguard to Mosley himself.

Standing with the fascist thugs while he and his ilk harangued the crowd.'

'What?' Faye's eyebrows rose.

Ellie recounted Beryl's tale. Her friend sat, silent.

'I don't know what to say,' she said, eventually. 'I thought Walsh was... dubious in some ways, but I thought we were both on the side of the angels, even though he'd be a somewhat tarnished cherub. I never thought he might be an active helper to people like that! DI Kent thinks he's a good, an effective, policeman.'

'Would the detective inspector know about his... extracurricular activities?'

'I doubt it...'

'Are you going to tell him?'

'I suspect I ought to, though... it's not the thing to do, to tell tales... about one's colleagues.'

'I can see that might be awkward, but, what if they're doing wrong?'

'Define wrong. It's not against the law to go to rallies and he's entitled to have his own political views...'

'Beryl tells me that these rallies almost always end in violence. The speakers whip up the crowds who've come to listen, encourage them to take the law into their own hands. If Sergeant Walsh is helping them do that, shouldn't his colleagues and his bosses know about what he's doing?'

Faye heaved a heavy sigh.

'I suppose so, but it goes against the grain...'

Ellie didn't have chance to reply, as the intercom buzzed and Ron's voice announced the arrival of John Smith.

'We'll talk about it later,' Faye said as she stood to open the door to her brother.

Still in uniform, John Smith carried his jacket over his arm; his short-sleeved white shirt had damp patches.

'Hello, Ellie,' he greeted her and took a seat, leaning forwards with a frown on his face. 'What gives, sis? Something up, is there?'

'What d'you mean?' His sister was cagey.

'There are rumours about you and a stabbing, yesterday. And, surprise, surprise, the folk in my nick expect me to know about it, seeing as how I'm your brother.'

John tried and failed to keep a light tone, his irritation not far beneath the surface.

'No one's been stabbed,' Faye said.

'But?'

Briefly, Faye outlined the previous day's events.

'Your DI...?'

'Was round here to take statements as soon it was reported.'

'As was my godfather,' Ellie added.

'But you're off the case?'

'And tied to my desk. Ellie picked Vincent West out of our rogues' gallery this morning.'

'He'll be long gone by now.' John exhaled, then pressed his lips together.

'Phillip placed a constable downstairs too,' Ellie said.

'I thought I spotted someone but thought it might be a mate of Ron's. I'll bet he's not pleased at having to share his cubby hole.'

'And we've changed the lock and have a telephone now.' Ellie pointed to the black Bakelite apparatus, its large handset and curly cord sitting above a metal dial. She felt absurdly proud of the thing.

'Sis, did you really go round to Hunter's home?'

'Yes. And before you start, I know it wasn't a particularly clever thing to do.'

'You're telling me!'

'I got a right bollocking for doing it.'

Ellie observed the exchange between brother and sister.

They were physically alike, with high foreheads and long faces, though John's square-cut jaw softened to a pointed chin in his sister. They were close; the bickering was an outward expression of it. They looked out for each other. Ellie wished she and her sister could be like that, but Marguerite simply wouldn't understand her.

Her gaze lit upon the knife, lying on the table. Would Faye tell her brother about this afternoon's threat?

'I should co-co,' John said, above Faye's mute protest. 'Alright, alright, but what'd you expect? Aside from that, everything's alright at Union Grove?'

'Everyone's very sympathetic,' Faye answered. 'Though I feel completely excluded.'

'Get used to it. It's the safe thing.' John's demeanour changed. 'Oh, I meant to ask, is Bob Lowe one of yours? He was round at Dad's depot, asking about things going missing, took a PC from our station with him.'

'Yes, he's Union Grove. Kent assigned him to follow up the thefts. I hope he was suitably discreet about where he got his information?'

'Said there were complaints from residents about lorries driving through their quiet streets in the dead of night, so he was asking why there was any activity at all going on in the small hours. When they got to the depot, he asked for the stores inventory. That depot manager is going to be in hot water.'

'With his bosses or with us?'

'Or both? If he's taking backhanders to look the other way, he's an accessory to theft.'

'It would be classic gang style, paying off those with petty authority,' Faye said. 'Especially now, when there's so much that's changing. I'll ask Bob about it if he's in tomorrow.'

'Right.' He gave his sister a meaningful look. 'About Mum and Dad…'

Ellie felt her lips begin to twitch. This was a repeat of her own conversation with Phillip the day before.

'Do they have to know? About what happened, either last night or this afternoon.'

'This afternoon?' John questioned, his eyebrows rising up his forehead. 'There's more?'

'Ellie was followed, chased,' Faye began.

John turned an exasperated face towards her.

'I went to speak with the boyfriend of the murdered nurse,' she began to explain.

'Murdered nurse...?'

'Violet Taylor was murdered, she didn't fall,' Faye said. 'We know that now.'

John looked from one to another.

'Oh no, not again! Why were *you* going to see this man, Ellie? Don't tell me — because Faye can't. Don't you realise that she's deskbound for a reason, because it's dangerous! She must leave the investigation to her colleagues, her *police* colleagues.'

'I didn't think going to Terry Carmody's would be dangerous,' Ellie said. 'I'd been to his flat before. I know him. He talks to me.'

'And what happened?'

'Two men were watching Terry's building. They followed me and I... I think they intended me harm.'

'They were armed,' Faye interjected, pointing to the knife.

John got to his feet.

'Looks like Army issue. Too many of these out on the street now.'

'They almost caught me.' Ellie paused. She didn't like to think of how close they had come to doing so. 'But a group of nurses were coming out of the gate to the SLH. They escorted me into the hospital. I was fortunate. I... I think they thought I was Faye.'

'You have reported this?' John asked, looking from her to his sister.

'Yes, I rang Sergeant Walsh. He's on his way,' Ellie answered, opening her palms and tensing her fingers. This was getting very stressful.

'But he's taking his time,' Faye murmured.

'It was frightening, but I'm alright,' Ellie said, determined not to seem cowed. 'Never give way to a bully. That's what these people are, really, isn't it, bullies? Criminals who want to get and to do whatever they want, regardless of anyone else and cause a lot of misery in doing so.'

'Yes, my dear,' Faye said. 'Bullies are exactly what they are. But they're bullies with knives and guns and a lot of men, and women too, willing to do their bidding. One individual can't stand against them alone. That's why we have laws and the police.'

There was a knock on the flat door. Then the sound of a key turning in the new lock. It was Beryl.

'What's going on?' the nurse asked, wide-eyed and anxious. 'There are all sorts of rumours over the road. Something about your being chased and attacked, Ellie?'

Ellie repeated a brief version of events. She really didn't want to go into it all again.

Hands on hips, Beryl took a deep breath and raised her eyes to the ceiling.

'Those bastards! But you're alright?'

'Yes, no damage done,' she said, feeling decidedly damaged.

'We must be doing something right,' Faye said, with a humourless smile, 'if they're trying so hard to frighten us off.'

'Humph. And what's being done about this attack then?' Beryl demanded.

'Ellie's reported it,' Faye responded, raising her fingers to signal to her brother that he should keep silent. 'It only happened this afternoon.'

Beryl looked unimpressed and spoiling for a fight. John was watching, mouth pressed into a thin line. Storms were brewing.

'It's already a week since Vi died and we're no nearer finding her killer!'

'That's not the case, Beryl,' Faye said. 'We're a lot further forward with finding out what happened in Fairview House, which will lead us to who killed Violet Taylor.'

'What about that sergeant I met the other day?' Beryl tried another line of attack. 'Has Ellie told you about him?'

Oh no. Not this now!

Ellie felt an overwhelming urge to run away, to escape.

She wanted quiet. It was all too much. The threats to Faye, being chased this afternoon, Beryl's bleak unhappiness, Antoine's return. She had to get away.

Ordinarily she would have gone for a walk on the Common, but that wouldn't be a good idea, given recent events. Yet there was one place where she could walk in safety. The hospital gardens.

'I'm going out,' she announced, flatly, and stood. 'When the police arrive, send to the SLH to find me.'

She walked out.

Ten minutes later she was alone in the quiet shadows of the gardens. Her policeman guard had been deposited in the SLH canteen, where dinner was keeping him occupied.

Night-scented stocks filled the air with perfume and tiny pipistrelles darted between the trees. Ellie breathed deeply. The lights of the hospital and of the nurses' home were becoming distinct as she sat, sliding back on to the bench beneath the roses as if she could dissolve into the thickening light.

She heard laughter and sensed rather than saw a knot of nurses leaving the nurses' home and moving towards the rear gate. Going for a night out. It had been so lucky that a similar group had been leaving that afternoon.

The world of gangland crime was a violent place; she hadn't realised before what her godfather's job entailed, what risks he ran. Perhaps this was why his wife had left him, being unable to bear the constant anxiety. He would be angry when he was told about this afternoon's incident and she would have to suffer another lecture, but that was the least of her worries.

Now her best friend was running similar risks. And it was doubly hard for a woman. How would Faye ever have a meaningful relationship, marriage, motherhood? Had this contributed to her break-up with Nick?

Men were few and far between in the SLH. The hospital was a place where women could learn and grow, unfettered by male expectations or lack of them. Yet women still needed men and men still needed women, not everyone was like Beryl and procreation was necessary for the species to survive. And there was always love.

That, she had begun to realise, was the nub of her problem. She didn't want to live without love.

She loved her job and the independence it brought her. It was what she wanted. She loved the SLH too; she would never want to leave it. It was far from perfect, like any institution, but the hospital and its people had rescued her when she needed rescue, had offered her a haven, a place of safety. Just as it had done that afternoon.

Yet this wasn't enough.

She wanted romantic love and love returned, intimacy and absolute trust, a future shared. And, perhaps, a child or children. She prized her independence and her career, but she needed more.

How could Antoine fit into that picture? She had been unable to dismiss him for good. What did that mean? Could anything come of their relationship? And Antoine would make demands; all men did. All spouses did – she qualified her thought – it wasn't only men. But she had missed him so badly…

A clanking sound came from the direction of the main hospital building. It was the largest of the fans kicking in.

Faye had brought her into the SLH, two years ago, when she was down on her luck and at the end of her tether. Since then she had become part of the hospital and it was part of her. Now it was Faye who was having such a difficult time. She hoped it would all blow over; Faye was made to be a detective.

Right now, that detective would probably be wondering where she was. And worrying.

Ellie sighed. Time to leave this delightful solitude, time to return to Westbury Court.

FRIDAY

42

FAYE

The squad room was bustling and busy. People came and went; even the clerical staff seemed to be hurrying.

Nobody would meet her gaze, not even Lydia. Had she contracted a contagious disease? Walsh greeted her when she arrived, but then went off somewhere. Was that deliberate? Was everybody avoiding her?

Faye had risen early, having had difficulty sleeping. She knew she didn't look her best, with puffy eyes and pasty skin. Ellie had been asleep when she left, which was probably a mercy after the drama of the previous two days. Faye had scribbled a note to her, asking about the maker's mark on Violet Taylor's ring; in the chaos of yesterday afternoon, she hadn't asked about it. She suggested Ellie telephone her at Union Grove with the information.

Once in the office she'd turned to the construction file. She needed to occupy her mind. She couldn't get out on the streets, but she could read and she could think.

She opened out the Ordnance Survey maps and, taking a red pencil, marked the Rose and Crown quarry and Nine Elms Depot. The two red circles were directly linked by the curving black lines of railway tracks. A thick mass of black lines ran into Nine Elms, many coming from Clapham Junction, one of the largest stations in Britain and a major confluence for trains from all over the south.

The railways and their depots were important in this case, she was sure. She began to trace the lines running *out* from Clapham Junction, looking for rail yards like Nine Elms. To the southwest was the depot she'd seen near Wimbledon; to the west, towards Heath Row, was Feltham Depot. Southwards was Selhurst, near Purley and the limestone quarry and to the east, Hither Green Depot. All formerly Southern Railways depots, now owned by British Railways and one, at least, had seen thefts, while another was next to a cement factory.

Was the security as lax at the other depots as it seemed to be at Nine Elms? The staff wouldn't have changed, but British Railways probably hadn't had time to establish its authority. A perfect opportunity for organised crime. Had these other, former Southern Railway depots lost consignments of materials too?

Bob Lowe had probably checked by now. She rose to see if he was at his desk, but it was empty, so she made a mental note to tell him to include the cement works next to Wimbledon Park depot.

On a different tack, if the gang was making concrete slabs for pre-fabs, they needed somewhere to cast the slabs before delivering them to building sites. She needed to look for a works or factory site they owned. Those details might be in the accounts of the companies associated with Hunter.

She noticed that the door to DI Kent's room was slightly ajar. He must be at Union Grove today.

Faye didn't know what she was going to do, if anything, about Walsh's alliance with Mosley and the Union Movement. The code of silence was deeply embedded in her psyche. You didn't tell tales, no matter what. It was a very basic rule of the ranks. She couldn't, she shouldn't do it.

She reached for the file containing the documents for the Hunter companies and laid out the accounts on the desk, company by company. None of the sites listed in the property companies accounts seemed suitable as concrete factories, they were mostly residential. Then she moved on to the building company.

These accounts were surprisingly up to date and only a glance was needed to tell her that the company's business was struggling. It relied on small public projects, usually for south London councils; she would ask Phoebe if Lambeth had given contracts to the company. As expected, private work was limited, given the strict regulation of building materials. The company hadn't, as far as she could see, got any contracts for prefab housing, it had several addresses which could be works or yards. She noted the address.

She noticed the rights issue. The firm needed funds but didn't borrow; there were no new loans. Perhaps banks wouldn't lend to them. So, it issued stock to investors. The shareholdings of Henry and Abigail Hunter, Derek Brodie and someone named Ralph Iverson increased by the year's end, so, Faye assumed, they had all bought new stock. By April 1947, London & Surrey's balance sheet looked much healthier.

Where had that money come from? Hunter's criminal empire was the obvious answer, but that would be difficult to prove.

One possible source could be the Greville Street robbery. It had taken place on the fourteenth of February; she remembered because it was St Valentine's Day. Could some of the money from the sale of the stolen diamonds have funded the cash injection into London & Surrey?

If she could link the Hunters to the Greville Street job through Violet's ring and show that the proceeds from the robbery were invested in a Hunter company, a so-called legitimate business, she would be well on the way to bringing the whole of the Hunter empire crashing down.

The first step was crucial; then they could get a court order to scrutinise all Hunter's financial affairs and ask questions about the source of the funds pumped into the businesses. Everything depended on showing a direct link between the Hunters themselves and the Greville Street robbery.

Faye looked up sharply at the sound of a door closing. Inspector Kent had returned to his office.

If she was going to tell him about Danny Walsh she would have to do it now. To break the unwritten rule, the code of the rank and file. Never grass to the brass.

Yet Ellie was right; if Kent didn't know about Walsh's sideline, he ought to. It was a question of the trust necessary between colleagues. She could and should go and speak with him about it.

'Come.'

He answered her tap on the half open door straight away. He was sitting behind his desk.

'Faye, come in,' he said. 'Danny's brought me up to date with the Violet Taylor case.' He took a deep breath. 'You did good work, followed your instincts and were persistent, all of which is commendable. It is clear, too, that you have an aptitude for detective work. *But*, that does not change my negative opinion of you.'

Faye didn't know what to say. Thanking him for the praise seemed inappropriate so she said nothing.

'You are foolhardy and reckless, although now you've seen what danger that places other people in.'

'You know about Ellie?'

That would explain why everyone was tiptoeing around her.

'The Chief Super called me last night about it. Your friend is now under strict instructions to stay at home in your flat or at work in the hospital, accompanied there by the constable assigned. At worst, her pursuers were waiting for her, or you, to show up, which means you're targeted. At best the men were simply watching the Carmody flat for anyone of interest. We can't be sure. In any case, she didn't get a good look at the two men, so there's no point in bringing her in to look at mugshots.'

'Any news on West?'

'None. Is there anything else?'

'There is one thing, sir.' Faye's palms were sweating. 'There was another Union Movement rally in Ridley Road on Sunday afternoon,' she began.

'What of it?'

'A friend and former colleague of mine was there, she…'

'I hope you're not going to add unsuitable neo-fascist connections to my list of your weaknesses.' The DI turned over pages on his desk. He didn't bother to look up.

'No, sir, but as it happens, she saw someone else from this station there, taking part.'

Kent's head snapped up; he glared at her.

'Who?'

'Danny Walsh, sir.'

Kent's eyes narrowed.

'Sergeant Walsh is an experienced and effective police officer, Constable Smith. Be careful what you say.'

No longer a detective constable, then. Was that a hint to keep her mouth shut?

No, she wasn't doing that. In for a penny…

'He was there, sir, acting as a bodyguard for Oswald Mosley himself.'

The detective inspector's emotionless stare was fixed on her face. As the seconds passed, Faye grew more uncomfortable; she could almost hear the pulsing of her own blood, but she didn't look away.

'I think your friend must have been mistaken, Smith,' Kent said. 'And you shouldn't question the integrity of your fellow police officers.'

'But she's very relia—'

'Especially those who have championed your cause, such as it is.'

Had Walsh been trying to change Kent's mind about her? Faye swallowed hard. Now she felt even worse about ratting on him, as the DI no doubt intended she should.

'Is there a reason why you are still here, Smith?'

'No, sir.'

'Then…' He flicked his hand towards the door as if waving away a troublesome insect.

Faye strode out.

Back at her desk she took stock.

Although it went against all her instincts, she had just done the right thing. Knowing that didn't make her feel any better about it. If Kent didn't believe her, or didn't want to, that was his choice. She had done her duty; it was up to him now.

'Hey, hello?'

It was Lydia, waving her hand in front of Faye's face.

'Sorry,' Faye shook her shoulders. Pay attention.

'Message for you.' Lydia handed her a folded message chit and returned to her desk.

Talk of the devil... It was from Danny Walsh. He'd spoken with Soapy and had more info. He told her to meet him, urgently, at Cavendish Road station in an hour's time.

Faye glanced at her watch. The call had been received thirty minutes ago. That didn't leave her long. The keys to the squad cars were hanging up on the peg board – she could collect a set and go.

But she had to stay at her desk. To leave would be to flout the DI's specific instructions and those of Chief Superintendent Morgan. Yet Danny had summoned her. She took her orders from him. The new information must be important.

Faye glanced around the room. Bob wasn't at his desk and Lydia was the only other person there. After last time, she hesitated to ask the SSO to accompany her. She looked at her watch again.

This was ridiculous. Her sergeant had instructed her to meet him in a police station. She would go, although she would, at least, tell them she was coming. Faye picked up the phone. After three rings, the desk sergeant answered.

'Morning, it's your favourite woman detective here,' she said. 'Is my sergeant, Danny Walsh, there?'

'No. Why?'

'He's on his way and so am I. When he arrives, tell him I'm leaving now, would you?' Faye said.

'Okey-doke,' the desk sergeant replied. 'I'll leave a note too, just in case.'

Faye looked at her watch again. Walsh was probably *en route* to Cavendish Road, time was passing. She picked up her bag and crossed to the peg board.

43

FAYE

Faye scanned the roadside for a parking space as she drove, in second gear, around the warren of residential streets near Cavendish Road police station.

She should, she *must*, be careful. This could be a trap. Get as close to the station as possible.

The only space to park was about a tennis court's length away from the rear of the station yard. Faye pulled up to the kerb and consulted her watch. Walsh was probably already inside, waiting impatiently for her arrival. She slipped out, locked the car and hastened towards the entrance.

A clunking of car doors came from behind her and a quick glance revealed three men, hats pulled low over their faces, striding away from a recently parked car about four houses down. They broke into a trot. There was no point in pretending she hadn't seen them; it was obvious what they were after. She took to her heels, running for all she was worth, fists pumping the air.

Fast and fit, she might be able to out-run them. It wasn't far and she had a head start. If she was lucky there'd be someone in the station yard; she could see that the railing gates weren't padlocked. Once inside, she could shout for assistance and then the tables would be turned. The pursuers would find themselves the prey and then banged up in the cells. Then they'd have some questions to answer.

A white van powered along the street in front of her and, with a screech of brakes, swerved up onto the pavement directly in her path. Two men leapt out.

'Help!' Faye yelled as loudly as she could and prepared to try and hurdle the bonnet of the van. 'Help! Murder!'

She hit the bonnet and slithered down onto the ground, barely keeping upright. The closer of the two men grabbed her arm. She grappled with him, raising a knee sharply into his groin.

'Fuck!'

He let her go, spinning into the road and clutching himself, but his accomplice was blocking her way. She was caught between him and her pursuers, hard on her heels. It was hopeless – she couldn't fight them all. But she could make her capture difficult; difficult enough so that someone would hear and raise the alarm. She backed into the tall rose hedge of a front garden, ignoring its briars and thorns and faced her foes.

'Help! Help! Murder!'

She kicked out at the next man who approached, but he jumped back, smartly. The rose briars bit into her skin, beneath her thin cotton blouse.

The other men closed in. They had a job to do and they were going to do it.

'Help! He—'

A fist connected with her jaw and her head snapped backwards.

———

THERE WAS a jolting pain along the right side of her body. Her jaw ached. Her head felt fuzzy and, when she opened her eyes, she saw little, only the inside of a bag or sack. She tried to spit a foul-tasting rag from her mouth, but the bag over her head was too tight to allow it.

Another jolt. She was in a moving vehicle, probably the back of that white van, lying on her side and tied at the wrists and ankles. Every time they hit a bump in the road she was shaken and jounced. Tensing muscles, she pulled and shoved herself into an upright position, leaning against the side of the van. Rose thorns pricked at her skin.

It was airless and dim and she couldn't see. But she could hear.

London, like any big city, had its own soundscape. She might be able to work out where she was. She calmed her breathing and tried to relax, to concentrate on listening.

Sounds.

Engine noise. A halt, the motor turning over – traffic lights, perhaps. Pulling away, then another stop. More traffic lights; she could hear the engines of other vehicles around and alongside them. A main road, then, with lots of sets of lights not so far apart.

That narrowed it down to about a thousand London thoroughfares.

If she was still in London? She might not be. She'd no idea how long she'd been comatose for and how far they had driven.

A snatch of chimes from an ice-cream van. Children's voices – it must be a school playground, a primary school, given the pitch of the voices. In the distance an emergency siren. It sounded like London, though where in London it was impossible to determine. The van stopped again.

She thought back to the ambush. They'd been waiting for her. It had been a trap. And she had walked right into it. Who had set it up?

Lydia had given her the message but might not have read it. Even if she had, she could have believed it to be genuine. The general switchboard took messages, wrote them on chits and pinned them, folded over, to the board outside the switchboard booth. Anyone could read one, anyone could write one.

Of course, the ambush wouldn't work if there'd been a partner in the car, who could have radioed for help and followed the van, even if they couldn't prevent the kidnapping. Then half of the station would have given pursuit. After what happened on

Wednesday every police car in south London would have been chasing them.

No. They had known that she was alone.

That meant someone at Union Grove was in on it, someone who saw her leaving. Perhaps the person who had written the message in the first place. There was a traitor in the squad, someone working for the Hunter gang.

Lydia and Bob had been the only people in the squad room and DI Kent had been in his office. Was it one of them? She didn't like to think so, but it had to be.

They were moving again. Her head hurt and she felt nauseous.

Where was she being taken now? To Henry Hunter?

And what would happen then?

Why the kidnapping and the bag over her head? If they were going to kill her, why keep their destination secret? A corpse couldn't tell anyone where she'd been.

It didn't make sense. But she dreaded finding out why.

The van stopped and a passenger door opened as its engine idled. She could hear gates or large doors being opened and they bumped over a kerbstone or step. Had they entered a garage or compound of some kind? She heard a clang as the gates closed behind them.

Then cooler air rushed in as the van doors opened and hands grasped her arms to pull her out.

44

FAYE

The bag was dragged off her head and she shook her hair out of her eyes.

The light hurt. The place had a cold, hard smell, of oil, metal and chemicals.

She screwed up her eyes, focusing on what was in front of her. A brick wall, with narrow windows near the high ceiling. A bare light bulb hung down, its light weak and indistinct. A warehouse or industrial building. Grimy machinery, forklifts, concrete mixers stood in the shadows.

Their concrete factory. Where they made the concrete into slabs.

She tried to pull her hands apart and ropes cut into her wrists, which were bound, behind her, to an upright chair.

'Detective Constable Smith,' a bodiless male voice said. 'Welcome.'

Henry Hunter?

A tall, broad-shouldered man walked around to stand in front of her. Derek Brodie. He wasn't wearing a jacket and he nonchalantly rolled up his shirt sleeves. A man about to begin a job of work.

Faye swallowed hard.

He must know that she knew who he was, yet he'd shown

himself to her. Her insides grew cold. This meant she was going to die. But what would happen first?

'I thought it was time you paid us a different kind of visit,' Brodie said.

He pulled the cloth from her mouth and stared down, mouth twisted and clamped tight closed. She salivated and licked her lips. There were noises from behind her, a rasping sound, like a blade being sharpened, then an unnerving, high-pitched snigger.

Faye forced herself to hold Brodie's gaze.

'What do you know about Carl Carmody?' he demanded.

So. They wanted to know what she, what the squad, knew.

'He's the younger brother of Terry Carmody, boyfriend of the nurse, the deceased nurse, Violet Taylor. He did odd jobs for the Hunters at their home; Henry and Abigail, your boss and his wife.'

Brodie's face was like stone, though she could have sworn there was a reaction, almost imperceptible maybe, but there.

'It's where we met,' she couldn't resist adding.

'Yes,' he said, bending down so that his face was inches from her own. She steeled herself not to recoil. 'I remember.'

He stood and, so swiftly that she didn't see it coming, struck her hard across the face.

Faye gasped. Her head rang and her skin stung. Tears sprang to her eyes.

'Be polite, detective constable.'

The sniggering was louder.

'The laughter you can hear,' Brodie explained, 'belongs to Carver West. Come and introduce yourself, Carver.'

A short, thick-set man entered her vision, jigging from foot to foot and leering.

'Carver visited your flat a couple of days ago.'

'Came to see you,' the man said, his eyes eager. 'To help you understand. Saw your friend instead – made me a cup of tea, she did. A real looker, I wouldn't have said no… But she was expecting a guest.'

Faye detected a slight lisp, an added sibilance.

'So he didn't get to do what he's named for. Did you, Carver?'

Giggling, West produced a chiv, waving it close to Faye's face. The blade glinted; it looked diamond sharp.

'He can be very creative with that,' Brodie said, pleasantly. 'But I won't let him play with you if you tell me what I want to know.'

West danced out of her vision again.

'Carl Carmody.'

Her brain raced. Why keep asking about Carl? He must realise they knew that Carl had been murdered.

'We know the overdose wasn't self-administered,' she began. 'Carl wasn't an addict – his pills would have made him very ill if he took narcotics regularly, his whole body would have reacted. The post mortem showed no signs of that.'

Brodie stared down at her. His arms were folded across his chest; beneath wiry black hairs was the distinctive badge of the Surrey regiment, a tattoo. He lifted his right hand and she flinched.

His mouth twisted into a smile as he stroked his chin.

'And...?'

'He saw the murder of Violet Taylor. She was wearing a ring that Terry, Carl's brother, gave to her. We think it got her killed, because it had been stolen from Abigail Hunter. Carl stole it.'

Brodie looked amused.

'Go on.'

'Carl was with his friends, associates of yours. Violet saw and came to take him home, but someone recognised the ring she was wearing, which had gone missing some time before.'

She stopped and licked her lips again.

'I don't know exactly what happened next, perhaps someone demanded the ring back and Violet refused to hand it over. There may have been a struggle. Whatever occurred, it resulted in Violet hitting the ground head first four floors below. Murder, or manslaughter at the very least.'

Brodie seemed satisfied with her answers. He waited.

Why? Why wasn't he pressing for more information? Unless he already knew.

It occurred to Faye for the first time that Vi's killer might be Brodie himself. Was he trying to find out if the police suspected him? But he'd know that, especially if there was a spy in the squad. There must be more to this than that. It wasn't worth kidnapping and killing a police officer for.

It didn't make sense. Her abduction would have serious repercussions for the Hunter gang.

Phillip Morgan might hold back when there had been a threat, but there would be a reaction from the police when one of their own, and a woman at that, was taken. Walsh and others like him would get to crack heads on the street at last.

Every misdemeanour, every non-payment of a fine, would be an excuse for taking people in and questioning them. The lucky ones would emerge bruised, but not seriously hurt. At the very least Hunter's businesses, criminal and legitimate, would be severely disrupted and maybe evidence and knowledge might emerge from the woodwork too. No crime boss would choose to court that sort of crackdown, not even one as big and powerful as Hunter's. What could be worth that? What Brodie was doing was completely counterproductive.

So why do it?

Did he fear that they'd made the link between the Greville Street job and the Hunters? That would scupper the gang for sure. But Brodie hadn't questioned her about that.

Faye's eyes didn't leave Brodie's face. His eyes flicked to look beyond her and he nodded. She willed herself not to turn. What was going to happen now? These were men who had seen the worst that humanity could do. What weren't they capable of?

Brodie was now contemplating her, his head slightly tilted to one side, one eyebrow raised.

An idea was forming at the back of her befuddled brain... Who would benefit from the police stamping down, physically as well as otherwise, on the Hunter gang? Could Brodie be doing this on his own behalf? Was he turning on his boss?

Then she remembered her earlier suspicion about Brodie and

Abigail Hunter. If she was right and they were having an affair, Brodie's days would be numbered if Hunter found out. Could Brodie be planning a palace coup, with Abigail's connivance?

'Can we have her?' A new voice said behind her, close to her ear.

'If you've finished with her?' The extra sibilance again.

She held herself rigid, she would not give them the satisfaction of looking round. But she couldn't control the shaking.

'No.'

What?

'Ain't she going out with the *frauleins*? Someone'll pay good money for her. She's a fighter,' another voice said. 'There's plenty like to break 'em.'

'And I deserve some fun for that kneeing.'

One of those who abducted her.

'No. Mr Hunter has something special in mind for this particular detective,' Brodie said, smiling at her with cold eyes. 'We owe her. Remember the Clapham South tunnels we had to move out of pronto? This is the bitch who got them closed down and did for Les Allen. A good mate of mine, he was.'

There were growls and grunts from behind her.

So, this was by way of retribution too. Yet, something wasn't right here... Since when did men like Brodie give explanations to their subordinates?

'Mr Hunter wants to send a message,' Brodie continued. 'Don't mess with the Hunter gang. Maximum impact. So put her out, then proceed with the plan.'

Plan? What plan? What did he mean?

A cloth pad was put over her nose and mouth. It reeked, a sweet, not unpleasant smell. Knock-out drops of some kind. She struggled, her feet slipping on the gritty floor. It wouldn't be long before she...

Faye lost consciousness.

45

ELEANOR

'No, not there! You'll have people tripping over the string,' Ellie called to her police bodyguard, who she had co-opted into helping with the fete. 'Use the whitewash to mark out the area, we'll peg it later.'

The hammering of tent pegs and the shouts of volunteers competed with traffic noise. Nurses, other hospital staff and local people were erecting stalls, tents, marquees and platforms. Further along the lane the funfair folk were setting up their booths and rides and snatches of hurdy-gurdy music added to the hullabaloo.

Anticipation hung in the air. Plenty of homebound commuters, emerging from Clapham South Underground station, came over to gawp. Some of them were given tasks to do.

There's so much to do!

Get as much as possible done today, then tomorrow morning would be less frenetic, when exhibitors and stall holders would arrive. Faye had warned her that everyone would want things — the best pitch, the front place in the marquee, the last slot in the dog show — and all of them would expect to be able to make their case to her, in person. So she was anxious to get as much done now as she could.

Faye.

Where was she? She was supposed to have arrived to help at six o'clock and it was already half past. Ellie was uneasy.

'Miss Peveril?' A round-headed man in shirt sleeves, wearing bright red braces, approached her, his hand outstretched. 'Horace Cain, Deptford Showground.'

'Mr Cain. Is everything going well?'

'Yes, thank you. We'll be ready to open by eight.'

'Not tonight, Mr Cain. I discussed this with your lady wife. As usual, the funfair begins only once the fete is opened formally. We can't have people jumping the gun.'

'We have our costs to cover, Miss Peveril. We want to start earning as soon as possible.' He hooked his thumbs into his braces.

'Once the fete is open, you can do so to your heart's content, Mr Cain. You've got the whole of the weekend. You'll make a tidy profit, I don't doubt.'

Cain screwed up his face and looked as if he was going to argue, but Beryl's arrival distracted him.

'Hello, Beryl. You still here then?' he greeted her.

'Certainly am, Horace. You trying it on again?'

'He certainly is,' Ellie added.

The showman grinned.

'After the speeches tomorrow then.' He laughed and strolled away.

'Beryl, have you seen Faye?'

'No.' Beryl frowned. 'Isn't she here?'

'No, but she should be. Can you take over here while I go and check the flat? She may have gone up to change.'

''Course. Let me know. After everything that's happened...'

But the flat was empty and Ron hadn't seen her since very early that morning.

Ellie telephoned Union Grove and was put through to the squad room. After several rings a woman answered.

'WPC Sweetham.'

'Hello, Constable Sweetham. It's Ellie, Ellie Peveril, Faye Smith's flatmate – you may have seen me at Union Grove yesterday. Faye's spoken of you. I'm calling from our flat. Is she there?'

'No, she left earlier this afternoon. Why?'

'I was expecting her to be here at six and she hasn't shown up yet. After recent events, I – I'm beginning to get worried.'

'Hmm, I understand. Sergeant Walsh might know. I— He's not here right now, but I'll ask him when he comes back. I know he's on 'til eight tonight.'

'Thanks. I'll be here for a short while, but then I must go back to work. A message left with the concierge at Westbury Court will reach me.' She gave Lydia the number.

Perhaps Faye had been delayed, or she'd called in at Cavendish Road station. She'd just check there before she returned to the Common. When Ellie dialled the number the phone was answered quickly. She recognised the voice of the desk sergeant.

'No, Faye hasn't been here since Monday,' he answered her question. 'We were expecting her this afternoon, to meet a – hold on, I'll get the message — a colleague from CID, a Sergeant Walsh, but she never showed up. I took the call at three o'clock, I wrote it down. When you see her, remind her that she still hasn't paid her subs, would you?'

Ellie frowned as she replaced the telephone handset onto its cradle. Something wasn't right about this.

She jumped as the telephone rang.

'Hello, Ellie Peveril here.'

'Ellie, it's Danny, Sergeant Daniel Walsh.'

'Sergeant.' Ellie's reservations about the sergeant had melted away, overridden by her anxiety. 'I'm worried about Faye. She's missing. Cavendish Road say that she was going to meet you there this afternoon, but…'

'What?'

'To meet you at Cavendish Road.'

'Are you sure?'

'Completely. I've just spoken with the desk sergeant.'

'Right.'

There was a short silence.

'Sergeant Walsh, Danny... Are you there, Danny?'

'Yes, I'm here. Stay where you are. I'm coming round, but I'll put out an alert for Faye before I leave here. Where else could she have gone?'

'I'll see if she's gone to the SLH.' She could telephone Jean and set her to search. 'The only other place is her parents, but I don't want to upset them.'

'I'll get someone to go round there, asking to deliver a message, very low key. See you shortly.'

He hung up. Clearly, Walsh thought something was amiss. Ellie's presentiment of disaster returned. She began to stride up and down the living room.

Policing was dangerous work, but Faye had chosen to do it. Detection was what she was good at, but it carried such risks. She should never have gone to that man's home; the problems had all happened since then.

Ellie stared out onto the activity on the Common, not seeing the bustle, not sensing the jolly anticipation.

She was certain that something awful had happened to her friend.

46

ELEANOR

The intercom buzzed.

'That sergeant's here again.' Ron's voice sounded tinny. 'He's on his way up. Have you heard anything?'

'No, Ron.' There was a rap on the door. 'Excuse me, he's here.'

Walsh didn't waste time with courtesies.

'What time were you expecting her home?'

'Six o'clock. She was going to help with setting out the fete, but never arrived. She's not at the hospital either, I've checked. When did you last see her?'

'This morning, briefly, at Union Grove,' he said.

'She left a telephone message at Cavendish Road station at three o'clock,' Ellie said. 'She said she was meeting you there.'

'I certainly didn't arrange to meet her.'

'I expected her here at six, like I said. Over an hour ago!'

'I'm afraid Faye has been lured away,' he said. 'A colleague at Union Grove told me she gave Faye a message purporting to be from me at about two o'clock. It asked her to meet me at Cavendish Road in an hour's time. I suspect she decided to meet me there and telephoned the station to say so.'

'Wasn't she supposed to be staying at her desk?'

'She was,' Walsh admitted, ruefully.

'Who wrote that message?' she demanded, eyes narrowing.

'I don't know. What I do know is that it wasn't me. You spoke with WPC Sweetham, who passed the message on.' The sergeant pursed his lips. 'I've put out an urgent alert on Faye.'

'That gang's been after her already. Do you think they've finally got to her?'

'I — I don't know.'

'Aren't you supposed to be protecting her? This is insupportable! That the police can't even protect their own.'

She didn't know whether to be angry with Walsh or anxious for her friend. She was both!

'Ellie, she's a responsible adult, a police detective and she's had her orders. It's up to her to follow them. She can't be molly-coddled and she wouldn't want to be.'

'She's the one attracting the gang's hatred.'

'That's as maybe, but it's our job and hers to bring them to justice. None of us are popular – Faye knows the score.'

'Did she know the score when she visited that gangster's home?'

Walsh took a deep breath.

'Faye did that on her own account. Nobody knew she was going to do it, otherwise we'd have stopped her, something I'm pretty sure she was well aware of.'

'Is that what this is about?' Ellie felt her voice rising in panic. 'Is she being punished for going to that house? Will they kill her for it?'

'I don't think they'd dare,' Walsh replied. 'Killing a copper, doing it deliberately, isn't something even a crook like Henry Hunter would order. Especially a woman. It would mean a full-scale war with the police. They might have taken her, but I don't think they'll kill her.'

'So why kidnap her then?' Ellie demanded.

'I don't know! I've contacted the detective inspector,' Walsh continued. 'He's probably also spoken with your godfather, Ellie. If Faye's missing, we'll turn south London upside down looking for her. Everyone will be out on the streets.'

'Then you'd better set about it! And you should speak with John,

PC John Smith, Faye's brother, as well.' Ellie said. 'If you can get hold of him. He's at the Battersea Bridge Road station.'

Walsh nodded acquiescence. 'I will.'

'Hello?' It was Beryl at the door. 'Has she turned up?'

Ellie shook her head.

'No,' she said. 'We know she left Union Grove for Cavendish Road station, but she never arrived there.'

'So… what could have happened?'

'We don't know. She received a message, supposedly from the sergeant here, asking her to meet him at the station.'

'I didn't leave any message.'

'We think it might have been from someone working for the Hunter gang,' Ellie said.

'Oh.' Beryl's face fell. 'Christ on a bike!'

'Not good news.'

'A lot of nurses lodge around Cavendish Road,' Beryl volunteered. 'I'll go over to the hospital and speak with Matron, get the word out to see if anyone saw anything.'

'Good,' the sergeant said. 'That could be helpful.'

'If you want search parties,' Beryl looked up at him, her hostility towards him clearly forgotten, 'there'll be plenty of volunteers.'

'I'll bear that in mind, if we need to search the Common,' Walsh said, as the nurse left. 'I'll go and wait for the DI downstairs, leave you alone.'

'Can't I do something?' Ellie pleaded. 'Please.'

'Right now, no. There's nothing for you to do but wait. Stay here in case she comes back.'

After he left Ellie washed the crockery in the sink. She put away various items of clothing, re-sorted the drawers in her bedroom, thought about cleaning the windows. In the end she sat in the living room, staring into space.

The bell of the church on Malwood Road rang the hour. It was eight o'clock.

She shook herself and went out onto the terrace. Dusk was falling. Soft hurdy-gurdy music sounded from the funfair site.

Below her Clapham Common had been transformed. The red and blue roundel of the Underground sign flickered into life, casting shadows onto a mini forest of tented stalls and marquees amid the trees. A deep chasm of shadow ran between the rows of stalls that ran from the Underground station to the deep shelters entrance, their canvas roofs catching the light from the South Side streetlamps.

Her pulse raced as she looked directly into the wide entrance of the rifle range, the silhouettes of painted targets standing out against the lights of the South Side behind. Too many bad memories. She had come so close to death there and so had Faye. Now it could be happening again.

Concentrate on the here and now, she told herself.

She began counting the stalls, linking them to the map of the fete in her head. Tombola, the Lost and Found, Pin the Tail on the Donkey; it would be buzzing tomorrow, full of people looking to enjoy themselves and to forget their cares. To have fun, a jolly day out. And she would have to ensure it ran smoothly.

Could she? Carry on as if nothing was awry when her friend could be lying dead or dying? She prayed Faye would be found before then.

Ellie sensed Beryl come to stand by her shoulder.

'I knocked, but you were miles away,' she said. 'I've spoken with Matron. If the police want to organise a search of the Common, half of the SLH will volunteer. Look.'

She pointed off to her left beyond Westbury Court. The lights were on in the police station house next door. Walsh emerged from its front porch and strode off towards the South Side.

'I feel so helpless,' Ellie said.

'I know. Me too. I... I'm sorry I argued with her. I didn't really believe she was a class traitor, that was me being a doaty bampot, getting on my high horse. I never know when to keep my mouth shut. She was only trying to do her job, I wasn't being fair.'

'She understood you were upset, Beryl.'

'Aye, mebbe.'

The Scot moved towards the terrace doors to go inside.

'I'd forgotten what was important, that Faye was my friend and a good friend at that. I was so caught up in my own ideas… and… the grief.'

'Pain does that,' Ellie said. 'It pushes out everything else.'

Beryl shrugged. 'I should'na have let it.' After a pause she continued. 'I'll be away now. I'll go over to the SLH first thing in the morning, then I'll come here.'

'Alright.'

'Oh, I saw Nick, Nick Yorke, outside the SLH – I told him about Faye being missing. I thought he ought to know. He might call.'

'I'll expect him, then. Good night, Beryl.'

'Good night.'

Ellie's gaze moved on to the funfair, cordoned off by its heavy ropes. The hurdy-gurdy music had ceased and the rows of coloured bulbs were dark, though the fair's generator still rumbled. Someone must have tested the candy floss machine; the sweet and slightly burnt odour of spun sugar hung in the air. She could smell it, even this far away. Light seeped round the edge of curtains already drawn closed in the windows of the caravans, as the fairground people made ready to retire for the night. They would have a long day tomorrow and an early start.

The doorbell buzzed.

'Beryl said Faye was missing,' Nick said as she opened the door. 'Has she turned up? Is there any news?'

'Come in. We think she may have been abducted.'

'Abducted? When, why?'

Ellie led him onto the terrace and they sat.

'One of the gangs her squad is pursuing. There have been… a number of incidents recently…'

She told him, briefly, about what had been happening.

'My God! Why didn't anyone tell—?'

Nick put his head into his hands. When he looked up his face was haggard. Suddenly he appeared much older.

'So what is this? Some sort of ghoulish power game?'

'We don't know.' Ellie reached her hand across to him, but he didn't see it. He was staring into the evening shadows. After a while he began to speak.

'I don't talk about the war,' he said. 'People don't. It's best forgotten. If you can manage it, it's best to look forward, not back. But this... this brings it back.' He paused.

Ellie didn't know what to say.

'I was on convoy duty in the Atlantic. There was a stretch of water, mid-Atlantic, when we were out of range of the planes. Our air cover would turn back and yet the planes from the further shore couldn't reach us. It was called "The Black Pit" and that was where the U-boats would wait.'

He had, she saw, returned to that time and his ship.

'They hunted in packs. We didn't know when or where they would strike. They'd sink us if they could, although it was really the merchantmen they were after. When they hit we would hear the explosion and see the smoke and flames and know that we'd failed. All we could do was try and find survivors, but even that was perilous. I felt helpless, impotent.'

In the darkness she couldn't make out the details of his face anymore.

'But at least we could fight back. And we got them sometimes. There would be a boom under water, then the wreckage would surface. A vile death, beneath the waves in the blackness, knowing that there was no possible escape, but I revelled in their destruction. It meant I wasn't powerless.'

He was silent for a while and she wondered if she should interrupt his reverie, but he continued.

'When I came home, well... My salvation was finding Faye. I saw her at the school and... I couldn't believe my luck that she could love me. Then she decided to become a detective. And she's Faye – if she decides to do something she's determined to do it well. The idea of family... well... so much for that. And it's dangerous work. I couldn't keep her safe. I'd be powerless again. I couldn't live with that.'

Faye had spoken about the break with Nick, but Ellie hadn't appreciated Nick's side of things.

'You need a drink,' she said. 'Come inside.'

Ellie poured them each a tot of the precious gin and added soda water.

'Here, a nightcap.' She handed the little glass to Nick.

'Thanks,' he said, as he gazed, hopelessly, down at her.

She wanted to take him in her arms and comfort him, to make him feel better.

And to feel his strong arms wrapped around her would bring her comfort too. She had never felt such longing.

'Cheers,' he said, clinking glasses.

'Chin chin.'

She returned his gaze, moving closer towards him as she sipped. He didn't step away. Ellie tilted her head back. Perhaps...

'I'd better be going,' he said, turning to put down the glass. 'Thanks for the nightcap. I'll be back tomorrow morning, if that's alright. Goodnight.'

Ellie blinked.

She exhaled with relief.

What had she been thinking? In his anxiety for Faye, Nick had opened his heart to her, such a rare thing. Was she so lonely that she would exploit this dreadful situation? Thank heavens she hadn't made a complete fool of herself!

'Goodnight,' she said and went, annoyed with herself, to let him out.

Temptation. Temptation snaked it's way its way into her heart and she'd almost succumbed to it.

The serpent is craftier than any beast of the field, Genesis 3:1.

Ellie didn't bother with pyjamas, then reconsidered and pulled them on. She flung the windows wide and climbed into bed.

47

FAYE

A harsh, grinding sound set her teeth on edge. Metal scraping upon metal. It cut through the fug in her brain.

She forced heavy eyelids open but saw only darkness; there was a blindfold over her eyes. The filthy gag was in her mouth again and, when she reached to remove it, she found her wrists were bound. She felt the pick of thorns in her flesh – was she in the back of the van again? If she was, it was stationary. Her head was thumping and her limbs felt leaden.

Ungentle hands grasped her forearms and pulled her along, until she fell, plummeting head first, but the hands hauled her upright. Her legs wouldn't do as she told them to. She was dragged, feet trailing along the ground, supported by the hands, more hands, holding her beneath the arms. She couldn't support her own weight. She needed the hands.

Her brain began to clear.

Where was she?

A whisper of cool breeze brushed her face.

Outside.

She concentrated on co-ordinating her movements and her legs answered her command. She began, unsteadily, to put one foot in front of the other.

'She's coming round,' a voice said in a hoarse whisper.

'Doesn't matter, we can put her out again later,' muttered another.

Why? What's going to happen?

Panic surfaced and she beat it back down.

There was a pause and one set of hands let her go. She sagged and staggered, falling to earth.

Grass. Dry grass and parched soil. Definitely outside.

Listen for sounds.

There was no traffic noise – was she out in the countryside? Had she been driven out of London?

'Up you come.'

She was pulled to her feet again and marched along. Sometimes it was uneven underfoot; at other times she was walking on a hard surface.

What was that smell? Burnt sugar.

Silly. It couldn't be.

Candy floss!

Was she at a fairground, maybe in a park? At Battersea, or Deptford? No, there were no river sounds. There was always life and movement on the river, no matter the hour. And there would be the thick stink of silt; the river was low after the long, dry summer, even at high tide.

What about Clapham Common? Could she possibly be so close to home?

If she was at Clapham South there would be sounds of some kind. Like the Thames, the South London Hospital never slept.

She concentrated, listening for familiar noises, holding her breath. Sure enough, in the silence she heard the distant rumble of the giant hospital fans and closer still, the growl of a generator. The Deptford Fairground people always brought their own generator.

She *was* on Clapham Common! At the site of the hospital fete!

On home ground. Her thoughts pivoted to escape. If she was near the SLH there would be people about, whatever the hour. Nurses or porters walking across the Common as they started or ended their shifts. There might be policemen going to and from the police station house. If she could get away from her captors, even for a few brief moments, she might attract attention or help.

Faye flexed the muscles in her legs and arms; she had to be ready to run. For now, she played half comatose.

One of the men dragging her, the first to speak, was wheezing. He couldn't be very fit. If she could get free she would almost certainly be able to outrun him. It would all depend on disabling the other man and fleeing as quickly as she could.

'There it is,' he said, a little louder. 'Look.'

Faye slipped a foot out of a shoe and, scuffing the ground, kicked it away, hoping her captors' attention was elsewhere. If her escape attempt failed, she could at least leave some indication that she had been here, to tell those looking for her – because she knew people would be looking for her – where she was.

There was no reaction. They hadn't noticed.

Where were they taking her? Wherever it was, it must be close now; the wheezing had increased considerably – he wouldn't be able to carry on hauling her along. She sagged again, why make things easy for him? She pretended to stop herself from falling and kicked off her other shoe.

'Hey, she's losing her shoes!' the breathless man said.

'Quiet!' the other hissed. 'You'll wake the dead.'

'But her shoes—'

'It doesn't matter. Nobody's going to know they're hers, even if they're found. Besides,' he chuckled, 'everyone'll have something more interesting to gawp at. Here. We're here.'

What did he mean, *something more interesting to gawp at*? What were they planning for her? Her blood turned to ice.

Must get away.

The second man let her go. It was only for an instant, but Faye took her chance.

She elbowed the wheezing man in the groin and spun round, but before she could spit out her gag or rip off her blindfold, her arms were pinioned by her side.

'Oh no you don't.'

Her ears rang with the blow. Pain flooded across her head.

'Fucking bitch.' Wheezer spat out the words.

'Leave it. She'll get hers.' He laughed. 'Put her out again. We can carry her inside.'

She'll get hers — what was going to happen to her?

She began to struggle. It was to no avail. The pad was placed over her nose and mouth again and she began to lose consciousness.

SATURDAY

48

ELEANOR

The clock said six thirty, but she wasn't going to get any more sleep. She had tossed and turned all night, tense and anxious about Faye and regretting the events of late last evening. She might as well get up and make herself a mug of tea.

Bone weary and forcing her eyes open wide, to banish sleepiness, Ellie blew on the surface of the tea and took her mug out onto the terrace, still in her pyjamas. Below her the tented village looked different in daylight, its dark shadows driven away by the sun. The South Side lay in the shade of the SLH buildings, but it already felt warm. It promised to be a glorious day.

She should have felt so differently this morning; it should have been such a good day, the culmination of months of work and preparations. Instead, she felt a hollowness inside, a presentiment of dread.

There was a knock on the door and Beryl joined her on the terrace.

'Morning. Any news?'

Ellie shook her head.

'Nothing at the SLH either. I've never seen so many polis on the streets round here. The station house must be empty.'

'Nick called round last night. He's in a bad way.'

Beryl nodded, frowning. She was about to speak when the buzzer sounded.

Perhaps it would be better news. Ellie hurried to open the door.

Nick. At first, he wouldn't meet her gaze. Embarrassed, perhaps, at unburdening himself to her, opening his heart? Or maybe he'd reflected on what had almost happened? Ellie looked away. She was very conscious that she was in her pyjamas as she led him out onto the terrace.

'Any news?' he asked.

Before Ellie could reply, the buzzer sounded again.

Sergeant Walsh stood there and for a moment hope sprang. Was there news? But his tired, defeated face told her the answer, he wore a tired and beaten look. He followed Ellie inside, raising an eyebrow as he caught sight of Nick.

'Faye's friend,' Ellie said, brusquely. 'Well?'

'Nothing. I'm sorry,' he said. 'We've turned over everywhere we know they operate – clubs, drinking dens, yards, offices and some more besides. Nothing. Nobody admits to having seen Faye at all. None of our paid informants, nor the tramps and beggars.'

'Surely someone has seen something?' Ellie said, frustration growing.

'No one's admitting to anything, and...'

'What?' Beryl demanded.

'It's...' Walsh hesitated. 'All my instincts tell me that this is wrong. It's as if everyone is holding their breath waiting for something to happen. Yet I can't get anything out of anyone, however I try.' He ran his hand over his unshaven, stubbly chin.

Ellie noticed the dried scabs of blood on his knuckles. Was that how he'd been trying to get information, beating it out of people? She found that she didn't care, as long as he found out what was happening.

'Have you contacted Faye's brother, John?' Nick asked.

'Yes, he and his station are knocking up anyone on their manor who might have any information, and we can hope, but I doubt they'll find anything. They're also dealing with... the river.'

A DEATH IN THE AFTERNOON

Ellie caught her breath.

'The divers have done from Chiswick to Battersea but are waiting for the tide to turn.'

The doorbell buzzed again. It was a bleary-eyed and dishevelled Phillip Morgan.

'We're doing everything we can, Ellie,' he said, as he hugged her. His chin was smooth. Somehow he'd managed to shave. 'I'm calling in every favour I'm owed.'

'Thank you, Phillip. I know you'll leave no stone unturned, but…'

'I know my dear.' Her godfather gave her a bleak smile. 'Detective Inspector Kent is with Special Branch right now. They may have access to information that we don't have.'

'Come outside,' she said. 'The sergeant's here.'

'No, I won't stay. I've got to get back to it.' He paused, then bowed his head. 'I encouraged her to join the force, Ellie. I got her a place in CID, I feel it's my responsibility.'

'It's what she wanted.'

'Yes, but I enabled it to happen.'

'Phillip, would they… could she already be dead?'

'I doubt it,' Phillip replied, swiftly. 'Really. To murder a serving police constable would be a level of escalation I don't believe that Hunter, or Caplan, for that matter, would consider sensible.'

'But, if they're not going to kill her, why take her?' She frowned. 'She'd be able to identify them.'

Ellie didn't want to contemplate what might be happening to her friend. Besides, there was another idea forming in her mind.

'Phillip, I think…'

'Yes?'

'Perhaps you might think this sounds bizarre, but I'm certain we should be on the lookout for… something unusual, out of the ordinary. I know I can't be specific, which isn't helpful, but, if Faye's been taken, she'll know we'll be looking for her. If she can, she'll try to let us know where she is. Try to help us find her. Give us some sort of signal.'

'You're probably right, you know your friend,' Phillip said. 'Though, what sort of thing did you have in mind?'

'I don't know... That's just it...' Her hands fell to her sides. 'Anything... different.'

Suddenly she needed to be doing something practical.

'I should dress,' she said.

Sergeant Walsh came in from the terrace.

'Morning, sir,' he said.

Nick followed him. 'I'm Faye's former boyfriend. If I can help, in any way,' he said. 'I know her parents...?'

'Yes, thank you. They should be told that she's missing and that we're doing everything we can,' Phillip replied. 'Could you..?'

'Yes, of course.'

'I'll carry on, sir,' Walsh said and, at a nod from his superior, he left, accompanied by Nick.

Beryl was leaving too.

'I'm off to my own place to change,' the nurse said. 'I'll see you later, at the fete.'

'Could you wait for me, one moment more, Phillip?' Ellie asked. 'There's something I need to tell you. It's important. I won't be long, then I'll walk down with you.'

Impatient to be off, her godfather, reluctantly, agreed.

Ellie slipped into her room and pulled on slacks and pumps. A summer suit of cornflower blue hung on the wardrobe door. She would change into it later, to greet the dignitaries and listen to the speeches. Despite everything, she had to look her best today. She was on show as a member of the SLH management and the hospital needed all the good press it could get. She pulled her hair back into a ponytail; she could dress it later.

When she returned to the living room Phillip stopped striding up and down.

'What is it, Ellie? I've wasted enough time here already.'

'It's the Hunters, Henry and Abigail. It's possible that they may be attending the fete today.'

'What!'

'The hospital invites representatives of all its potential contractors to the fete and that includes London & Surrey Ltd. The invitation may have been passed on to the directors, the Hunters. I'll check in the office if the invitations have been accepted.'

'My god, Hunter's coming here, having a day out, while we scour London looking for one of our own, more than likely taken by *his* gang. That'll take some nerve,' he said. He frowned. 'Are we judging this all wrong? Is he determined to provoke a reaction?'

'I don't know, but do you think it might be of significance?'

'Yes. Maybe. Check to see if they've accepted and let me know, ring this number.' He scribbled a telephone number on the back of one of his cards. 'A message will find me, wherever I am. I'll tell Robert Kent and the sergeant.'

'Phillip...' Ellie hesitated, it wasn't for her to tell him how to do his job. 'Faye's brother John is a policeman. He's likely to be here today, at the fete. I couldn't say what he, or Nick, would do if they came face to face with Hunter. Maybe tell your men not to share this information generally?'

'I will. Good thinking.'

They had reached the vestibule.

'I've got to get back to the Yard, see if I can get any more resources. Take care.' He kissed her forehead. 'Don't give up hope.'

'I won't.'

She waved him off then crossed the lane to the Common. Early volunteers were at work, finishing off stalls or bringing in items that they had not thought suitable to leave overnight. The place had a positive energy about it, unlike the deserted site of the night before. Enthusiastic gardeners were milling around the marquee, anxiously clutching bags and boxes full of produce, arriving early to secure the most advantageous positions. Stall holders were unloading their vans and stocking their stalls.

Ellie gritted her teeth. The fete was important to the SLH; it was the public face of the hospital on show. It had to go well.

For the next few hours, she must put her worries aside and do her job.

49

ELEANOR

A ripple of polite applause greeted the mayor of Lambeth as he trundled, sweating in full regalia, to the microphone at the front of the stage. Ellie slipped from her seat at the end of the front row and stood to one side amid the encircling crowd. She had been told that the Hunters had accepted their invitation and she was curious to see this couple, one of whom was so feared. She counted along the rows and seat numbers until she came to their allotted seats.

Surely this wasn't them?

A respectable-looking couple, a middle-aged, but still handsome woman and her dapper, summer-suited and bespectacled husband, both attentively watching the mayor. He looked like an accountant!

She counted again, with the same result; there was no mistake. A broad-shouldered, grim-faced man sat to the other side of the woman, his gaze shifting, his eyes never still. He looked much more like a gangland boss ought to look. The seating arrangements must have got mixed up.

As she turned to go, her gaze swept across the crowd standing opposite. She recognised many of the people in it, staff from the SLH as well as local people; there was Pru Green with Maurice

Grover, looking relaxed, several canteen staff and some of the porters. And...

Antoine Girard.

She caught her breath as her stomach seemed to plummet towards her shoes and a ripple ran up her spine. What was *he* doing here?

He looked very dashing, wearing a navy-blue blazer and cream trousers. He was laughing and looking into the eyes of a chestnut-haired young woman, his hand resting upon her shoulder. For a second his eyes met Ellie's, before she looked away and shrank back into the crowd.

So much for his promised commitment and devotion.

How could she have been fooled? Again.

Stupid. Stupid.

Ellie strode away towards the lane, oblivious to her surroundings. She weaved through clusters of folk who were admiring the decorated lorries and floats parked there. Somewhere in her subconscious she noticed that children were licking ice lollies, so an ice cream van had opened early, despite strict instructions. A small knot of young people had congregated at the ropes that cordoned off the funfair, waiting for the speeches to end and the fun to begin.

'Ellie! Ellie!'

Glancing briefly over her shoulder she caught sight of Antoine following her, manoeuvring through the crowd, the brunette hurrying behind him. This was the last thing she needed right now! Ellie increased her pace.

'Ellie.' He darted in front of her and blocked her path, his breath coming quickly with the exertion. 'I want to—'

'Miss Peveril, excuse me, Miss Peveril.'

She turned to see Horace Cain coming towards her.

'Mr Cain?'

'Someone's been in the fairground. Overnight. Kids, probably, the little bugg— beggars. My people always check the rides before we open, to ensure they're safe, so that's alright, but I don't like the idea of anyone tampering with my equipment.'

'Are you certain someone's been inside?

'Yes. I found cigarette butts and there were scuff-marks on one of the wooden walkways.'

'Where, Mr Cain?' she asked.

'In the fairground!'

'Yes.' Ellie was trying to be patient and keep her voice even. 'Is all the machinery safe? Will you be able to open?'

'Yes, but we can't have people in the fairground after dark and unsupervised.'

Something unusual, out of the ordinary.

'Show me.'

Cain turned on his heel and marched towards the fairground, ducking under the heavy ropes that were there to deter entry.

Ellie followed him through the fairground with Antoine and his companion tagging along.

Cain halted beside the waltzers.

'Here. Look.' He pointed downwards.

Ellie peered at the grass and a couple of cigarette ends. She bent down to see better, scanning the ground around.

What was that? Something just underneath the platform of the fairground ride. It looked like a…

Shoe. It was a shoe. Ellie stretched to reach the object and drew it towards her.

It was Faye's shoe! A grey court with a low heel; Faye had been wearing those shoes yesterday. She was certain.

Faye was here!

'Antoine, go and get Beryl, she's on a sideshow called "Pin the Tail on the Donkey", it's not far. Tell her to come here and bring Sergeant Walsh with her.'

'D'accord. "Pin the tail…" But what's going on?'

'I don't have time to explain.'

Cain was looking impatient now.

'Can you just do it, please?' she insisted.

Antoine left, brunette in tow, as Ellie knelt to examine the ground again. Cain was right – the parched ground was scuffed and marked, the grass flattened. It looked as if something heavy had been dragged over it. Her insides shivered – a body? Pray not.

She should tell Cain.

'Mr Cain, this is important,' she said, rising. 'A local woman has gone missing. Hasn't been seen since early yesterday afternoon and we believe she may have come to harm. She's my age and height, with fair hair—.'

'It's Faye,' Beryl shouted, hurrying towards them. 'She means Faye Smith.'

'Of course, you've met her before!' Ellie clapped her hands to her cheeks. 'How stupid of me! She used to do my job.'

'Faye!' Cain's eyes widened. 'Missing? Why didn't you say so before?'

To Ellie's relief, Beryl was followed, not too far behind, by Sergeant Walsh. Walsh nodded a greeting to Horace Cain.

So, the two men knew each other; that could be useful.

'Look.' She offered Beryl the shoe, which she stared at then took.

'Faye's,' Beryl said.

'Found just here, by those cigarette butts.'

'Kid's got in last night…' Cain said.

Walsh squatted down to examine the ground.

'Filtered,' he said as he picked up one of the cigarette ends, brandishing it before them. 'Kids don't smoke filtered. Too expensive. This isn't kids.'

'So who was it? And what have they to do with Faye? She must be here somewhere. We must search.'

'Look, Miss Peveril. We've abided by our side of the arrangement.' Cain put his hands on his hips. 'We're not opening until the fete is open. But we have to open then. You can't stop us doing that.'

'I'm sorry, Mr Cain, but Faye was wearing shoes like this one, which was found right here.' Ellie waved the shoe. 'She must be here somewhere. She might be injured or unconscious.'

'We checked around last thing. Before turning in. There was no one here then.'

'But someone came in during the night, we can see the evidence of that here.'

'I've explained to Miss Peveril, Danny,' Cain appealed to Walsh. 'We can't conduct a full search now.'

'We're wasting time,' Ellie said. 'We need to search before the fair opens.'

'We're opening as soon as the speeches end.' Cain had a determined look on his face. 'We've done what you asked, but you agreed that we could open then.'

'You'll open when I say you can, Horace.' Walsh waved his warrant card at Cain. 'But we'll try to be quick.'

'We need to search everywhere,' Ellie said. 'The rides, the side shows.'

'That'll take hours! We're supposed to open in ten minutes.'

'Can't your people help us search?' Ellie pleaded with Cain. 'They know their way around better than we do. They'll be quicker. Please?'

Horace Cain folded his arms.

50

FAYE

Someone was thumping her skull. Beating an implacable rhythm. She couldn't understand who was doing it, how it was happening. Dealing with the pain demanded all her attention. She had to make it stop.

She forced her eyelids open. The pain began to recede as her eyes focused. No one was striking her. The pain was inside her head.

She saw a bright scene in triplicate, quadruplicate or more. There were women bound to chairs, all gagged. Lots of women; the image repeated, again and again. She blinked to clear her vision, but the picture stayed the same.

She couldn't be seeing right. She closed her eyes and opened them again. The figures were still there.

She turned her head sideways. So did all the women.

Reflections, they must be reflections. Mirrors.

That was it. She was surrounded by mirrors.

Around her were struts and beams, gearing and crankshafts all painted in primary colours, reds and yellows, blues and golds. All was hard metal or painted wood; her body was the only softness. Swags of bright fairground bulbs, chopped and abbreviated, lit the scene.

She tried to make sense of the reflections. Where was she?

Then she heard Danny Walsh's voice in her head – *'pretend we were working in the central gearing room, so, when the mirrored walls were turned outwards, we could see up the girls' skirts when the horses were on the rise.'*

That was it! She was inside the central room of a fairground ride, its multi-panelled, mirrored walls facing inwards, though they would swivel open when wanted, to reflect the prancing horses. She was inside a merry-go-round.

The repeating red vertical reflected in the mirrors was the central post around which the wooden platform rotated. The floor planking didn't quite reach it; there was a gap of about two feet between the pole and the raw edges of the wood. Looking up, she saw gears connecting to struts fanning out from the centre to carry the horses.

Her chair stood on the platform, about an arm's length away from the gap round the central post. She couldn't allow the chair to fall once the merry-go-round started to move. If it toppled over, she would go with it, into the gap, her limbs ground between platform and pole. If, by some miracle, she slipped through unscathed, she would be pounded by the struts and arms supporting the turning platform, mangled and broken. A certain and horrible death, delivered by a machine built for innocent pleasure.

Terror pierced the dull miasma in her brain. No sharp volt of electricity could have caused greater shock or travelled more quickly through her nervous system.

No, no! NO!

She would die.

It was so unfair. Tears sprang, unbidden, to her eyes as she struggled, in vain, against her bonds. Her heart was pounding. She had to do something! Had to get free!

Get as far away from the central pole as possible.

She leant forward, taking her weight on her feet and pushed backwards. The chair inched back, but her hands, bound at the wrists behind her, hit a flat surface. The multiple reflections, versions of herself, showed her that it too was a mirror. There was nothing against which to rub her bonds, to break the fibres of the rope.

If she couldn't free herself before the machine started... Her blood ran cold in her veins.

Panic rose again and she struggled to force it down.

Do something!

Faye felt the rope that bound her wrists. It felt like hemp; there was a slim chance she could separate its individual strands and break them. She began to try and work her fingers into the cable, pulling and plucking.

If she was lucky, it was early in the morning. She couldn't hear any traffic, but it was a Saturday, so there wouldn't be a rush hour. On the other hand, if the fete was underway there would be more noise, of music and clamour, people chattering and laughing, enjoying their day out. So, it was probably early.

Her mind detached itself and she began to recall how she had got here. She had been kidnapped by thugs reporting to Derek Brodie, lieutenant to Henry Hunter. This was Hunter's doing. She felt a spurt of anger and hatred and redoubled her efforts to part the strands of the rope, adrenalin surging. She would escape!

Faye flexed her fingers. Already cramped and aching, she could feel her fingertips becoming raw. Yet the strands of rope felt as strong as ever. Tears of frustration ran down her face, but she had to keep at it; she didn't know how much longer she'd got. Her fingernails snagged and tore as she picked at the fibres of the rope, praying that they would split and break, give her something to work on.

Concentrate, she told herself. But her mind floated free, worrying at another puzzle.

Why was Hunter doing this? Revenge? According to the sergeant, Hunter took care of such things personally. Yet he hadn't confronted her, let alone threatened her in person. Why? And why chose this elaborate method of murder?

'*Mr Hunter wants to send a message. Don't mess with the Hunter gang. Maximum impact.*' Derek Brodie had said.

So that was it, a message. That was why she was here.

The horribly mangled body of a Metropolitan Police detective killed almost in front of hundreds of people who were out for a good time at a fete. Perhaps they would hear her muffled screams.

It was even grisly enough to make tomorrow's front pages, her death splashed over the Sundays. The Met would look incompetent and ineffectual, unable to protect its own, and it would prompt all sorts of questions, on the streets as well as in the news, possibly in Parliament.

A noise. What was that?

An amplified voice, its words indistinct. Was someone testing the PA system?

No. There was applause.

It was the speeches; that was why it was so quiet. It wasn't early, it was lunchtime! People were listening to the speeches. Ellie was probably sitting in the front row of the audience. So near and yet so far.

But – it seemed that they'd finished. Was the fair about to begin? Had she so little time left?

No!

Frantic, she pulled and dragged at the strands of rope.

Then she heard the PA system again, a different voice. Thank Christ!

There was a rumbling, a muttering. People were growing restless, anxious for the fun to begin, but Faye had never wanted self-important wind-baggery more.

Keep talking, she prayed, keep speechifying.

And she worked at the rope with bloody fingers.

51

ELEANOR

Cain put his thumb and forefinger to his lips and whistled. Four or five young men, fairground barkers and ride operators, came hurrying up.

'Bill, go roust out the others. We have a missing woman on our hands and she may be in our showground. We need to check all the rides and sideshows before we open. Gianni, check the rifle range too – it's over by the South Side. Mabel...' this to a young girl who had also come running, 'bring Sherlock.'

She hurried off and, within minutes, Bill returned with a gang of fairground folk.

'Most of you know Faye Smith from the hospital, she's missing and possibly unconscious, somewhere around here,' Cain explained again. 'If she's in our showground we need to find her. Now get a move on. Start over that side, nearest the entrance. Fan out and look inside all the booths and machines.'

The fairground men strode over to the perimeter, prompting hopeful glances from a, now sizeable, crowd that had formed outside the cordoned area, impatient, waiting for the speeches to end and the fete to be opened officially. There was a collective groan as they turned their backs and began to search.

'We're going to have to open soon,' Cain said.

'Well, you can't,' Walsh said. 'I'm sorry, Horace, but—'

Cain jerked his thumb towards the cordon. 'You try and keep that lot out.'

'My boss, Detective Inspector Kent, is on the way, bringing uniforms.'

'If they get here in time,' Beryl said, glancing at the growing crowd.

Mabel returned, running. She was clutching the rope lead of a scruffy-looking border collie, its eyes clouded by cataracts.

'That Faye's shoe?' Cain reached for the shoe that Ellie still carried, then crouched in front of the dog. 'Here, boy. Have a good sniff.' He held the shoe out to the dog. 'In his day, Sherlock was one of the best finding dogs you'd ever see at the circus.'

The dog sniffed at the shoe. After a few seconds his tail began to wag and thump the ground.

'Good dog, good Sherlock.' Cain removed the lead. 'Now, find her! Off you go!'

Ellie and the others watched as the dog zigzagged, less than speedily, across the grass, sniffing all the while. Then it tensed, its head went up, pointing forward and it trotted, purposefully, along the path.

'If she's here,' Horace said, striding after the dog, 'he'll find her.'

They all followed.

Prolonged applause sounded in the distance. It appeared that the speeches had finished. A mechanical pipe organ started to sound out the Toreadors' March and there was a buzz of noise. Time was running out.

'They're wanting in,' one of the barkers said. 'They'll be ducking under the ropes if we don't take them down soon.'

The dog had veered from the path.

'Where's he going?' Ellie asked as Sherlock ran around the base of a large carousel, its elegant painted horses seeming to look down at the scruffy creature with disdain.

Then the dog changed direction and trotted over to the oval dodgems' rink. The operator had removed the canvas side panels and the rubber-encircled cars on their poles were parked at the side of the ride. Sherlock disappeared beneath it.

'Sherlock, where you going?' Horace called. 'There's no room under there. She can't be there.'

The dog reappeared, tail wagging.

'Come on, find her.' He offered the dog the shoe again. Again, Sherlock ran beneath the dodgem's rink.

'Boss.' A fairground man strode up, accompanied by John Smith, sweating in the heat, his uniform jacket unbuttoned. 'We're going to have to let them in soon. Otherwise, it could turn ugly.'

'I'll go and talk to them,' Walsh volunteered.

'It'll need more than that,' John said. 'There's too big a crowd. Any luck?'

'Look!' Ellie pointed to Sherlock, who had re-emerged, this time bearing a shoe in his mouth. It was the partner to the other one.

They clustered around the animal, who was looking up hopefully for a reward, having dropped the shoe at Horace Cain's feet.

'Good dog,' he said, petting its head. 'Problem is, there's only about six inches underneath there. She can't be under there.'

Walsh was already on his knees peering under the wooden step.

'You're right,' he said. 'So how did her shoe get there?'

'She must have kicked it off!' Ellie said. 'Trying to leave some sign to help us find her.'

'Sounds like my sister.'

'It's a message for us. It means she's here somewhere, I'm certain,' Ellie added.

'But where?' Walsh asked.

'We've looked in the rides,' the fairground man said. 'No sign of her. Sergeant, if you're coming? And we could use your help too,' he said to John and Nick.

'Yes, yes, but...'

'She *must* be here.' Ellie wasn't giving up.

'Boss!' Another of the barkers called, waving at Cain. 'They're in.'

Ellie didn't need telling. It was too late.

The first group of young men and women, laughing and smiling, were inside the fairground. Children darted along wooden and grass walkways between the booths and rides. At the dodgems they demanded that the operator open the wooden barrier and let them run for the cars; they climbed up the steps to the merry-go-round. Swing boats creaked as passengers climbed aboard.

On the carousel a young man wearing a red bandana took their pennies, before helping some of them clamber up onto the backs of the sculpted wooden horses.

'Boss?' He called across to Cain, as he stood at the lever that activated the carousel.

'No, we haven't searched there yet,' Beryl objected.

'The dog's already looked,' Cain said. He nodded to the young barker.

The bandana man gripped the top of the long lever and pushed it forwards.

'No, you can't. We haven't—' Ellie cried.

To no avail.

Hurdy-gurdy music started, distorted in its slowness at first, then jaunty. The merry-go-round began to turn and the horses began, gently, to rise and fall. The riders urged their mounts on with shouts, anticipating the eventual acceleration.

The day's real enjoyment was underway.

52

FAYE

The wooden platform started to turn, slowly, then increasing in speed.

No! Stop! No!

Faye strained muscles and sinews, pulling at her bonds and stretching her chin to work the gag out of her mouth, but she was tied too tightly. Her breath was coming quickly and she felt her heart rate accelerate.

In desperation, she tried to shout, to call out, despite the gag, but her muffled cries were drowned out by elongated hurdy-gurdy notes, which quickened to become a popular tune as the merry-go-round got up speed.

Mirrors flashed with shards of light reflected from above. Through the hole at the foot of the central pole, Faye saw the massive concrete block holding steady as the merry-go-round moved around it.

There was a clanking as the gearing, out of sight above and hidden below, began to work, raising and lowering the horses and causing the whole contraption to vibrate as it moved more rapidly, shuddering and jolting. Faye felt her chair resonate and start to move.

Was this it? Was this her end?

No.

No. She wouldn't allow it!

She braced her bare feet hard against the wooden boards to hold her chair in place. If she kept up the pressure, she could prevent it rattling and jouncing, moving gradually towards the gap. Her body tensed, keeping her legs locked in position. She had to keep them rigid.

The infinity of images blurred as sweat ran down her forehead and into her eyes. Her blouse was clammy and wet. She made herself breathe evenly and thanked her lucky stars that she'd done the early morning runs and got fit. But, fit or not, how long could she keep this up?

The whole room groaned and shifted — the merry-go-round must be at full velocity now. Only her braced position held the chair against the wall, preventing it from toppling into the gap and taking her with it. But her limbs were growing tired and she felt the chair juddering, moving sideways. Her feet, damp with sweat, were losing their grip. What she needed were the heavy police-issue brogues currently languishing in the bottom of her wardrobe at number twenty-two.

She gritted her teeth and pushed harder. Her whole body strained to keep her legs rigid and her feet flat onto the floor. The music reverberated around her skull and the reflected light flashed and sparkled on the mirrors. She felt her concentration wavering.

Keep pushing, she had to keep pushing.

Then the revolving platform began to slow. Her chair ceased shaking. Soon she would be able to relax.

But not yet. If the platform came to a halt too jerkily, she could be jolted into the central gap to wait, like the prancing horses held in stasis, for the next ride to begin, when she would be consumed by the machine. She prayed that the carousel came to a smooth stop.

It slowed. And slowed. And stopped.

Faye gasped. Her leg muscles spasmed, shaking after the effort. Tears of pain ran down her face.

Her respite wouldn't last for long. The wooden platform shook as children jumped down from their painted steeds and the music played on. Soon there would be another set of willing riders and the whole thing would start again.

She didn't have much time. She couldn't repeat that effort; there had to be another answer. Think!

She had to find something to hold on to or, better still, find a way out.

She peered around the interior and multiple other Fayes peered with her, studying the edges of the mirrored panels. The panels fitted seamlessly one into the other, but there must be a door; the fairground people had to enter to check that everything was working properly. Somewhere there must be a door and a door handle.

There!

A slim metal handle; difficult to see because of all the reflections, but it was there, about a third of the way around.

Faye tensed her legs, took the whole weight of the chair and, with a little jump, shunted it sideways. She did it again. And again. Her thigh and calf muscles burned with pain and her hair tumbled forward around her face, but she could gradually move around the platform. If she could just get round to the door she might be able to open it and get out. Why hadn't she thought about this before?

There was a shout from outside, heard above the hurdy-gurdy music. It was the ride operator, telling the riders to hold on tight. The merry-go-round would be starting up again soon.

Mouth pulled back in a grimace of desperation, she quickened her actions.

Almost there.

As the platform began to revolve around the post again she made one last desperate effort.

Yes!

She braced her legs to stop the chair moving and felt behind her for the handle. It was higher up than was comfortable, but she could reach it. She depressed the handle and pushed.

Nothing. The door didn't budge. Perhaps it opened inwards?

She couldn't risk pulling it open now; it could catapult her forwards into the gap around the central pole. She'd have to wait until the merry-go-round halted again, but she knew she couldn't brace herself again for long. She needed help.

Use the rope!

Impervious to all her attempts to pull its strands apart, it was now covered in blood. Maybe that would make it more pliable. Wincing, she rubbed her raw and bleeding fingertips on the strands of rope, pushing her fingers into the gaps between them. Then she yanked her wrists apart.

The rope stretched. Not enough for her to free her hands, but enough to give a little leeway.

The chair legs rattled against the wooden platform, reminding her of her immediate peril. She hooked the rope around the metal handle. She would still have to brace herself and keep the chair steady, but this might help.

The velocity of the carousel increased and 'You are my Honeysuckle' was replaced by 'If You Were the Only Girl in the World'.

53

ELEANOR

The funfair quickly filled with people. Queues snaked around the popular rides and families wandered along the walkways and on the grass, licking ice creams or eating the bright pink spun sugar of candy floss. Ellie cast wild glances around, looking from one ride or stall to another.

'Where is she? We have to keep looking! We can't give up. She must be here somewhere!'

Her shoes were here; that meant something, didn't it? Faye was trying to tell them that she was here. Ellie grew more desperate as the crowds milled around them.

'But where?' Beryl said, too short to see much among the press of people. 'Dammit! Bloody hordes, couldn't they wait?'

'She's somewhere around here,' John said. 'She has to be!'

'I agree. Faye's here,' Walsh said, his face despondent. 'Or was here.' He scanned the mass of people. 'I used to love funfairs, I told Faye—' Then his expression changed. 'Hang on a minute.'

He spun round and began shoving his way through the crowd, prompting yelps and cries of annoyance. John plunged into the throng behind him.

'Where are they going?' Beryl demanded.

'I don't know... Wait, I think he's going back to the carousel,'

Ellie, so much taller, replied.

'Then so are we!' Beryl started to elbow her way after the men, not caring who she buffeted aside. 'Gangway!'

Ellie tried to follow, but Beryl's shoving had made people bad-tempered and unco-operative, blocking her way. She couldn't seem to make much headway, yet she caught glimpses of John up ahead. She gritted her teeth and pushed again.

'Excuse me, excuse me.'

Why didn't people let her through? She could have shrieked in exasperation. There were so many people!

'Ellie.' A hand grasped her lower arm. It was Antoine.

'Follow me,' he said into her ear and pushed ahead of her, reaching behind him for her hand. Taller, bigger and more intimidating, he was able to forge through the mass of people. Together, they made their way towards the carousel.

Ellie could see the sergeant, clambering onto the moving platform, where he clung to an upright while gesticulating, summoning them.

'Get this thing turned off!' he yelled to John, below him in the crowd. 'There's a room. Around the central pole, if I can remember right. Full of mirrors.' He disappeared from view as the merry-go-round turned.

John leapt onto the platform, where he remonstrated with the fairground barker, eventually grabbing the long activating lever. But the barker wouldn't let go.

'Hey you! Frenchie!' Walsh shouted, pointing, as he swung into their field of vision again. 'Go and get my boss, DI Kent — Detective Inspector Kent. He'll be by the perimeter rope or at the Lost and Found with CS Morgan.' Then he plunged into the maelstrom of whirling carousel horses.

A central room, he'd said. Faye could be here. Inside the machine.

Ellie sprang after him up onto the fairground ride. The horses rose and fell, their supporting poles sliding forward and back through slits in the wooden floor. She saw Walsh stagger as he cannoned into one of them and blood poured from his forehead, but there was no time to stop and help. She had to get to the room at the heart of the merry-go-round; she could see its painted panel walls between the gallopers.

She wound and dipped past wooden horses, rocking back on her heels and side-stepping around the gilded, impassive equine faces. Children shouted and laughed, stuck out their legs and waved to onlookers watching from the ground, where the surrounding crowds merged into a multi-coloured blur at the edge of her vision. The repeating motion and bright colours disoriented her. Strident, rolling music reverberated in her head, growing louder as she neared the centre.

Blinking, she told herself to focus. Focus on the task! Get to the room at the heart of the carousel. She dodged the final line of horses and landed flat against the panelled walls at the centre of the ride. She put her ear to the wood and tapped on the elaborately decorated panels. It was hollow! Just as the sergeant had said.

Feet braced to combat the bucking of the wooden floor, Ellie circled the central room, feeling for the depression or protrusion of a door handle.

There it was! She'd found the door!

She grabbed the handle and tugged at it. No use. She pushed and it gave a little. So, it opened inward – perhaps something was in the way.

Get this door open!

Ellie stood back and kicked hard at the door, which opened, then closed again. There *was* something blocking it, preventing it from opening. She tried again. There was a clattering from inside. The door flew open.

Dazzled by light, she couldn't work out what she was seeing.

Strings of electric bulbs zigzagged across and around the space. Gears were cranking; everything seemed to be moving, circling. Nausea rose in her throat and she felt light-headed. She swallowed hard and focused on the central post, painted a bright red; it helped her distinguish between the multiple mirrored images and reality.

There was a muted cry from her left.

Faye!

Perilously close to the gap between the revolving platform and the central pole, her friend was lying on her side, struggling to keep her head raised, away from the edge, neck sinews straining taut like cords. Bound to a chair with a gag in her mouth, tears streamed down her face.

In two strides Ellie hauled her and the chair back from the drop. She pulled the gag from Faye's mouth.

Faye spluttered and sobbed. 'Thank you, thank you.'

She looked up at Ellie, then down at the struts passing, ever slower, below the gap in the floor. 'I thought I was going to die.'

Ellie glanced down. She could see the post sunk into the concrete block and the supports for the wooden platform. If Faye had tumbled through the gap... she would have been battered beyond recognition, lost consciousness and died. An awful death. The nausea returned.

'It's alright,' she said, sniffing and swallowing her own tears in an attempt at reassurance. She reached to untie her friend's bonds. 'Everything's going to be alright now.'

Walsh barged through the door, one side of his face covered in bright blood. He took one look then turned to shout from the doorway.

'She's here!'

The merry-go-round finally came to a halt as the hurdy-gurdy music ceased. Walsh knelt to help untie the ropes around Faye's wrists and lift her to her feet.

'Thank you, thank you.' Faye spoke between sobs.

'Hush, we've got you now,' the sergeant responded.

'Alright now, it's alright now.' Ellie repeated the words like a mantra, embracing her friend. 'Come on, let's get out of here.'

'All the fun of the fair,' Walsh said. 'We've got half the Metropolitan Police scouring the capital looking for you, and we find you only a hundred yards from your own doorstep.'

54

FAYE

'Careful, careful now.'

Ellie's voice was close to her ear. Her friend's arm was around her waist, holding her tightly, helping Faye support herself as they threaded between the now stationary steeds. Her legs seemed to be made of water; she could barely stay upright.

Beyond the canopy of the merry-go-round, she looked up at a bright azure blue sky. The air was filled with fairground noise, music, laughter, the sounds of people enjoying themselves. The SLH summer fete. Normal life.

She was going to live. Made weak by relief, Faye couldn't stop the tears.

Walsh leapt down to the ground to help her climb from the carousel, but John was already there, reaching up, face strained with love and concern. She caught sight of Nick, hovering beside him.

'Sis, you alright?' Her brother spoke into her hair, as he pulled her tight to his chest and she closed her eyes. 'Thank God you're alright.'

Faye nodded, unable to speak.

'Let her sit down,' she heard Ellie say.

As John released her, Faye collapsed onto the steps of the merry-go-round. John sat close beside her, with Beryl on her other side.

'Thank God we found you!' Beryl exclaimed.

DI Kent came striding from the direction of the South Side, Antoine Girard in his wake.

'Where was she?' he demanded.

'Inside the merry-go-round controls, in the machinery,' Walsh replied. 'It was lucky we got to her. Ellie, Miss Peveril, insisted the fairground people conduct a search. If we hadn't found her, she'd be a bloody mess by now.'

'Who took you?' Kent said, crouching in front of Faye. She could see he was trying hard to hide his impatience. 'Did you see who it was?'

She sniffed and mopped tears away with the back of her hand. This was her boss; she had to look professional. A male DC wouldn't be grizzling like a girl.

'Derek Brodie, sir,' she answered.

'Brodie! So, it was as we thought. The Hunter mob!'

'He said it was a message from Hunter, but—'

'This will not be tolerated!' Kent's face closed upon itself, his mouth a thin line.

He rose, turned on his heel and marched off.

'No, sir! Stop! Stop!' Faye called after him, but, amidst the noise of the fair, he was already out of hearing. 'Danny, stop him! You have to stop him!'

'He's not stupid. He won't do anything untoward in public. He'll be professional when it comes to dealing with Hunter.'

'Hunter's here?' John exclaimed. 'Here. At this fete? Here!'

'Yes—' Ellie began.

'How? Why?'

'He was invited. His company is competing for a hospital building contract,' Ellie said.

'You invited a gang boss to your fete!' John was incredulous, glaring, with mouth open.

'The directors of the company were invited, long before we knew anything about the criminal connections,' Ellie tried to explain.

It was too convenient, Hunter and his wife being there, at the very place of the messy execution of a police detective, and a woman police detective at that. It all fitted together. Faye was convinced she was right.

'It isn't her fault.' Antoine tried to step between Ellie and a furious John.

'My godfather knows,' Ellie continued. 'The police know.' She cast a pleading glance towards the sergeant.

'Listen! Listen to me!'

No one was listening and this was important. Faye tried and failed to stand. Yet everyone else was on their feet. They'd all forgotten about her. Except Nick. Their eyes met.

'Listen!' he shouted above their arguments. 'Listen!'

'Will you all please stop it!' Faye yelled loudly.

Everyone looked down at her.

'Danny, stop the DI retaliating, stop him doing anything – and I mean anything – that could be seen as retribution.

'Explain,' Walsh demanded.

'We're being set up. This isn't Hunter's doing at all, I doubt he knows anything about it, but we're meant to think it's him. Go now! I'll explain later. I'm right. I'm sure I am.'

The sergeant hesitated and Faye turned to Ellie.

'Then you go, Ellie, please, you go!' she pleaded. 'Tell Phillip, tell him I'm saying that we do not retaliate, we do nothing! Otherwise it's playing directly into their hands. He mustn't arrest Hunter. It's important! Once this starts it'll be too difficult to stop.'

'I—?'

'I don't have time to explain, but I know I'm right.'

Ellie looked at her, nodded and started out in same the direction as DI Kent.

'Danny, listen. Brodie used Hunter gang members, but I doubt it was at Hunter's behest and it wasn't in his best interests either.'

'Is Brodie working for himself? Is that what you're saying, that this is a gangland coup?'

'It could be, I don't know, perhaps Caplan is behind it. But I think Abigail Hunter may be involved too.'

'You told me that you thought there was something between Brodie and Abigail Hunter. Is that why...?'

'Yes. No. I don't know. I can't explain it all and we don't have time. Stop Kent and Morgan from taking any action until they've heard me out. Tell them to come to the flat. Now. Go!'

Finally, Walsh set out at a trot.

John looked at his sister, an eyebrow raised.

'Go with him,' she said. 'Make sure.'

He ran after Walsh.

Faye realised that the tension in her limbs had returned and she forced herself to relax.

Nick sat down beside her, his lips clamped together and his eyes sad. He was, she could see, fighting the urge to reach out and embrace her and she so wanted to be held, safe and well. It almost overwhelmed her; if she gave the slightest indication... Faye held herself as rigid as when she was inside the carousel.

He passed a hand over his face.

'How do people live with this?' he asked, looking away.

Beryl reached to hold Faye's hand, distracting her.

'Relax, Faye. You can't do any more. It's up to them now.'

Faye nodded.

'And Faye?'

'What?'

'I'm sorry. I'm sorry I was such a bampot, blathering on about class and corruption. I know you wouldn't do any of that! I was just—'

'It doesn't matter, Beryl,' Faye said, beginning to smile. 'It really doesn't matter.'

'Erm, excuse me.' It was the carousel operator. A small crowd was waiting for a turn on the merry-go-round. 'Can I get this going again now?'

55

ELEANOR

Ellie pushed through the throng of people, hoping to catch a glimpse of the DI's distinctive black hair up ahead, but she couldn't see very far in front of her at all. She had lost him. It didn't matter; he'd be headed to the Lost and Found tent, where Phillip had set up headquarters. She knew where that was.

Antoine caught her up. His pretty companion seemed to have disappeared.

'Where are we going?' he asked.

'To the Lost and Found, you were there before. Come on!'

The Frenchman helped to forge a path and soon she could see the large Lost and Found sign hung high above the heads of the crowd. There were fewer people here and the grassy area around the tent was cordoned off to hold a children's play pen. The DI and several uniformed police constables stood inside the cordon with the three people she had seen earlier that day listening to the speeches. Kent was speaking, though she was too far away to hear what was being said.

'Hurry!' Ellie called to Antoine. 'I don't think the inspector is in any mood for idle chitchat.'

Whatever it was the DI said, it certainly seemed to upset the others and two of the constables stepped in to restrain the big man, who was handcuffed and bundled away.

He must be the Derek Brodie Faye had spoken of.

That meant the bespectacled man *was* Henry Hunter.

The gang boss shook off Kent's hand as the DI took his arm to lead him into the tent and she could sense the menace, even from afar. Hunter spoke to the woman — he seemed to be giving her instructions — then accompanied Kent into the tent.

'We've got to stop him arresting Hunter,' Ellie said and took to her heels.

Up ahead a third constable followed the inspector inside. Abandoned, Mrs Hunter hesitated, but after a few seconds she marched off in the direction of the Underground station, just as Ellie rushed past the constable standing out front.

She cannoned through the tent flap into the shady interior, closely followed by Antoine. Halting, abruptly, in the centre of the tent, she doubled over, her hands on her knees as she sucked the air into her lungs, gasping for breath. All the occupants of the tent stared at her.

'Detective Inspector, I must speak with you!' She gasped. 'I insist!'

'What?' DI Kent exclaimed, glaring.

'Please!'

The inspector stared; his mouth was working, though he said nothing.

'Phillip, please?' She appealed to her godfather.

Hunter's eyebrows arched.

Phillip took charge.

'Outside,' he said and began to usher Ellie and Antoine out of the tent.

'Not you!' Kent pointed to Hunter. 'Stay here. See to it,' he ordered the constable beside the tent flap.

'What do you think you're playing at, Ellie?' Phillip demanded. 'What the hell's going on? And what are *you* doing here?' This was to Antoine, who was hovering by Ellie's side.

'It's a set-up,' Ellie began, breathlessly. 'Faye is convinced that Hunter doesn't know anything about her kidnapping, or the attack on me, or the bogus engineer in our flat.'

'What?'

'But she said Brodie took her,' Kent countered.

'Yes, but she had more to say. We're supposed to think Hunter's to blame, that's what Faye said. It's a stratagem, the police are being used,' Ellie explained, her breathing returned to normal. 'She asks you not to arrest Hunter, not to retaliate, not to do anything, in fact, until she's had a chance to speak with you.'

Phillip looked thoughtful.

'This is—' Kent spluttered.

'Sir!' John Smith ran up, followed by a red-faced Sergeant Walsh, who was sweating heavily.

The two senior policemen acknowledged the newcomers.

'We're being set up,' Walsh said, wheezing for breath. 'I'll leave the full explanations to her, but I think Faye's right. This is a gangland coup, using the Metropolitan Police to put it into effect. It all fits, sir. Everything. There's been something odd about this all along. Derek Brodie and,' he lowered his voice, 'Abigail Hunter, possibly in cahoots with Zack Caplan.'

'Interesting,' Phillip said, his anger forgotten. 'You and Faye are certain?'

'Yessir.'

'Right.' The chief superintendent took a deep breath, looking into the middle distance. 'Then we've no need to hold Hunter,' he said turning to the uniformed policeman standing beside the entrance to the tent. 'If we need him, we can always pick him up again later. He's not going to run, he's got too much at stake here. Constable, let him go.'

'But sir, isn't that…?' DI Kent began. He lapsed into silence as Hunter emerged.

'My solicitor will be pursuing this matter,' Hunter said to Phillip. 'This is police persecution. You will be hearing from him and me.'

His eyes, Ellie noticed, were glittering, cold and menacing. He no longer resembled an accountant. More like a reptile, of the deadly kind. Her skin crawled.

'I will await his letter with interest,' Phillip replied.

Hunter grunted as he stomped away, disappearing into the throng of people.

'Where is Faye now?' Phillip asked John. 'The hospital?'

'She's gone back to the flat,' he replied. 'Beryl will give her the once over and Faye can go to the SLH for a formal check-up later.'

'And you are?' the inspector asked.

'Constable John Smith, sir. Faye's brother.'

'May I suggest we all join her?' Walsh added. 'She can explain this better than I can.'

'I won't,' John demurred. 'I'd better tell our parents that we've found Faye and she's alright. Tell her that I'll be round later.' He disappeared back into the crowd.

'Westbury Court then,' Phillip said.

The DI nodded, but his mouth was a thin line.

Ellie had complete faith in her friend, but she hoped that Faye had got this right. It would finish her career if she hadn't.

'I'm sure she's right, sir,' Walsh said.

'She had better be, sergeant,' Kent muttered. 'She had better be.'

56

FAYE

'I believe that Derek Brodie is behind it all,' Faye said, looking around the room at them all. 'Probably with the connivance of Abigail Hunter, with whom, I believe, he was having an *affaire de coeur*.'

'And they killed Vi?' Beryl asked from her perch on a kitchen stool.

'I think so... well, Brodie did.'

Faye glanced at Walsh, who was sitting on the sofa next to the DI. He gave a slight nod of the head.

'Violet was killed because she was wearing a ring stolen in a Hatton Garden robbery carried out by members of the Hunter gang last year, organised and led by Derek Brodie,' she explained. 'Abigail Hunter kept a ring from the robbery, or perhaps — yes, that would fit — Derek Brodie gave it to her. Carl Carmody stole it from the Hunters' home in Wimbledon, where he did odd jobs.'

'Which was very foolish,' Walsh interjected.

'I think Carl thought he was safe. Perhaps, while he was at Ridgeway Drive, he'd seen Brodie with Abigail and had suspicions about their affair. Carl may have been emotionally unstable, but he wasn't stupid. So, believing that he had a hold over Abigail, he helped himself to a ring, to give to his brother, so that Terry could propose to Violet with a ring.'

Faye paused, to let it all sink in. The noise of the funfair could be heard through the open windows.

'Did Terry know?' Beryl asked. 'That the ring was stolen?'

'I don't know,' Faye replied. 'Carl may have told him some tale about it.'

'Because... if he did... he placed Violet in danger.' Beryl's face was unreadable.

'I don't know, really,' Faye repeated. 'Anyway, Abigail probably suspected that Carl had stolen her ring; he was in her house, alone and unsupervised. She sent Brodie to find him and retrieve it. He was supposed to frighten the life out of the boy. But Brodie had other ideas, mainly, I believe, because he thought Carl might know about him and Abigail. He wanted Carl dead, before he could tell Hunter. Brodie struck lucky in finding Carl at the flat in Fairview House; he sent the thugs away and set about beating him.'

'Carl's body showed signs of a thorough-going beating,' Walsh added.

'Violet had seen Carl on the balcony; she went to the flat hoping to extricate Carl from the other louts, but Derek Brodie opened the door. He immediately recognised the ring on Violet's finger as being the one belonging to Abigail. The ring was important,' Faye explained, 'because it linked Hunter and his wife with the Hatton Garden robbery.'

DI Kent and CS Morgan exchanged glances.

'*But* if Hunter found out that Brodie had given it to Abigail, it had another significance; it could also reveal Brodie's cuckolding of his boss and Abigail's infidelity. The ring had to disappear and its wearer be dealt with.'

'So Brodie threw Violet off the balcony!' Beryl said. There were tears in her eyes.

'I think Brodie killed Violet to silence her,' Faye said. 'Then he doused her in alcohol, tried to pour some down her throat and threw her body off the balcony. Violet wasn't drunk, she didn't fall while inebriated. She was trying to help an unfortunate young man. Violet's reputation is unsullied. Tell everyone that, Beryl. Make sure the *Gazette* prints the real story.'

'I will.'

'And no one can criticise the SLH by association either,' Ellie said. Faye nodded in agreement.

'Carl, too, had to be silenced,' Walsh prompted.

'Yes. Carl was seen running away from the flats, but Brodie probably put the word out that he was looking for him.'

'When we went round to see Terry on Saturday morning, he hadn't seen Carl since Friday,' Beryl said. 'Terry assumed his brother had come in late on Friday night and gone to work early the following day. But did he go home at all?'

'No, it would have been much too dangerous,' Faye answered. 'Carl was on the run. But he couldn't avoid his pursuers for long.'

There was a small silence as everyone absorbed what Faye was telling them.

'Why didn't he go to the police?' Ellie asked.

'With what? Brodie had the ring — that was the evidence. Without that, it would have been his word against Brodie's and I've no doubt that Brodie would have acquired an alibi,' Faye continued. 'No, I think Carl was trying to get to Hunter. He had information about Brodie and Abigail to trade. Also, he probably wasn't thinking straight, he'd not taken his medication for over twenty-four hours.'

'But Carl never reached him,' Beryl said.

'No, Brodie or his men got to him first.'

She paused and looked around the group before continuing.

'I think Brodie and Abigail have been planning to take over the Hunter gang for some time, possibly encouraged by Zack Caplan. Brodie was his boss's go-between with Caplan, so they could have met without raising suspicion. My visit to Ridgeway Drive gave them the perfect opportunity, providing a credible reason for some retaliation, to make it look as if Hunter was on the warpath against the police. There was a personal connection too, it would look like revenge. After all, it was Ellie and I who exposed the gang's Clapham South base.'

'Did they know who you were when you went to Ridgeway Drive?' Ellie asked.

'I don't think so, not at the time,' Faye answered. 'In fact, I think that element was a bonus. All they wanted was a reason to "retaliate".'

She licked her lips.

'First, Vincent West and the stabbing of the uniform, actions designed to intimidate. We assumed Hunter had ordered it, when in fact it was the lovers' idea. When he heard about it, Hunter could hardly admit that it wasn't him; to do so would make him look weak. Second, my kidnapping and eventual death. It was no coincidence that it was to take place here, at the fete. It would be a very public place for an execution and a neat revenge for what happened in the deep shelters close by. Plus, Henry and Abigail Hunter would be in attendance.'

'And the men who chased me?' Ellie asked.

'Probably set to watch the Carmody apartment, to see who was trying to talk to Terry,' Walsh said. 'They might have mistaken you for Faye or recognised you as her flat mate. Either way they wanted to scare you.'

'They succeeded!'

'It all fitted with the plan,' Faye said. 'And for the conspirators, it had the added benefit of the connection directly with you, sir.' She looked directly at Chief Superintendent Morgan, who was standing by the doors to the terrace, smoking his pipe. 'Via your goddaughter. It made it even more personal.'

'And you think the plan is?' Phillip Morgan asked.

Walsh turned to look at Faye. She took a deep breath.

'I believe the plan was to provoke an all-out "war" between the Hunter gang and the police. Derek Brodie told the thugs who abducted me that he was doing his master's bidding. I wondered at the time why he bothered to explain, but, once my corpse had been discovered and my colleagues were demanding answers on the streets, one of them was bound to squeal. The Metropolitan Police, which would, by then, be under fire in the press and in Parliament, would believe that Henry Hunter needed to be destroyed in any way possible.'

'His Majesty's Police do not indulge in gangland warfare,' DI Kent said, sharply.

'But we crack down, don't we?' Faye said, with a glance at the chief superintendent. 'Sometimes harder than others. We would target Hunter, there would be chaos. He'd be charged with my murder, then Brodie would make his move and turn King's evidence, ensuring his former boss got the hangman's noose. He would take over as head of the gang, having negotiated a lighter sentence. I, of course, wouldn't be around to say otherwise.'

'It makes sense,' Morgan said. 'But how, exactly, did you arrive at this conclusion?'

'A series of coincidences, which weren't really coincidences, all linked with the death of Violet Taylor,' Faye replied, with a glance at Beryl. 'The story of a drunken fall didn't add up and a local informer on the periphery of the Hunter gang clearly knew more than he was saying. When I visited the Hunter home, I came across Derek Brodie, looking like he belonged there and deduced that there was a very close relationship between him and Abigail Hunter. So I began to wonder.'

'Faye told me about her suspicions,' Walsh acknowledged. 'But I admit, I didn't take them seriously at first.'

'My visit to Ridgeway Drive prompted them to act. Someone had told Brodie about the invitation to attend the fete, probably Abigail Hunter. Were their invitations only accepted recently, Ellie?'

'Yes, on Wednesday,' Ellie answered. 'I asked Jean to check.'

'*After* I visited Ridgeway Drive,' Faye said. 'The fete was the perfect place for my execution, in the presence of Henry Hunter and his wife. It wasn't just the police it might provoke... I suspect my brother would cheerfully have punched his lights out, had he known Hunter was there.'

'This is very good work, Faye,' Chief Superintendent Morgan said.

'I was very slow in putting two and two together,' Faye said, shaking her head. 'My problem was that Abigail was surprised to hear of Carl Carmody's death, so I didn't associate her with his killing. I don't know why her lover didn't tell her about it, perhaps she wouldn't have approved. In any event, Abigail didn't know that he was dead when I went round to her house. That threw me off the scent, but I eventually worked it out; that everything was done to allow Abigail Hunter and Derek Brodie to take over the Hunter gang.'

'And they tried to use the Metropolitan Police to do their dirty work for them!' DI Kent exclaimed.

There was a brief moment of silence.

'You've arrested Brodie,' Faye said. 'And I'll be able to identify those who kidnapped me on his orders.'

'Yes, Brodie will be charged with your kidnapping and attempted murder, Faye and that's for starters,' DI Kent said.

'And Abigail?' Faye asked.

'That will depend on what we can get out of Brodie,' the DI replied. 'That is to say, if he'll shop his lover. He may not.'

'Either way, Abigail Hunter will have some explaining to do, not least to her husband,' the chief superintendent said. 'She might try and talk her way out of trouble, but I doubt she'll succeed. Henry Hunter will put the facts together soon enough, especially when we charge Brodie with the kidnapping and planned murder at the fete. I'm fairly convinced he'll work it out.'

Faye narrowed her eyes. Would CS Morgan make sure of that, she wondered?

'I wouldn't be in Derek Brodie's shoes for all the tea in China,' Walsh said. 'Even inside. Hunter has men who work for him there too.'

'He deserves everything he gets,' Beryl said. 'Doubled.'

She sat back with a great sigh.

'Brodie will be kept in solitary for his own protection,' Morgan said. 'He'll stand trial and justice will take its course. If Brodie dies, it'll be by the hangman's noose, not by the extended hand of Henry Hunter.'

57

ELEANOR

'So, the killer has been apprehended,' Antoine said. 'What happens next?'

He sat in the same armchair as before, but this time holding a glass of pale ale.

'He'll be charged and stand trial,' Ellie answered. 'And I hope that, at the least, he'll be incarcerated for a very long time.'

'I seem to have walked into a penny dreadful,' the Frenchman said. 'Police inspectors, murders, diamond robberies... It would be amusing if it wasn't so dangerous.'

Ellie frowned. It wasn't funny.

'I can tell you that I didn't find it amusing this afternoon,' Faye interjected.

'No, I'm sure...' Antoine coughed, embarrassed at his misjudgement.

In the silence that followed they could hear the music and hum of activity at the fete; it wouldn't close for another half an hour, at ten thirty.

'I'll just...'

Faye stood and went outside, where the streetlamps on the South Side illuminated their little terrace. As the doors closed behind her much of the noise was shut out.

Antoine gazed across the room at Ellie, who began to grow uncomfortable under his scrutiny. She pushed herself away from the table she was leaning on and went to perch on the arm of the other armchair, crossing her legs.

'Why are you here, Antoine?' she said. 'You and your pretty companion seemed to be having fun earlier. I'm surprised you stuck around.'

'Ahh, I see,' he said, putting his glass down. 'You are jealous.'

'I most certainly am not!'

'Are you sure?'

'Completely.' Ellie was vehement. How dare he presume to think so? 'I'm... disappointed,' she continued. 'In you; you're hardly the lovelorn suitor you proclaimed yourself to be the other day, you certainly haven't wasted any time finding yourself some other female company. And I'm mainly disappointed in myself, for beginning to believe you.'

'I see. I am insufficiently lovelorn. Obviously I should be pining for you, wasting away in a garret, or one of the old St Thomas's towers at the very least. *Alone and palely loitering.*'

Despite herself, Ellie found her lips beginning to curve into a smile. She compressed them, raised her chin and looked down her nose.

'You have an unhealthy preoccupation with Keats,' she said, primly. 'It's not—'

'You must allow me to introduce my cousin to you,' he overrode her. 'Stephanie. She is the daughter of my mother's sister and is visiting friends in England.'

'Your cousin.'

'I thought she would find a south London summer fete diverting and perhaps we would run across you, while we were here.'

Ellie's cheeks flamed; she felt very foolish. She must have sounded like a jealous harpy.

'It's none of my business,' she said, focusing on her slippers. 'I realise that, but—'

'I meant everything I said, Ellie,' Antoine said, quietly. 'But I'm not going to become some sort of hermit while I wait for you to admit me back into your life. I will go out with friends, go to the cinema, to pubs. I know it mightn't be the same as if you were with me, which is what I want, but I'm going to do it anyway.'

She couldn't blame him for that, she supposed. She looked across at him. His help had been useful that afternoon, though his presence had prompted questions from her godfather, who'd been unaware of the Frenchman's return.

Exactly what she was going to tell her parents she didn't know. And him soon to be a divorcé now, too. That wouldn't go down well. Though better than if he was married!

'Will you come to meet Stephanie?' Antoine gave a half-smile. 'She is very curious about the Englishwoman who I've left France for. I suspect there are several of my relatives in Ligugé waiting for her to report back.'

This time Ellie smiled.

'What do you suggest?'

'Supper. Next week some time. We could eat near St Thomas's then walk along the river, if you would like?'

This was all moving very quickly. She would have to make it clear to Stephanie that she wasn't committed to her cousin in any way.

'Stephanie knows,' he added. 'About us. About how I deceived you.'

'You told her?'

'Yes, there was no point in keeping it secret.'

Hmmm. It seemed he was being open and truthful.

Maybe that would be alright? A walk along the Thames on a warm summer's evening would be very pleasant and Stephanie would be a sort of chaperone.

'Very well, I'll check which evening is best for me.'

'I'm free on Tuesday and Wednesday,' Antoine said, as he rose. 'Now, I will not outstay my welcome.'

He knocked on the glass of the terrace doors and waved his

goodbye to Faye. Ellie showed him to the door. She hoped she hadn't just made a very big mistake.

'Are you two...?' Faye asked as she re-entered.

'Not yet,' Ellie answered.

'Danny Walsh is crossing the South Side, on his way here,' Faye said.

Five minutes later Walsh was sitting in the armchair recently vacated by Antoine.

'What happened?' Faye asked, impatient to find out. 'Any news on Abigail? Come on. Tell.'

'Abigail Hunter has been seen at the Hunter house on Ridgeway Drive.'

'Trying to brazen it out?' Faye said. 'She's got guts, I'll give her that.'

'Brodie's been charged. He didn't take it well.' Walsh smiled. 'He's been transferred to the Scrubs. Brixton was thought to be a bit too local.'

'What about the men who kidnapped me?'

'We've picked up two of them and there's an alert out for the others.'

'Good.' Ellie was glad justice was being served.

'And Violet Taylor's death? And Carl Carmody's?' Faye asked. 'Has Brodie been charged with those?'

'Not yet, it'll depend on what forensics find, officially, in flat four eleven, and if we can persuade witnesses to come forward from the Belvedere Estate. We'll have uniforms round there tomorrow, knocking on doors. People are going to be woken up on a Sunday morning.'

'Violet Taylor was seen at the door of a flat owned by one of Hunter's companies, there's a witness to that, though you'll need to persuade him to talk to you,' Faye said. 'I suggest you speak with Staff Nurse Beryl MacBride about that.'

And the best of luck doing that, Ellie thought.

She hoped that Beryl would now be able to heal. She wanted her old friend back, her dry as bone sense of humour, her pointed commentary on life.

'There's the trajectory of the falling body to look at, and we can see if any more of the party goers identify Carl Carmody as one of the youths on the balcony,' Faye said. 'There's a case to be made if we conduct a proper investigation.'

'There's a case against Brodie for Violet Taylor's murder, true. I suspect it's heading my way.' Walsh grinned.

'And the Greville Street job? What about Hunter, or his gang, for that?' Faye asked.

'A small matter of evidence,' the sergeant replied. 'Without the ring, we have nothing to connect the Hunter gang and the robbery. Unless we can persuade Brodie to spill the beans, but that wouldn't help him much and might put Abigail in a difficult position.'

'The cash injection?'

'Something to follow up, to track down the source, but that's for the Inland Revenue, not for us.'

'Why not? It should be for us.'

Ellie wasn't entirely sure what they were talking about, yet she knew that, if her friend thought it worthy of pursuit, Faye would pursue it or make sure someone did.

'We need to understand how Hunter finances his legitimate businesses and the same goes for Caplan. Where did Hunter get the funds to pay for the rights issue? We need a court order, so we can demand all his financial records.'

'You can go through all of the accounts when you're back at your desk,' Walsh said.

'We need that court order pdq,' Faye insisted. 'Before he has time to destroy all his records.'

'Alright, alright.' Walsh raised his hands in surrender. 'I'll just have to persuade the DI.'

'I have faith in you.'

The sergeant grimaced, looking uncomfortable, as Faye glared at him, gaze unwavering.

Rarely had Ellie seen the moral high ground so ruthlessly exploited, even in Cathedral Close. She swallowed down a laugh.

'And there's the construction fraud.'

Faye hadn't finished yet.

'We know the Nine Elms Depot had stores stolen and Bob — Detective Sergeant Bob Lowe,' she clarified when Ellie looked puzzled, 'is checking other south London rail depots. I'll bet there were stores stolen from them too. The industrial yard I was taken to is likely where the gang mixes its cement and stolen sand to make concrete and PRC panels. The warehouse floor felt gritty underfoot, as if a load of sand or aggregate had been deposited there and there was a lot of equipment. If we can find the place there should be plenty of physical evidence.'

'Faye, it could be anywhere in London,' Walsh said. 'Unless, of course, you can tell us where it is?'

'I was out for the count for part of the drive there,' Faye replied. 'But I can tell you this – it'll be somewhere in the rectangle between Hither Green, Croydon, Feltham and Battersea rail depots. It'll be on or near a major road that has a succession of sets of traffic lights in close proximity and road works, located near a primary school. Look for a warehouse or industrial building, with a perimeter fence and a gate — a compound. Oh yes, and it'll have a trail of rose briars and petals leading from the front of the building into the building itself.'

Walsh's mouth dropped open and his eyebrows rose.

In this mood, Faye was unstoppable.

'That *must* be enough to go on,' Ellie said, smiling at him.

His gaze softened.

'If you say so. Now...' He rose. 'Those rose briars won't be around for too long, I'd best get onto it.'

Ellie accompanied him to the door, but he turned to look back at Faye. 'Oh, the boss says have a day off, Faye, get yourself a once over from a doctor. I don't suppose that will be difficult given your contacts.' He inclined his head towards the South Side and the hospital. 'He'll expect you at Union Grove on Tuesday morning.'

'At Union Grove?' Faye looked hopeful.
'That's what I said.'
'You mean she's still on the squad?' Ellie asked.
'At Union Grove, Detective Constable Smith.'

TWO WEEKS LATER

Danny Walsh thrust a copy of yesterday's *News of the World* into Faye's hand.

'Look at the *Screws*!'

It was folded back at an inside page. She scanned it, her eye caught by a prominent photograph of a nightclub. Round, linen-topped tables were scattered in front of a glittering stage on which a willowy singer crooned into a microphone.

'Adelaide Hall sings the blues,' was the headline. 'Famous songstress performs at the Black Cat Club, Soho.'

At the table near the front was Henry Hunter, wearing a white tuxedo and smoking a fat cigar. He was accompanied by two young women.

'Hunter!'

'Yeah, but not just him,' Walsh said, pointing at the man sitting at the table behind. 'Look.'

'But... that's Radlett! His Honour Mr Justice Radlett!'

'Yep.'

'Ha.' Faye bared her teeth. 'Technicality my .... That's why we didn't get the court order in time.'

'I suspect so.'

'But that's... that's...' Faye banged the rolled-up newspaper on the desk, startling the other occupants of the squad room. 'How can we do our job when the bosses have judges in their pockets? And politicians too. How?'

'Calm down,' Walsh said. 'This is how things are, you know that. That's what we have to deal with.'

'I know, but... sometimes...' She sighed.

After a moment she looked at him sidelong, a mischievous glint in her eye.

'And it comes to something when even colleagues can't be trusted,' Faye began.

'What do you mean? Are you looking at me?' Walsh bridled.

'I most certainly am.'

Walsh blinked, he seemed to know he'd been insulted but couldn't work out how.

'I didn't clock you as a fascist sympathiser?'

'Ahhh,' he grimaced. 'I see... No. I've been... infiltrating certain groups to monitor their activity. Mosley may have monied backers, but there are elements that no one, not even those on the political far right, would finance. They resort to all manner of extortion and robbery to fund their activities.'

'Ellie's always said that the Nazis were nothing but gangsters,' Faye said. 'Racist fearmongers and terrorists too, but always gangsters.'

'I got close to the leaders of the British League,' Walsh continued. 'I've been able to gather some very useful intelligence. Who shopped me?'

'Beryl saw you with Mosley,' Faye said. 'She told Ellie, who asked her godfather for an explanation.'

'The chief super shopped me! Bloody hell! You can't even trust the brass these days.'

'Beryl won't take "No" for an answer and Ellie can be very persuasive.'

'I wish she'd try and persuade me.'

'So do half the men in south London. Oh, by the way, I don't think *you're* from south London either.'

TWO WEEKS LATER

Walsh raised his hands in surrender and smiled.

'My father's name was Waschler. I was born in Kracow, a Polish Jew, in 1916, before my parents fled to Britain at the end of the Great War. But I grew up in Mile End and I'm a British citizen. As British as you are!'

'I knew it! An East Ender! I knew you weren't from Lewisham!'

'Well, I live in Lewisham now.' Walsh looked sheepish.

'Look, I, too, have a confession to make,' Faye said, flushing. 'I... I reported you to the DI.'

'Yeah, the boss told me,' Walsh replied.

'You're not angry that I told tales?'

'About that? No. It was the professional thing — the right thing — to do.'

'Good.' Faye smiled too. 'Will you carry on? With the cloak and dagger work?'

'I doubt it, too many people know me now. I'll stick to straight policing, at least for a while.'

The door slapped back against the wall as Lydia burst into the room, her eyes bright, wanting to share her information.

'Have you heard? Has everybody heard?'

Everyone turned to look at her.

'Derek Brodie's been found dead, hanging in his cell at Wormwood Scrubs,' Lydia divulged, with relish. She enjoyed being the centre of attention. 'Suicide, apparently, or at least it looks that way.'

'I don't believe it for a minute,' Walsh said. 'It's Henry Hunter's doing.'

So Brodie wouldn't face justice after all. Phillip Morgan was wrong; Violet's killer would escape the hangman.

'I wonder if Abigail Hunter knows?' Faye mused.

Abigail and the Hunter children still lived in the house in Ridgeway Drive, although Henry Hunter hadn't been seen there since shortly after the SLH summer fete.

'Hunter isn't famous for the milk of human kindness,' Walsh said. 'My money is on him informing Abigail of her former lover's demise in person. A fiver says that he's at the ex-marital home pronto, to twist the knife, if he's not been there already.'

Nobody was prepared to take the bet.

'So that's that.' Faye sat on Walsh's desk. 'The state can't even keep prisoners in safe custody and Henry Hunter's dark reputation is cemented further. And what about us, having to police against that backdrop?'

'We carry on,' Walsh replied. 'That's what we do. It's all we can do. Come on, Faye, we got a good result; we arrested those responsible for your kidnapping and attempted murder; we charged Brodie with the deaths of Violet Taylor and Carl Carmody.'

'Though he'll never be convicted,' Faye interjected, but Walsh continued.

'We've avoided the Met being made a gangland cat's paw *and* closed one of the Hunter gang's depots for making concrete from illegal materials.'

'Hmm, I've been talking with my sister about that — she works in the council planning department. Did you know that the wartime regulation about building firms having to declare the source of their materials was relaxed for a while? It's back now though; we ought to talk with councils about ensuring that it's enforced, get them to do some of the work for us. Make sure the gang doesn't start up the same racket somewhere else.'

'Faye, does that brain of yours ever stop whirring?'

At that moment DI Kent walked into the room and beckoned to Faye to come into his office.

'Uh-oh.' She slipped off the desk and followed him.

'You've heard?' he asked, closing the door behind her.

'About Brodie, yes.'

Kent walked over to the window and looked out.

'I want you to visit Abigail Hunter.'

'You what, sir?' Faye snapped her mouth closed. 'Why? She's hardly going to look upon me as a friend. I got her lover put inside, which led, indirectly to his death! And...'

'You're known to her already,' Kent explained, turning back to face Faye. 'A familiar face and female. I think we've been missing a trick by failing to consider the women. You and Lydia have started something and I intend that the squad carries it on. But this isn't an order, Faye... given the circumstances.'

'You mean that she may have known about the plan to kill me?'

'Yes, but I'm not sure she did. What do you think?'

Faye considered before replying.

'Abigail knows how dirty her husband's business is, so she's no saint, but I don't think Brodie confided in her. He certainly didn't tell her about Carl Carmody's killing, so he may not have told her about his plans for me. It's ironic, I suspect Hunter trusted his wife more than Brodie did, yet Abigail betrayed the first for the second.'

'Hmmm, well, I'm not asking you to befriend her, but she's vulnerable now. You might offer her an escape route if she needs one. In exchange for information, of course.'

'She's hardly going to squeal, boss; her continued existence depends on Henry Hunter believing that she won't talk to the police. But I'll go to Ridgeway Drive, if she'll let me in.'

'Good. You might get nowhere now, but it could pay dividends in future, you never know.'

In future. Did that mean she had one, a long-term future, here in the squad?

'So you... Sir, you want me to stay with the squad?'

'Yes.'

The DI looked Faye directly in the eye.

Had Phillip Morgan insisted, she wondered? Would DI Kent be looking for reasons to rid himself of her? Or... could her work have convinced Kent that she was worth persevering with?

'Let's be clear, Faye,' he said. 'I wasn't enthusiastic about your joining this squad at the outset, but Phillip Morgan convinced me to take you. If you stay, I expect to see a change in your attitude.'

'Yessir.'

'You *must* obey orders. You ignored a direct order, not to mention your training, when you went to Cavendish Road alone;

TWO WEEKS LATER

when you'd been told specifically that you shouldn't leave your desk.'

'Yes, sir. But sir, I genuinely believed Danny, Sergeant Walsh, had summoned me. I—'

The DI raised an eyebrow and a finger.

'Listen. You've been lucky,' he said. 'You're lucky to be alive, let alone in my squad. You're useful, I'll admit, you even show signs of becoming a good detective – Morgan's right there. Your independent thinking is part of that, as is that obsessive quality that all the best detectives have.'

Obsessive?

'But you need to understand that you can't go it alone. You're part of a team. Possibly, just possibly, if you learn that lesson you might have a career in front of you. You might even earn your stripes and get to direct a team of your own, but neither will *ever happen* unless you learn to take orders. Do you understand?'

'Yessir. I do, sir.' Faye stared at him, wide-eyed, desperate to impress upon him that she understood. 'I've learnt my lesson.'

'We'll see,' he said, dismissing her.

Relieved, Faye closed the door to his office behind her and leant against it. The room was still full of chatter about the news about Derek Brodie. DS Turner was deep in conversation with DC Ford; Bob Lowe was on the telephone at his desk; he acknowledged her look with a raised hand. Danny was joking with Lydia, who was resisting his demands for more tea. Other squad members went about their business, while a woman from the typing pool delivered type-written sheets to desks.

It began to feel like it might be home.

Yet there was one thought still simmering away at the back of her brain.

The thugs who kidnapped her knew that she would be alone. Someone had told them. Someone from Union Grove. Faye was determined to find out who it was.

AFTERWORD

A Death in the Afternoon is fiction, a work of the imagination.

The Metropolitan Police first admitted patrol women in 1918, but it wasn't until much later that it began to treat female recruits seriously. In 1948, Faye would not have been unique, but she would have been very unusual. Police corruption was endemic in the Met during the 1940s and later. The practice of 'taking a drink' was widespread and was described to me by the son of a south London police officer who served at that time. It was not until the appointment of Sir Robert Mark as Commissioner in 1972 that this was tackled in a comprehensive cross-force way.

Post-war Britain suffered a crime wave and in London several dominant criminal gangs emerged; I have fictionalised those gangs in the novel. Scotland Yard created a Special Duties Squad to gather information and smash the gangs at street level. They operated without the bureaucracy attaching to usual police work and were never questioned about sources. The 'Ghost Squad', as it was known, was extremely successful.[1] I have based certain aspects of Faye's unit on the work of that squad.

The immediate post-war period was one of huge change as the Attlee government put their 1945 manifesto into practice. Central government and local authorities assumed some responsibility for

AFTERWORD

dealing with the societal problems that beset individuals. This included introducing a National Health Service, nationalising utilities and national infrastructure and the creation of the 'safety net' of national insurance and national assistance for those temporarily out of work. A million new homes were planned (often prefabricated) and the school leaving age was raised to fifteen. Often referred to as the establishment of the Welfare State, a broad acceptance of this agenda was conceded by Parliament and this hegemony continued until Margaret Thatcher in 1979.

Abroad, Britain withdrew from empire, largely because she could no longer afford to maintain it. India and Pakistan became independent, as did Burma and Ceylon (Sri Lanka). In some old dominions or protectorates, British soldiers remained stationed, notably Palestine and Malaya, but here, too, the British gradually withdrew or were forced to leave. The focus shifted to the Commonwealth.

The British Nationality Act of 1948 gave right of entry and British citizenship to citizens of Britain's colonies and the *HMS Empire Windrush* docked at Tilbury in June 1948 carrying immigrants, invited mainly from the Caribbean. Many were billeted upon arrival in the deep shelters in Clapham.[2] The nearest Labour Exchange (Job Centre) was in Brixton, where the newcomers went seeking work. They gravitated naturally to live in that direction and 'Black Brixton' was born. Many were better educated than the native working classes and many were men who had served in the armed forces, especially the Royal Air Force (RAF), over 6,000 of them, in World War II.[3]

Instead of gratitude and welcome, they were met with suspicion and growing hostility. Often, the police were openly and casually racist, like many of the general population. I have tried to include this in the book, while at the same time trying not to be offensive. I may have got this balance wrong and I apologise if people found this to be the case, but I have leant towards authenticity, mainly because I don't want to airbrush out of the book some unedifying elements of British history. There are also recent modern parallels;

a government welcoming immigration, without being prepared for the impact on a population already seeing services under pressure.

Sir Oswald Mosley formed the Union Movement in 1948, to bring together several right-wing groups. This included populist rabble-rousers, who promoted mass meetings and street violence. Then, as now, there were riots, attacks on places of worship, the demonising of minorities and blatant racism.

JULIE ANDERSON

NOTES

AFTERWORD

1. Documented in Kirkby, Dick (2011) *Scotland Yard's Ghost Squad: the Secret Weapon Against Post-War Crime* (Yorkshire: Pen & Sword Books).
2. A tour of the deep shelters is regularly conducted by the London Transport Museum as part of their 'Hidden London' programme. Find out more at London Transport Museum (ltmuseum.co.uk).
3. Murray, Robert N. (10996) *Lest We Forget: Experiences of World War II West Indian Ex-Service Personnel* (Hertford: Hansib Publications).

ACKNOWLEDGMENTS

Many thanks to those who have helped me write this book, some with their special knowledge and expertise, particularly my fellow Clapham Writer, John, who was generous with his memories of that time, growing up as the son of a south London police officer. I was also helped by the British Association of Women in Policing. Thanks also to Lamberth Archives and the Black Cultural Archives in Brixton.

To my coterie of early readers (small but select), Miv, Annette, Helen and Jonathan, thank you again for your input at a relatively early stage in the development of this book. To my editor, Sue Davison and to Adrian and Rebecca at Hobeck, many thanks, especially to Rebecca, who was kind enough to read this when I was unsure about aspects of it and helped me resolve my difficulties.

Above all to my husband, Mark, who read and re-read the many versions of this book, patiently pointing out inconsistencies and inaccuracies.

JULIE ANDERSON

ABOUT THE AUTHOR

Julie Anderson is the CWA Dagger long-listed author of three Whitehall thrillers and a short series of historical adventure stories for young adults. Before becoming a crime fiction writer, she was a senior civil servant, working across a variety of departments and agencies, including the Office of the Deputy Prime Minister. Unlike her protagonists, however, she doesn't know where (all) the bodies are buried.

She writes crime fiction reviews for *Time and Leisure Magazine* and is a co-founder and Trustee of the Clapham Book Festival.

She lives in south London where her latest crime fiction series is set, returning to her first love of writing historical fiction with *The Midnight Man* and *A Death in the Afternoon*. Julie is currently writing the third book in the trilogy.

Website: https://julieandersonwriter.com.

ALSO BY JULIE ANDERSON

The Midnight Man

The Cassandra Fortune Mysteries
Plague
Oracle
Opera

HOBECK BOOKS – THE HOME OF GREAT STORIES

We hope you've enjoyed reading this novel by Julie Anderson. To keep up to date on Julie's fiction writing please do follow her on social media or check her website https://julieandersonwriter.com.

Hobeck Books offers a number of short stories and novellas, free for subscribers in the compilation *Crime Bites*.

- *Echo Rock* by Robert Daws
- *Old Dogs, Old Tricks* by AB Morgan
- *The Silence of the Rabbit* by Wendy Turbin
- *Never Mind the Baubles: An Anthology of Twisted Winter Tales* by the Hobeck Team (including many of the Hobeck authors and Hobeck's two publishers)
- *The Clarice Cliff Vase* by Linda Huber
- *Here She Lies* by Kerena Swan
- *The Macnab Principle* by R.D. Nixon
- *Fatal Beginnings* by Brian Price
- *A Defining Moment* by Lin Le Versha
- *Saviour* by Jennie Ensor
- *You Can't Trust Anyone These Days* by Maureen Myant

Also please visit the Hobeck Books website for details of our other superb authors and their books, and if you would like to get in touch, we would love to hear from you.

Hobeck Books also presents a weekly podcast, the Hobcast, where founders Adrian Hobart and Rebecca Collins discuss all things book related, key issues from each week, including the ups and downs of running a creative business. Each episode includes an interview with one of the people who make Hobeck possible: the editors, the authors, the cover designers. These are the people who help Hobeck bring great stories to life. Without them, Hobeck wouldn't exist. The Hobcast can be listened to from all the usual platforms but it can also be found on the Hobeck website: **www.hobeck.net/hobcast**.